THE MISTRESS ENCHANTS HER MARQUIS

Christina McKnight

La Loma Elite Publishing

Copyright © 2017 by Christina McKnight

All rights reserved.
ISBN: 1-945089-13-X (Paperback)
ISBN-13: 978-1-945089-13-8 (Paperback)
ISBN: 1-945089-12-1 (Electronic book)
ISBN-13: 978-1-945089-12-1 (Electronic book)

La Loma Elite Publishing

All rights reserved. No part of this publication may be reproduced, distributed, or transmitted in any form or by any means, including photocopying, recording, or other electronic or mechanical methods, without the prior written permission of the author, except in the case of brief quotations embodied in critical reviews and certain other noncommercial uses permitted by copyright law. For permission requests, write to the author, addressed "Attention: Permissions Coordinator," at the address below.

Christina@christinamcknight.com

Dedication
To My Readers~

Each day I'm able to sit behind my computer and escape into another story is a blessing. Thank you for your unwavering support!

Prologue

Baltimore, Maryland
June 1818

    Elijah Watson, the eighth Marquis of Ridgefeld, stood on the dock, seamen and crew hustling around him. The brisk afternoon breeze swept off the Chesapeake Bay, washing over him as he stared at the growing city before him. The wind surrounding him and solid footing beneath his feet did nothing to alleviate his sorrow and heartbreak, but he needed to complete this journey—an adventure his grandfather had called it when they'd set sail from Liverpool on the newest clipper from the Hudson's Bay Company, the *Cameron de Gazelle*. Neither had dreamed it would be their last voyage together.

    He never would have allowed his grandfather to convince him it would make a grand adventure for them if Eli had known what was to come…

    They'd sailed to Africa, South America, across Europe, and the Orient—journeyed by land to every part of England and Scotland in search of treasure; Eli had never imagined Melville Watson, the seventh Marquis of Ridgefeld—Melly to his closest friends—would take ill on passage to the New World.

The sickness had struck so quickly—taken so much from the man—he'd wasted away in five short days, reduced to nothing but skin, his bones protruded at every angle. It had been utterly devastating for Eli to witness the man who'd raised him, clothed him, fed him, sent him to University diminish before his eyes. The ship's doctor had labeled it consumption and demanded his grandfather be quarantined from the other occupants of the ship. Only Eli was brave enough to venture into his grandfather's sick room to care for him, spending his days hidden on the ship, embarrassed by the tears and sobs that would not halt. He needed to be strong, lend his strength to the elderly man to fight his sickness, but Eli had been weak.

"Pardon, m'lord?" A hand settled on Eli's shoulder. "Will ye be need'n ta go somewhere specific?"

Eli turned to see the ship's captain, concern etching his face. "Captain, I..." The burly man, his clothes filthy from their near thirty days at sea, shook his head. "My apologies. Yes, I have an address, but it is nearly two years old."

"I be head'n ta see me family." He lifted his pack for Eli to see. "The docks ain't the proper place for a lad like yeself once darkness sets in."

Confused, Eli wondered what the man offered—transport from the harbor to Baltimore proper, a meal, a bed for the night, or only a warning to seek a safer area before the sun fell below the town's skyline.

A gusty, cold wind hit Eli's back, soaking straight through his coat. The hair on the back of his neck stood on end, though if it were caused by the chill settling on the harbor or the warning in the captain's words, Eli did not know. In fact, he was far too exhausted to care.

His eyelids drooped; he was drained.

"Is there an inn close to Market Street?" He would benefit from a hot bath and a few hours of rest before attempting to locate the woman he'd journeyed across the Atlantic to find.

The captain's eyes narrowed, and he scratched his balding head. "Market Street, ye say?"

"Yes, the last correspondence I received had an address off Market Street." Eli and his grandfather had researched the city of Baltimore before purchasing their fare to America. The town was growing by the day with industrial, manufacturing, and shipping trades. It was a new world of growth and opportunity—though his home country did not see it as such. Eli had come for exactly those purposes. "It was postmarked almost two years ago, however. I fear the person I seek may have moved on already."

"Ah, well, the area ain't no better than the docks, m'lord," Captain Constantine said. "But if'n ye hurry, ye should arrive afore dark and be safely inside. I'd offer ye a ride, but I be goin' the opposite way. If'n I don't hurry, me horde of heathens will eat me supper afore I arrive."

Eli chuckled along with the man, but while the captain's stomach shook with his deep laugh, eyes crinkling at the corners, Eli was hard-pressed to find his jovial spirit.

The captain seemed to notice his dour mood and his laughter ended abruptly. "I be sorry we didna make it ta port afore ye gran-da passed, lad. Ol' Melly was a kind man, ta be certain. Good man, such a shame…"

Elijah suppressed the tears stinging the backs of his eyes and threatening to fall. He refused to cry before the captain. "That he was, Captain, that he was." He cleared his throat and gazed at the buildings the crew had told him were the city of Baltimore. "I will hail a hackney and depart for Market Street. Do not fret."

"Ye send word ta the ship if'n ye fall inta any trouble, ye hear?"

"I certainly will, Captain," Eli reassured the man; though it was unlikely he'd find anything other than trouble while in America. He only prayed his business here would be handled swiftly, and he could seek passage back to England with all due haste. "This is not my first time in a foreign land."

"I be in port for several days, then we sail for Canada." The captain nodded and then turned and walked toward a waiting carriage, shouting greetings to the occupants of other ships as he passed.

With a final wave, the man was off.

Leaving Eli alone. Depressingly alone.

He hadn't lied about his familiarity with traveling. Nor had he been completely honest. He'd seen the world. Traveled to exotic places, and met interesting people, even explored an ancient pyramid in his youth, but never had he traveled unaccompanied.

Melville Watson, his grandfather, had been by his side on every adventure from the time Elijah was born.

His guardian in childhood.

His mentor in adulthood.

His father in every sense of the word.

Now he was gone, buried at sea—taking with him a huge part of Eli and leaving behind a gaping hole so large, Elijah feared nothing was left of him.

Despondency nearly dragged Eli to his knees, his entire being weighted by grief.

This voyage had better be worth the great man he lost.

Eli moved quickly toward the carriages and carts loitering on the street, awaiting their freight. He hoisted his and his grandfather's travel packs higher on his shoulder and lifted his arm, waving to a hack driver nearby.

The driver gave a solid shake of his reins and pulled forward to meet him. "Last fare of the day, guv'nor."

"I will count myself lucky, then," Eli called, tossing his bags into the hack before claiming the seat beside the driver. "Market Street, if you please. An inn with vacancies is preferred."

The driver eyed him for a moment, a puzzled look on his face. "Ya be one a those British guv'nors."

It had been over forty years since the colonies claimed their independence from England—over a decade before Elijah's birth. King George III hadn't forgotten the slight, and it appeared the great people of Maryland hadn't either.

"I am, but I have family in Baltimore." Eli hoped mention of family—accompanied by his most charming smile—would ensure that the driver delivered him without further delay.

"What kinda kin do ya have on Market?"

Elijah had wondered the same thing since the captain had spoken of the unsavory area. "A female very near and dear to my heart, sir." A woman who'd taken his heart when she'd fled England—long before Eli was of an age to give it willingly. His chest, above where a person's heart should lie, ached...pleading to have the delicate, broken piece of him mended.

Thankfully, the driver did not seem to notice Eli's sarcasm, and he nodded, giving his reins another shake. The hack's mismatched pair of horses sprang forward and settled into a leisurely pace as they advanced into the city.

The driver hummed a good-humored tune as he traversed the crowded, late-afternoon streets, weaving around a carriage with a broken wheel only to veer sharply in the other direction when a group of men stumbled into the road, their arms raised in salute before passing a bottle between them.

"Yellow-livered drunkards!" the driver shouted as they passed. "They be gettin' themselves dead, sure as sunshine in June."

"What is that man doing?" Eli shouted over the clopping of the horses.

"That's Samuel with Peale's Gas Light Company lightin' the street lamps." The man gave a soft chuckle. "And ya high and mighty King say we're the uncivilized gents."

Eli had read about the use of hydrogen for lighting. There was word that neighborhoods in London were installing the gas-powered inventions in their homes, and they'd soon be on every street corner. It seemed Baltimore was advanced in this arena.

They continued in silence, Eli free to take in the rowdy city around him—the people were so alive, scurrying here and there. However, one man looked much like the next as they finally turned onto Market Street. It was a working-class neighborhood with storefronts and several warehouses. Light shining brightly from second and third-story windows told Eli people lived above where they worked.

"Only a few more minutes 'til we're there, guv'nor."

The street narrowed, eliminating the space for pedestrians to walk along the road as the buildings encroached on the path they traveled, blocking the sunlight and darkening the road. It was fascinating the way the structures loomed without collapsing inward.

His grandfather would have marveled at the sight, as well.

Before long, the street widened once more, allowing people space to walk and making room for hitching posts for horses. Laughter, loud shouts, and male voices raised in song floated Eli's way, and Market Street veered to the right as a large building encased with windows came into view. Even here, a mile inland, Eli could smell the fresh, clean ocean air—unlike London's rank outdoors. As they drew closer to the building, he noticed a shingle hanging from the post on the street side.

McDowell Inn and Tavern.

Eli slipped an envelope from his coat pocket and read the hastily scribbled address on the paper:

31 McDowell Street
Baltimore Maryland
America

Could it be this simple to locate her—or at least the last place he'd known her to reside? Someone inside must remember her. His grandfather used to regale Eli with tales of her—the way she lit a room, the way she commanded attention, and the way every man hung on her every word.

The driver turned onto a narrow lane and brought the hack to a stop. "Five cents." He held out his hand and awaited his coin.

Eli fished around in his trouser pocket for the American currency he'd traded his British shillings for aboard the ship and retrieved a half-dozen shiny cent pieces.

"Is this McDowell Street?" Eli held the envelope out for the man to see. "Thirty-one McDowell Street?"

The driver glanced at the number on the envelope and over at the sign hung on the inn. "Yep. Finest inn and tavern this side of the Atlantic!"

Elijah looked back to the large building before him, noting the discarded rubbish that lingered in the small yard, several piles raked up against the actual building. Paint peeled around the door and window frames. The riotous sounds from inside escaped through several missing windowpanes on the first floor. This close to the dock, he supposed it was the finest inn within hackney distance of the Atlantic, though it did not appear to be an establishment any proper woman would enter—let alone call home for almost a decade.

He had no more grabbed his bags and jumped to the ground when the driver pulled away, his laughter rising above the commotion coming from the inn.

The late marquis—his grandfather—would have enjoyed a few hours among the rambunctious crowd within McDowell's. Sharp pain etched through Eli once more. His grandfather was gone. Elijah was now Lord Ridgefeld, a marquis. It was a title he'd been raised to inherit, but not this soon, and certainly not in this fashion.

He sighed.

For Eli, a warm bath, a decent meal, and a soft bed were in order.

Then he would seek more information.

Until then, his mind could not be trusted to work properly.

Hoisting his bags once more, he pushed through the small gate, which creaked loudly and hung from one hinge, the other having rotted clean through. He lifted the hanging gate back into place and made his way to the double doors. A bell sounded above his head when he entered, but it was unlikely anyone would hear it over the shouting, and—was someone playing the piano?—singing coming from deep within the inn.

This dilapidated, rowdy tavern and inn was the last thing Eli had expected to find at thirty-one McDowell Street; however, it was the only clue he had.

He prayed it was enough, and the voyage had not been a complete waste of his time—and his grandfather's final days.

"May I help you, sir?" A man, obviously the proprietor, judging from his neat garb and combed hair, looked Eli up and down as he walked behind the high counter. "Are you here for a meal, a drink, or a room?"

"All three," Eli replied.

The scrutiny left the man's expression, and a welcoming smile settled. "I'm Joshua Jenkins. You've come to the right place. One room left for the night."

"It must certainly be my lucky day," Eli mumbled. The last hack of the day at the docks, and now, the final room at the inn. If his luck held, he would attain what he'd journeyed to America for and be homeward bound by the following night.

Certainly, everything could not be this simple.

"This way, sir." The innkeeper started down the corridor in the direction of what must be the tavern room. "The cook is here for another few hours if you are hungry. You'll need to eat in the tavern. Right through that door there."

The man gestured toward a set of double doors, pushed open wide to reveal several tables, a long bar counter littered with empty pint glasses, and a piano—every available seat was taken.

"Busy night?" Eli asked, pausing to have a look inside.

The stench of stale liquor and unwashed bodies assaulted him—likely he gave off as pungent an odor as the crop of men gathered in the tavern.

"Every night is a busy night," the man said. "Finest inn and tavern this close to the Atlantic." Jenkins slipped his thumbs into the waist of his trousers and rocked back on his heels. "Even the fine mayor of Baltimore frequents my tavern."

As if to prove his point, Jenkins stepped forward and pointed to a man sitting close to the piano—a woman on his lap. "That is Mayor George Stiles right there."

Eli whistled through his teeth, hoping he displayed the appropriate measure of appreciation for Jenkins' elevated status. America and its citizens took no stock in British titles, but apparently they treated elected officials as their upper class. To think, a man could be born a dirt farmer and be elected as mayor of a great city with hard work and dedication. It was an enlightened concept. One he and his grandfather had debated the merits of on more than one occasion.

The woman on Stiles' lap laughed and hurried to her feet when the mayor attempted to slip his hand beneath her skirt. She turned toward the door, calling something over her shoulder to Stiles before acting as if she would flee the room, but the good mayor grabbed her skirt and pulled her back onto his lap. She landed with a giggle, her back pressed to the man's chest as his hand slipped around to cup her breast.

As Eli stared, her gaze met his—

Eli took a step back. It could not be… certainly, this was not she.

The bags he carried slipped from his shoulder, and Eli kneeled, riffling through the contents of one until he found what he sought.

A miniature portrait—a smiling woman, a baby in her arms, and a large hound at her side.

The woman had aged considerably since the portrait was commissioned; her once ebony hair was now shot through with grey, her skin no longer the pale color preferred by the English, and her hips were considerably more rounded. But still, it was she.

She laughed and turned back to the mayor when Eli attempted to hold her stare.

Alice Watson.

Elijah's mother.

And the woman who'd fled England a month after his birth in pursuit of a man—leaving behind her the memory of Eli's father who'd died before his birth.

She'd abandoned her only son—leaving him to be raised by his grandfather.

Undoubtedly, she'd done well for herself if she was wed to the mayor of Baltimore.

Eli continued to stare at her—a woman he'd known through sporadic letters, a few portraits, and his grandfather's stories.

The mayor noted his glare, whispering something to Eli's mother and nodding in his direction.

"Do you know Ally?" Jenkins asked in surprise.

But Eli remained silent as he watched his mother disentangle herself from the man's lap and move in his direction.

She stopped before him and placed her hands on her hips, taking in Eli's appearance from head to toe. "Can I help you, sir?" Her British accent had lessened over the years, but it was still detectable. "It is insolent to stare at a person as you are."

His heart sank further than it had in the long days since his grandfather's passing—if that were possible.

Eli had always assumed that when he came face-to-face with his mother, she would know him—that deep down, a mother would always recognize the child they'd given birth to. But not a hint of recognition crossed her face as she frowned at him, tapping her foot with impatience.

"Have we met?" Her tone rose a notch in irritation, yet her stare scrutinized his face. Did she notice his resemblance to the generations of Ridgefeld men who'd come before him?

"We certainly have, *Mother*."

Her eyes widened in shock before narrowing on his face as if she studied his every feature—but then Stiles called for her.

"I will only be a moment, love," she called over her shoulder, but the merry tone in her voice had disappeared.

The room grew silent as his mother continued to assess him, her expression going from disbelief to inquiry to horror.

"Will you not introduce me to your husband, Mother?" Eli glanced toward the piano where the mayor had stood and was now headed in their direction.

She flinched when Stiles arrived at her side and held his hand out for Eli to shake it. "I'm Mayor George Stiles," he greeted. "Is there trouble, Ally?"

"No, I—" His mother stumbled over her words, looking between the pair.

"My mother was preparing to introduce her son—the one she abandoned in England over twenty years ago—to her husband."

"Her *husband*?" Jenkins and Stiles exclaimed in unison.

"You are married?" Stiles turned to Eli, his mouth gaping.

The man certainly must jest. If Stiles were not his mother's husband, then why was she here… with him… sitting upon his lap?

Elijah's stomach churned—it could not be… Alice, his mother, would not lower herself to such a deplorable level…

"Tell me you are married!" Elijah fumed, prepared to avenge his mother's honor. "Mother?"

"Elijah." She stumbled over his name as if she'd never spoken it aloud. "You must leave. Go back to your grandfather and England—where you belong." She grimaced, averting her eyes and inching closer to Stiles. "Come, Georgie Pie." She turned, running her fingers down the mayor's sleeve in invitation as she sauntered back to the piano, her hips swaying with each step.

Stiles leaned in close and whispered, "Find your own ladybird." He laughed. "Or, if you can wait a few days, I just might be done with old Ally, and you can have her."

Elijah stood frozen as the pain in his chest almost pulled him to his knees—the immense agony could only mean one thing. His heart, fractured from his grandfather's passing, was now completely shattered.

The man leapt and ran after Eli's mother, pinching her posterior as he moved past her, inciting a round of laughter from the other men in the room, including Jenkins, who stood behind Elijah.

Alice Watson had abandoned her only son to move to America—the land of opportunity and dreams—to become a common strumpet, nothing more than a courtesan.

She'd rather live the life of a harlot than be a mother to him.

"Your room, sir?" Jenkins ventured up a narrow staircase farther down the hall.

"I've changed my mind. I will not be needing a room this night." Elijah kneeled, pushing the portrait back into his bag and closing it tightly, then slinging both onto his shoulder once more.

"A meal or a pint?"

Jenkins' inquiry echoed through the corridor as Eli retraced his steps and fled out the front door and through the hanging gate—not bothering to right it on its broken hinge.

Chapter One

Derbyshire Countryside, England
April 1819

    Miss Samantha Pengarden looked up at the looming storm clouds as the gusty winds whipped her skirt around her legs and tendrils of her auburn hair came loose from her coiffure. At least, she'd seen fit to don her sturdy walking boots for her outing—for she may very well be caught in a sudden spring downpour before she reached Hollybrooke Manor. She could barely make out the vast country home of Lord Cummings in the distance over the rolling green hills several miles outside Derby. The small town was the closest thing to civilization Sam had seen in over a fortnight.
    A single droplet of rain fell, hitting her nose and dripping off the tip to the front of her gown. When she'd departed the manor no more than two hours before, the day had dawned clear with not a cloud on the horizon. After the hectic days of travel from

London and the many hours spent preparing for her sister's wedding, the warm breeze had felt welcome on her face.

Sam took hold of her skirt and quickened her pace. It would not do to have her gown ruined by the coming storm—with four women traveling in one carriage, there was limited space in the boot for all their needed wardrobe and other necessities. Her eldest sister, Marce Davenport, had demanded they pack sparingly for the trip.

It would have suited Sam fine if she had been excluded altogether—not that she was against her sister, Jude, marrying Lord Cartwright; however, she had only just begun to settle into her place in London. She enjoyed everything about her days spent calling on newfound friends, rides in Hyde Park, afternoons at the modiste's, and evenings at the opera, playhouse, or any number of soirées. Many a night, she took to bed as the promise of a new day dawned.

It was thrilling, to say the least.

The dashing men clamoring to place their name on her dance card. The women insisting she call them friend. The matrons giving her the evil stare because of her beauty and appeal.

Since she'd left London, none of those things had come to pass.

Here in Derbyshire, Judith Pengarden—her identical twin in almost every visible way—was the shining star. Set to marry an earl in two days' time, all attention was directed at her, leaving Sam confused and alone—forgotten and neglected. Not a speck of it was fair.

Everyone would agree that Sam was the one who drew notice. With her deep, raspy voice and graceful poise, she was the sociable sister to her twin's reserved ways. They may look exactly alike, but it was Sam who received envious stares from the other debutantes in ballrooms, not Jude.

But she kept that fact to herself, for another lecture from Marce about her vanity was not to be endured quietly—and any argument during her eldest sister's scoldings always ended with the offending sister banished to her bedchambers and denied outings for days on end.

It was as if she were a child, old enough to leave the schoolroom but not yet a mature woman having reached her nineteenth spring.

Sam huffed when several more raindrops landed on her face, neck, and her exposed wrist above her glove. She would have been wise to bring a hooded cloak with her, but she'd never expected to seek extended hours away from Lord Cummings' manor—especially on a walk far from his land.

Consequences.

Another word Sam had come to loathe hearing from Marce's mouth.

The wind howled through a stand of trees not far off the road, tearing her skirt from her hand, and Sam stumbled, righting herself before she fell to the hard ground. Bruised knees, ripped gown, and sopping wet hair was not how she sought to return to the manor brimming with guests arriving to bear witness to Jude and Simon's special day.

Maybe she'd catch a cold from the moisture and take to her bed until it was time to return to London.

Not likely—her luck could not be that stellar.

The sound of approaching carriage wheels, horses' hooves, and the jingling of reins had Sam spinning around. Someone was coming down the lane—and she looked no better than vermin, thankfully not drenched vermin as yet; but if the rain increased, it would only take a few moments for her hair and gown to be saturated.

Although, the thought of returning soaked through to her skin, her hair plastered to her neck, and her boots sloshing, had Sam restraining her laughter, though it escaped as a snort instead.

She clamped her lips tightly as a large traveling carriage with four massive, black horses pulling at the reins barreled toward her. The coachman hunkered down on his bench as much as possible, exposed to the elements as he coaxed the beasts onward.

Did the man not see her?

Sam leapt for the rutted road as the carriage neared with no signs of slowing down, let alone stopping to offer assistance. People this far north of London were certainly lacking in manners—it would have been best to turn down Lord Cummings' offer to host Jude and Cart's wedding in his impressive garden; however, Jude had little dowry to speak of, and Cart was still diligently working to return his family coffers to what they had once been.

Had Sam known the barbaric nature of Derbyshire, she'd have argued against journeying into this wild, rolling countryside—unknowingly filled with runaway coaches and vision-impaired drivers.

She stood several feet off the road, safely out of the carriage's path as it ambled past her. The curtains were drawn, hiding the occupants within.

Likely more guests arriving at Hollybrooke Manor. With her luck, they'd be disembarking their carriage as she strolled down the drive, rain dripping from her windblown hair and her boots squishing with water.

Splendid.

"Halt!" The man's shout could barely be heard over the thrashing of the coming storm and the carriage. But the coachman pulled tightly at the reins and began to slow—coming to a stop about two hundred feet from where Sam stood.

She eyed the carriage as the coachman jumped down from his perch and lowered the steps, pulling the door wide. Inside, she saw an extravagant dark burgundy velvet interior as a lamp swung to and fro, casting a dim glow on the man exiting the conveyance.

The lamp at his back threw a shadow in her direction and darkened his face, making it impossible for Sam to see his features. He could be missing all his teeth or wearing an eye patch, and Sam would be none the wiser. He sauntered toward her as if oblivious to the pelting rain that had only grown in intensity. She glanced skyward; surprised to notice that the clouds, which had loomed in the distance, were now solidly above them, their grey bellies rolling much like the landscape before her.

The man's height grew the closer he approached—certainly over six feet.

A tendril of warning ran down Sam's spine when the man stopped in front of her until he brushed his dark hair from his forehead and a smile settled on his lips.

All caution—and common sense—fled in that moment.

The man... he was... dashingly handsome.

Stubble clung to his sharp jawline as if he'd missed his morning blade. His eyes—a deep cocoa—matched his wayward hair, currently being blown back across his forehead. Straight, white teeth were revealed by his smile... and a single dimple formed high on his right cheek.

Relieved she did not stare into the toothless face of a pirate with an eye patch, Sam's attention returned to the man's eyes. Something lay behind them—sorrow, perhaps—which belied his smile.

"My lady?" he asked.

"Oh. Yes?" She'd been so distracted by his appearance, she'd missed what he'd said.

"I asked if you require a ride somewhere," he repeated. "The storm appears to be gaining steam, and I cannot, in good conscience, allow a woman to remain unattended out here in the middle of nowhere."

"You must not be from Derbyshire."

"Pardon?" His brows drew together, creating a stream of rain that gushed down his nose.

She'd spoken her inane thought aloud.

Marvelous.

Not only was she becoming increasingly drenched as the seconds passed, but now she appeared addlebrained, as well.

"I am bound for Hollybrooke Manor, but I am in no hurry and can deliver you home safely before continuing on my way," he said.

Maybe her luck was improving. She decided to test his offer. "Yes, I would much enjoy passage home."

"And your directions?" He glanced over his shoulder at his coachman, who waited patiently. "I do not know the area, but if you can give my driver your location, we will be on our way. Come, allow us to seek refuge from the storm."

Sam looked between the carriage, the man before her, and his coachman. If he were journeying to Hollybrooke Manor, then he was either a friend of Lord Cartwright's, or an acquaintance of Marce's. He could not mean her harm—certainly, a man with such a heavenly smile could not cause anyone injury.

With a shrug, she led the way back to his carriage. The wind at her back blew her tangled hair forward as she sloshed through the muck, the deepening mud attempting to hold tightly to her boots.

The rain hammered against her the entire way, making its way down her neck and into the back of her gown. Embarrassing, yet unavoidable, she feared. There was no sense in fretting over something she was incapable of doing much about.

Sam accepted the coachman's hand and hurried up the steps into the dry, warm, expensively adorned carriage.

Her rescuer must have sensed her hesitation or noted her delay in selecting a seat. It would be the height of impropriety to mar his lovely velvet bench with her rain-soaked bum. When she realized that he remained in the elements while she debated her next move, she quickly sat on the rear-facing seat and awaited him.

He alighted, and they settled into silence as the driver closed the door and made his way to this perch once more to await her directions.

"I fear I am traveling in the opposite direction of Hollybrooke Manor," she said, brushing her hands down the front of her gown to push away any water that hadn't soaked her clear through to her undergarments. "And it is quite a distance to ask you to travel."

He cleared his throat, his inviting smile returned. "It is no trouble. I can have my driver turn the carriage around and head back toward Derby. Where is your home located exactly?"

"London." She clasped her hands in her lap, knowing her request was absurd, but he had offered to transport her home—and her home *was* in London… and it was where she desired to be. At around eight miles per hour, even with stopping overnight to rest the horses, she could be home by the next evening.

Meeting his wide-eyed stare, Sam suspected she would not be arriving home until she journeyed with her sisters after the wedding. "Very well," she sighed. "I am staying at Hollybrooke Manor, as well, but I would much prefer to be in London."

"If it were within my power—and not against several laws and highly indecent—I would rush you back to London with a swiftness unparalleled, my lady."

"Alas, I understand why you cannot," she concurred, her lips turning up in a grin.

He moved over to the window and drew the curtain back, leaning slightly out the opening to be heard over the growing storm. This gave Sam the opportunity to take in his own posterior—as divine as his face, as it turned out.

"On to Hollybrooke, Mathers!" he shouted before regaining his seat.

Sam's gaze was fixed on his fingers as they expertly undid the top button of his wet overcoat to reveal only a slightly dampened white linen shirt beneath. She swallowed to be rid of the spittle that had collected at the sight of his neck as he attempted to fix his neckcloth. Surely this man was a figment of her imagination, his dark complexion with midnight hair and dark brown eyes were not the standard Englishman's appearance. She should be frightened by his intense features, hard jaw, and broad shoulders; but then he smiled once more and the dimple returned.

The carriage swayed as the coachman commanded them to be on their way.

"I am Elijah Watson." He paused, and the sadness she'd noticed in his eyes returned. "The Marquis of Ridgefeld."

A marquis? What had she expected with the lavish adornment of his traveling carriage? Velvet cushions with nary a blemish, except where the excess rain drained from her person and onto the material.

"Are you surprised?" he asked, his brow raised in question as the smile fell from his face. "Do I not look like a grand marquis?"

She took him in from head to toe before answering, and she noted he sat a bit straighter under her scrutiny. She tapped her forefinger against her chin when she spoke, narrowing her gaze. "If you are not indeed Lord Ridgefeld, then you did a superb job of commandeering the most luxurious town coach I have ever had the pleasure to see—especially this far from London in the wilds of Derbyshire." Sam made a show of widening her eyes in fright. "Tell me we will not be set upon by the law before we arrive at Hollybrooke Manor."

The sorrow fled him once more as his eyes lit with merriment at her jest. His chuckle was deep and genuine, filling the enclosed carriage.

Chapter Two

Elijah hadn't laughed since boarding the ship for America the previous May. Now, his chuckle echoed in the carriage. It was the sound of a man who laughed often. The thought sent a shot of guilt through Eli—and he suppressed his merriment with an awkward cough. Since returning to England, and his family estate close to Liverpool, there had been little cause for happiness— only the sting of loneliness at his grandfather's absence. In a way, his enjoyment during the last several minutes struck him as a betrayal to Melville Watson's memory. His time of mourning was not over... truly, the one-year requirement for women to mourn the deceased, denoted to be proper by his countrymen, would never fulfill Eli's need to pay homage to the late marquis.

Honoring his grandfather was the purpose of his journey to Derbyshire—to speak with the curator and special exhibits acquisitions representative for the British Museum in London. Both Lord Cummings and Lord Cartwright were in residence at Hollybrooke

Manor for the next several days until Cartwright departed for an extended trip with his new bride.

And so, Eli had made the twelve-hour carriage ride when the invitation arrived. He'd known Cartwright had been acquainted with the late marquis, but was unaware his grandfather had consulted with the man after several of his exploration excursions. Cartwright had examined, identified, and catalogued several pieces for the museum's national records.

Eli would not complain or discourage the opportunity to be away from his country estate since reminders of his grandfather were in every room—hung on every wall and adorning every table; only feeding his sense of loss.

The distraction posed by the woman across from him was welcome, as well, though a sense of shame settled, thinking that any distraction was necessary. Eli should allow himself to feel the agony of losing his grandfather, for it was his fault the great man was gone before his time.

There was something wholly unfamiliar about the woman with him—maybe it was the slant of the coy smile she tried to hide when he laughed. Or the way her reddish hair—the light in the carriage showed it to be dark auburn—hung untamed about her shoulders, wild with abandon from the winds. Or possibly the way he'd happened upon her, on a deserted country lane in the middle of a sudden rainstorm without even the benefit of a cloak to shield her from the harsh weather. Then again, it might be her ability to bring a spot of gaiety after so many months of mourning the loss of the man he considered closer to him than a father.

Mathers, his valet, who was also serving as his coachman for the journey to Hollybrooke, rapped on the top of the carriage to alert him that they'd nearly reached their destination.

And make him aware of the startling fact that he'd spent the last several minutes appraising the woman across from him as if she were an object—a piece to be admired and treasured.

"May I ask your name?" His question hung heavily in the air. When she remained quiet, he feared she'd refuse his request, so he continued, "If I am to arrive for Lord Cartwright's wedding, chilled through to my skin with a drenched woman on my arm, I should at least know my companion's name. Not to mention the damage done to my carriage from our wet clothes."

Her breath hitched, remorse filling her eyes as she took in the harm she'd done to the velvet bench. "My lord, I am sincerely apologetic for any damage I have caused your carriage."

"The carriage is merely a possession and is of little actual value to me." He placed his hand at his heart. "It is human life—and the preservation of it—that concerns me. You could have been injured, or worse, set upon by highwaymen out there alone."

"Or a wild beast?" she hissed.

"There are wild beasts about?" She'd been in far more danger than he'd assumed.

"That is yet to be determined." The spark in her eye said she jested with him yet again. "Cummings' land has not seen any unlawful activity in two decades. I know because the man is more than happy to go on and on about the vast greatness of his family holdings. If you ask me, perishing on the side of the road during the storm would have been the most entertaining thing to happen in all of Derbyshire in *three* decades."

He wanted to inform her that loss of life was never an entertaining occurrence, but instead he smiled, suspecting she jested once more.

"I am Miss Samantha Pengarden. My family and I are in attendance for the Cartwright wedding, as well."

"It is certainly nice to have made your acquaintance before my arrival, as I will not know another person present," he admitted, lowering his gaze. He'd lived a life of travel and exploration, but London and society were not things his grandfather had found interesting. Therefore, they had avoided the city and the *ton*, as a general rule.

The last time his family had mixed with the *beau monde*, his father had found himself saddled with a bride. Not many years later, Eli's mother was with child, and his father dead. No more had he been born than his father's bride fled England, leaving the aging marquis with a babe to raise.

A long lock of red hair fell over her shoulder, a droplet of water falling on her hand where it was clenched in her lap. She quickly swiped it on her skirt. "May I ask how one attains an invite to a wedding when he is not known to either party… surely even a marquis, such as yourself, must wonder?"

He'd found the invitation quite puzzling until he read the note attached. "This is the final time Lord Cartwright and Lord Cummings will be in England at the same time for the next two years. You see, I have a rather large donation to make to the museum and wish to discuss it with both men before deciding that London is the finest place for the pieces."

"It is a superb museum, for certain," she said, nodding. "I have been dozens of times."

"Would you agree it is superior to The Louvre in France?" He was interested in her opinion, not that he'd ever consider shipping his grandfather's prized possessions outside the country. A woman who attended museums was not as common in his part of England, where most labored every day at the shipyards or manufacturing houses to gain enough coin to feed their families. Most of the *ton* preferred to stay closer to London, rather than brave the sparsely populated countryside in Liverpool.

She flipped her hand, pushing her hair back over her shoulder before aiming a serious glare in his direction. "The museum in London is the only museum I've ever visited."

"But you hold it in such high regard."

She lifted her chin as if shocked another would question her judgment. "Certainly, my lord."

"I meant no offense, Miss Samantha." The carriage jerked to a halt. "It seems we have arrived. It is not London, but we will soon be dry and fed."

"I do believe, Lord Ridgefeld, a dry gown is preferable to journeying all the way to London sopping wet." She pulled the carriage curtain back and gazed out the window. "It seems that no one has noted my absence—and more guests have arrived. I must look a fright. Can my good fortune last long enough for me to hurry through the foyer and up the stairs?"

Eli attempted not to stare again. The woman was beautiful… even in her drenched state. He could only imagine her stunning splendor once she was outfitted in a clean, pressed gown, her hair piled atop her head or hanging in long curls down her back.

She turned back to him, an auburn tress falling forward to hide her slender neck. "Oh, bother, Lord Cartwright is already coming this way."

"I will attempt to distract him while you slip inside."

"You would do that for a perfect stranger?" She eyed him, biting her lip uncertainly.

"But we are not strangers. Not any longer," Eli paused in an attempt to stifle his next words. "However, I do not take issue with agreeing that you are perfect." Perfect? If he knew anything for certain, it was that perfection didn't exist—at least not in any place or person he'd encountered in his lifetime. Although Eli suspected he'd found it in the least likely place—Derbyshire.

The carriage door swung open, and Mathers reached in to assist Miss Samantha in her descent.

She dropped her gaze, a rose-tinted hue blossoming on her cheeks as she stood and took his coachman's hand to exit the carriage.

"Thank you for rescuing me from the storm—and any wild beasts that may roam the area, my lord." She cast the words over her shoulder and took the first step down from the carriage, her sly smile returning.

"My pleasure, Miss Samantha," he called, but she was to the ground and speaking quietly with Lord Cartwright before hurrying into the house as he exited.

What had he been thinking calling her perfect?

He was not the man to enter into witty banter with another—especially a woman. Lord Cartwright had witnessed their arrival... together... her gown soaked... both with a smile upon their faces.

He knew not a soul but her; though it was likely everyone in attendance would know his name long before suppertime.

"Lord Ridgefeld? Elijah?" Lord Cartwright asked, holding his hand forth in greeting. "It is a pleasure to make your acquaintance."

"Thank you for the invitation, my lord." Eli took the offered hand with a smile, happy to be back on track and addressing the reason he was here. "It is very nice to finally meet face-to-face, as well. I stumbled upon many letters of correspondence between you and my grandfather. I do hope it was agreeable I contacted you."

"Of course, of course." Lord Cartwright gestured toward the open entry door. "Let us be out of the rain."

"Certainly." The man before him was not what he'd expected when Eli had decided to journey to Derbyshire. Lord Cartwright could not be more than three years his senior. He was neither stodgy, nor elderly, but appeared the proper gentleman. The correspondence between Melville and Lord Cartwright had dated back over seven years—the man must have still been at University at the time.

Elijah followed Lord Cartwright into the foyer as a footman rushed past him to help Mathers unload his trunk. Eli spotted Miss Samantha as she rounded a corner at the top of the stairs and disappeared... his ease with her. It was a burden he'd lived with since leaving America. The sense of being alone even when surrounded by others. For those brief moments in the coach, he hadn't felt that way.

Lord Cartwright chuckled, obviously noticing Eli's distraction. "Thank you for bringing her back safely. I fear the woman would have been stranded in the storm long past nightfall if you hadn't happened upon her."

"Her sudden appearance was a surprise as I hadn't seen another soul since passing through Derby earlier in the day."

"Yes, this part of the shire is rather remote and rustic; however, when Cummings offered his impressive gardens with ample space for guests for the nuptials, I could not turn him down." Cartwright glanced about the foyer. "His family has taken rather magnificent care of Hollybrooke Manor."

Eli couldn't disagree. The floors were polished until they shone, and the stair railing could be used as a looking glass—it reflected the many candles from above, making the area glow brighter than a windowless room should. Deep voices could be heard down the corridor, and the sound of female laughter sounded from another direction. It had been years since he'd attended a gathering this large—and by society standards, this hardly counted as anything more than an intimate gathering.

Mathers and a footman entered, carrying Eli's trunk as they moved toward the staircase.

"Ah, yes, Lord Ridgefeld." Cartwright took in his disheveled state. "I am certain you wish to change and remove the travel dust from your person. The butler will show you to your room. Please send word if you are in need of anything."

The rain had removed most of the dirt from his clothing, but his linen shirt still clung to him damply—his neckcloth altogether forgotten where it hung limply at his neck. "Thank you, my lord. I look forward to meeting your intended and Lord Cummings when I am properly attired."

"Dinner will be served in an hour's time. You are welcome to join us or take your meal in your room."

"And do call me Elijah—or Eli." He smiled, realizing he rather liked Cartwright and saw why his grandfather had taken so well to him. "I am still hard-pressed to recognize Ridgefeld as me, it was always my grandfather."

Cartwright set his hand on Elijah's shoulder, a rare moment of intimacy over a shared loss. "Melly was a great man, an inspiration—and a proud grandfather. You may not know this," he lowered his voice as if to impart a secret. "He sent me many letters over the years when you and he were traveling—from Africa, Scotland, and even India."

He'd known the marquis had spent many late nights writing, but Eli had always assumed he wrote of their exploration and discoveries in his journal. Maybe he did not know his grandfather as well as he'd assumed.

"My grandfather was a man entrenched in adventure—seeking a new journey at every turn," Eli said. He'd come here to take his mind off his loss, not to spend time wallowing. Though he welcomed meeting another who obviously missed the marquis, as well. "It is only right his treasured finds be appreciated by all."

"Lord Cummings and I are very grateful for your consideration of the British Museum to house his collection—"

"I know there is nothing of great worth, but it is everything he worked his entire life to discover. If even one person—or child—is inspired to seek out their own adventure because of my grandfather's passion, then his life will hold meaning for many years to come." Eli was uncertain why he'd shared so much with Cartwright. He cleared his throat before continuing, "Either way, I am not entertaining any other museums. My grandfather trusted your counsel with antiquities, and I intend to do the same."

"We appreciate that, Elijah." A bell sounded deep within the house. "It seems time has passed quicker than I expected. That is the dinner bell. I understand your need to wash up. I will have a meal brought to your room."

"Thank you, my lord."

"Let us dispel with the formalities. This is a quiet country gathering—truly, not much more than family and a few close friends. Call me Cart."

A friend? Lord Cartwright saw him, Elijah Watson, as a friend—and he couldn't help but like the man more. "Thank you again for the invitation."

"The men will congregate in the study for drinks after the meal." Cart turned toward the sound of the other guests moving toward the dining room. "Please join us if you are feeling rested enough. If I do not see you this evening, do have a pleasant night."

Elijah nodded and headed toward the stairs, following the butler to his assigned bedchamber. During his long carriage ride, Eli had looked forward to arriving at Hollybrooke and seeking his chambers to await his meeting with Cartwright and Cummings—completing his business and departing soon after the wedding ceremony.

To his amazement, he found himself hurrying up the stairs, delighted with the prospect of an evening in the company of Lord Cartwright—a kind *friend*—and his guests.

Chapter Three

Sam halted, pushing the door to the servants' stairwell open an inch, and listened. No footsteps sounded. No sound of movement nearby. All the guests were busily playing parlor games in the salon—allowing their meal to settle and taking time to visit before everyone retired for the evening.

It had been simple to make her escape once the men joined the women after they'd imbibed their drinks and enjoyed their cigars. Her ruse of feeling chilled ever since being caught by the storm was believable and partly true. Even after changing into a fresh gown and donning a shawl, she still found a shiver traveling through her, and her voice was raspier than normal.

Peeking down the hall in both directions, Sam verified that no one lingered within sight. She stepped from the stairwell and silently closed the door behind her. She and Jude had spent years sneaking about their home, Craven House, undetected by Marce, their eldest sister. Hollybrooke was far larger, and therefore affording more opportunities to scurry about unnoticed.

Her slippered feet made a soft pattering noise as she quickly slinked into Lord Cummings' study. She left the door as she'd found it—partially open. The men had been overly kind, leaving a strong fire in the hearth that sent warmth and light to every corner of the room, creating shadows as the wind howled outside. It was the perfect setting for the entertainment she had planned for her evening.

Her only concern was the lingering stench of cigar smoke that shrouded the room. It would clear soon enough, though.

Sam would have thought twice about leaving the group and skulking about in Lord Cummings' office if Lord Ridgefeld had attended the meal—but as course after course passed and the women retired to await the men, Elijah hadn't joined them.

Now, she hoped to find what she sought before scurrying back to her bedchambers without anyone seeing her. Her maid had assured her they were here—stacked among all the other books. A scandalous secret the Cummings' servants took great pleasure in sharing with visiting servants.

If Cummings knew his secret had been spread to all his guests, he'd release all his servants immediately—but as yet, he hadn't heard, giving Sam ample time to slip in and collect a sample from his collection.

Lord Cummings was not foolish enough to hide his scandalous collectibles on the shelves nearest the door where anyone could happen upon them—especially with several elderly men and a few matrons in attendance. Unexpected heart palpitations were a serious risk if the aforementioned group were to find such scandalous items. She surveyed the room, furnished with all dark, cherry wood pieces—massive desk, tall chairs, tables both large and small—and shelves lining every wall except the one that housed the bank of windows to her left. Her eyes moved back to Cummings' desk. If Sam had something she wanted to hide, the best place was behind her, allowing her to guard her treasure.

The shelves behind his desk were set high, permitting a table to be nestled below, cluttered with assorted ledgers and paperwork all neatly stacked and organized. The man was not the most interesting fellow—all proper and gentlemanly at every turn. It was shocking to think he'd actually acquired such an indecent thing and sheltered it within his home. The light from the hearth was barely enough to read the titles on the spines—the angle attaining more shadows due to the desk.

Sam had been told the set included ten thin volumes, their covers crafted from the softest leather, each only about six inches tall. None of the shelves before her held such books. Time was slipping by, and the men could decide to adjourn once more to the comfort of the study, a room their wives and other female guests would not venture into without an invitation from their host.

"Where are you hiding, you pesky things?" The fire crackled in response, calling for her to search harder—and faster—or she'd never locate them. She thought for only a brief moment she should have enlisted Jude's help, but her twin had been more than clear with her. Her sister had put her thieving ways solidly behind her and would not jeopardize Lord Cartwright's trust by embarking on another of Sam's schemes.

This wasn't a scheme, though. She had no plans to steal and sell the books, nor even keep them; she merely wished to peruse and return them before anyone was the wiser—more specifically, before Lord Cummings suspected anything was afoot. As the curator of the British Museum, his home was brimming with ancient artifacts. If someone sought to steal a piece, there were several rooms housing far more valuable items than his study. No, what Sam sought was not a thing of monetary value, though of educational value, certainly.

Namely, *her* education.

Cummings…she needed to see the room as he did, see his personal domain through his eyes.

Sam paused, closing her lids and channeling all she knew of men, which wasn't much. She'd spent innumerable hours with Garrett, her brother; however, he'd spent so many years surrounded by four sisters that he certainly did not project an accurate portrayal of what men acted and thought like when not surrounded by the fairer sex.

Opening her eyes, Sam took in the room as a man arriving home after a long day of conducting business—whatever business a man with unlimited funds need handle—and appraised the room.

Yes, a drink would be welcome after a long day addressing museum business. Sam walked slowly to the sideboard, her strides long and exaggerated—mimicking the overconfident saunter she'd witnessed time and again from men who saw themselves as above those around them. She surveyed the decanters on display—three held liquids of varying shades of brown, one held a clear liquor, and one a deep burgundy. She itched to select the last as it likely held table wine, but that would not be Cummings' selection, and she could not bring herself to sample the darker spirits. The compromise—the clear decanter.

A line of tumblers sat to her left. She poured a small portion into the closest one. There was no need for waste. Sam was attempting to get into Cummings' mind, not fall deep into her cups. The night was only beginning, and she planned to use it wisely.

Sam sniffed the clear liquid—her nose filled with the smells of Christmastide. A distinct odor of juniper and pine reached her, similar to the holly branches they hung about Craven House.

Cautiously, she took a sip and swallowed quickly. While the least visibly harmful, it burned the entire way down her throat and warmed her stomach—her chill from earlier gone. Not an altogether horrible sensation, but not one she'd partake of on a regular basis. It was satisfying to know what Garrett sought when he poured himself a drink—even now, she felt her nerves flee, and she settled into her task once more.

Cummings was a single man—his mother long gone from this earth, no wife or children, no female relations in residence. He would have no need to hide the collection or place them high so little hands did not stumble upon their wickedness. Though, neither was he an overt man—arrogance of social standing did not lead him to disregard all propriety. No, he would not display them openly for viewing. Besides, they were of a very private nature.

Not close to the door or on the shelf behind his desk.

The shelves closest to the hearth were lined with baubles that were for visual effect, and the bank of windows left no room for the collection.

That only left a few areas.

Sam stared at the massive desk, moving her inspection to one side and then the other. She noticed a shelf lined with portraits—his father, mother, and several older charcoal images. The shelf was shrouded in shadows. Sam took each framed picture, careful to handle them with extreme care, and set them aside—revealing a row of thinly bound books.

Her breath hitched as she ran her finger down the spine of one. The leather was soft to her touch, though it should be hardened by age—brittle from years of explorers devouring them from cover to cover, examining each hand-drawn image. Maybe even pausing to try what the illustrator suggested as they moved from one page to the next. No, someone took great care with this collection, certain to oil each cover from time to time to prevent deterioration.

Examining the binding of each book was difficult in the dim light. She needs must remove one from its place and bring it closer to the hearth to make certain it was what she'd risked discovery to find. The way her pulse raced indicated there was little doubt what lay within these tiny books.

Sam stilled and listened. Even the voices from the salon had receded. Either everyone had retired, or the festivities had settled for the night. She must make her selection, replace the pictures, and hurry back to her room.

If she asked Lady Theodora, Cart's little sister, she'd insist Sam take the first book—any book lover understood the importance of starting at the beginning of a story, not in the middle.

The decision was made—and she agreed. Any education must start at the very beginning or one might miss something important. And how utterly embarrassing if Sam ever gained the chance to use her forthcoming education and missed something of great import because she'd started in the middle. Sam had three days to study all ten books. Certainly, that was ample time to make her way through each in proper order.

She took the first leather-bound book from its place. A thin layer of dust coated the exposed top edge, the only portion accessible to the elements of the room. No one had removed the books in many years—which meant the chance of someone noticing one missing was slim, especially if she only took one at a time and replaced the portraits carefully in their exact places.

The hearth was only a few paces away, and Sam hurried to its welcome light to delicately open the volume.

In Physica Educationem in Caritate: Volumen Unum.

An Education in Physical Love: Volume One.

No author listed. But why?

Sam had studied Latin enough to translate the title—exactly what she'd come searching for.

A shiver ran through her. Was it anticipation? Trepidation? Shock?

It was certainly a tremor of eagerness, a foreboding of what was to come.

Leaving London for the wilds of Derbyshire would not be as dreadfully dull as she'd suspected. She could barely still her hand long enough to hurry back and replace the portraits. She itched to turn another page—and begin her education in matters of the flesh. Jude would be well versed within a matter of days. Garrett was a man, and had therefore likely partaken of the nude female form on far more occasions than Sam was willing to ponder. And Marce—their eldest sister, she was cultured in the art; the way her hips moved, her knowing smile, and the way she turned her neck at just the right angle to afford the best view. All things Sam had witnessed during their outings in London. Her sister was aware of the pleasure a man could give to a woman, she was certain of it.

That left only Sam and Payton—who, at seventeen and unmarried, *should* be too young to know or even suspect what happened between a man and woman within their marriage chambers. She could not push from her mind all she'd learned about her youngest sibling—namely her tendency for games of chance and the mounting debt Marce had been required to settle on her behalf. Could the young woman—truly past the age of being merely a girl—know more than Sam?

Sam moved back into the shadows and replaced the portraits—curbing her need to open the book to the first image.

Everything as it should be, she paused once more and listened for any movement in the hall outside the study. Nothing. Silence. Deep, resounding quiet.

A few more moments would not hurt, especially if the entire household had retired for the evening—it was more likely she'd encounter another guest on the floor above as she navigated the endless corridors back to her room. But once inside, she'd be free to examine the book at great length for, unlike Craven House, Sam had been given her own bedchambers.

She sat on the edge of the chair closest to the hearth, affording her enough light to inspect the volume. It was almost weightless in her hands—an object so small could not possibly hold an education so vast.

Her hand shook as she ran her finger over the title, stitched into the soft leather by hand.

Sam wet her lips as one foot tapped the floor in anticipation.

She would not wait until she reached her chambers to explore the treasures within, she could not. Every inch of her trembled as she flipped the book open to the first drawing—and her mouth fell open.

The image should be terrifying to an innocent woman with no intimate knowledge of the nude male form. The glaring picture staring back at her was…it was…shocking, to say the least.

The male sex organ was certainly not compatible with her own passageway.

Certainly, this could not be drawn to size—the organ extended from the man's nether region, standing proud. Erect. Was that the term?

Fully engorged. It was a drawing; however, the member appeared to throb on the page.

A sheen of moisture broke out across her forehead and on the back of her neck.

Sam glanced toward the door, fearing someone had entered with her unaware.

No one had invaded her privacy, so Sam turned back to the page before her. The man's face was etched with ecstasy, his head thrown back, and his eyes clenched shut. Even his hands were in tight fists, and his mouth set in a compressed line. Had the illustrator enlisted the aid of a true naked male?

At the thought, a spark of damp heat settled between her legs as if her body knew exactly how his member would fit within her. Sam was not ignorant of the fundamentals of animal reproduction—they'd once had several horses in their stables.

She set her finger upon the photo of the man, tracing his exquisite form from head to toe. It was inconceivable that every nude male was as impressive as the illustrator had made this one. Closing her eyes, Sam conjured up her own image—committing the drawing to memory for later pondering; however, her imagination would not allow her to disregard her new understanding so quickly.

Her eyes popped open when she realized the man had taken on a very familiar appearance in her mind's eye, right down to a certain dimple.

Sam's gaze skipped to the open door of the study—to see the exact face her mind had conjured without her permission.

Lord Ridgefeld—Elijah—stood silently in the doorway.

He cleared his throat and stepped over the threshold. "My apologies, Miss Samantha. My intent was not to startle you; however, I also was not in favor of interrupting your concentration."

"My lord!" Sam glanced down at the open tome on her lap and slammed it closed with a bit more force than was proper or necessary, only causing his attention to be drawn to the book she held. "Lord Ridgefeld," she stammered. "I was unaware anyone was still about the lower floor."

His gaze fell to the book she attempted to hide within her skirts as her face blossomed with heat to match that between her thighs.

Chapter Four

Elijah had escaped her notice for several moments, affording him the luxury of taking in her appearance without giving her the same opportunity. His grandfather had always stood by his claim that a true person could only be witnessed when they weren't aware they were being watched. That was certainly true of Miss Samantha—he'd noticed her smile, but the coy upturn of her lips hadn't only been bestowed upon him. No, her mouth had had that enthralling smile when he'd walked into the room—her eyes closed tightly. It was the reason he hadn't announced his presence sooner.

They'd shared a secret, however brief the moment had been.

"…I was invited by Lord Cartwright to join him after I settled in." Eli removed his stare from the book previously in her lap, which was now clenched to her chest—pushing her breasts higher. It was highly improper to notice a woman's attributes—and utterly unsuitable to dwell on them while conversation came to a halt. "I can see he is not here, so I will bid you good evening."

Eli nodded, forcing his gaze to her face, but it was more captivating than the sight of her bosom straining against the material of her gown. He should turn away now, flee the room and return to his chambers—or better still, depart the house altogether and allow the falling rain to chill his rising temperature.

Every instinct told him to leave—but something deep within urged him to stay.

"The men departed over an hour ago, my lord." Sam's breathy words made her voice raspier than normal—not that he was aware what was *normal* for her. "I believe if you hurry, they may be in the billiard's room."

He'd explored a bit of the main floor after he'd descended the stairs. There was no one about, and he'd feared he'd taken too long with his meal and assisting Mathers with his unpacking.

"I will leave you to your evening." Elijah gave Sam a curt bow before turning to depart.

"My lord?" He halted mid-step. "You were not at dinner. Is everything as it should be?"

She'd noticed his absence? Eli wanted to close his eyes, and burn this moment into his memory—to appreciate it later. It had been years since anyone had worried thus. His grandfather had taken a parental step back after Eli left for Eton, his grandson on his way to becoming a man and not in need of a nursemaid.

It had escaped Elijah how much he missed having another person think of him, ask after his well-being, and notice when he was not about.

Eli slowly turned back toward Samantha, noting she'd slipped the book behind her and settled her hands in her lap.

"It was a long journey." Elijah would not comment on his hesitancy to be surrounded by so many strangers—each seeking to know him and where he'd come from, the only guest unknown to everyone in residence. But that was not completely accurate. He'd made Miss Samantha's acquaintance, however briefly. "I took my meal in my room." He glanced to the floor in contrition—unsure why he sensed his absence had displeased her.

She'd brushed her long locks and tied them back with a green ribbon that matched the sash of her gown—and highlighted her auburn hair. The glow from the hearth behind her illuminated her long tresses. He could almost envision her in a nightshift, sitting before the warmth of a fire and reading a tale of adventure. Maybe even a story similar to the adventures his grandfather had taken him on. Would she sit, rapt, as he recounted his tales of their exploits?

"What were you reading?" He strode farther into the room, uncertain why he wished to stay and learn more of Miss Samantha. It wasn't decent to be in a room alone—after dark—with a woman one was not wedded to; still, he could not resist the need to be close to her. "May I see it?"

She stood quickly, holding the book behind her back. "I…well…I was about to depart for my room."

"I will not keep you, then," he said, moving to a shelf, appearing to inspect the row of books. He hadn't any intention of selecting one, but her interest alone was enough to have him seriously scrutinizing the titles.

"I was only seeking a book to keep me occupied while here." She glanced over her shoulder to a corner shelf. "But I found something interesting."

She made to slip past him, but he spoke before she could depart. "Since you are vaguely familiar with Cummings' study, might you offer any suggestions for a book for me?"

He would not dwell on her reasons for being in Cummings' private study looking for a book and not the library.

She turned slowly, careful to keep her book hidden from sight. His interests were piqued. And the resulting curiosity was hard to hide.

"What type of story do you find to your liking, my lord?" Her voice trembled. "While I am not overly familiar with Lord Cummings' collection, many are organized in a similar fashion."

"You assume I enjoy stories of flights of fancy and tales of fiction?" He raised his brow in question, hoping she'd take to the conversation and remain. When he found the time to read for pleasure, he almost always secured a tale of exploration and adventure.

He kept his focus on the shelf closest to him, avoiding her wide-eyed stare and the corner he'd caught her inspecting moments ago.

"However, I *do* enjoy tales of adventurers, pirates, and even the occasional spy." He ran his hand along the books on the shelf, spotting several authors he'd never heard of. Even with his grandfather's impressive collection of books, there were still writers who'd escaped his notice. "Tell me, Miss Samantha, if you were to select a book—which I see you have—what would it be about?"

Eli turned to her then. Her face had turned scarlet, and her eyes did not exactly meet his, instead focusing on his shoulder.

Surely, the woman was hiding something—and he intended to find out what.

#

Sam tightened her hold on the book behind her back as her face flared red, no doubt. Thankfully, the flames in the hearth had diminished enough to hide her blush. Had he seen the book in her lap before she was aware of his presence?

For his indecorous scrutiny of her, Sam should show him exactly what she was reading before he'd interrupted her thoughts—he needn't know her musings swarmed around his naked form: the curve of his back, the width of his shoulders, the tight, corded muscles his trousers hid, and the firm roundness of his posterior. Even his dimple, hidden if not for his smile.

Thoughts a proper young miss shouldn't be pondering alone in a stranger's study where anyone could stumble upon her. All of Sam screamed she was glad it was Lord Ridgefeld who'd interrupted her highly inappropriate meanderings. She—and her siblings—had never been proper misses. Raised within the walls of a rumored bordello, the Craven House women had been plagued by scandal and ruin since long before their mother's passing.

Part of her enjoyed that Lord Ridgefeld knew nothing of her family and her upbringing, especially her unfortunate bastard birth. These new rumors hadn't taken hold of every London ballroom as yet, and Marce desperately hoped each of her sisters would secure a husband before old gossip came back to haunt them—and make favorable matches impossible.

He awaited her response.

Though she didn't know how to answer. Should she be honest and show him what she'd come for? There was little chance they'd meet again after departing Derbyshire for their respective homes.

Would he take her for an indecent woman? Would he seek out Lord Cartwright or Lord Cummings to reveal her wicked secret? Would he call attention to her lewd interests?

All things any gentleman had a right to do, but she feared none of these.

"I think I would favor a story with passion," she confided, testing his reaction and saying the word aloud for the first time. It rolled off her tongue like any other, yet it sent a shiver of anticipation through her. "…and adventure."

She risked a glance in his direction. He was still inspecting the shelf, but his back had stiffened and his gaze lingered on a single book.

"Passion and adventure are tightly woven in many stories—for isn't passion an adventure in and of itself?" His slow inspection resumed, and he moved to the next area. Thankfully, he was on the complete opposite side of the room from *In Physica Educationem in Caritate*, and his book selection would hopefully be fulfilled long before he rounded the room and found Cummings' intensely private collection. "And no adventure is complete without the fulfillment of passion—whether it be desire for treasure or the touch of skin to skin."

He glanced over his shoulder, and Sam averted her eyes once more. He could not possibly know of

Cummings' risqué novellas, nor that she'd located them and held the first volume to her back. Was she bold enough to show him?

"Do you think a book can capture both passion for treasure and the touch of skin, my lord?" Sam turned and paced to stand before the fire, needing what little warmth it gave to keep her trembling at bay, though it wasn't the cold evening draft that sent waves through her. The heat soaked deep through her gown, warming her backside, similar to the way Lord Ridgefeld's intense stare sent warmth cascading down the front of her. "I consider education a treasure no person should shy away from."

She'd sensed his gaze upon her as she moved across the room, likely assessing her question. "I suppose it depends greatly on the subject of the education garnered within the book."

"Are you a man who values discussions of the weather and other inconsequential things when women are near?" Sam was uncertain why it mattered so much to know whether he found worth beyond her beauty. She would be the first to admit she hadn't sought attention using her stellar talents beyond her charm.

Intellect was Jude's ability.

Cunning was Payton's skill.

And Marce, her persuasive capabilities were legendary.

Sam had been given her beauty, and beyond her grace, men did not seek to know if she possessed a wit to rival her exterior exquisiteness. She'd always found it suspect that a man would tie himself to a woman without knowing if she possessed the common sense necessary to find her own way out of a horse stall without assistance.

Eli sat heavily in the chair Sam had vacated moments before. "I have found meaning and importance in discussions of all topics. I once found myself stranded during a monsoon in South America. I—as well as the other locals—were made to strip naked and press our bodies close to avoid freezing." Her eyes widened at his words. "Come now, Miss Samantha," he prodded. "You cannot think that all discussions about the weather hold little...*passion*."

Sam longed to demand he tell her of the passions he experienced during his stay in South America. Had he fallen in love? Had he been made to leave the woman behind and return to England? Why did she care in the first place?

There was so much she didn't know about him— far more than she did, in fact.

What was a man of noble English birth doing in South America, where disease and famine were rumored to run rampant among local villages?

The thought of another woman sitting somewhere halfway around the world, dreaming of Lord Ridgefeld's naked body was too much for her to process. Without realizing it, her eyes traveled from his head to the toes of his Hessians, and back again.

His smirk told her he knew exactly what she was picturing—and he didn't seem annoyed or put off by it. He only folded his hands across his lap and allowed her to look her fill. While she thought of his time in South America and whether he'd taken a lover, Lord Ridgefeld apparently was not. He seemed solidly in the present, assessing her as she did him.

"I have shared my outlandish story," he said, tilting his chin up, and for the first time in their short acquaintance, he looked the arrogant nobleman he was—his eyes challenging her. "Are you prepared to offer a showing of your trust in me?"

How had their conversation turned to the subject of trust—especially between two people who'd been strangers only hours before?

However, if she were to obtain more information about his adventures, then she need be a bit more forthcoming. "Certainly, what do you have in mind?"

Unexpectedly, he stood and took the few steps to stand before her, only stopping when their noses were scant inches apart. "I would see the book you are so overtly hiding behind your back."

"I have no book, my lord," she murmured.

He could not push. He would not. No man would demand a woman show him what he sought—then again, he was demanding nothing of her. It was merely a request, a show of trust as he'd so adeptly called it.

"Oh, but we both know that is a falsehood, Miss Samantha." His warm breath cascaded across her cheek, sending yet another tremble through her. Did the man have any idea how his closeness affected her? Certainly, he would not cause her such discomfort if he did…or maybe this was transpiring exactly as he'd planned. "The book?"

Blessedly, he stepped back, but held his hand out, waiting for her to set the tome in his hand.

"My lord," she breathed. "I cannot."

"You cannot, or you will not?" he asked, his voice deepening.

Yes, he knew the *precise* effect he had on her...and he enjoyed it immensely.

"I never pictured you for a scoundrel, my lord."

"Call me Elijah," he countered. "Any woman who dares insinuate I am a scoundrel should call me by my Christian name because, I regret to inform you, you do not know me at all. However, if you insist on using the term, I shall live up to its meaning."

He snaked his arms around her waist, grazed her neck with his lips and for a brief moment she feared he'd kiss her. Right there in Cummings' study, the door open wide for any passerby to see. Instead, he did something she dreaded far more—he snatched the book from her grasp.

"Let me inspect what you seek so hard to hide." Elijah took the book and turned from her, pacing back toward the door from which he'd entered. When his steps faltered, she knew he'd opened the cover to the first image—or more than likely, he was fluent in Latin. She wished she could assess his face when he fully saw the risqué book she'd been about to abscond with. His shoulders stiffened once more, and she feared he'd be repelled by her improper choice of reading material.

"My lord—"

A deep rumbling filled the room, and it took a moment to recognize the sound. The blasted man was laughing—at her.

No one dared laugh at her, just as he intimated no one dare call him a scoundrel.

Her face flamed with embarrassment—it gnawed at her insides, making trails with knife-like strikes.

He'd begged her to trust him—and now, he laughed at her.

"Miss Samantha." He pivoted to face her. "I must admit, you are full of surprises…surprises so grand, you can make a male of my ilk blush like a freshly introduced debutante."

His eyes sparkled with merriment as she turned her glare on him. He certainly was *not* blushing—not even in the slightest.

"I have not partaken of anything so…scandalous…outrageous…and enthralling since my time in West Africa. Did you know there is a native tribe which inhabits a part of Ghana that doesn't wear a stitch of clothing? Not a single loincloth to be had in the entire village. Men, women, and children, alike, walking about as naked as the day they entered the world."

The wretched man was teasing her—and all Sam could do was picture him under the blazing desert sun without benefit of clothing to protect his skin from the harshness of the heat. In her mind's eye, she stood beside him, similarly dressed, or in this scenario, undressed. He reached his hand forward, entwining his fingers in her long hair, her only protection from the scorching sun above. Her throat was dry as sand, and her words stuck, her mouth unable to voice any sound; however, he seemed to understand her discomfort and took her hand, turning her toward a paradise oasis in the distance—why hadn't she heard the water before? Noticed a sanctuary from the heat lay within walking distance?

They began their trek toward the tall, shade trees—a waterfall peeking through the foliage.

The sand burned under her bare feet.

Again, Elijah came to her rescue, sweeping her into his arms and carrying her to safety—their blazing hot bodies pressed close…

"Miss Samantha?" The whisper was close to her ear—a deep, rich murmur of promise.

Her eyes sprang open. Elijah stood before her once more. Closer this time. The book long forgotten in favor of the here and now. They were in this moment, together and alone. No need to view such images on paper for they could not compare to the real thing.

Would Elijah show her the reality if she asked? Begged? Pleaded?

She barely stopped the question from passing her lips, though a sigh did escape.

"My lord?" The simple words, barely audible to her own ears, were all he needed to close the distance between them.

He pressed his lips to hers, demanding but in no way controlling. He sought permission as he allowed her to set the pace of their kiss.

Sam had not wanted to allow this moment, this gift, to slip away unexplored.

No book, no picture, no discussion could have prepared her for the glorious feel of his mouth moving against hers. The warmth of his lips sent a current of need pulsing through her.

Shocking herself—and *him* judging from the sudden jolt of tension that tightened his back—Sam slipped her arms around Elijah's waist and stepped closer to him, their bodies now connected from chest to thigh.

He parted his lips, his tongue blazing a trail across her bottom lip, hotter than the sun in the African safari.

It was a welcome heat, and a sensual thrill raced through her and pooled between her thighs at her most intimate spot.

Sam allowed her hands to explore his back, dipping low to settle on his rounded buttocks.

Yet another aspect of the male form that could not be adequately conveyed by a mere image on a page.

Too soon, he pulled back, and emptiness filled the space between them. He moved so quickly, her hands fell to her sides as he paced across the room toward the open door just as a servant entered, his arms laden with seasoned wood to stoke the fire for the night.

Sam hadn't heard him approaching, hadn't sensed anything but her heart beating erratically, Elijah's matching her rhythm.

"M'lord. Miss." The servant nodded as he passed them, likely anxious to have his task completed so he could retire for the evening. "Pardon the intrusion. I will only be a moment."

Elijah cleared his throat and nodded to Samantha when the man kneeled before the hearth, his back to them.

She dared a quick glance at the servant, his attention fully on his task before looking down to discover her two top buttons had become undone. How had that happened?

The ribbon that held her hair back only moments before now lay at her feet, discarded. She placed her hands against her heated cheeks.

Her heart beat so loudly, she barely heard Elijah's words over the heaving of her chest.

"I will bid you good evening, Miss Samantha." With a curt bow, he departed the room, leaving her decidedly alone—besides the servant—and highly unfulfilled.

Sam glanced around the room.

In Physica Educationem in Caritate: Volumen Unum was gone. Disappeared.

Stupendous.

Chapter Five

Eli took the stairs two at a time, following the sound of voices—female laughter and male chuckles—toward where he assumed a meal was being served. The delicious aroma of salted meats and fresh bread met him as he entered a large room. The massive table was nearly overflowing as men and women ate while a child ran to and fro around the room. A boy, likely less than two, sang at the top of his lungs as a woman reached out and snagged his arm, trying to coax him into taking a bite of the eggs tentatively perched on the fork an inch from his mouth.

It was utter chaos, yet it appeared only he noticed. Everyone else enjoyed their meals while speaking with other guests—some shouting all the way to the far end of the table.

He'd spent far too many years with only his grandfather for company.

The notion of entering the fray that was the breakfast room was scary. The room shrank around the gathering, certainly not large enough to hold everyone gathered. His heartbeat thrashed in his ears. Not loud enough to drown out the noise, but deafening to the point where it made the conversations unintelligible. Eli stood rooted to his spot just beyond the threshold, debating returning to the quiet safety of his chambers and requesting his meal be served there.

"Lord Ridgefeld!" Cartwright called to him, banishing any hopes of escape—at least until he'd been properly introduced and fed. The beat of his heart doubled, and the room exploded around him with noise and laughter. "Come in. Come in. I have many people for you to meet."

His grandfather had always described Simon Montgomery as a quiet, shy, introverted scholar, who shied away from situations unknown. It seemed his pending nuptials had disrupted his norm—for the better.

Eli stepped into the room as every eye turned to him. Utensils hung in midair, conversations ceased, and even the child stopped struggling against his mother's hold.

The sense that everyone knew everyone and he was the only outsider overtook him. Eli took a moment to straighten his already perfect coat and clear his dry throat.

Plastering a weak smile on his face, Eli continued toward Cartwright where he sat at the head of the table. At least twenty other gentlemen and ladies cluttered the room as servants came and went, delivering food and refilling empty glasses.

An open seat was pulled out for him next to the bridegroom. As he rounded the table, he noted that a very familiar halo of auburn hair sat across from his intended seat. His smile, a moment ago feeble, now spread wide with certainty.

The long night had been spent wrapped in dreams of her—his fingers running through her long hair, his mouth exploring hers, his hands slowly unbuttoning her blouse once more as he breathed deeply of her scent of lavender. He'd awoken several times, his body drenched in sweat from his passionate longings for a woman he barely knew. However, in his dream state, she'd whispered promises of banished loneliness and a yearning to be by his side forevermore.

"Lord Ridgefeld," Cartwright set his hand on Eli's shoulder and turned to face the woman who'd invaded and stolen Elijah's slumber the previous night. "My I introduce my intended, Miss Judith Pengarden."

"Pardon?" Eli stammered, his stomach tightened. "Miss Judith Pengarden?"

"Yes." Cartwright squeezed his shoulder, but Eli was helpless to look away from the auburn-haired vixen. "This woman is to be my bride."

She stood with a welcoming smile, not the coy slant from the study.

Any further utterance stuck in his throat. Cartwright's intended? Miss Judith?

It could not be. No, this woman—her name was Samantha, not Judith.

"My lord," she nodded in greeting before resuming her seat. "It is a pleasure to meet you. Simon has told me much about your grandfather. It is an honor to count you among our guests for our special day."

He saw no recognition in her eyes; she didn't betray their association in the slightest, and she nodded to him to take his own seat. This was impossible.

Cartwright knew they'd met—he'd greeted them outside the previous day…witnessed his intended departing Eli's traveling coach. The beat of his heart hurried once more, and a sheen of sweat rippled across his forehead. Unlike the previous night, this was not from erotic dreams of a maiden with a fiery wit to match her long tresses.

"I am also glad to be here…" His words trailed off, unable to add "Miss Judith." She was not Judith, or maybe she was, and it was he who'd been lied to.

"Elijah." Cartwright regained his seat and made introductions down the line of guests. "Lord and Lady Haversham—with their son, Neill. Mr. Jakeston and his wife, Ruby."

He continued down the table until Elijah finally recognized a name.

"Jude's siblings, Garrett, Marce, and Payton."

The sight of the trio was unexpected. Siblings? Not a single one appeared similar. Garrett and Marce had hair like spun gold, and Payton's mane was so dark, it verged on ebony while Cartwright's intended had hair of the deepest auburn. He could almost feel its length between his fingers—soft and bouncy with curls threatening to take over.

Each offered a polite greeting; however, Eli could barely muster a reply as his head swam.

He'd been invited—an honored guest—to Lord Cartwright's wedding in Derbyshire…and he repaid the man's kindness by kissing his betrothed, unbuttoning the woman's gown, smelling the lavender scent of her hair. Maybe Eli's most debauched act had been he and the woman's witty, flirtatious banter, their easy conversation—a connection far deeper than lust.

Eli was a scoundrel. A rakehell. A dishonorable lord. A depraved man of the worst kind. He'd dreamed most of the night of deflowering another man's bride. His chest tightened as he ran his fingers through his hair.

Activity started once more around him, a steaming plate loaded with eggs, ham, bread, and berries was placed before him. The savory scent nauseated him—or was it his wretched deceit that gnawed at him from the inside out?

There was little chance he'd be able to keep the food within his belly.

Eli should excuse himself from the meal, return to his bedchambers and pack his bags. Instruct Mathers to ready his carriage for departure. It was the proper course of action—and he truly needed to grab hold of his honorable nature, despite his disgraceful engagements from the previous night.

Blast it all. He was a marquis, a gentleman most noble—and the man his grandfather had been proud to call kin. How had he taken a wrong turn down this harrowing path?

And bloody hell, why did images of the siren keep swimming through his thoughts…even now, when he knew she belonged to another?

"Did you travel far, my lord?"

He brought his eyes from his plate to meet hers across the table, scrutinizing her before replying to her question. She—Miss Samantha—knew exactly how far he'd journeyed to reach Derbyshire, why now did she pretend ignorance? He'd answered her question the day before. Still, the inquiry required his reply, for he was cornered. He sensed the attention of several guests focused on him. "Over ten hours."

"That is quite a distance." She brought a bite to her mouth, delicately setting it upon her tongue, smiling as if it were the single best morsel of bread with jam she'd ever eaten. "You are more than welcome to stay at Hollybrooke as long as it suits."

"I am in no need of a permanent houseguest, thank you very much, Jude." It seemed their host had arrived. Eli dragged his intense stare from the woman long enough to see a tall, slight man enter the room. "You must be Lord Ridgefeld. It is a pleasure to make your acquaintance."

"I am certain you could use a companion around this massive house," Cart retorted, hiding his grin with another bite of toast. "My betrothed was only trying to secure your future, Cummings."

Elijah had met Lord Cummings once before. Long ago when he and his grandfather had visited London for the purpose of visiting the museum; however, Cummings hadn't left any lasting impression.

"I have much to do at my own estate, my lords," Eli retorted. "I have no plans to overstay my welcome."

Cummings took a seat and spoke quietly with Mr. Jakeston, giving Eli the opportunity to inspect the woman across from him as she and Cartwright shared a private jest. Her laugh was not the deep, throaty chuckle he'd become familiar with—no, it held the tone of a light breeze.

Her voice also rang like the melody of a cheerful song.

It was something easily masked, but the woman before him lacked the presence he'd enjoyed during his time with Miss Samantha. Miss Judith Pengarden was the mirror image of the woman he'd held in his arms in the study. The one he'd happened upon, reading a most scandalous old text. The same miss he'd wrapped his arms around, placing his lips to hers and drinking in her lavender scent as their mouths danced.

But the woman sitting across from him possessed no coy smile. She looked directly at him, not from under lowered lashes. He could not envision this woman stealing into a man's private study in search of a risqué novel no innocent female should even suspect existed.

"Are you feeling ill, Lord Ridgefeld?" she asked.

He'd been staring—impolitely. Studying her every detail: the length of her hair, the lift of her chin, the exact shade of her green eyes.

"Elijah?" Cartwright inquired, his severe tone said others had noted Eli's interest, as well.

He shook his head. "My apologies, my lord. Miss Judith. I think I find myself suffering exhaustion from my travels. I believe it would be wise to retire to my chambers and rest for the morning."

Concern knitted Miss Judith's brow, and Cartwright nodded his agreement. "Certainly. Long carriage rides are overly taxing on the body. Please send word if you need anything."

"If you will excuse me." Eli pushed his chair back and stood, avoiding eye contact with the woman across from him. Something was off—direly wrong. Could the woman so easily betray Lord Cartwright and then sit across the table from Eli with her betrothed at her elbow as if nothing untoward had occurred the previous night. "I will hope to see everyone later in the day."

Eli stumbled to the door, mumbling apologies as he passed guest after guest until he was finally free of the room. He threw a glance over his shoulder to see if any eyes followed, but no one paid him any mind—Cart and his betrothed were already deep in conversation amongst themselves. He listened to the chatter of conversation as he made his way back to the staircase.

Nothing was as it should be. Lord Cartwright's betrothed had hoodwinked him only two nights before they were to be wed—and with a stranger, no less. Though if you'd have asked Eli only an hour prior, he would have challenged anyone who called him and Miss Samantha strangers—correction, Miss Judith. Why the false name? Did the woman think she would not be found out, her duplicity not made known? Maybe betraying your intended was more acceptable if done with a stranger you were not likely to see again— therefore, any lingering guilt or reminders would be out of sight.

That would only put Elijah in the earl's crosshairs—he'd lusted after Lord Cartwright's betrothed. It didn't matter that she'd lied to him. He was the gentleman; he was supposed to be above reproach. He was the one who'd entered the study knowing full well they were alone—and their position would lead them both down an unsavory path.

Elijah Watson, the eighth Marquis of Ridgefeld, had compromised another man's betrothed. He only had himself to blame for his predicament. His blood ran cold at the thought—he'd become the man his mother would love, and one his grandfather would despise.

Only now, it left him wondering if he was his mother's son or the man his grandfather had raised to carry on their family name.

Elijah had many decisions to make—his course of correcting the wrongs he'd done first and foremost.

Chapter Six

Sam closed her bedchamber door. The hinges gave no groan of protest, well-oiled, much like every door in Lord Cummings' grand house. Not an item was out of place. Every floor, every stair rail, and every table was polished to shine. Marce took precise care of Craven House—it was all she could call her own—but there were still chores that never managed to be finished. It was not the case at Hollybrooke Manor. Servants were readily available should a guest need assistance, though that had not been the case the previous night.

Her evening and into the early hours of the morning had been spent imagining all the ways her time in the study could have gone had the servant not appeared to ruin everything and send Elijah fleeing for the safety of his chambers. The man hadn't even done her the courtesy of leaving the book she'd risked discovery to find.

Irritating.

However, she needed to put the thought out of her mind, especially if she were to make it through her busy day and not lash out at her siblings during their preparations for tomorrow.

The halls had been deserted as she'd attempted to follow Elijah and demand he return the book to her, but he'd disappeared. If she'd known where his room was located, Sam might have been so bold as to knock on his door; however, with so many guests in residence, and the sheer number of rooms at Hollybrooke, even she was not brazen enough to traverse the halls in search of signs of Lord Ridgefeld.

Jude had summoned her for breakfast at a most ungodly hour, likely requiring her assistance to entertain all her wedding guests. Instead, Sam had taken her time donning her morning gown, brushing her hair until it fairly shone before pinning it precisely in place—upswept to expose her long, slender neck—though she much preferred it hanging loosely about her shoulders. She'd taken even more time selecting the perfect slippers—not that she'd brought more than three pairs, but she pondered if white or cream better suited her pink gown. Then she sat at her dressing table to select the perfect adornments to accompany her outfit—finally settling on simple opal earbobs with a matching broach.

The plan was to arrive at the end of breakfast, hope Elijah was in the room, and simply take the seat next to him then demand he return what was hers—er, not hers exactly, but she figured that was splitting hairs.

Sam lifted her chin and hurried her pace toward the main staircase. It would not serve her well to miss the meal entirely and thus have to hunt Elijah down later or risk returning to the study for volume two of *In Physica Educationem in Caritate*. That was arguably the simpler task, but after a full night spent wrapped in a dream world with Elijah, she was eager to see him in the flesh—ascertain if he'd spent the dark hours in his own imaginary dreamland.

Even the thought of his name sent tendrils of need through her.

Her time in Derbyshire certainly would not go to waste. Cummings' study—and Lord Ridgefeld—offered the perfect distraction to keep her boredom at bay.

"Good morn, Miss…"

Sam focused on the man heading her way, his booted feet rung distinctively as one did not lift as high as the other, making a sort of scraping sound as he moved.

Not many could determine if they stood before Jude or Sam.

Countless people, even her own siblings, looked with questioning stares when they entered to find one of them in attendance, waiting for them to speak before identifying them by Jude's softer, more feminine voice, or Sam's deep, raspy one.

"Lord Chastain," Sam said, putting the man at ease. "It is lovely to see you and Ellington have arrived in time for the ceremony on the morrow. Jude is overjoyed you both could be here."

"We arrived late last evening, but everyone was abed." He gave her a warm smile. "I know Ellie is looking forward to time with you and your sisters. She misses you all so very much."

Since Lady Ellington married and became Lady Chastain, she'd been busy renovating her new home, a townhouse that had sat unoccupied for almost two decades. Sam could only imagine the workload both Ellie and her husband, Alex, faced.

"I very much look forward to seeing her, as well," Sam replied. "I am on my way to the breakfast room, will I find her there?"

"I delivered her to your sister's side only moments ago, but needed to return to our room." He gave her a quick bow. "Do enjoy the meal. I will return shortly. Until then, please keep an eye on her."

Sam couldn't help but laugh. "I will, my lord."

Ellington was of similar age to Sam and Jude, but since her marriage, Ellie had evolved into a true lady: her manners were impeccable, her poise and grace were becoming legendary in London, and her days as a pickpocket were clearly behind her. Much like her own sister, Jude, Ellie was not willing to jeopardize her husband's good standing by continuing any questionable activities.

In recent months, Marce had entrusted Ellie with keeping watch over Sam and Jude while at society gatherings. It would have been comical and utterly preposterous less than a year before.

Lord Chastain made his way down the hallway and entered the chambers two doors down from her room, his slight limp barely noticeable.

The sound of another pair of Hessians making their way up the stairs had Sam longing to duck back into her bedchamber to wait until no one was about. If she kept getting waylaid, she'd never reach the breakfast room before Elijah took his leave. She took comfort in knowing at least one chamber was crossed off her list when Lord Chastain entered his room.

Sam turned the corner, prepared to nod a greeting to whoever was coming her way and then avert her eyes and continue on without further conversation.

However, the familiar jawline and chocolate brown hair of the man who crested the top of the stairs brought Sam up short, her breath leaving her on a sigh. Why was Ridgefeld so bloody appealing? He was certainly no more attractive or charming than the dozens of other men she'd met in London. If anything, he was far too stuffy for her, a bit too proper, and…all thought fled when she noticed his intense glare landing on her, recognition dawning and then a look of utter puzzlement.

"Lord Ridgefeld." She gave him her most amiable smile. Anything to charm him into giving her the book back—and maybe convincing him to continue her education in the arts of the flesh. "I was on my way to the breakfast room to break my fast. Have you already eaten?"

Her question was met by his continued inspection, his eyes taking her in from head to toe and back again, finally settling on the broach at her throat. There was no sign of his dimple she'd become accustomed to seeing.

Unease gripped her, and she reached for her suddenly too tight collar.

"I am certain you were only moments ago enjoying breakfast." His glare snapped to hers as if inspecting her response to his words. "You favor eggs, ham, and fresh bread with jam, if I am not mistaken."

Her eyes widened. It was a favorite of all the women at Craven House, but how he knew this tidbit was surprising.

"You are certainly correct, and Hollybrooke Manor has one of the best cooks in all of England, or so Lord Cummings boasted on my first day here." Her words did nothing to soften his look. "Will you join me, my lord?"

"You know damn well we sat across from one another only moments ago and spoke of my travels and my family." His voice rose with annoyance. "Though, I cannot imagine how you hurried so quickly and changed your gown."

"Hurried to change?" Sam took a step back—despising herself for feeling the need to cower at his angry words. Had he gone insane? He was spouting nonsense, but the venom behind his words was unmistakable. "I only just left my chambers."

"I may have been fool enough once to believe the best in a woman, but that time has passed." A vein pulsed in his forehead, and his nostrils flared. "Tell me, Miss Judith Pengarden, did you always plan to betray your betrothed, or was our chance meeting truly serendipitous?"

Sam gasped for air as she attempted to hide her amusement. Of all the times for someone to mix up the sisters…this was certainly not the most convenient.

"Was our time last night only meant to be one final tryst, or do you plan to continue your charade of affection for Cartwright?" His shoulders hunched forward then, the anger leaving him. "Damn it, Lord Cartwright is a fine man. Will make a respectable husband and a marvelous father."

Her heart plummeted. "Elijah…I…" Her toneless response did nothing to curb his fury.

"Save your explanations." His hand sliced through the air, cutting off her words. "I am not interested in rationalizations or any justification you have created to elucidate away your duplicity."

"Allow me to explain this...it is only a misunderstanding, I promise you."

"Do you think your promises mean anything?" he huffed. "I have things to attend to. I should be going."

He made to push past her. Without thinking, Sam grabbed his arm to stop him. She supposed he'd learn his mistake soon enough, but not a part of her wanted them to be at odds until she could catch both Jude and Elijah in the same room together. Why hadn't she mentioned that Simon was to wed her sister—her identical twin sister?

"Please wait and allow me to speak."

"The only person I should be speaking to is Lord Cartwright." His threat stung, driving his accusation deep. "I have much to explain to him—apologies to give. Then I must take my leave immediately."

"You mean to tell him of our time in the study?" She leaned close, her hand still rested on his arm. "That is not necessary, if you will only listen."

"Listen to you weave another—more elaborate—web of lies?"

Every speck of closeness she'd thought existed between them vanished.

She'd never meant to deceive or mislead him in any way. Everyone in attendance was either family or a close friend. It had been many months since she'd had to explain to anyone that if they thought they'd met her or seen her somewhere, it was completely probable they'd met Judith instead.

The situation would be comical if it had something to do with anyone other than the man she'd spent the night dreaming of—wrapped in his solid arms, his lips blazing a trail down her neck and over her breasts, and his heart beating in unison with hers.

A blush heated her cheeks at the thought of his engorged member. Did it actually resemble the image from the book? It may be a bit longer before she discovered the answer to her question because at that moment, the only man who could tell her—or return her book and allow her to find her own answer—was seething mad.

"Do allow me to pass, *miss*." His voice was level and even, betraying none of the fury she sensed rolling just below the surface.

Chapter Seven

Eli peered at the woman, everything within him screaming for him to pull away from her and find his chambers. The hall was no place to discuss such intimate matters. Though, *no* part of him wanted to address the situation, only run and forget her treachery.

It was the thing he'd guarded himself against since his mother's final betrayal. Eli had been right to not trust another, never allow someone so close they could wound him.

He wanted to linger—demand she tell him why she'd lied to him, but from his own mother, he'd learned that people often have no notion why they do the things they do. His connection with Miss Samantha—Miss Judith?—had been true, to the point of being almost tangible. Just as his lips had touched hers, he thought he could grasp hold of their passion and never let go. The worst part was, he hadn't worried about trusting her. He'd taken her for who she'd claimed to be, and what she'd appeared to offer with no question.

Elijah had unwittingly caused irreversible harm to a man he respected. Lord Cartwright had asked for none of this, yet the most damaging part of the situation would fall upon him. It was within the earl's right to challenge Eli to a duel in Miss Judith's honor.

"We spoke of very private matters." It seemed oddly strange to be concerned about details of his past when his future was in jeopardy. "What you have done is treacherous."

A door opened behind him, closing quietly as footsteps rounded the corner.

"Miss Samantha, I thought you were on your way to the breakfast parlor." Lord Chastain paused briefly, eyeing her hold on Eli's arm. Her grasp fell away, freeing Eli to depart. "Lord Ridgefeld, a pleasure to see you again."

Chastain had called her Samantha—but she was Judith. Surely the woman hadn't made a habit of duping others, as well. At the same time, he found he was content to believe she'd set out to not only deceive him but others, as well.

Eli waited until Chastain started down the stairs before facing her once more.

She had the nerve to smirk, folding her arms across her chest.

Elijah turned in stunned silence, but Chastain had moved out of sight, none the wiser to the conversation he'd interrupted. Eli had been so certain the woman from the breakfast parlor, and the one before him were one in the same—Elijah had allowed his emotions, feelings of rage, betrayal, and shame, to overpower his intuitive nature.

His accusation and thinly veiled threat to go to Cartwright had been unmistakable. He'd meant his words to be hurtful, even if only a fraction of how much her deceit had injured him.

That was not completely true. He'd indeed sensed something strange—roughly different—about the woman below. They shared the same eye color and shape, their hair was the same hue, and their necks were similarly slender; however, this woman's voice held a deeper, throaty tone, her hair was a bit longer, and a certain essence of command filled her as she stared intently at him.

"Twins?" he asked. "You never mentioned in our time together that there was a woman roaming about Lord Cummings' home who was a mirror image of you."

"You never asked." Her chin lifted in defiance. "I did tell you of my three sisters here for the wedding."

"…but not that your sister—*your twin sister*—was to wed Cartwright!"

"It must have slipped my mind, my lord." A spark of mischief twinkled in her green eyes. "I might have been on the verge of telling you when your lips landed on mine."

"You expect me to believe that?"

"Do you have refutable evidence to the contrary, my lord?"

"Will you discontinue addressing me as *my lord*?" She'd been in his arms, their lips pressed together as their hands explored one another. He'd had quite scandalous thoughts of her since. Certainly, they had moved past formalities. "It is Elijah or Eli, blast it all."

Eli wanted to grab the woman and shake her—furious with the situation and with her—but, instead, he insisted she call him by his given name. It made little sense beyond his insatiable need to hear his name on her lips. He had no right to crave her as he did.

"Certainly, Elijah." She enunciated each syllable, giving far too much attention to the last as his name rolled off her tongue. It was as if she felt like the wronged party, and he was not the victim in her ploy. "It was not my intent to mislead you in any way."

"And you are Miss Samantha, not Miss Judith who is to marry Lord Cartwright?" He needed her to say it aloud. His attraction to her could not continue, but he needed to know he'd not done anything utterly damaging. Not that kissing an innocent, young woman wasn't detrimental—but it was repairable, especially as no one had witnessed their compromising situation.

"I am who I've always claimed. Samantha."

He continued. "Then I do owe you an apology for my outlandish behavior and accusations."

She eyed him suspiciously. "I accept your apology, Elijah, under one condition…"

He was unsure he'd agree to any condition, especially if it had to do with the naughty book currently stashed under his bedding in his chambers. "I am willing to hear what the condition is and assess if we can come to a truce."

"You are to call me Sam from now on when we are in private." When he didn't readily agree, she added as she took a step toward him, "You said some very hurtful things, Elijah. I would hate to see our animosity continue over a misunderstanding that was quickly rectified."

She took another step forward as if daring him to back down. He'd never been one to allow others to intimidate him, and this slip of a woman before him would not be his undoing.

"Sam. That is a man's name, is it not?" he asked.

"Just as Jude is a man's name," she quickly retorted. "My dear mother, the lord bless her soul, was fond of masculine nicknames. She was under the impression a woman could attain more if gifted with a strong name. As twins, barely larger than the palm of a man's hand, we needed all the strength we could get."

He felt his anger recede slightly, and he dug deeply to hold onto an ounce of the betrayal that had assaulted him when he'd entered the breakfast parlor. "I will address you as Sam while in private," he bit out through clenched teeth. Thankfully, he was only at Hollybrooke for an additional two days, at most. Another one-on-one meeting was unlikely to happen—no matter how much his treacherous body longed for it.

Their misunderstanding had indeed been rectified, yet Eli grasped for strands of anger...to remember what every woman was capable of, least he forget once more. He had no reason to remain furious at Sam, but his displeasure with himself was valid. Certainly, she should have been more forthcoming during their acquaintance, though he should not have been so quick to trust her, and then be even quicker when coming to an incorrect conclusion.

"Samantha Jane!" Her eyes widened, and she glanced toward the stairs as heavy boots thundered toward them.

"Samantha Jane?" Eli cocked one eyebrow.

"It is not Samantha Jane—it is plain Samantha," she hissed. "My dear brother thinks it funny to invent absurd middle names for us."

Before she could say another word, her brother had reached the top of the stairs and was almost upon them. "Sam," his breath heaved from his exertion. "Marce requires your attendance—immediately."

"That sounds awfully dire, dear Garrett Mallory," she cooed, returning his affection for names in a teasing manner they obviously had in common. "I will be down straight away."

"See that you are. It is most urgent." The man blinked several times and looked between Samantha and Eli as if noticing him for the first time and wondering what Elijah was doing alone in his sister's company. "Ridgefeld, is it?"

His scalp prickled at the man's intense scrutiny.

"Lord Ridgefeld rescued me from the storm yesterday, Garrett," she chastised. "Do be cordial."

"Rescued you, you say?" Garrett's eyes rounded in surprise. "You would have done us a far greater service by leaving her to the elements, I assure you."

"Might have saved me a lot of trouble, as well," Eli mumbled.

He chuckled along with Garrett, realizing he quite liked the man.

"Stellar to meet you, Ridgefeld." His chuckle subsided. "Call me Garrett, everyone does."

"It is a pleasure, Garrett."

"Ridgefeld, I hope to see you about. Samantha Constantine, we will await you in Cummings' study." Her brother sobered, his lips pressed together sternly. "Hurry."

Eli watched as the man retraced his steps down the hall and hurried down the stairs. "You look nothing like any of your siblings but Miss Judith." He'd gained a quick introduction to them in the breakfast room.

"We have different fathers—one mother," she sighed.

"I am not the first to inquire on the dissimilarities?"

"Someone mentions it at least a dozen times per year." Her shoulders straightened. "Have we mended our misunderstanding, my lord?"

As much as he wanted to hold onto his anger, it was not specifically directed at her. And he must let it go, at least until he departed Hollybrooke and was safely in his traveling carriage. "I think we have, Miss Samantha."

"Wonderful," her coy smile returned. "You shall escort me to dinner. Do not arrive late."

Eli allowed himself to smile at her demanding request—the woman was a hellion with no disguise. "Of course, miss. I would be delighted." Judging from her brother's comment, she'd been a handful her entire life. It was something he wasn't used to, a woman with a backbone who stood up and spoke her demands loud and clear—and didn't run off at the first sign of trouble. It was the only reason he was honoring her request without questioning her in regards to her commanding nature.

Sam—it sounded odd, even in his mind—pivoted and followed her brother down the stairs.

Eli would escort her to dinner and likely sit at her side to enjoy an entire evening of her coy laughter and peculiar banter.

The only question remaining was: what would occupy the next nine hours until he could see her again?

Chapter Eight

"Garrett," Sam shouted as she flew down the stairs, trailing her brother's long strides. "Do slow down. This gown makes it impossible for me to take more than one stair at a time."

"We've kept Marce waiting long enough." His severe words were at odds with his normal carefree demeanor. "Now, do hurry up."

"Heavens, what is so important?" Samantha took the final step to the main floor and sped up, grasping Garrett's arm to slow him down. "Is Marce upset I did not arrive in the breakfast parlor in a timely manner?"

Sam walked a fine line with her eldest sister. She and Payton had been lectured the entire journey from London about putting forth a positive impression and in no way were they to cause Jude any embarrassment before Cartwright's family and friends. They'd been paraded around as if they were a normal family, entertaining as if they belonged among the upper crust of society. With Jude's marriage to Lord Cartwright,

Sam supposed *her sister* did belong among them now, but where, exactly, did that leave her other siblings?

Were they to remain in the shadows, receiving invitations out of a sense of obligation?

Sam would not stand for such a thing.

"You did not attend breakfast?" Garrett asked. "I would have foregone the first meal if I had known it was an option."

He threw her a smug grin as they reached the closed door of Cummings' study.

There were several raised voices inside—she knew Marce's well, and the lighter tone of Jude's, but the loudest voice in the room was unfamiliar. It could be the heavy door distorted his words.

"I am not going to relish what lies on the other side of that door, am I?"

He stared at the closed door, his smirk vanishing. "All I ask is that you listen to Marce—and do not overreact."

"As if I ever overreact!"

"As if you do anything *but* overreact, Samantha Olivia."

Sam and Jude had never been apart. Much like the connection between Marce and Garrett—who shared a father—she and her twin had each other; always had at least one person they could depend on. And Jude was, at this very moment, preparing to leave Sam behind to marry Simon and start her own family.

Sam stood still, not reaching for the door nor having the energy to flee. There was nothing Samantha could do to change the situation besides beg Jude not to marry; however, Simon was a good, kind man who would take care of his wife and the family to come.

How could Sam do anything to jeopardize that future, even though it left her adrift without a stable person to anchor her to shore?

It was a childish way of thinking, especially with regards to her twin's marriage, but no matter how hard Sam tried to suppress her feelings of resentment and abandonment, they were still there. Always lurking just under the surface, threatening her control.

Garrett pushed the door wide to reveal Jude perched on the edge of the chaise, Marce in a high-backed chair close to the desk, dominating the room, and a man she'd never lain eyes upon pacing before the hearth. The room appeared different from the night before without the low light and the crackle of the fire.

Sam stepped into the room, and Garrett retreated, closing the door—leaving her and her sisters alone with the man.

Something about the set of Jude's shoulders had Sam rushing to her twin's side.

"Jude?" She lowered herself to the chaise and reached for Jude's face, turning it toward her. "Have you been crying? Has someone hurt you?" Sam would not stand for that...ever. "And you are pale as a ghost."

Jude clasped her hands in reassurance. They were freezing—the tips of each finger held a blue tint.

"Samantha." Marce's voice pulled Sam's scrutinizing stare from Jude's hands to where their eldest sister sat. "Do stand. I have someone here to make your acquaintance."

Sam risked another look at her twin, whose gaze had settled on the stranger pacing before the fire, but Sam hadn't time to inspect the man when her sister was so obviously hurting.

The room was alight with tension—Marce sat ramrod straight, and the man strode with solid, heavy steps back and forth from the corner of the desk, to before the hearth and then to the far windows, only to pivot and retrace his path. Heavy footfalls drew her attention; the sure stride and pattern very familiar to her. It was the same as her own pacing.

Heel. Toe. Heel. Toe.

Marce had complained for years that it sounded as if a herd of elephants was stampeding above her office, which lay directly below Sam and Jude's bedchamber.

The man's dark copper hair was cut precisely above his collar, and his eyes avoided hers.

She didn't need to see their color. They would be sage green.

The same as Jude's moss-colored eyes—which were the mirror image of her own.

"What is going on, Marce?" Sam moved to stand before her eldest sister, hands on her hips.

Her sister responded by standing to face Sam, her petite height almost a foot shorter than her twin sisters, affording Sam a view of her golden curls pinned to her crown.

The man cleared his throat and stopped pacing to halt with his back to the fire.

Perspiration had broken out across his forehead. He was nervous, as well he should be.

Fiery red hair came with a matching temper. The hair on the back of her neck stood on end as the man, his height several inches taller than hers, moved to stand before her as Marce retook her seat.

She understood now. Her sister was only there to keep Sam's temper at bay. To remind her of her status as a proper lady—no thanks to the man before her.

"As I live and breathe," Sam seethed. Jude's gasp filled the room. "The prodigal father has returned."

He shifted from one foot to the other and frowned, betraying his unease at the situation.

"Lord Beauchamp," Marce began a proper introduction. An introduction that should not be necessary between father and daughter. "This is Miss Samantha Pengarden, your daughter."

Sam assessed him, her eyes narrowing to mimic his. Upon closer inspection, Beauchamp's red hair was shot through with grey, his shoulders slender to match his lean frame, and his face was etched with age lines. His wrinkles showed a man who'd experienced much in his life, though not all of it positive.

They'd been told since they were old enough to notice other children had a mother and a father, while she and her siblings only had a mother, that Madame Sasha—their mother—had been Beauchamp's mistress. It hadn't turned sour until the elder Beauchamp demanded his son marry, and marry well.

Their mother and Beauchamp had parted ways, and he'd married quickly, without ceremony.

However, not before he'd left Sasha with a parting gift—his twin daughters in her womb.

Dexter Pengarden, Viscount Beauchamp, stared between them, as if unconvinced that two such identical women existed.

"What are you doing here?" Sam bit out through clenched teeth.

"I was invited—"

"You must be mistaken." She cackled at the ludicrous insinuation.

To prove her wrong, he pulled the invitation from his coat pocket and held it out to her.

Sam unfolded the invitation she knew all too well. She and Payton had spent several days hand-writing thirty identical slips to be delivered to all of their family and friends, inviting them to join Jude and Cart in Derbyshire for a festive garden wedding. This particular letter had been crafted by Payton, her tight, heavy handwriting unmistakable.

But who had sent it to him? Surely not Jude. Her sister would have asked her permission. Payton and Lord Cartwright were unaware of who'd fathered Sam and Jude. Even Garrett had never shown the least bit of interest in locating any of their sires. That only left one person—one woman with hair of spun gold and eyes that were wise beyond their years. The person they could all rely on to care for them—make sure they always had shelter, food, and shoes with warm stockings.

"Marce?" Sam challenged, turning to her eldest sibling.

A sob wrenched from Jude's throat, and her face lowered into her hands, her shoulders shaking with silent cries.

"I thought it was long past time for the pair of you to become better acquainted with Lord Beauchamp."

"What would bring that insane notion to mind?" Sam turned back to Beauchamp, who'd wisely remained silent but continued to inspect his offspring.

"You and Jude are taking your place among society." Marce shrugged as if her actions were not life-altering to her siblings. "It was not something I thought to happen, but it has; therefore, it would only be a matter of time before the pair of you crossed paths with Lord Beauchamp. I thought it best for it to happen here, among family and friends, as opposed to a crowded ballroom. Besides, the *ton* is bound to recognize the resemblance quickly enough—and rumors will spread. Your name will be linked to his, and the connection shared in every salon in London. I will not risk the pair of you being fodder for all the gossipmongers."

"That is not our concern." Sam cared naught if her father's name were embroiled in ill repute—or if she were linked to unsubstantiated rumors. Her entire life had been a scandal, from birth to present day. She'd grown up the bastard child of a viscount. The chanting of her schoolmates could still be heard—and it had been years since anyone dared speak of her less than honorable birth. "I—as well as Jude—do not care if disgrace lands squarely on his head. The scandal would be well-deserved. Jude and I will persevere."

She held Beauchamp's stare as she spoke, satisfied her meaning was heard. Let all of London gossip behind their fans about the twin women who looked suspiciously similar to Lord Beauchamp—even using his surname. The viscount deserved to be ridiculed, ostracized, and altogether spurned by proper society. He'd left the woman he'd claimed to love, to care for and raise his children while he moved on to another woman. One his family deemed *proper*.

"It is not him I am concerned about, Sam," Marce mumbled. "Jude is to wed on the morrow and will take her place at Simon's side as his countess. You will soon fall in love yourself—and I want no rumors to swirl around either of you."

"Jude, did you know about this?"

"I did not," her twin wheezed, attempting to lessen her sobs. "I only arrived a few minutes before you."

She'd been lectured about causing Jude any anxiousness before her wedding, threatened with being relegated to her room until the Season ended, and watched carefully since their arrival in Derbyshire. How was it that this man could sweep into the house and wreak such havoc on the eve of Jude's nuptials?

"I shall have Lord Cartwright summoned to throw him from the house—as he deserves."

"I am here to see Judith wed, and then I will take my leave, but not before." Beauchamp began his pacing once more, the study of his twin daughters coming to an end. "We shall be cordial if we see one another in London. There is no reason to cause gossip where there is none to be had."

"And what of your wife, my lord?" Jude squeaked.

It had been the reason he'd left Sasha before she'd grown large enough to know she was with child—and the reason he'd remained absent from their lives. Beauchamp had a wife who had longed for children of her own, and was unwilling to allow Jude and Sam to be a part of their lives, especially once the viscountess was carrying her own child.

Beauchamp dipped his head at the mention of Lady Beauchamp. Had he not informed his wife of his journey to Derbyshire? What had changed, if he was willing to face her wrath now but not all those years ago?

But it was Marce who answered the question. "She passed away five years ago during childbirth."

"You've been aware of this?" Sam threw the words at Marce harder than if she'd thrown a rock. "Why were we not told?"

Jude retreated back into her silent shell as she gently rocked back and forth on the chaise. She'd never been one for confrontations and raised voices.

"Your mother—Madame Sasha—forbade me from making contact with either of you," Beauchamp confessed. "I was respecting her wishes."

"*Respecting* her wishes," Sam repeated with a laugh. "You certainly did not respect her enough—love her enough—to remain and help raise your children. You did not respect her enough to willingly give your daughters all they deserved as the children of a viscount—illegitimate or not. You did not respect her enough to send funds to make sure we had food on the table and clothes to keep warm. You did not love Jude or me enough to be there when we needed you. You did not love us enough to come for us as soon as you could. You did not care enough to check on us after Mother died."

Sam's laugh turned into a deep moan as all breath left her—an emptying hollowness gripped her as loneliness set in.

It was unfair to burden Jude with her feelings, especially since she'd be wed tomorrow and leave for a trip to Cartwright's family estate. Marce was clearly not of the same mindset as Sam.

The room was closing in on her as Jude's sobs grew in intensity...Sam spun toward the door, needing air, needing space...needing something she couldn't define.

Her hand grabbed for the knob as she twisted and wrenched the door open, stepping into the hall. The sobbing followed her, bouncing off the corridor walls and echoing deeper into the house—a screech of fright from a passing maid was enough to stop Sam long enough to realize it was her desperate bawling reverberating through the house, not Jude's.

Sam fled up the stairs, tripping twice but righting herself quickly—only scraping one knee as she climbed, desperately needing the solace of her bedchambers.

Could she forget all that'd transpired in Cummings' study—go back in time to before Garrett had come to collect her?

The slam of her bedchamber door rang as she leaned against the hard surface, slipping down to the floor. Her legs shook, unable to hold her upright any longer, and she allowed the cries to leave her, deep howls of anguish pulled at her core and her chest heaved with each wail.

She hadn't any notion what to do, how to react, or what to say. Part of her longed to take hold of her father and never let go—while another part wished to go back a few hours, return to the upstairs hall—with Elijah.

Lord Ridgefeld was incapable of the many transgressions Sam levied against her father.

The marquis would never hurt her; leave her without any explanation or so much as a backwards glance.

Chapter Nine

Elijah breathed a sigh of relief when he stepped through the double doors and found he stood on a terrace overlooking Lord Cummings' gardens. The fresh air, room to move, and solitude were immediately soothing. He'd never lived in a crowded household, never understood the reality of living with siblings or relatives except for his grandfather. Any memory of a time when his mother was present eluded him, *if* there were any memories to be had.

As a child, the only sounds within his home were those he made. Grandfather encouraged him to explore their estate: hike around the pond, fish in the stream that fed the pond, climb the fruit trees—but these were all activities made more enjoyable with company.

Eli had only his grandfather as a companion. They'd spent years seeking out adventure, traveling the continent and abroad, collecting anything of interest. In short, his upbringing had been pleasurable. Love, laughter, and learning all in abundance for Eli.

That did not stop him from suspecting something was lacking—a void remained.

And he'd foolishly thought bringing his mother home to England could fill it. He'd created an image of a damsel in distress, awaiting her knight to rescue her. The harsh reality was…his mother was exactly where she wanted to be—far from her only son and her birth country.

Laughter invaded his reprieve as he slowly walked around a corner of the terrace, revealing a group of guests playing battledore and shuttlecock on an expanse of freshly trimmed lawn. A light breeze whipped the women's skirts about their ankles and pushed the men's hair into their faces. The storm from the previous day had passed, leaving only blue, cloudless skies. But the wind remained, a reminder of the fickle nature of England's weather patterns. It was good to see that it had cleared before Lord Cartwright's wedding, for certainly rain showers on one's wedding day could not be a favorable omen.

It had rained the night before his ship ported in Baltimore—his grandfather gone only several days and he out to find his mother. Eli should have anticipated his failure. How he wished he had remained aboard the *Cameron de Gazelle*, awaiting its journey to Canada and then its return to Liverpool without knowing the fate of Alice Watson.

However, he'd been alone. Depressingly alone. Not many spoke to him after his grandfather's passing, either because they attempted to give him space and time to grieve, or they did not know what to say to a young man who'd lost his only known relative.

Eli hadn't wanted to continue life alone. The desire to find his mother, bring her back to England, and create the family he'd lacked was the only thing that had driven him from the ship that day—on his fool's errand.

Mounting his white steed, in the form of a hack, Eli had located his mother.

The problem had been that he'd hoped to rescue her. He hadn't known *she* was the dragon he'd been sent to slay. She'd balked at the mention of leaving America—finally sending Eli scurrying back to Liverpool, alone.

Odd that the return voyage and his time in England since had seemed all the more vacant simply because his hopes for his future—one with his mother—were dashed for good. She had no interest in coming home, no interest in knowing her son, and certainly, no motherly devotion to Eli's happiness or understanding of his sorrow and loss.

The woman had single-handedly crushed him. It was much preferable to believe her letters had stopped arriving because she was in jeopardy and silently begged him to come for her. Not that she'd turned herself into a common harlot.

Anger—red-hot—settled within him once more at the thought. His mother, Alice, had everything she could dream of in England…a country home, unlimited funds, and a son who loved her despite all she'd done. However, for whatever reason, an existence dependent on a man was preferable to her.

Eli leaned against the railing, attempting to focus on the people in the distance—what game they played now, who was winning, and what they all found so enjoyable.

He'd discovered scarce moments of happiness since his grandfather's passing—and even fewer flashes of peace. Naively, he'd thought to find some sense of tranquility away from the place he'd called home his entire life, putting miles and hours of travel between him and every item that reminded him of the late marquis.

The elderly man's presence only followed him. If his grandfather were here, he'd be with the gathering on the lawn, laughing and enjoying the company of so many guests. He'd insist Eli join in, as well.

That had never been Elijah's way of things. He'd accompanied his grandfather during years of travel, but always stood in the background, watching the many people who sought out the marquis, hanging on his every word—awaiting any compliment sent their way by the old man. And he'd been generous with his good tidings, well-wishes, and praise. His grandfather had never failed to notice a woman's different hairstyle, or a man's extravagantly tied cravat knot.

"Lord Ridgefeld!" a man called to him from across the lawn, waving him over. "Join us."

Eli was in no mood to dive into merriment—nor did he seek to bring the other guests down with his dour temperament. Instead, he acted as if he hadn't heard the man call him. Lord Haversham, Eli thought he remembered the man's name.

It was time he moved out of view to avoid another call to participate.

He retraced his path back along the terrace, and past the doors he'd exited through. Green lawn no longer filled the area beyond the terrace, but a maze of flowers and shrubs with paths of white pebbles zigzagging from one rose bush to a tall hedge to a bench nestled between two bushes with blue blossoms.

Every plant was trimmed precisely in anticipation of Lord Cartwright and Miss Judith's wedding on the morrow. Not a single blossom dared wilt, not a leaf dared fall—the care of the garden was unlike any he'd seen before.

A crew of gardeners must have worked all morning to remove any damage done by the storm. Every blossom pointed heavenward, soaking up the rays from the sun as if not a drop of rain had fallen the previous day. The wind, so evident and harsh on the other side of the house, did not disrupt a single leaf in the garden.

The vision before him was serene. It pained Eli to think of the disturbance to the beautiful flowers and well-maintained shrubs that were to come. A morning surrounded by such exquisiteness, to sit among the plants, to inhale their scent, as Lord Cartwright entered into the bonds of marriage. It was a breathtaking place, but he understood the seclusion needed for the flowers to thrive, just as his peace had been irrevocably broken since his arrival at Hollybrooke, so would the gathered guests shatter the harmony of Cummings' garden.

Certainly, his way of thinking could not be correct. Happiness and joy begat happiness and joy. Would the flowers not bloom brightly, and the shrubs not stand taller when infused with the good cheer of the wedding party?

Maybe it was possible only Eli flourished surrounded by stillness, silence, and solitude.

He balanced his weight on the railing and crossed his arms.

Breathing in deeply, Eli closed his eyes.

The calm enveloped him, soothed his melancholy mood, and forced him to focus on the even beat of his heart. The same organ that hadn't long ago beat with an intensity he'd never felt. It had been the sight of Miss Samantha coming toward him in the hall that changed things. He'd been angry, felt betrayed, and for the first time, knowing he was alone at Cummings' house party hadn't been to his liking.

Then, his rage had subsided, and something altogether new overtook him. Her quick wit, sly smirk, and lifted chin—Miss Samantha appeared before his closed eyes. Her auburn hair trailing down her back as she'd fled the hall in pursuit of her brother. But her hair had been pinned atop her head that morning—it was another intimate moment he remembered. He'd wanted to call her name, ask her to remain with him, not to leave him alone.

Miss Samantha could in no way understand his sense of loneliness—her house, no doubt, always teeming with her siblings and activity. She was at ease in a crowd, welcoming the sight of guests and relishing their attentions. Or at least, that's what he imagined of her. Her lighthearted disposition left no doubt she was outgoing when surrounded by society, so at odds with Elijah's personality.

A part of him mourned the person he could have been if his father hadn't died and his mother hadn't abandoned him. His grandfather loved him—made sure he was educated, well-traveled, and the perfect gentleman; however, that did not mean some deeper part of him didn't realize something was missing.

He allowed stillness to take over once more, banishing thoughts of his mother, his grandfather, and a certain enchanting, fiery-haired maiden. With the banishment of those thoughts, the sounds of the wind blowing through the trees alongside the manor receded, and the laughter from the guests quieted.

The serenity found in complete silence, accompanied by the dark allowed delicate sobs to drift down to him. Heart-wrenching, soul-consuming, fate-shattering weeping invaded his sense of seclusion. If it were not for the rise and fall of the female cries, Eli would imagine it was his own inner turmoil finally coming to the surface, demanding to be recognized and dealt with.

Eli moved toward the sound, coming from farther down the terrace, back toward the doors he'd exited. Stepping down and onto the lawn, he gazed upward as the sobs carried on the breeze.

The sadness of her cries had Eli rubbing his chest where a deep ache had taken root—a combination of the sound from above and his own bottomless grief.

An intense need filled him, compelling him back into the house and toward the sobbing. If he were able to soothe the woman's hurt, would that also assuage his own?

Elijah was uncertain where the absurdity of that logic had sprung from, but he needed it to be true. Once inside the manor, the cries disappeared, blocked by walls of thick timber and a solid floor; however, he knew the general direction of the room facing the back of the grand home.

Hurrying up the stairs, Elijah was thankful he didn't encounter anyone as he took the steps three at a time. Once he'd reached the top landing, he took off in a sprint, his boot steps loud even with the thick rug below him.

Chapter Ten

Sam gathered herself enough to move to the large four-post bed dominating most of her guest chamber, but her aching sobs did not cease, though her tears had vanished a few moments ago. Normally, the peach-colored bed covering and draperies would have been light enough to brighten her mood, but now, the room had turned an offensive, bittersweet orange. Her tongue swiped across her dry lips, tasting only the salted remains of her tears—evidence of her conflicted emotions regarding Lord Beauchamp's appearance.

Father.

Her father.

The term was foreign to her and held no meaning beyond filling her with a sense of emptiness, bound to grow deeper with Jude's impending marriage.

How could Marce think it wise to invite the man to Derbyshire?

Beauchamp couldn't be bothered to journey across London to look in on his daughters, but he'd travel all the way to Hollybrooke? For what purpose?

She'd lived her entire eighteen years without a man in her life but Garrett, and she had done just fine. If the viscount expected her to fall in line and pretend to be the daughter he'd always known, the loathsome man did not know Sam at all. They had never met—in fact, he'd never taken so much as a passing interest in his offspring. She could not be the good daughter, just as he hadn't any notion how to be a father.

Of course, it seemed many people she'd thought she knew were doing things completely out of character. Marce's actions stirred Sam's sense of betrayal. Had it not occurred to her eldest sibling to at least ask her or Jude if they had any interest in meeting their father?

Jude possibly would have agreed to the invitation with a bit a coaxing, but Sam, no, she never would have approved. It was Jude's wedding, but this affected Sam's life as much as Jude's.

From what she'd overheard behind closed doors growing up, Beauchamp had shown a slight interest in having a child with her mother—that was until she and Jude were born, and not only was Sam a girl, but a pair of girls. The man had run for the hills.

Once, many years ago, when her mother would not buy her a baby doll she so wanted from the mercantile, Sam had screamed that if her father were there, he would have bought her the pretty doll—an entire shelf of dolls…because *he* loved her. It had been unfair, and she had yelled in a moment of childish indignation and fury. Sam remembered the way her mother had smiled and calmly walked from the shop, leaving Sam on the floor, crying. Jude had stood beside her, torn between following their mother and other siblings, or remaining with her twin. In the end, Sam had brushed the dirt from her frock and departed the store, Jude walking steadfastly at her side.

She'd never apologized for her harsh words, but that evening, Sam and Jude had heard Sasha talking with another woman in her study, something about being blessed to have given birth to girls, or the *horrid man* would have returned to take her child—or children as the case may be—and raise it as his own with his barren, cold-hearted wife.

She hadn't known whom they spoke of at the time.

And as Sam grew older and matured, she'd come to understand the neglect and heartache her mother had witnessed at Beauchamp's hand. It was too much to dream he'd changed, that he was now capable of putting the needs of others before his—or his family's—demands.

The bit of enjoyment she'd begun to take at Hollybrooke had been dispelled quickly, made all the worse knowing it would follow her back to London.

A light tap sounded at her door.

Sam attempted to swipe away any remaining tears from her face, but her palm only met dry skin. Had Marce come to confront her about her rude behavior? Maybe it was Jude come to cry on her shoulder—but Sam couldn't be the strong one in this situation. She was not the person anyone should lean on for support…she was falling apart, too.

The knock sounded again.

"Go away!" Her voice trembled, and she fell silent, but another, more insistence knock followed.

Sam stood and moved toward the door to send away whoever sought to disrupt her moment of weakness. She'd never been one to seek time alone. It gave way to many thoughts that were better left hidden, locked away deeply within her.

The knob was cold against the palm of her hand as she twisted and pulled the door open a crack.

If it were one of her sisters, they would have entered the room without warning or demanded entrance. It would embarrass not only her family but also her if a servant waited on the other side of the door.

"Yes?" Her eyes attempted to adjust to the bright light in the hall. She blinked rapidly to focus—her room had been shrouded in shadows as Sam hadn't bothered to pull the drapes or light a candle upon her return. She'd dismissed her maid until after the noonday meal for Sam had expected to be downstairs with the other guests. "I seek a few moments alone. You may return in an hour's time to tidy the room."

"Miss Samantha?" Sam narrowed her eyes, taking in Lord Ridgefeld standing outside her door. "Is everything as it should be? I was on the terrace and heard sobbing."

Spectacular.

A witness to her weakness.

It was not good enough Beauchamp had shown up and ruined her remaining days with her twin sister close, but now all the guests below had heard her wallowing in her own self-pity, bawling over the appearance of a man she hadn't met until now, and who, in fact, meant less than nothing to her.

She glanced past the marquis, searching for the huddle of guests who likely waited within hearing distance to absorb all the sordid details.

"Did my brother send you to check on me?" Her brow rose as if she were challenging him to deny it. It was highly improper for a man to call on a woman in her chambers, but that did not register with Sam before her question had been voiced.

"Certainly not."

"Is everyone speaking about me—and our unexpected guest?" Sam prodded. "You can let everyone know I am doing well. Your obligation is fulfilled."

"Is everyone speaking of what?" His eyes narrowed in confusion.

Sam pulled the door wide and stepped around Lord Ridgefeld, glancing down the hall in both directions. If an audience waited, they were out of sight and suspiciously quiet. Likely afraid to breathe and miss any tidbits of conversation that floated their way.

Her upbringing screamed no one was about, and that Elijah was here of his own accord.

"I assure you, I am alone, Miss Samantha." He'd taken a step back to allow her to pass, but without thinking, she grabbed his arm and hauled him into her chambers, shutting the door behind him. "I do not think this is proper—"

"Oh, do not be so felicitous, my lord." Sam moved back to her bed and plopped down. "I do not wish for an audience to hear me bawling. And, need I remind you, if you were concerned with propriety, you would not have knocked on my door."

"Very true. However, you were crying." It was not meant to be a question, so Sam held her tongue. "Tell me, Miss Samantha, what has upset you? I will attempt to set things right."

"Are you ever not the relentless gentleman?"

"I...well...no," he stumbled over his words, his posture stiffening.

Which brought to mind another image—a drawing to be exact, of another thing, stiff and large. Sam felt the blush creep up her cheeks. In her dreams...in the hall...Sam could not avoid the images from the wicked book.

"Call me Sam," she blurted. Why did the man make her feel so at ease and at the same time on edge with something very close to need? She'd never needed another—beyond her twin, of course. "I mean, my family calls me Sam, you are free to do the same."

He gave her a weak smile as he strode across the room and lowered himself to sit in a straight-backed chair.

The mere sight of him pushed all thoughts of her father's surprising appearance from her mind. She was alone, in a room with Elijah...and the last thing she wanted occupying her thoughts was Beauchamp.

Elijah shifted in the atrocious chair, attempting to find a more agreeable position; unfortunately, the seat did not afford one.

Finally, he settled for slouching ever so slightly, extending his legs and crossing them at his ankles.

Sam laughed when he folded his arms across his chest.

"Is something funny?" he inquired.

"You have the appearance of a petulant child." She shouldn't find even a hint of joy on a day such as this, but Sam noticed her wit flee whenever Elijah was near.

"Mayhap I feel like a petulant child at the moment," he retorted in jest, though Sam saw the change in his expression, as if a bank of clouds had settled over him. "Now, what has you upset, Sam?"

She set her hands on either side of her on the bed and sat a bit straighter. The man had the uncanny ability to push her troubles away. He'd done that exact thing when his carriage had pulled up alongside her on the road, offering her transport back to Hollybrooke before the storm unleashed its fury on her. Before his arrival, Sam had only thought of being gone from Derbyshire and back in London—surrounded by hordes of elegantly dressed people where she'd thought she belonged. But in the last day, she hadn't thought once of returning—and suspected the crowds of people only kept her inner turmoil at bay.

"I am feeling better, never fear." The last subject Sam wanted to address with Elijah was why she'd been crying. It was silly, truly. A woman crying over her father and his rakehell ways. Certainly, there were far more sorrowful things in the world.

He eyed her suspiciously. "I do not believe that for a second. Your sobs were heartbreaking. I will know why."

It was a command, yet his posture remained at ease.

"Samantha." His tone softened, and he sat forward, moving his hands to rest on his knees. "Sam, do not think I have not been through my own trials and heartbreak."

Heartbreak—he kept coming back to the word. The farthest thing from her mind was heartbreak, but what did Elijah know of it? Had he loved a woman only to have her rip his heart from his chest and crush it under her dance slipper? Or worse yet, was he still in love with a lady who did not return his affection?

It was a shocking—and impossible—thought. At some point, Sam had come to think of the man as hers; no other woman had a right to him physically or emotionally.

"Tell me what you know of heartbreak," Sam mumbled, avoiding eye contact, fearful of what he'd see in her green stare.

"That is certainly not going to happen until you inform me what sent you to tears," he refuted.

Sam pushed to her feet and crossed her arms, pacing toward him only to reel and walk back toward the bed.

"If you will not tell me, then I will have to guess." One brow rose, and his smile returned as he tapped his chin in thought. "Let me see…"

"You will not guess, my lord." Unless he'd already heard gossip below stairs—which was highly probable. It would injure her further to know he'd sat before her all this time and knew exactly what had brought her to tears but was forcing her to say the words aloud.

"Oh, I assure you, I am most adept at hide and seek, Miss Samantha." He chuckled and sat back once more in his slouched position. "My grandfather was known to lose—or as he called it, *hide*—things about his estate. I spent many hours finding items he'd misplaced."

"This is not hide and seek," she countered, pivoting once more to face him.

"Hidden or lost emotions are no different than misplaced physical items."

The notion that he could somehow deduce what had upset her was not appealing, but she had no intention of speaking of her family's shame—especially with Lord Ridgefeld, who was little more than a stranger.

"Are you missing a pet back in London, mayhap a kitten?" His eyes widened when Sam's mouth betrayed her, her lips curling slightly. "Oh, I know…a parakeet!"

"Heavens, what would ever make you think I have a bird?" Sam couldn't help but laugh at his obvious jest.

"Well," Elijah sat forward once more, taking her in from head to toe. "Sometimes, it takes more than one guess. Allow me to think."

He made a production of closing his eyes and sighing loudly.

Sam tapped her slippered foot on the bare floor.

Finally, his eyes sprang open. "I know, you forgot your favored gown in town and now you will be forced to borrow a maid's garb for the wedding tomorrow morning."

"Do not be ridiculous, my lord." Sam sighed with exasperation. "If I had forgotten my gown, I would simply borrow one of Jude's.

"Your sister is marrying Lord Cartwright tomorrow, which will leave you alone. You will miss her companionship. Mayhap you even—begrudgingly—envy her finding Cartwright."

Sam turned back toward the bed to hide her look of utter shock. Her own musings spoken aloud. It was true, she did feel all those things, though she was hesitant to admit to envying her twin in any way; however, it gave Sam something to latch on to—something that had nothing to do with Beauchamp, his sudden, unexpected arrival, and his abandonment of his twin daughters over eighteen years prior.

"You are quite accomplished, indeed," Sam said, twisting toward him once more. "Though I am very happy for Jude. She is in love. Simon is her perfect match—their temperaments and interests align closely. They will suit each other well."

"However, this leaves you alone," he prodded.

"Certainly not," Sam said with a chuckle. "I have Marce, Garrett, and Payton."

"But Payton is little more than a child."

"She has reached her seventeenth year, my lord." Sam heard the hostility in her tone and wished she could take it back, but Elijah didn't seem to notice. "She will be presented to society next season; that is if she can control her vices for another year."

"I do know a thing or two about being alone—and the sorrow it brings to a person." The dark shadow returned to his eyes. "I have lost, but am trying to move forward."

Sam was instantly remorseful for her insensitivity. "My apologies, Elijah." She sank into the tall-backed chair that matched his. "You lost your grandfather recently, and here I am, laboring over Jude's marriage and departure from our townhouse. All the while, I should be content she is still with us and happy beyond anything I've ever seen."

Elijah sighed. "That is not *why* I brought up my recent loss, Sam."

If he said another word after uttering her name aloud, she didn't process it. She could listen to him say her name—whisper her name, yell her name, sigh her name—for the rest of her stay in Derbyshire.

"Are you listening to me at all? Here I am, a poor sap, baring my soul, and you are not so much as hearing me." Elijah stood, stepping before her chair. She tilted her chin upward to see his face and avoid staring at his midsection—knowing what lay just a bit south of his waistband. "As I was saying, the best medicine for melancholy is distraction."

She wondered if he suspected he'd been her distraction since his arrival. And, oh, what a wonderful diversion he was. She made the foolish mistake of lowering her chin, her eyes shifting from his face to his lips, and farther down to his broad chest straining against the thin linen shirt below his coat.

She gulped, bringing her eyes back to his. "I am accomplished in the art of distraction."

"I have no doubt," he whispered as he leaned close. "Were you in the study last night looking for a distraction?"

"My book!" She'd almost forgotten about the set of volumes and the one he'd taken with him the previous night.

"Correction, Lord Cummings' book."

"Possession is what matters, my lord."

"Then I would say I am the rightful owner of the book because it is in *my* possession."

"I want it back," Sam demanded, her stare hardening. "You may collect it and bring it to me."

"I will do no such thing." He laughed, standing straight once more. "Besides, the proper thing to do is return the book to its rightful place…before anyone notices it is missing."

"And if I do not want to return it yet?" Blast it all, Sam wanted another peek at its wicked pages. Maybe more than a peek—she'd collect the entire collection, but that would certainly draw attention to the bare shelf. "I have not learned all I seek to know."

"I think it best you find another distraction—one that is not as ruinous."

It would be disastrous if she were found in possession of the scandalous book, but Sam could think of no other way to learn the ways of the flesh without questioning Garrett—which was *not* an option—or begging Ellie to confide what the marriage bed held.

But…she did have another option, and he stood right in front of her. "Are you offering to teach me, my lord?"

Chapter Eleven

"Miss Samantha, I do not think this is something we should be discussing." *Behind closed doors*, he wanted to add but smartly kept that bit to himself. Bloody hell, the woman had trapped him using his own words. "I think it best—"

A coy smirk lit her face, halting his words of caution. It was the same smile he'd noticed when he plucked her from the side of the road before the storm. "But, my lord, you recommended a diversion." She pushed her bottom lip out in a pout when he shook his head, unable to speak at her suggestive remark. She looked up at him from under lowered lashes. "I will be an eager pupil."

The woman was a siren. A minx sent to throw him off course. She was doing a stellar job of it. "Why don't I escort you downstairs or to the lawn area? The other guests were playing battledore and shuttlecock on the west lawn earlier."

"Not the type of distraction I was thinking of, Lord Ridgefeld," she cooed, her tongue darting out to slide across her plump lower lip.

Was it him, or did she put extra emphasis on *Ridge*?

His treacherous body responded.

She was a proper miss. Young and innocent, but she played the part of a seasoned courtesan. A woman well-versed in the talents needed to seduce a man—even a man as honorable as Eli.

"Then I have another idea, one you will certainly be more agreeable to."

His head tilted a bit to the left, his interests piqued. "Go on."

"We are both in need of distraction, are we not?"

He'd come to Derbyshire for that exact reason, but hadn't expected his journey to include the maddening, auburn-haired beauty before him who led him to question everything he thought a noble marquis was. "You are correct."

"Why not allow ourselves to be *each other's* diversion while in residence at Hollybrooke?"

Eli was not so gullible as to agree to her proposition without further explanation. "And, exactly how do you see this scheme going?"

"Well, we shall provide one another company during our stay—much as we are now."

"Much as we are now?" He was in the bedchamber of an unmarried, innocent miss, surrounded by a manor full of guests—in a stranger's home, no less. Their association was already far past the point of being anywhere near orthodox.

Eli glanced over his shoulder at her rumpled bed coverings, then to her gown closet with her things neatly arranged. Everything as it should be...more to the point, *he* was the only thing out of place.

"It is not sensible for you and me to keep one another company in such a way, Miss Samantha." He spoke her name slowly as if she were unable to grasp the meaning of his words. The room closed in around him. He stood too close to her, so close he could smell her fragrance of juniper berry, a change from her normal lavender scent. After less than a day, he thought he knew her usual perfume preference? "Though, I do concede I enjoy your company immensely."

He shouldn't have allowed the last words to cross his lips.

She smiled triumphantly and clapped her hands vigorously. "Then I propose we attempt to make the next couple of days tolerable for us both...no more sulking, no more melancholy, and more entertainment. You will set aside your grief, and I will overcome my coming loss."

He should in no way agree to her proposal. The wise decision would be to turn around immediately and slip from her room unseen. To forget their time in the carriage, their time in her chambers today...and, if he were truly smart, ignore their time together in the study. However, Eli was reluctant to sour her delightful mood by rejecting her suggestion outright.

Her request was a simple one: two days, or what remained of their time in Derbyshire, with his company as a distraction. She was requesting nothing but his time—which Eli had in spades.

"To clarify, we will accompany one another while in a proper setting?"

"If that is your wish, my lord," she conceded with a nod.

"Very well, then," he replied. "I would like to know more of what you propose."

Sam leapt from her seat and wrapped her arms around him, pulling him close for a tight hug. "It will include…"

Her words trailed off as all Eli could think about was her arms wrapped around him. The feel of her breasts pressed to this chest. The way her hips aligned with his. And that, when she spoke, her breath lingered at his neck…warm and inviting.

He suspected he would regret his decision to go along with her plan—he only hoped he was far from Derbyshire before his remorse truly sank in.

Sam released her hold—far too soon, but also too late to dissuade the stirring within him—and bounded back to the bed. She seemed completely unwitting of the scandal it would cause if he were discovered in her private chambers. Even *if* a chaperone had been present, it would be exceedingly inappropriate.

There was no hiding how aware he was of her exquisite beauty: her hair begging to be released from its trappings to fall wildly down her back, her gown a bit too snug across her breasts, and the way her skirt rose, revealing a quick glimpse of a shapely white ankle as she'd hopped on her bed.

His manhood jumped in response.

Her bed.

Her rumpled, sleep-disturbed bed.

Large, plush, and covered in a soft peach and white coverlet. In fact, the entire room was decorated with feminine pieces, from the white writing desk in the corner to the brass chandelier hung high above the bed. The chaise close to the window was a creamy white with pillows matching the drapes.

He focused on her troubled demeanor to keep his own wayward thoughts from moving into actions.

But even with all this light, bright décor, the room was cast in shadows with the draperies tied tightly shut and not a single lit candle. It was much the way Sam appeared when he'd first walked into her chambers—surrounded by shadows, as if stalked by what haunted her. Though it did not diminish her outward glow.

His own chambers were in direct opposition to this one. The color palette was dominated by varying shades of the darkest blues with large, oversized pieces of dark cherry wood furniture. Not a speck of soft color or delicate, girlish adornments could be found in the room.

Thankfully, she hopped from the bed and hurried to the closest window. Pulling back the heavy drape, Sam pinned it in place with the tie and rummaged through the writing desk before retrieving a slip of paper and a pencil, its tip sharpened to a deadly point.

Eli feared for a moment she would return to her place on the bed, but again, luck was in his favor as she took the seat next to his once more.

She cleared her throat, setting the paper on the small table between them. "Now, it is my understanding you are unfamiliar with the guests in residence, is that correct?" When he nodded, she continued, "Very well, I will task myself with familiarizing you with everyone: names, titles, estate location, and interests. Is that agreeable?"

"Certainly, it would be most helpful."

"Marvelous." She leaned over the table and scribbled a few hasty notes on the paper.

From his vantage point, he could not read what she wrote.

"What are you to gain from our arrangement?" Her interest in him puzzled Eli greatly. She was a stunning beauty, poised and elegant, blessed with a charming wit to match. He, on the other hand, was a social outcast by choice. While widely traveled and educated—all thanks to his grandfather—Eli was not a society man. He was a gentleman, thanks once more to his grandfather; however, he'd never attended a soirée or playhouse in London. He was most at home at his country estate or gallivanting across the wilds of England, Scotland—or even the deserts of Africa.

Adventure was what he craved, what he missed most about his grandfather. However, could he find the kind of thrills he was used to in the arms of Sam?

The twinkle in Miss Samantha's eyes told him she too sought adventure, although Eli suspected that partaking of an exploit among society was far more dangerous than exploring the caves in Egypt.

#

Sam was utterly shocked Elijah had agreed to her request. She kept her eyes on the paper before her to keep hidden how much she looked forward to their arrangement. If she'd known she would open her bedchamber door to find Elijah standing there or that she'd propose this plan, then she would have thought it through beforehand, instead of scrambling now to figure out how best to use their arrangement to her advantage.

Dare she admit what she desired from their association? Maybe an ounce of truth would not be awful to admit.

"It is simple, my lord." And it was rather simple, at least in Sam's mind. "You will escort me about Cummings' home: to all gatherings, meals, and entertainments. It will appear I am being courted by a marquis, a quite dashing gentleman." Sam paused, giving him a wink. "This will show any eligible gentlemen I am a prize. I have heard the best way to gain the attention of men is to appear unattainable." And no doubt it would impress her father greatly.

"Are you seeking attention, Miss Samantha?"

"Does not every woman?" she replied, setting her pencil aside.

"I would not know what a lady seeks."

The man acted as if he hadn't ever been in the company of women. "What about your mother...mayhap a grandmother, aunts, or female cousins?"

His chin dipped, and she noticed that his hands were clenched tightly into fists in his lap. "My grandmother died long ago—I barely remember her— and I have no other female relations. It was only ever Grandfather and me."

"Then I can help you in another way, as well." Elijah was affording her the perfect diversion to keep her boredom—and father—at bay until they departed for London. "I shall give you an education in women. I am certain you wish to find a match at some point."

If he ever journeyed to London, the marquis would find himself hounded by every matron, their simpering daughters in tow. Sam leaned closer to him, unable to think of other women being in his presence. Or worse yet, Eli finding the women's company enjoyable.

Sam had witnessed many pitiful debutantes ushered around the ballroom by their mothers and introduced to men of every caliber: some old and wealthy, some young and titled, and others revolting but well connected with superb lineage.

Outrageously deplorable.

She and her sisters were all expected to wed, but they were not forced upon every gentleman they encountered or sold to the highest bidder.

Her place on the fringes of society afforded Sam the opportunity and freedom to move about almost unnoticed. Though her beauty did draw much attention, and it was normally of the scandalous variety—which she'd allowed on a few occasions. A chaste kiss in a darkened hallway, a dance with a most handsome lord pressed a bit too closely, and even a ride in one lord's enclosed carriage.

However, Sam had never involved herself in a tryst of any sort.

Do not doubt she'd been propositioned—sent flowers and extravagant gifts, but Marce had insisted she return each with a stern note that their impure advances were not welcome.

Would Marce approve of Sam spending time with Lord Ridgefeld?

"I have not thought overly much of attaching myself to a lady," he replied.

"Then this will also work in your favor. There are a few young women here, and likely their mothers will sink their razor-sharp talons into you as soon as they hear you are unwed, titled, and wealthy."

He rubbed the back of his neck. "Allow me to ponder this…you will gain the notice of men, and I will ward off marriage-minded mothers?"

"I guess that is very true," Sam agreed with a laugh. However, she would not mention that having Eli at her side during her time at Hollybrooke would also keep her father away, reducing the chances of him seeking a private word with her or, heaven help her, making Sam cause a scene before everyone gathered. At this point, she had nothing to say to Beauchamp. She was uninterested in any apology he might feel obligated to issue nor any promise for a future association of any sort. "Does this meet with your approval?"

"We both agree to conduct ourselves in a suitable manner?"

"Certainly, my lord," she said.

"You will introduce me to gentlemen of note, while keeping the matrons' talons from sinking into me?"

"That will be the easy part." Her empty stomach fluttered as she awaited his answer.

He allowed a low, long sigh to escape, turning his gaze to his lap. "We will not find ourselves in a compromising situation—after leaving your bedchambers today?"

She hesitated to agree. On one hand, she found Elijah safe and non-threatening. On the other, she desperately longed to learn more about the physical side of an intimate relationship, and he was the only person who could help her with that. He would never agree to teach her. However, there was no reason to share with Eli what she truly sought.

"No, we will accompany one another only in public areas," she conceded, hoping he did not notice her wording was open to interpretation. The study had been a very public area; however, their time there was without the prying eyes of any other guests. "If you agree, I will expect your company for the evening meal."

"I do agree. However, what are your plans for the rest of the day?" He eyed her suspiciously as if he expected her to dissolve into tears once again when he left the room. "We can begin immediately. Mayhap I can escort you on a walk through the garden, or we can join the gathering on the lawn."

She hadn't any idea where Beauchamp had gone after she'd fled the study, but Sam was not ready to face the man just yet—or the questioning stares of the other guests. By dinner, she would need to compose herself. She was expected to attend and be at her family's side as they reveled in their final meal before the ceremony on the morrow. Even if her father showed for the repast, Marce would never risk a scene by seating Sam close to the man. Until then, she had much to occupy her time and energy.

"I believe I have a gown to be fitted for the wedding," Sam said. "But I will see you this evening."

Standing, she realized she did not want Elijah to depart, but it would not benefit either of them if her maid arrived and caught them alone in her bedchambers. He stood, as well, and trailed her toward the door.

"I have one last request, my lord," Sam said, setting her hand on the doorknob but making no move to turn it.

He paused before her, so close she could smell the fragrance of his freshly laundered shirt. "I do not think one final request could do any harm."

His warm breath brushed against her cheek and down her neck, making it difficult for her to remember what her entreaty was. She itched to touch him: her fingers running through his neatly combed hair, and her lips meeting his once more. It was only overshadowed by her desire to have his hands discover her body, his tongue exploring her mouth, and his body pressed tightly against hers.

"Your request, Miss Samantha?" he whispered.

The space between them sizzled. "I long to have a certain book returned to me." Was that the request she'd had in mind? She hadn't any clue. "Please, my lord," she cooed, leaning close to his ear, bidding the rest of her to remain under her control even as she yearned to touch him. Her entire body hummed with a longing her mind did not fully understand.

He was so very close.

She pulled back and looked into his eyes, begging him to give in to her request. Having the book returned, allowing her to gaze at images of other nude forms, would surely take her mind off *his* body.

He leaned toward her, filling the space she'd left between them. He was going to kiss her—right here, in her chambers. Instead, he halted, his lips a fraction of an inch from hers. If she pushed out her lower lip just a bit, it would graze his.

Her hand fell from the knob, and Sam prepared to wrap it around him when their lips met…*if* their lips met.

The silence between them stretched endlessly as Sam awaited either his answer or his lips.

Every nerve ending in her body tingled with anticipation.

"There is no chance of that." He straightened, pulling the door open. When had he grasped the knob? "If you seek to continue your scandalous education, you will need to return to the study for another volume, for I will not be returning the first to you."

Sam expelled her breath as he strode through the open door and into the empty hallway. His footfalls gradually faded as he made his way to his own chambers, his door opening and shutting soundly after he'd entered.

It was only then Sam realized he'd denied her final request—but his actions vowed something far more alluring than what the combined books promised. There was little need for her to return to the study for another volume.

Lord Ridgefeld—Elijah—would afford her the distraction she desired…and the satisfying promise of so much more.

Chapter Twelve

Eli stood before the looking glass as he fumbled with his neckcloth. The blasted thing had given him so much trouble it had lost its pressed appearance three attempts ago. He should never have excused his valet in favor of dressing in solitude. He was bound to be tardy for escorting Miss Samantha to supper if he did not settle on a knot and accomplish the task quickly.

Making a good impression was imperative; however, arriving unburdened by secret longings for Sam was far more important.

Mathers had spent the better part of an hour with his straight blade to Eli's jawline. It was essential for him to make a notable impression on Cummings and Cartwright. If not, the men might very well turn down the Ridgefeld donation. With Sam at his side, she was certain to steer him in both navigating the meal and any entertainments planned for their evening. Thankfully, there was no ball or dancing, making Eli's formal shoes and stockings unnecessary. The loathed finery was a necessary evil for some, but he'd managed to avoid their torture most of his adult life.

He'd settled on his Hessians, black trousers, a crisp shirt, and a coat. He was at ease, yet presentable. Fashionable without appearing the peacock.

If he were at his estate, he'd have recently finished meeting with his steward and would be preparing for a brisk walk about his property and stables to check fencing, the horses, and crops—trailed the entire way by the horde of cats that earned their keep as rodent catchers. Cook would have his evening meal readied when he returned from his daily activities.

Did other lords take such an interest in their estate's condition?

Elijah couldn't help but think that he'd been raised in a vastly different manner than most men of the *ton*. He'd never lived a life of luxury—he worked hard, every day, whether it was at his family home or on one of his many adventures with the late marquis. His hands were calloused from swinging a pickaxe for days on a dig in Austria. His legs were muscular from walking behind a plow in Africa when he'd helped a community plant row crops. His skin was tanned from his many sea voyages. These were experiences—adventures—many noblemen would never know. And also memories he'd cherish; maybe one day share with his own children.

Sam had asked if he planned to wed soon, and he'd lied, saying he hadn't thought of it and denied it was something he was interested in at present. The fact remained that he would, at some point in the near future, take a wife and start a family—or face the possibility of living alone except for the servants at his estate. Very much like stockings and formal shoes,

London would soon be another necessary evil, for what other way could he become acquainted with suitable females?

If there were another way, Eli would be interested to know. Country parties seemed not at all horrid; however, one need be acquainted with the host and hostess to garner an invitation—which was exceedingly difficult when one was unfamiliar with polite society.

He would journey to London in the near future to transport his grandfather's extensive collection of antiquities and artifacts. Certainly, there would be enough time to explore society for a week—maybe longer.

Eli could stall no longer in his chamber if he planned to arrive in time to partake of the meal with the other guests. Except for the morning meal, he was unfamiliar with any other people in attendance. It was also likely he'd already forgotten the names of the many people he had met thus far.

"The mail coach it shall be," Eli mumbled, his fingers fumbling as he tied the rather simplistic knot. They were in the country, after all, certainly profligate neckcloths were not required. He turned one way and then the other, inspecting his handiwork. "It will have to do."

Retrieving his coat, Eli slipped into the garment, allowing its restrictive tailoring to settle across his shoulders. If it were up to him, he'd don a far less limiting jacket; however, his valet had assured him the fit was indeed proper, even though he did not favor it.

Eli stepped into the hallway, pulling his door securely closed. The wall sconces had been lit, casting a glow down the corridor in both directions. At first, the deafening silence unnerved him. Everyone must have journeyed downstairs already.

The sense of being utterly alone was nothing new to Eli, but the unfamiliar house had him straining to hear the odd noises given off by the old manor. A gowned figure rushed around the corner, her slippered feet making not a sound as she hurried toward him. She passed under a sconce, illuminating her auburn hair and making her appear as if she wore a heavenly halo. The thought almost had him laughing as Sam was in no way angelic.

He kept the comment to himself, fearing he'd mistaken Miss Judith for her twin once more.

"Lord Ridgefeld," she breathed, her words leaving her on a pant from her hurried movements down the hall. "I thought you had abandoned me to the wolves."

Her hair was pinned securely atop her head, much the same as earlier. The halo he'd seen wasn't imagined, but the precise style she'd been intending. Her gown—of the purest azure—only complimented her fair skin and mossy eyes.

He cleared his throat when his eyes dipped, inappropriately, to the low neckline of her fitted gown. "I made a promise, Miss Samantha." He held out his arm, and she set her fingers lightly at the crook of his elbow. "And a man can only be judged by the promises he keeps—or destroyed by the words he forsakes. Or so my grandfather says—" he paused, uncertain what had brought the odd adage to mind. "I mean, what he used to say."

He sounded the perfect dolt.

"My apologies," he said. "It is lovely to see you again, Miss Samantha. I do hope your day was more enjoyable as the time progressed."

Her hold tightened on his arm at the mention of her less than composed time in her bedchambers. "I sincerely hope my evening is more pleasant than my morning, my lord."

"I will do all in my power to make it so." It was a promise he hoped to keep. "Shall we?"

When she nodded, they started down the hall and rounded the corner to the main staircase. Voices from the gathered guests drifted toward them along with some soft female laughter, deeper male chuckles, and other jovial conversation—each carrying over the other, making it impossible for him to discern anything that was said. Eli longed to be a part of it all, but still, his unease held him back from taking the first step down the grand stairs. Sam halted at his side as if noticing his tentative steps.

"I hear there were a few scattered storm clouds expected through the night," he commented.

She appeared more than happy to delay their arrival a bit longer. "That is correct, my lord. However, I suspect the heavens would not dare ruin Jude's wedding day."

"Lord Cummings' garden is certainly prepared for the ceremony." Eli remembered the precisely manicured roses, shrubs, and pathways. "He is most definitely taking Lord Cartwright's pending nuptials to heart."

"They have been friends since their time at Eton, Lord Ridgefeld," she replied. "Not as close as brothers, but certainly more than mere friends—or so my sister insists."

"I look forward to gaining a closer acquaintance with the pair." Eli took the first step down with Sam following suit.

"Do not surround yourself with them all evening or," she paused, a smile tugging at her lips, "we shall find ourselves falling into a slumber borne of boredom."

His deep bark of laughter bounced off the tall walls as they turned on the landing to take the final few steps into the foyer. He glanced over at her, noting the way her eyes twinkled with mischief. "I genuinely doubt I could ever be lulled into sleep with you so near."

"Oh, do not make a promise you are unable to keep," she retorted, allowing her own laughter to bubble out.

Eli glanced to the foyer, only then seeing the group frozen in their places, watching him and Sam take the final step.

He could not comprehend their odd expressions. One woman's eyes were rounded as if in astonishment at what she saw, another hid her smile behind her fan, and two gentlemen—Lord Haversham and Mr. Jakeston, he believed—exchanged a knowing look.

Sam's gloved fingers dug into his arm, her nails biting his skin through his coat sleeve.

"Good evening, Lord and Lady Haversham." Her words were tense as if uttered through clenched teeth. "Mr. and Mrs. Jakeston. It is a pleasure to see you all again."

Eli risked a glance at Sam. Her lips were pulled back in a smile, but it didn't resemble the genuine grin he'd noted she wore on several occasions since their meeting.

Though he was uncomfortable with the foursome's stares, Sam seemed outwardly unaffected by their notice.

He pulled at his neckcloth, suddenly a bit too tight for his liking.

"We were overjoyed at the invitation," the woman on Haversham's arm said. "It was lovely for Lord Cummings to open his home to us—children and all."

"Are you referring to us?" Jakeston set his hand at his throat dramatically. "You wound me, my dear Lady Haversham."

The dark-haired woman on his arm swatted at him. "Do not sound so affronted, Harold. You and Brock are well aware of your childish behaviors—and likely, proud of them."

"I dare say, I take grave offense to that," Jakeston retorted. "I have been ever the gentleman since my arrival, Mrs. Jakeston."

"You jumped into the pond earlier!" his wife contended.

"I most certainly did not!" Jakeston argued. "Haversham threw my mallet into the murky, frigid water—and then pushed me in after."

"Jakeston was being the proper gent and rescuing Cummings' property from ruin," Haversham said, stepping in to aid his friend—but in no way offering a convincing explanation. "He only needed a spot of help to remember his gentlemanly obligation to fetch the mallet."

"Was it gentlemanly to then trudge through Lord Cummings' home, allowing the filthy pond water to mar his floors?" It was Lady Haversham's turn to narrow her eyes at her husband.

"Let us be off," Sam whispered, leaning close to Eli's ear. "These two are likely to continue their debate until the sun rises on the morrow." She pulled on his arm, stepping around the two couples. "We will see you all in the parlor."

They moved toward the voices coming from the other gathered guests as Haversham and Jakeston appeared to act out the scenario at the pond. It must have taken place while he and Sam had been in her bedchambers.

Eli chuckled. "I would have relished seeing that."

"Oh, I am certain the pair will offer continued entertainment during our stay." The tension left her as they neared the parlor. "They bicker and banter much like a wedded couple."

They stepped through the open door in unison, Eli grinning like a fool with Sam proudly on his arm.

"Sam!" Payton called, leaping from the chaise lounge she shared with another young girl. She dashed across the room and grabbed Sam's free hand. "There are to be cards after our meal—and Marce says I can play!"

The dark-haired girl bounced before them as if not noticing Eli at Sam's side. The young woman had sat between Sam's older siblings at the breakfast table.

"That is very gracious of our sister to allow," Sam said, squeezing the girl's hand before glancing toward him. "Lord Ridgefeld, this overexcited young woman is my youngest sister, Miss Payton Samuels."

She dropped Sam's hand and took a step back, curtseying deeply before him. "My lord, it is a pleasure to make your acquaintance." Standing straight once more, the young woman glanced over her shoulder, and Eli noted a petite blonde woman nod her approval.

"And it is a delight to meet another of Miss Samantha's siblings," Eli responded. "I look forward to a rousing game of cards later. Will you save me a seat at your table?"

A blush blossomed in the girl's cheeks, and he was uncertain from where his charming question had sprung. "Of course, my lord, but I do hope you brought extra coin."

He had no time to answer as the young woman bounded off to regain her seat next to the other girl.

"If you value your coin, do not take a seat at Payton's table."

Eli glanced at Sam, his brow furrowed. "Why ever not? Is she an accomplished player?"

"Heavens no," Sam confided. "She is a superior cheater."

"No!" Eli glanced back to where Miss Payton was seated, her head now tilted toward the girl beside her as they chatted in hushed tones. "I do not believe it."

"Do take my warnings to heart," Sam said, pulling him farther into the room. "Marce has the gaming debt slips to prove it. I am unsure if my sister is happy Payton mastered counting cards or if she'd rather continue to pay the debts Payton incurs by being a horrible player. It is said she gained the tendency to scheme from her father."

Sam's humorless tone said she spoke the truth.

Cartwright and Miss Judith moved to greet them, and Eli was taken aback once more at the resemblance shared by the sisters—they were identical in appearance. It was little wonder he'd mixed them up.

"Good evening, my lord." Miss Judith offered a warm smile. Tonight, the sister's gown choices could not be more different. While Sam's neckline plunged low, allowing an expansive view of her mounded breasts, Miss Judith's was secured high on her neck. They had both settled on blue gowns, but while Sam's choice was almost a vibrant, sapphire hue, Miss Judith's was more of what a young woman was expected to wear—a light pastel color not too different from a bright sky on a clear day.

Eli couldn't help but notice that the sisters avoided eye contact, and Sam stiffened on his arm. "And to you, Miss Judith. Thank you again for extending the invitation."

"Oh, once Simon explained the situation, I readily agreed," she said. "We will be away from London for some time. I would not want the museumgoers to suffer the loss of such a delightful collection because I am dragging Lord Cartwright to the country."

"There is no dragging needed, my sweet plum," Cart reassured his intended, patting her arm gently. "I would follow you to the ends of the Earth."

Sam snorted, garnering a stern look from her twin.

"Your gown is stunning, dear sister." Miss Judith addressed Sam for the first time. "You look exquisite, as always. I am delighted to see you are feeling better."

Eli wondered if the comment was in reference to Sam's afternoon spent within her room, but kept the question to himself, content to wait for a private moment.

"Thank you, Jude. If you will excuse us. I find I am in need of refreshments."

"Lord Cummings has several options on the side table," Lord Cartwright cut in, looking similarly uneasy with the overwrought atmosphere between the sisters. "We can speak again at supper. Cummings is interested in seeing the list of items you plan to donate to the museum. The man can speak of nothing else but our meeting."

"Certainly, Lord Cartwright." Eli agreed.

"Come now, Simon. Can you not convince Lord Cummings to go one meal without discussions revolving around antiquities?" Miss Judith's sharp stare had her soon-to-be husband nodding in agreement.

"It is only another twelve hours he must wait to view the list." Lord Cartwright rubbed his jaw in thought. "I will speak with him. Though, he is our host…"

"And I am the bride."

"You will not hear any argument from me," Cartwright readily agreed, placing a chaste kiss to Miss Judith's cheek. "My apologies for introducing the matter to the conversation."

Her light, melodic laugh filled the space between them. "I will forgive you anything."

Elijah nodded as the couple moved toward the door where Lord Haversham, Mr. Jakeston, and their wives appeared.

There was much he longed to ask Sam, but his simple question would have to suffice with so many people gathered close. "Is all as it should be, Miss Samantha?"

"Things are rarely as they should be," she replied, forcing a laugh—though he wasn't certain whose benefit it was for. "Let us move to the refreshment table."

He noted her need to change the subject and feign interest in the table along the far wall. Two servants stood at the ready to pour sherry or something a bit stronger for the gathered guests.

As they moved across the room, Sam nodded to several people and issued greetings to others, but she made no move to halt for further conversation, favoring to continue on. Her eyes scanned the room continually, only pausing briefly as she took in the twenty or so people gathered. It was as if she searched for someone specific—but they were not present. Her shoulders relaxed, and her hold on him loosened.

Eli wondered if she had another reason for offering to stay by his side during their time at Hollybrooke.

"Who do you plan to introduce me to next?" he asked. "I fear I've forgotten the names of the few people I met this morning. What about that man over there?" Eli nodded quickly at a man standing alone by the windows. He hadn't taken his eyes off Sam since they'd entered the room. The man, Eli's senior by at least a decade, glared at him and Sam, a pinched expression on his face. His fists clenched and released before he turned sharply to look out the bank of windows into the growing darkness.

Sam accepted a flute of sherry from a servant before responding. "That is Lord Gunther."

"Lord Gunther, you say?" Certainly, Eli had never met him, but something about the name was familiar. "Where have I heard that name?"

"In *The Post*, I dare say. He and Cartwright became entangled in a scandal not long ago."

"And the man still received an invitation?"

"The invitation ended the disagreement between the pair." She quickly glanced at the man one last time before guiding Eli back to face the door. And somehow convinced the man that his pursuit of Lord Cartwright's new sister-in-law was wanted—and, dare she say, expected. "He was actually the reason I embarked on my walk the other day—and the reason I was almost caught in the storm. He has confessed his affections for me and has been quite smitten for several months now. He cannot reasonably comprehend I do not hold the same fondness for him."

Her assurance did nothing to assuage Elijah's spike of jealousy. "Is there something wrong with the man?" he prodded, unwilling to allow a change in topic.

She took a long sip of her drink, her eyes focusing on the door once more as another couple entered the room. "Oh, nothing is wrong with the man *if* one is resigned to live in a home that hasn't seen a proper dusting in over a decade—or thinks a grown man collecting porcelain dolls is not a bit peculiar."

"Dolls?" Eli couldn't help but take a closer look at the man.

"An entire upstairs room filled with them—too many shelves to count. And I would likely be added to his collection were I to be interested in his courtship."

"Interesting," Eli mumbled.

"Certainly not as interesting as the man over there." She notched her chin at a rail-thin gentleman with lank hair standing a bit too close to Lord Cartwright by the door.

"Who is he?"

"Only the premiere auction house owner in all of London, Mr. Lewis Stanford." She leaned close to Eli, as if her next words were so interesting she feared others hearing them. "It is rumored the man dresses in women's finery and walks about the London streets after dark."

Eli snorted, unable to keep his mirth at bay—at the precise moment Mr. Stanford started in their direction. "He certainly has a narrow waist perfect for stays."

"Yes, but it is said he uses apples to fill his top." She raised her flute to hide her smile. "Lady Chastain said she saw him at Covent Garden once. He bent over to pick up his fan after it had been knocked from his grasp, only to have the apples bounce to the ground and roll under the feet of the moving crowd."

"You jest!" he hissed as Stanford halted before them, issuing a greeting to Sam and a curt bow to Eli.

"Mr. Stanford," Sam greeted. "It is lovely to see you again. How long has it been?"

"I am uncertain, Miss Samantha." The man beamed with pride at Sam's recognition of him.

"I know, it was at Covent Garden...am I right?" she asked.

The man's cheeks flamed. "I...well...," he stammered, squirming.

"No," she acquiesced. "It was last month when I attended your shop with my sister."

Stanford visibly relaxed, though his eyes remained guarded. "That was certainly when we last saw one another. Cartwright said you would introduce me to Lord Ridgefeld."

Sam smiled. "Mr. Stanford, allow me to make Lord Ridgefeld known to you."

"Melly's grandson, correct?" Stanford turned to Eli, Sam forgotten. "I see the resemblance. Cartwright tells me you plan to donate your grandfather's collection to the museum."

"That is correct, Mr. Stanford." Eli eyed the man, his shrewd gaze that of a true businessman.

"Everything?"

"I do not understand."

"Is it your intent to hand over all of your grandfather's antiquities to the museum?"

The hair on the back of Eli's neck stood on end at the man's overzealous interest. "Yes, everything I do not plan to keep for future generations."

Stanford reached into his front coat pocket and fished around, removing a small card. He held it out to Eli. "Here are my directions. If you are willing to sell anything, I'd be very interested."

"My grandfather was not one to make a profit—"

"Be that as it may, you are now the marquis." Stanford wisely paused when Eli's shoulders stiffened at his inference. "Sad loss, to be sure. Melville was a resourceful man—a tough tradesman."

"You did business together?" He'd never heard of Stanford before now and had come across nothing in all of his grandfather's paperwork mentioning either him or his business.

"Oh, no." Stanford shook his head. "We met several times, but we were never able to come to an agreement on anything."

Eli didn't doubt that. His grandfather rarely gave up any artifact he discovered, preferring to keep it close or bring it to the museum for study.

"It was nice to see you again, Mr. Stanford," Sam stepped close. "I believe my sister is requesting our attention."

"Very well," Stanford bowed. "Please call on me if you find yourself in London, my lord."

As the man scurried off, Eli could imagine him in stockings and heeled boots.

"Who is next?" Sam tapped her finger against her glass, taking in all the guests in the room.

"I thought you said your sister was requesting our attention." He looked toward Lord Cartwright and Miss Judith, but they were engaged in conversation with their host—who'd arrived at some point without Eli noticing. "Miss Judith does not appear to need us."

"I have other sisters."

Eli glanced to Miss Payton, who'd left her perch on the chaise to speak with another fiery-haired woman. He'd met her that morning—Lord Chastain's wife if he were not mistaken.

Once again, Sam brought her flute close to her mouth and whispered, "See the blonde woman—standing with Garrett and staring daggers at me?"

It was the woman who'd nodded to Miss Payton earlier. "That is your eldest sister, correct?" He couldn't keep the shocked tone from his voice. "She looks nothing like you—or Payton."

"We are half-siblings—we share a mother," Sam answered. "My sister's name is Marce. Since our mother's death, she has raised us all…at Craven House, once, long ago, the most notorious bordello in all of London—some have claimed, all of England."

"You jest," Eli said a bit too forcefully, catching the notice of Lord Gunther by the window along with several others he'd yet to meet.

Chapter Thirteen

"I never jest about scandal, my lord," she hissed with a deep, throaty laugh. "And it would behoove you to keep your voice down. Everyone in attendance is well aware of my family situation, as it were." Well, except for her long-lost father's inopportune reappearance in her life. In fact, if it hadn't been for Elijah, Sam would have claimed ill and stayed in her room for the evening.

"You were raised in a bordello?" His eyes rounded, and he made no attempt to act as if he sought to mingle with anyone else in the room as his body turned fully toward her, his back to the other guests with Sam pinned between his towering frame and the wall. "Your mother was a…a…"

"Madame," she offered the correct term. "Madame Sasha. And for a while, my sister was Madame Marce, but the immoral side of Craven House is long gone. The most that takes place behind our doors now are high-stakes card games. And do not look so utterly shocked."

"Lord Cartwright is aware—"

"Everyone in this room is aware," Sam confided, taking pleasure in his stunned stare. Beauchamp, the only man to know firsthand the pleasures to be found at Craven House, was not present. She'd been relieved to not spot him among the guests…and she dared to hope that he understood he'd overstepped and retreated from Hollybrooke altogether. "Do not stare so intently. Truly, the circumstances surrounding our births and upbringings are not newsworthy here. I had a childhood similar to those of other London youths, complete with schooling and such. Marce—and my mother before her—made certain we were raised as ladies. "

"My apologies, I did not mean to offend you or your family." He held her stare as he spoke. "I am unfamiliar with the ways of town life."

"Your astonishment does not offend me, nor do you need ask my forgiveness." It was odd that her family circumstances had always been something she hid when possible. When she'd attended soirees and the opera with Lord Chastain or Lady Haversham, she'd always been guarded with her name and connections—but she hadn't hesitated or experienced any anxiousness when telling Elijah. Now was not the time to dwell on the reasoning behind her forthcoming nature with him; however, it could have much to do with their kiss or his discovery of her in Cummings' study, clutching that wicked book. Or maybe it was the way he'd spoken to her, soothed her hurt earlier until they both laughed, her tears forgotten.

"Do not look now, but your sister—the blonde one—is headed our way," he whispered. "What warning have you for her?"

Marce fairly floated in their direction, ever the poised lady, though many would never address her as such. It was a shame their eldest sister spent most of her time caring for their home, her siblings, and any person who sought out Craven House as a refuge. She refused every invitation for herself, except when it came from a close acquaintance—or furthered her objectives to marry off her siblings.

"There is no warning grand enough for my dear eldest sister." Unknowingly, Sam had inched closer to Eli, their shoulders now touching as Marce bore down on them—her expression less than friendly but ever cordial. "Sister."

Marce scrutinized her as if to judge how angry or hurt or disappointed Sam was with Marce's interference in her life, and Jude's.

Sam only notched her chin higher, determined not to give her sister a glimpse of the betrayal that filled her at Marce's meddling.

However, she only stepped forward and wrapped Sam in a hug. The sight likely looked comical to those around them, as Sam was a full head taller than her petite sister, though that had never stopped Marce.

"Samantha." Marce pulled back for one more intense stare before releasing her. "Please, introduce me to your companion."

"Elijah Watson, the Marquis of Ridgefeld, may I present," she paused before continuing, knowing her sister would be angered by Sam's next words, but there was little she could do while surrounded by so many people, "Lady Marce Davenport, my eldest sister."

True to form, her sister bristled at the use of her title. It had always confused Sam why her sister did not acknowledge her status as the daughter of a duke—the legitimate daughter of a duke, no less.

"It is an honor to make your acquaintance, my lady," Eli replied.

"It is only Marce." Her sister winced, and Sam felt a spike of remorse. "I'd like to thank you for collecting Sam before the storm washed her away."

"When I set out that morning, I had no intention of rescuing a damsel in distress; however, it pleased me greatly to have been on the road at that exact time, or there is no doubt Miss Samantha would be suffering a chill from the cold downpour."

A grin lit Marce's face as she was clearly taken with Eli's dashing discourse. The man did not know it, but he had a charm that was severely lacking in London.

"Garrett and I are very fortunate you were on your way to Hollybrooke." Marce turned to Sam once more. "And thank you for introducing Lord Ridgefeld to our guests."

"Of course." None of the guests were Sam's choice, for if she'd had any voice in the guest list, she would have scratched Gunther immediately and likely burned Stanford's invitation. Though, both men were close with Lord Cartwright. Sam supposed the bridegroom should be allowed to have his friends present.

"Oh, speaking of Garrett, he is requesting me at his side—the soon-to-be dowager Lady Cartwright has arrived." Marce nodded to them both. "Do excuse me…and wish me luck. The woman is a viper if I have ever met one."

Elijah chuckled, as if unaware how tense their conversation had been. "Do send for me if you need any assistance, my lady."

"I surely will," Marce said. "I look forward to conversing more during our meal."

Sam couldn't help but smirk. Before departing her room to find Eli, Sam had sent her maid to the formal dining room to switch their place cards. She'd known Elijah, as a marquis, would be seated close to the head of the table, while she would be farther down. Even an informal country party need follow proper seating protocols—but for a new pair of mink-lined gloves, her maid was more than happy to make certain Lord Ridgefeld was seated next to her mistress—and far from her sister or Beauchamp, if he chose to attend the meal.

If Marce noticed her sly smile, she ignored it as she floated toward Garrett, who attempted to slip from Cartwright's mother's hold.

"Dearest sister!" A sweet voice sang behind them. Sam turned to see Lady Theodora, a smile upon her face with her book clasped to her chest. "Did you hear the wonderful news?"

Lord Ridgefeld raised a brow, a silent inquiry about yet another sister.

Sam shook her head before continuing. "I have not, Theo—but before you tell me, I'd like to introduce you to a friend of mine." The word sent a jolt through her entire body, from her toes to the tips of her ears. "May I present Lord Ridgefeld to you, Lady Theodora Montgomery? Elijah, this is Cartwright's sister. And on the morrow, officially my family by marriage...another sister."

Elijah made a grand gesture of bowing deeply to the child. "Lady Theodora, the pleasure is mine."

She giggled and dipped into a curtsy. "Do call me Theo or Lady Theo if I am to call you Elijah."

"A lady such as you must call me Eli," he said with a wink, sending Theo into another round of soft laughter and drawing the attention of the other guests. "Now, what news have you for *us*?"

When had she and Elijah become an 'us?'

The girl's enthusiasm always astonished Sam. "Yes, Theo, tell us the grand news."

Sam wouldn't admit that she'd already heard from Jude—and overheard Theo's mother ranting over the decision shortly after their arrival at Hollybrooke.

"I depart for Miss Emmeline's School of Education and Decorum for Ladies of Outstanding Quality in Canterbury immediately following Cart's wedding." Theo hopped up and down once more. "Simon has agreed to allow me to journey alone—with only my maid as chaperone while he and Jude continue on to our country estate."

"Miss Emmeline's…what?" Eli asked. "You must tell me of this school."

Theo's eyes fairly twinkled with delight. "It is a boarding school for girls. Mother has agreed to allow me to study there until I am presented to society."

"That is wonderful news, Theo." Sam smiled encouragingly. "I know you will do well. Lady Theo is perhaps the most intelligent woman I know."

"Then I am happy to know her, as well," Eli said. "I look forward to hearing all about your time at school when next we meet."

A bell sounded, and a servant cleared his throat before addressing the group. "Dinner is served, ladies and gentlemen. Please make your way to the dining hall."

Sam noted Marce moving in her direction, but Eli offered her his arm, which she gladly took before they turned to follow the other guests from the salon. Beauchamp had had the sense to remain absent.

As they moved down the hall toward the wonderful smells of duck, fresh bread, and other savory dishes, each fighting to have their aroma greet the hungry guests first, Sam leaned close and whispered, "It is said that Cummings' cook was brought all the way from Bucharest near the Black Sea."

"The man has much in the way of rare items in his home." It was the first mention of Cummings' risqué collection of books, and Sam's cheeks heated at the thought. "Cummings is full of noteworthy surprises."

They entered the room, servants at the ready to seat Lord Cummings' guests as they located their places. The long table was set with candelabras and sparkling, polished silver trays overflowing with meats and cheeses. Another deep bowl steamed with soup. It was a feast meant to honor Lord Cartwright and her sister's coming union.

Her twin and her betrothed sat to the left of Lord Cummings at the head of the table, with Cart's mother and Marce to his right. The seat next to Marce was suspiciously empty. Had it been intended for Lord Ridgefeld?

It didn't matter.

"Our seats are here," Eli ushered her toward the foot of the table, their cards propped upon their plates—their names written in Jude's heavy-handed script. "We are next to one another, Miss Samantha. What a wonderful surprise."

Payton and Theo had already taken their seats across from Sam.

Unfortunately, Stanford appeared at her elbow as a servant pulled a chair back for the man to sit. Her maid had certainly not earned her new mink gloves.

"Miss Samantha," the man purred. "It seems we will be sharing our meal."

Not if Sam could help it, but there was little to be done as Lord and Lady Chastain took the seats next to Payton and all the other guests located their places.

Sitting, Sam wedged her chair ever so slightly to better face Elijah and hopefully discourage Stanford's unwanted attentions.

"Ladies and gentlemen," Cummings said, standing to gain the attention of every guest. "We are gathered here at Hollybrooke to celebrate Lord Cartwright and Miss Judith Pengarden. Let us feast, drink, and be merry!"

Everyone cheered, raising his or her glass in salute. Sam couldn't help but join in the revelry. Her sister was to be married in just a few short hours. Nothing would be as it was. Upon her return to London, Jude's side of their room would be emptied—her dresses removed from their closet, her brushes gone from their dressing table, and her writing desk moved to Lord Cartwright's home. Her new stationery and calling cards would read *Lady Cartwright* with her new directions.

No longer were they Miss Samantha and Miss Judith—an inseparable pair.

Jude the rational one, and Sam the hellion.

The Mistress Enchants Her Marquis

Who was Sam to be without her twin by her side?

Chapter Fourteen

"Oh, certainly not, Lady Theo," Eli cautioned. "The wilds of Africa are far more dangerous than the moors of Scotland. I once witnessed a crocodile leap two feet from the water to snap its jaws around a bird flying above."

At the *Ooohs* and *Ahhhs* issued from both Miss Payton and Lady Theo, Eli smiled contently, risking a sideways glance at Sam, who used her fork to push the remaining morsels of food around on her plate. She'd been unaffected by their debate regarding the dangerous nature of society. In fact, she'd kept her eyes trained on the remnants of pheasant and avoided discussions with everyone at the table. Her mood drifted from lighthearted to melancholy as the evening progressed; even her quick wit and their entertaining banter had died to silence as course after course of savory deliciousness were placed before them.

Eli had been under the impression they'd both agreed to banish their gloom.

"The meal is distinct from any I've tasted before—in all my travels," Eli said, hoping to draw her from her sullen silence. "Many of the spices I have never sampled before."

Lady Theo and Miss Payton chatted happily amongst themselves, leaving Eli free to dedicate his attention to Sam once more.

"Now, I must ask your opinion on something. Do you think Stanford prefers lavender or peach-scented perfume?" His question was whispered, unheard by the other guests over the many conversations around them; however, she did not acknowledge him. "A penny for your thoughts, Miss Samantha?"

A servant stepped forward and removed his plate, turning to Sam next. "May I, miss?"

"Oh, certainly. I am finished." She set her fork aside and shifted, allowing the servant room to collect her plate. "Thank you."

"Miss Samantha." Eli caught her eye before she had time to return it to the table. "You seemed rather distracted—which I thought was my duty—during our meal. Is anything amiss?"

She shook her head, her mouth opening to speak, but Lord Cummings stood, once again signaling for everyone's attention. The man seemed to enjoy his obligations as host, as he'd spent the entire meal speaking with anyone who would listen.

"Ladies." Cummings' robust voice echoed off the walls enclosing the room as servants hurried to and fro, removing plates and clearing the serving dishes. "While it has been great having you underfoot, I am afraid you have overstayed your welcome. If you will be so kind as to retire to the drawing room, we will join you shortly."

Everyone laughed—with the exception of Sam—as the women stood, preparing to depart the room.

Sam stood quickly with barely a weak smile for him before turning and following the other women out.

A man, tall and lanky, slipped into the room as the doors shut solidly behind him, cutting off the chatting from the women as they journeyed back to the drawing room—leaving Eli alone with the other men. He kept his seat when Lord Cummings and several of the men moved to the sideboard, the host pouring each a large tumbler of port.

It gave Eli time to inspect each gentleman. They would be his peers if he chose to remain in London for a spell after delivering his grandfather's collection to the museum. Lord Haversham and Mr. Jakeston stood chuckling at something Lord Chastain said. Eli was too far away to overhear the jest, but Jakeston slapped his friend on the back when his laughter turned to coughing as if he'd choked on his port.

Stanford, the auctioneer, had wandered toward a shelf along the far wall and examined a row of books. Cartwright, Cummings, and Gunther stood at the sideboard, refilling their cups as the final man, who'd slipped into the group only after the women had departed, stood several paces away, speaking to no one. From the turn of the man's head, Eli suspected he listened to Lord Cartwright's conversation.

Maybe he too was unfamiliar with those in attendance.

Elijah stood and strode toward the man, his auburn locks and the set of his chin oddly familiar. He could at least make the man feel welcome—as Sam had done for him the day before.

"Have you just arrived at Hollybrooke?" Elijah asked, stopping before him.

"Earlier this morning, yes." He appeared relieved to have someone to speak with. "Lord Beauchamp."

"I am Elijah, Lord Ridgefeld," he responded with a nod. "I only arrived yesterday. You did not attend the meal."

Beauchamp glanced around, beads of sweat appearing across his forehead. "No, I had other business to attend to. Are you a friend of Lord Cartwright?"

"Yes—and no," Eli said with a chuckle. "My grandfather and Lord Cartwright were well acquainted. I am here with museum business." When the man only nodded, Eli asked, "And you? Are you a friend or part of the family? I understand the gathering only includes a limited number."

"Yes—and no." Beauchamp made use of Eli's explanation. "I am family—here to see my daughters."

"Oh," Eli didn't bother keeping his interest at bay. "Will they be joining the party shortly?"

Beauchamp grimaced and glanced again at the closed door. "I believe they are with the other women. Which is surely safer for all involved."

Elijah hadn't any idea what the man meant, but Lord Cartwright appeared at his elbow then, holding out a tumbler of port to each of them. "Ah, Ridgefeld, I see you have met our surprise guest."

"I have. Lord Beauchamp was telling me he arrived today and that his daughters are with the women. I am looking forward to meeting them."

Cartwright laughed, and Beauchamp blanched, all color draining from his face, and even down his neck before the pallor disappeared beneath his cravat.

"Did I say something amusing, my lord?" The other conversations in the room had quieted, and all attention was on Eli—or maybe it was Beauchamp. Tendrils of recognition connected…tall and rail-thin, hair of burnt-red, and eyes the color of—

"I am Dexter Pengarden, Viscount Beauchamp. Miss Samantha and Miss Judith are my daughters."

Could it be? Sam had spoken nothing of the man and had insinuated Lady Marce had raised her and her siblings.

A whistle of shock sounded behind him.

It was encouraging to hear he wasn't the only person in the room reeling in utter surprise.

"I…well…" For not the first time since arriving at Hollybrooke, Eli was stunned into wordlessness. "It is very nice to make your acquaintance, my lord." But was it nice? It was not difficult to deduce that it was this man's arrival that had sent Sam into a tailspin.

"Do not worry, Ridgefeld," Cummings said, joining the small group. "You are not the only one surprised by the appearance of Lord Beauchamp. I fear we are all still whirling with disbelief."

"Enough, Cummings," Cartwright hissed. "Come, my lord. Let us speak over here."

The pair moved to the far end of the room, out of earshot of the others, and Elijah was left with his mouth gaping open. Had this been the true reason Sam was crying earlier?

Why would her father's arrival at her sister's wedding cause her such upset? Eli glanced around the room, each man only now starting on their drinks—it would be at least an hour before they joined the women again.

"Lord Ridgefeld?"

Eli's mind had been elsewhere, unaware Gunther had moved from his position against the wall to stand beside him.

Exactly the man Elijah had no interest in speaking with—he'd sat at Lord Cartwright's end of the table during the meal but sent barely veiled looks of discontent in Eli's direction.

"Lord Gunther, is it?" Eli said by way of greeting.

"Yes." The man narrowed his eyes, and his shoulders tensed. "May I speak frankly?"

"Certainly." Though Eli hadn't a clue what the man could possibly have to discuss—frankly or otherwise.

"Have you said or done something to injure Miss Samantha?"

The question caught him off guard. He'd wondered what had altered Sam's demeanor since this morning, but that Gunther suspected as much, as well, meant the man was at least partly familiar with Sam.

A jolt of pain coursed through Eli's jaw, his teeth clamped tightly to hold back any foolish outburst. Instead of issuing a scolding retort, Eli breathed deeply and exhaled. "I haven't any notion of what you speak, my lord."

Gunther took a menacing step forward. "It is only I was invited as a possible suitor for Miss Samantha, and I swear the woman is avoiding me. I think you know something of the matter."

She certainly was avoiding Gunther, but it was not Elijah's place to enlighten the poor fellow to that fact.

"I regret to inform you that I will be of no help in the matter." Eli had no reason to trust Gunther—and Sam's aversion to his attention only solidified things. "Miss Samantha and I have only recently gained an acquaintance. She has taken me under her wing to introduce me to the other guests."

"Good to hear, my lord." Gunther sighed in relief. "I had heard from my servant that he saw you exiting Miss Samantha's private chamber earlier."

He'd been careful to survey the corridor in both directions when he'd departed Sam's room—Eli hadn't seen or heard anyone close. "Your servant must have confused me with someone else." Foreboding coursed through him. If a servant had, indeed, witnessed his departure from Sam's room, it would not be long before their host was informed. Eli could not allow the man to see him react in any way.

If the man pressed, Eli would have no further explanations to give. Not another guest could vouch for him—except… "I went for a walk earlier today about Lord Cummings' estate. Across the lawn and by the pond in time to see Mr. Jakeston's untimely fall into the water." Lord Haversham had seen Elijah walking, even motioned him to join the group on the lawn, but Eli had acted as if he hadn't seen the man's gesture. He hoped it was enough to keep anyone from speculating further on Eli's whereabouts that afternoon.

Thankfully, Gunther laughed. "I would have given a hundred pounds to see that. Is it true Lord Haversham pushed him into the frigid water?"

There was no going back now—Eli could only make sure the man believed his every word and no future questions arose on the subject. "Actually, Lord

Haversham was attempting to help Jakeston extricate a mallet from the water when the man took a tumble."

It was the story he'd overheard after descending the stairs earlier. The hectic commotion surrounding the fall would likely prevent anyone from remembering who exactly had been present to witness the incident.

Greatly benefiting Eli and his much-needed alibi.

Glancing over his shoulder, he noted Lord Cartwright, Garrett, and Lord Beauchamp had disappeared from the room.

Eli took a long drink from his glass. "Will you excuse me?"

With a satisfied nod, Lord Gunther moved toward Stanford, reassured Eli posed no threat to his coming courtship of Miss Samantha. Which for all intents and purposes, was true.

However, he and Sam had struck a deal—and Eli expected her to see it to completion.

And in turn, he would see his side through until he departed Hollybrooke.

The thought of leaving the guests behind in favor of the solitude of his estate no longer filled him with a sense of ease.

Despite all that had happened since his arrival, or maybe in spite of it all, Elijah was having an enjoyable time. He could not deny it was mainly due to Sam.

And at the moment, something deep inside him knew she needed him.

He set his empty glass on the sideboard and slipped through the door, closing it quietly in his wake.

He retraced the path back to the drawing room they'd met in before the meal had been announced. The double doors were open, affording Eli a clear view of the entire room.

Suspiciously missing, along with Sam, was Lord Cartwright, Garrett, Lord Beauchamp, and Lady Marce Davenport.

Chapter Fifteen

Sam wanted to throw something, hurl it as hard as she could into the dying fire in Cummings' study hearth—unfortunately, everything in the room was worth far more than she. Had her father not instilled in her and Jude how little he valued their existence? No, she would never treat another's possessions with the wanton disregard her father had with his own children.

Her feet pounded against the hardwood as she carved a path back and forth before the hearth, her cheeks aflame, but Sam was too preoccupied to notice beyond the fire that coursed through her veins.

True, no person was a possession, but to be wanted, to be cherished, to be treasured as much as Lord Cartwright—or even Lord Cummings—did the objects he collected would fill her with a sense of belonging, especially now with Jude leaving her. No one seemed to understand the deep-rooted isolation Sam experienced every time Jude was not by her side.

It had rocked Sam to her core when she had departed the dining room, trailing the other women, only to walk straight into Lord Beauchamp. She'd prayed he'd left Hollybrooke after their confrontation that morning, but it seemed he was naive enough to think staying in residence would win him some sort of forgiveness from his daughters.

And it very well might from Jude, but Sam was in no way ready to hear the viscount's rationalizations for the deplorable neglect of his *family*. Yet, Beauchamp wasn't any more family to her and Jude than the man who swept their chimney flue at Craven House—actually, at least Sam recognized that man, knew his name and disposition…Beauchamp was a perfect stranger.

An imperfect stranger.

How could the scoundrel think that showing up at Hollybrooke would gain him anything?

The notion had Sam coming up short and halting her frantic pacing. Beauchamp must certainly expect something from her—or worse, Jude. What other reason could he have for accepting Marce's invitation?

Sam had fled the others, needing a private, quiet place to think and mull over what she was to do next.

Cummings' study was far enough from the other guests to afford her the privacy and silence she craved. No one would search for her here. It was likely Jude had been called from her own celebration to locate her twin. She had been far more reserved and distant since their arrival at Cummings' estate. Sam understood. Jude hadn't meant to leave Sam out or make her feel unwanted; unfortunately, that was precisely what Sam was fighting. No longer did she and Jude stay up late, exchanging gossip and giggling until the morning sun began to light the London sky. No, now, Jude shared those talks with Lord Cartwright, the man she loved.

Regrettably, she *did* envy her sister's happiness.

Though they'd been without a mother or father, at least they had one another; which at times was preferable. A sister was superior to a friend, as well—they could bicker, argue, and disagree, but always come back to one another.

Jude had always recognized Sam's need to garner the favor of those around her. Her twin had even gladly accepted her place in Sam's shadow at society entertainments.

Fresh tears fell once more. Sam hadn't felt them rising through her anger, but now they streamed down her cheeks, creating burning trails until they fell from her chin.

Sam brushed the moisture away. She need only stay strong until Jude was properly wed on the morrow, then she could return to London and live as she had the last year. Yes, a side of her bedchamber would be empty, but she could fill it with new baubles—maybe even a permanent bathing tub. Certainly, her days and evenings would be lonely without Jude for company, but Sam could spend more time with Lady Chastain—or possibly take a suitor or two, there were always gentlemen seeking her favor. And there was always Payton. Her young sister would need guidance as she prepared to enter society—why could Sam not dedicate her time to this good deed? Though, only scarcely a year younger than Sam and Jude, Payton was no longer the child Sam seemed to think of her as.

However, none of those things would fill the spot where a part of her heart would be missing—not gone, but far away and out of reach.

Would Payton agree to share a bedchamber with her if she begged?

Sam shuddered at the thought. Heavens no.

What of Lord Beauchamp? Had he spoken with Jude, convinced her he was sorry for all he'd done? All he *hadn't* done. Did he actually feel remorse for the past—deserting a woman he'd claimed to love and the children that love had brought into existence?

It was all too overwhelming.

Sam rubbed her temples to alleviate the pounding in her head. While it soothed some of the ache, it did nothing to realign her swirling thoughts.

There was no reason for her to join the gathering in the drawing room. Nor could she seek out her chambers. Her siblings would not allow her to wallow in self-pity. They would demand she talk to them about her pain, her anguish, and her despair. Sam wasn't prepared to labor through such a conversation as yet—may never be ready to discuss her father's appearance and her twin's coming departure.

She stared into the flames as they licked at the logs, throwing a wave of heat across her skin. It would be so easy to allow them to engulf her—extinguish her sorrow, wipe it from her being.

Taking a step closer, Sam begged the blaze to draw out her grief. To take it from within her and destroy it in its flames.

"I suspected I'd find you here."

Sam yelped in surprise.

The deep, whispered words had her taking a step back from the hearth as she patted her hair back into place before turning. She hadn't heard the study door open and then close behind Elijah, but a part of her soared to see him there—certainly not her heart, but some part of her recognized what he offered her.

"I met your father, Lord Beauchamp." He continued toward her before stepping to her side and turning to stare into the hearth. "Is he the cause of your pain?"

Her eyes narrowed, scrutinizing the fire and avoiding the man beside her. Sam was uncertain how much to share with Eli. He was only slightly less the stranger than Beauchamp; however, he'd proven his caring and compassionate ways. "A great portion of it, yes." Her voice quaked, betraying the hurt she'd attempted to hide.

"Why? I would assume a person would feel a measure of happiness to see their father."

"Of course, any other person might…though, today was the first time I've ever laid eyes on the man." She didn't dare glance in Eli's direction, couldn't handle the pity she would see in his eyes. It would only serve to crush her more. "Jude and I have known his name, obviously, as we share it, but he has never been a part of us."

"Us?" His tone remained quiet.

"Craven House—Marce, Garrett, Jude, Payton and me. And before she passed away, our mother. Beauchamp walked away, leaving us all, to take his place as viscount. His father gave him the option of marrying a proper lady and one day taking his place as Viscount Beauchamp, or being left with only what was entailed to his estate and not a shilling more." Sam sighed, bringing her hands forward toward the heat as a chill ran down her spine. "He chose the option that afforded him the most—his family lands, holdings, and coins. He married soon after we were born."

"I am sorry."

"As am I. However, none of this is your doing, my lord." Sam turned toward the darkened room, putting the glow from the fire at her back and a shadow masking her face. "But I often wonder if he ever thought of us—rode past Craven House hoping to see us outside. Did he remember our birthday or see a jewelry chest in a shop and long to buy it for us?"

"Something you cannot know unless you ask," Eli replied. He remained facing the flames, giving her a piece of the privacy she needed.

"That is easy for you to say. You know nothing of such heartbreak, of growing up knowing your father was so close but didn't care enough to seek you out or want any type of relationship." Sam shook her head, exhaling to calm her nerves. She need remember none of this was Elijah's fault—but he was the one present, at her side, willing to listen. "My apologies. I am upset beyond reason. I think it best I retire to my chambers for the evening."

"I would not, if I were you."

"And why not?"

"Your brother and Lady Marce are awaiting you there," he confided. "I slipped past your open door and saw them inside. I feigned a need to seek my own chambers, but snuck down the servants' stairs to locate you."

"Why did you think to find me here?" she mumbled, finally risking a glance at him.

"It was either here or on the road leading toward London, and it is dark and cold outside. Not to mention the threat of wild animals on the hunt." His hand found hers where it hung at her side, his fingers entwining with hers. "Do not doubt that if I hadn't found you here, I would have called for a horse and rushed out into the night in search."

Sam's head ached ever more when she allowed a light laugh to pass her lips. "You would risk the wilds of Derbyshire after dusk for me?"

"I would risk far more than that, Samantha."

"Well, it is a good thing you are not in the place my father was, or mayhap your choice would be altered significantly." She longed to think the best of Eli, but he was a lord—just as her father was—and she would never think undesirably of him for making a choice that benefited his future and his family name. "Gentlemen are sometimes put in very hard predicaments. I think I shall retire now. I will seek privacy in Payton's chambers until I am certain mine are my own once more."

Sam pulled her hand from his, and their fingers slid apart, though she felt the squeeze of his hand as he attempted to hold her there. Lord Ridgefeld was in attendance at Hollybrooke to conduct business, not soothe or rectify a long ago wrong done by another man. "You are not the only person in this room abandoned by someone whose only goal in life should be to love, protect, and cherish their child." His voice wavered, halting Sam.

She'd been so carried away with her own life circumstances she hadn't thought of Eli's situation—

why he'd been raised by his grandfather. Each time he'd mentioned the late marquis, his eyes had lit with love. She'd assumed he'd lived a content and happy life. Then again, how many people thought the same of Sam and her siblings?

"Let us sit, Sam," Eli whispered, taking her hand once more and tugging her toward a lounge close to the little heat coming from the hearth. "I have a story to tell you."

"I am in no mood for a cheerful story—"

He refused to release his hold. "There is no cheer to be found in this tale, I assure you. However, you may realize you are not as alone in your situation as you think."

Sam wanted Eli close, but didn't want to listen to his fabled story, concocted to soothe her frayed soul. She longed to escape to an empty room, cry until there were no tears left, and fall into an exhausted sleep—awaking to a new day. Only then could she fathom donning her gown of rich golden silk and joining her family in the Cummings' gardens for her twin's morning wedding.

"All I ask is for you to listen," he coaxed.

For some unknown reason, Sam gave in and sat beside Eli on the lounge. She would listen to his story, though she could not promise to find meaning behind his words.

He took hold of both her hands, threading his fingers through hers once more.

Sam could not take her eyes off them as Elijah began his story, his words soft, spoken in reverence.

"I lived with my grandfather for as long as I can remember." Eli squeezed her hand once more. "He was a loving man, an honorable man, an adventurer at heart, and he never shied away from bringing a boy along on his expeditions. I spent my first birthday in Rome, my fifth birthday in the Orient, and my ninth birthday trudging through the Amazon. He is the man I hope to one day be."

Elijah was wrong if he thought his story not a happy one—or that he wasn't already as noble and pure as his grandfather.

She looked up when he did not continue to see a single tear holding at the corner of his eye.

"I mention those specific places because they capture my life on very special days—days that should be filled with family, home, love, laughter, and celebration. Instead, my grandfather, bless his kind soul, took me to explore the world so I would not dwell on the two important people who should be present in my life…but were not. One taken far too early, and one absent by choice.

"The marquis did everything in his power to make sure I was not surrounded by an empty home—full with remnants of parents I had no memory of. He did not shower me with extravagant gifts or treat me as anything but a boy needing a proper upbringing. He taught me love, compassion, and loyalty."

"Loyalty…something my father knows nothing of."

"Is that true?" Eli asked. "He was loyal to his father, he was loyal to the Viscountship. I think, if anything, he lacked the ability to love."

Sam let go of an unladylike snort.

"He is here now, is he not?"

"Yes, but to what end?" Sam pulled her hands free and looked at Eli, his face etched in concern. "Why come to us after all these years?"

"Does it matter so greatly?" he protested. "He is here—"

"And will likely depart and disappear again as soon as he attains what he desires."

"That is a possibility, but allow me to finish my story."

"Your lesson about love, compassion, and loyalty was not the culmination of this lecture?" Sam's tart reply did not deter Elijah.

"Certainly not, Miss Samantha." A soft smile settled on his lips, and her breath stuck in her lungs. "Your father returned to you of his own free will. I, on the other hand, was not so fortunate. I put someone who meant everything to me in jeopardy to gain something I thought was lacking in my life. And I suffered horrible consequences. I lost my grandfather, and the person I went halfway around the world to find, turned me away with barely a glance."

"Oh, Elijah, I—" Sam reached forward, uncertain why, but knowing she needed to feel him—and he needed the same. "Tell me what happened to your parents…why you lived with your grandfather."

Her fingers grazed his cheek, but he didn't pull away as she'd expected. Instead, he brought his own hand to hers, pressing her palm against his warm skin.

"My father's demise started long before he met my mother. You see, he was much like my grandfather, but prone to risk-taking of an extreme nature." Eli turned his face and placed a kiss on the palm of her hand, sending a tingle through her entire body. "My mother,

Alice Watson, loved my father for his adventurous ways. There was never a dull moment to be had with the pair. However, when my mother found she was with child while on a trip to Africa, my grandfather insisted she journey back to England to await my birth."

Sam suspected this was the part of the story that was in no way happy. "It must have upset him to send your mother away."

"My father or grandfather?"

"Your father, of course." It was similar to her love for her twin. It would be devastating when the possibility finally sank in it could be several months before she saw Jude again.

"No, I do not believe either man was dismayed at the departure of my mother for England."

"What happened next?" Her question left her with a sigh of anticipation. "Did your mother arrive safely in England?"

"Certainly, or likely I would not be sitting here," he said with a sorrowful chuckle. "However, my father fell to his death from a high ridge when he and my grandfather quarreled over selecting a dig site. My father got so angry, he stalked off into the night…"

"And the marquis never saw him again?"

"Oh, no." Eli shook his head, releasing her hand. "He was found early the next morning, or at least what the scavengers hadn't eaten of him."

Sam gasped, her hands clutching her throat in shock. "That is awful!"

"Perhaps, perhaps not." Eli shrugged. "We cannot know what today would have held if my father hadn't perished."

"And your mother?" The story could not be any worse. "Did she die of a broken heart when she found out?"

"Not exactly. She gave birth to me, and shortly after, fled to America."

"She never returned?"

"She sent letters—about twice a year—but a little over a year ago, they stopped arriving." If possible, a far deeper sorrow shone from his eyes. "I feared she was in trouble and needed my help. I convinced Grandfather to accompany me to America—Baltimore to be exact—to find her."

The pit of Sam's stomach dropped, suspecting no good news was to follow.

"You both sailed to America?" She hadn't quite known the extent of his travels until this moment.

"Yes. Unfortunately, only I arrived safely." Eli jumped to his feet, rubbing his palms down his face. "I am sorry, Sam. You are the first person I've told the complete story to. It has not gotten easier to speak of since my return."

"We do not need to discuss it at all," Sam protested. "Your meaning is clear."

"No, it is not. You see, when I finally found my mother, she didn't even recognize me—her only son. She told me to return to England and leave her be." Eli pivoted toward the study door and strode to a nearby chair. He grasped the back, and his knuckles turned white. "I begged my grandfather to journey to America with me to collect my mother. He died because of me, because I needed more than he could give. Because I could not be grateful for all I had. I had to discover more about the woman who'd birthed and then abandoned me. The marquis died, and it was all for nothing. I am completely and utterly alone in this world."

"We are not so different, you and I," she mumbled through the heartache she felt on his behalf.

"That is true. However, if my mother were to return to England—show up unannounced on my doorstep—I would not turn her away. I would not wonder what her ulterior motive could be. I would open my arms and welcome her."

"It is not that simple, my lord." Sam stood and crossed the room to stand before him. "I truly wish it were, but..." Her lips pressed together, conflicting feelings coursing through her. Sam was uncertain if she were capable of forgiving Beauchamp.

Eli set his hands on her shoulders, gently kneading them.

Sam's gaze dropped to their feet, afraid he'd see the reasoning in her stare.

"How does one begin to forgive a man who allowed his children to grow up in impoverished circumstances while he dined at his club, traveled around England, and wore coats worth more shillings than our yearly food staples?"

"The way I would push aside the fact that my mother would rather live as a woman of loose morals in an American saloon than return home and have all the pretty gowns she could dream of...have an entire estate and London townhouse...and receive invitations into every home in England." His hands moved from her shoulders up her neck, and he leaned close. "One does not need to forget in order to forgive."

Their lips were almost touching. "What if I do not want to forgive?"

"Then happiness and contentment will be forever out of your reach." His warm breath fanned her lips.

Happiness and contentment—those were both things she longed to achieve...someday. She had never suspected they'd be permanently out of reach. How had Jude attained what might always be denied her?

"You are not a woman to allow such a thing to slip away, are you, Miss Samantha Pengarden?"

He didn't wait for her answer but pulled her closer; every inch of their bodies touching from breasts pushed against his solid, muscular chest to their knees, her skirts the only thing preventing his warmth from touching her in places she hadn't known were frozen.

Sam tilted her chin upwards slightly to look into his eyes, her response at the ready.

She expected to see pity and sympathy, but his gaze held neither.

Desire. Not lust, but affection mixed with adoration.

Eli's lips parted before settling against hers.

She ached with the need to touch him, explore every curve of his body as his hands did the same. It was as if Eli's kiss—his kiss alone—was the only thing that could restore life to her, make her believe forgiveness was possible. That healing from her deep wounds was not only possible but also immediately attainable.

This kiss was far different than the one they'd shared—in this very spot—the night before. Sam moved her hands up and down his back, pulling Eli closer still. Every part of her screamed if he let her go, if he pulled away, it would mean the end for Sam. He was the only reason she breathed.

He set a demanding tempo, first arduous as if he too would cease to be if their lips parted, but then the pace lessened as the kiss turned from need to a slow, building craving. A longing with no end—a yearning that no amount of passion could quench.

A warmth spread through her, settling between her thighs as her desire built. Her body knew what she needed, even though Sam did not.

Eli pushed his fingers into her hair, pins falling to the floor when her long tresses fell about her shoulders.

A moan escaped her as his lips left hers, trailing a fiery path down to her chin and pressing light kisses down her neck—and lower still. Sam tilted her head back to allow him greater access to what he sought. His lips pecked a soft path along her collarbone and dipped to the swell of her breasts, just above her gown's low neckline.

Sam explored his backside, moving her hands lower and lower, and his mouth did the same to her front.

Ecstasy.

"Samantha," he sighed. His fingers untangling from her hair as they grazed the curve of her neck to join his mouth at her heaving bosom. "You are exquisite. Every inch of you is pure perfection."

The beat of her heart thumped through her entire body as her legs quivered.

His back tensed, and he pulled back ever so slightly.

Sam wasn't ready for the sensations coursing through her to end; nor was she prepared to withdraw her hands from their current exploration of his round arse.

However, it appeared Eli was not ready for that either. He brought his lips back to hers, his tongue darting across her lower lip.

The notion of living in this moment for all eternity would be the grandest fate Sam could wish for herself. With his body against hers, his lips possessing hers, and his hands caressing her from neck to waist…if there were a heaven, this would be it.

She would give herself completely—and freely—to Elijah and the sensations he was causing within her. All he need do is ask, and she would give all to him.

Sam had always imagined herself to be half a person, Jude the other.

Never whole without her twin.

But it was not true. Jude was not the missing part she needed to be complete.

She needed this…this desire, this passion, this hunger to never cease, for she would perish without it.

"Pardon, I did not mean—" A familiar lyrical voice started, immediately cutting off. "Sam? Lord Ridgefeld? What are you…I should… What is the meaning of…" Jude's voice rose higher with each word.

Elijah's back flexed, and Sam's hands fell from his backside as they both took a step back—away from each other.

Glancing over Eli's shoulder, Sam noted the shock on her sister's face, her mouth hanging open and her eyes wide as saucers. Part of Sam wanted to give her sister a smug grin, show her that even though she was abandoning her twin, Sam would fare well without her. But more importantly, she longed to share how much she'd come to adore Lord Ridgefeld with the only other person who'd understand.

"It is not what it appears, Jude." Her satisfied grin won. "I was upset, and Lord Ridgefeld found me in tears. He was only comforting me..."

Sam kept her stare locked on Jude's, afraid to glance at Eli, his back still to her twin.

It was exactly as it appeared, and would have progressed further if they hadn't been interrupted.

Eli turned, taking a small step closer to Sam. "Miss Judith. I can offer no explanation for what you have witnessed. I—"

Jude held up her hand, silencing Eli. "It is none of my concern what took place in this room. I am here to collect my sister. I must speak with her regarding," Jude paused as if determining the correct thing to say in a situation such as they'd found themselves, "a delicate family matter."

"He knows of Lord Beauchamp," Sam confessed. "Lord Ridgefeld, thank you for lending me a shoulder to cry on. It was very noble of you. Do give my sincere apologies to your valet if I have ruined your coat."

She hurried to Jude's side, noticing for the first time how affected her sister was by their father's appearance. Her eyes were red and swollen, her face flushed, and her hands clutched so tightly, her knuckles turned white—possibly to halt their shaking. Though, some of her upset was surely caused by catching her twin in a most indecent embrace with a man.

The scandalous nature of their situation kept Sam from meeting Elijah's gaze. She knew his burned a hole in her—she could feel it—and she could not lift her eyes from his knees.

Sparingly, Elijah cleared his throat and shoved is hands deep into his pockets. "Ladies," he said. "I will allow you privacy and return to the other guests."

He slipped past them and out the door before Sam could muster the courage to meet his eyes.

They stood in silence for what seemed like an eternity before Jude turned to depart.

"Jude, let me explain—" There was not much for her to say unless she confessed everything. To do that, Sam would need to understand her connection to Elijah. Was he truly only a distraction to keep boredom at bay while she was in Derbyshire, or had their relationship turned to something far beyond friendship?

"There is no need. Lord Ridgefeld is a very handsome man. He comes from a decent, respectable family," Jude mumbled, matter-of-factly. "You could have set your sights on a far less desirable gentleman. You will want to fix your hair and straighten your gown before we meet with Marce."

Jude stepped to the side, allowing Sam to flee for the safety of her room.

Chapter Sixteen

The morning dawned clear and bright, not a cloud on the horizon and no chance of showers ruining Lord Cartwright and Miss Judith's special day. Below his window, Eli watched as servants hurried to and fro; carrying large floral arrangements, massive trays of meats and cheeses, and chairs for all the guests. A long table had been arranged upon the lawn to accommodate all the guests after the nuptials were complete.

Eli spied Lady Marce and Lord Cummings directing servants in and out of the house as the garden was transformed into a whimsical fairy tale of gold and deep burgundy ribbons, flowers, and table decorations. He would be hard-pressed to remember a setting as perfectly beautiful as the one below.

A gentle rap sounded at his door, and Mathers hurried from Eli's dressing closet to answer.

"Your master's presence is requested by Lord Cartwright in Lord Cummings' study."

Eli glanced over his shoulder to see his valet nod to the maid and close the door.

"My lord—"

"My ears work remarkably well, Mathers," Eli said with a chuckle. "I will make my way down now."

As he departed his room, Elijah wondered if Miss Judith had spoken with her betrothed about the compromising situation she'd found Sam and him in the previous evening. He'd half expected Lord Cartwright or Sam's brother to be pounding on his door before midnight, calling for pistols at dawn—on the lawn. However, now he saw they would not seek a bloody mess where the guests would dine.

The halls were empty at this early hour, many guests still deep in slumber or preparing for the late-morning wedding.

Eli entered the room to find Lord Cartwright studying a large book spread open on the table.

The sandy-haired man glanced up, motioning Eli to enter.

Lord Cartwright stared at a large map of the Americas, lightly trailing his finger across the paper in a grid-like pattern.

"I can return later if that suits you better," Eli said.

"Later I will be tying myself to the most beautiful, cunning, imaginative woman I've ever had the pleasure to meet." Cartwright finally glanced up from his intense study of the map. "My apologies. My sister brought this blasted map to me a few moments ago. Says there is an error somewhere on this page and bounced out of the room. Imagine, challenging me when I should be meeting with you and then preparing to shackle myself to a fiery-haired woman for all eternity."

When Eli made no comment, Cartwright continued, "You know several scientists have explored the topic of monogamy among warm-blooded creatures. They found every indication mammals are meant to secure a life partner and spend their days completely devoted to that one creature." He looked to Elijah for comment, but flapped his hand instead, dismissing the topic. "Ah, well, that is neither here nor there, as it were. And Theo's map challenge will also have to wait. Is now an optimal time to discuss what your grandfather wished to bequeath to the museum?"

"If the time suits, but I can also wait until the morrow, if you prefer." They'd planned to meet today; however, it was rather unconventional—in Eli's way of thinking—to expect a man to conduct business on his wedding day. "I also do not mind putting this off until you return from your wedding travels."

"Certainly not." Cartwright closed the tome and motioned for Eli to have a seat before Cummings' desk. "However, it is my aim to meet you in London when you arrive to deliver the treasures."

"You may not be interested in any of the pieces, my lord," Eli rushed. "Nothing is of great value or significant history—though that was not the point of my grandfather's collection."

Cartwright settled into the seat across from him. "Elijah...it is agreeable I call you by your given name?" When Eli nodded, he continued, "I do feel like our acquaintance spans years. Melly often wrote of you and spoke highly of you on our few brief meetings."

Elijah pinched the bridge of his nose and blinked rapidly to keep his treacherous tears unshed, focusing on Cartwright once more. "The marquis was a kind, generous, and loving man. I was blessed to have him not only as a grandfather but also as a father figure."

"And I know he felt blessed, as well. He spoke many times about his vast collection." Cartwright leaned forward in his chair. "But I must confess I was shocked to learn you wished to donate his collection—in its entirety."

He'd been taken aback, as well—his man of business venomously speaking out against his intentions, though none of the items were entailed to his estates. Therefore, Eli was free to do with them as he pleased—or better yet, as his grandfather would have wished. "They will be enjoyed and cherished far more in a place where many can view and experience them and learn of Grandfather's many adventures."

Cartwright nodded as if agreeing with Eli. "Yes, I have many letters to go with the pieces. Notes he wrote me during each exploration trip."

"I will also be sending his journals and inventory catalogs. It should help with labeling and dating all the artifacts as he kept meticulous notes referring to each piece: where it was found, the date, and any local knowledge about the item." Elijah had stumbled upon the chest holding his grandfather's handwritten journals by accident. They even included many from before Eli's birth, when his parents had traveled with the marquis. His mother had been quite the adventuress, exploring underwater caves and digging in trenches alongside Eli's father and grandfather. "They will all belong to the museum as long as you promise the exhibit will always be free of charge to visitors."

Cartwright tapped his finger against his chin. "It took some convincing, but Cummings agreed to open a portion of the museum for visitors to enjoy without collecting a fee."

"It is what my grandfather would have wanted," Eli said, leaving no option if Cartwright wanted the collection. "He always said that it wasn't about the artifacts found or their value, but about the journey of discovery—and the memories made."

"The exhibit is certain to inspire other young explorers to follow in Melly's footsteps," Cartwright agreed. "Now, what about you? Do you plan to continue in your grandfather's footsteps? Travel the world, seeking adventure."

It was the topic Eli had been waiting for, suspected he could not avoid. "I will remain in England. I have no plans to travel neither outside the country nor away from my estate but to bring Grandfather's collection to the museum. Mayhap the future holds something outside of England; however, not in the coming year."

"Very good." Cartwright fell into silence as he scrutinized Eli. "May I ask a rather blunt and highly incongruous question?"

Eli lifted his chin in confidence, his mouth tightening. "Of course, my lord."

"Jude frequently conveys it is rude to pose a question of a sensitive nature," he sighed. "So, I have adjusted my manner and request permission to ask such things before blurting out what I wish to know."

"That is a commendable compromise. I am here as your guest; therefore, feel free to ask anything you wish." *As long as it isn't related to Sam, our time alone, or our intimate relationship*, Eli longed to add. "I have nothing to hide."

He had much to hide, including his budding affection for Sam.

"It has been brought to my attention that you and Miss Samantha were caught in a rather delicate situation last night..." Cartwright broke eye contact and proceeded to inspect his freshly trimmed nails, obviously uncomfortable with the conversation. "You see, Jude is worried about her sister, and while I agree that Sam is of a mature age, her actions and words since arriving in Derbyshire are rather out of character and suspect for her."

"And you've been sent by Miss Judith to inquire as to my intentions?"

Cartwright flopped back in his chair, his eyes closed as he nodded vigorously. "Yes, that is exactly what I've been sent to do. Not my idea, mind you, but important to Jude."

"I can assure you that things were not as they appeared," Eli confessed.

"Things are rarely as they appear. Something I—and Jude—know well, Lord Ridgefeld, which is why I have been sent to speak with you regarding the incident and not either of Miss Samantha's older siblings." Cartwright shuddered at the mention of Garrett and Lady Marce. "They are a ferocious pair, to be sure."

"I appreciate your and Jude's discretion on the matter." Though Cartwright owed Eli nothing.

"I do not see that there is a *matter* at all, but my soon-to-be bride is not so certain." Cartwright folded his hands in his lap and stared at the far corner of the room. Eli glanced in that direction, expecting to find a timepiece or bauble that had caught his attention, but the area was devoid of anything significant. "Lord Ridgefeld, may I again touch on a delicate matter?"

The inquisition was not yet at an end. There was more Cartwright had been sent to convey—but whether it came from Miss Judith or Sam, he did not know. "Of course, my lord." The hairs on the back of his neck stood on end. From the man's uneasy posture, his next words were not going to be to Eli's liking, and the earl knew it.

"What *are* your intentions with Miss Samantha?" Cartwright gazed at anything but Eli—currently inspecting a picture on the desk in front of him. "Do you plan to pursue a courtship?"

"We have only just met, my lord." Eli attempted to keep the shock from his voice—or at least disguise it. But he'd be a bloody fool to admit he'd thought of just that scenario since their meeting on the deserted road. "I am acquainted with few people here, and Miss Samantha kindly offered to make introductions. I was in no position to turn down her assistance."

"I can understand that," Cartwright mused. "However, I think…correction, Jude wishes you to know Miss Samantha is experiencing a bout of emotional turmoil—her words, not mine—at the sudden reappearance of their father. I have been informed you are well aware of this development."

"I am." Eli couldn't decipher exactly what was transpiring between him and the earl.

"Very good. So you understand that Samantha is not precisely herself at this moment, which Jude believes has caused her to latch on to you, giving you a false sense of her true feelings toward you." Cartwright took a deep breath and expelled the air slowly. "Jude suspects her feelings are not genuine, but come from a place of desperation, confusion, and fear."

Eli sat up straight. "Are you saying that—"

Cartwright held up his hand to halt Eli. "I am saying nothing. This comes from Jude, who I might add is quite adept at matters of the heart, as it were. And is the only true expert on her sister's heart, outside of Samantha herself."

"I am certain what has transpired between Miss Samantha and me has nothing to do with matters of the heart, my lord."

"That is good to know," Cartwright's posture went slack, releasing pent-up tension that Eli hadn't noticed. "This is all Jude asks…if you do find yourself with an affection for Sam—which neither of us is against—she asks that you allow Samantha the time she needs to process her father's appearance without you as a distraction. Once you arrive in London with your grandfather's collection, you are welcome to pursue her with vigor—if you are interested. You will have our blessing and that of her two older siblings."

"What of Lord Beauchamp?"

"That does not signify," Cartwright said, dismissing any mention of the man. "His wishes are of little note to Jude and her siblings, including Samantha and her future. He is not her guardian, and therefore, will not be consulted about her choices for the future."

Eli would likely need time to process everything alongside Sam. He'd ventured to Derbyshire in hopes of being rid of all the reminders of the man he'd lost to his own selfishness; in no way had he come seeking to find a bride—or even a dalliance or flirtation.

"Now, where your intentions lie in a month's time, neither of us can be certain, but for the time being, Jude thinks it best that you depart to give Samantha the space needed to come to terms with everything."

"Are you throwing me out?" Eli asked to gain more insight.

"Of course not." Cartwright waved his hand, dismissing the accusation. "Stay for the wedding and the feast to follow, but, please, keep your distance from Samantha and depart with first light tomorrow."

Eli could only nod, his next action undetermined. If he stayed and ignored Sam, she'd think him a scoundrel, especially after the previous evening: all that was said, all that was shared, and all that was confessed.

"Are we in agreement?" Cartwright pushed from his seat.

"Absolutely, my lord." It was the only response Eli could give, although it couldn't be further from the truth.

"Wonderful." The earl's ready smile returned. "Without further delay, I have a wedding to dress for. If we do not have occasion to speak again, I look forward to seeing you in London when we return from our trip."

Eli followed suit, standing as they both moved toward the study door.

"Good blessings on your wedding, my lord," Eli said with a stiff bow. "I wish you and Miss Judith all the best in the years to come. I am delighted to know my grandfather's collection will be well cared for and enjoyed by the masses. Until London."

"Thank you for understanding, Ridgefeld." Lord Cartwright walked from the room, leaving Eli to stare after him.

Cartwright was correct in his thinking—Sam needed time without Eli as a distraction to determine the relationship she wanted to embark on with Beauchamp. It was similar to what his grandfather had done for him. Eli had been afforded the space, time, and resources to determine if he craved a connection with his mother. If he should journey all the way to America. If Alice Watson, his mother, longed for a relationship with her son. At the time, Eli would have forgiven her anything—wiped the past from his memory to make a place for their future.

It was only right Elijah give Sam the same opportunity.

His only desire was that she not experience a second heartbreak as he had.

Chapter Seventeen

Sam took her place in the second row as instructed by Marce. The garden had been transformed into a magical area with carefully manicured shrubbery and paths lined with gold ribbons, flowers of the perfect shade of burgundy to accentuate Jude's fiery hair, and tiny candle holders hung in the branches above her head. It was morning, but the sparkling light from above cast an enchanted glow on all the guests.

It was breathtaking—all of it.

Even the table set for their feast was utter perfection with tall-backed chairs with alternating gold and burgundy bows tied for decoration. The tabletop was arranged with exquisite place settings for all the guests—children included. The aroma of roasting meats, fresh bread, cheese, and delicious sweet desserts drifted across the expansive garden and lawn. Sam's mouth watered, though she'd eaten only an hour before.

Everything was flawless, as Jude deserved—and Simon, as well.

The pair had met under improbable circumstances but beat the odds—as Payton called it—to find love, happiness, and hope for a bright future.

All things Sam had come to realize might be out of her reach.

Thankfully, Jude had come to her the night before. She hadn't relished her twin barging in on her and Eli's private moment, but the discussion they'd had after he departed was one of true enlightenment. Jude hadn't planned to marry and leave Sam, forgetting about her. No, they would continue to be close. They were sisters. More than sisters...twins. They shared a unique bond, something even Marce and Garrett did not possess. Jude would not give that up, even though she was to wed Simon.

Possibly the most startling revelation had come when Sam had expressed her unwillingness to forgive Beauchamp and her desire to see the man gone—and not returned. Jude felt the same, but she was willing to hear their father's side of the story. When she had children, she did not want the stigma of her own fatherless upbringing to affect them. Jude did not have to trust the man, but at least her children would know their grandfather—their lineage.

"May I take this seat, Miss Samantha?"

Sam looked up to find Lord Gunther, staring at the vacant seat beside her.

"Ummm, this seat is spoken for. I do apologize, my lord." She smiled to soothe any insult. "But I believe we are to sit across from one another at the meal to follow."

"Very well." He gave a curt nod and moved to sit several rows behind Sam.

She turned slightly to search the gathering crowd. Elijah hadn't yet arrived. What was keeping him? He hadn't broken his fast in the dining room either, though she'd heard he was meeting with Lord Cartwright in Cummings' study.

She'd taken her time eating, refilling her plate twice and imbibing nearly a full pot of tea, which had eventually sent her fleeing to her room in discomfort before Eli had shown his face. They hadn't seen one another since Jude had walked in on them embracing. Sam longed to see him, let him know all was as it should be, and Jude would keep everything to herself.

There had been much shared by them, yet Sam suspected they could have talked late into the night; their conversation before the fire moving to the lounge and their voices quieting to whispers.

She'd experienced serenity for the first time. Moments of utter relinquishment: of everything she need confess, of all that worried her, of all that weighed her down.

And he'd reciprocated in kind; sharing parts of him that not another soul was privy to. He hadn't said that much, but Sam knew it to be true. He was not a man who clung tightly to others, open to sharing his past. Unlike Sam, who could not seem to let go of those closest to her.

Mr. Stanford walked down the path, his covetous eyes settling on the empty chair beside her.

She quickly set her fan and reticle on the seat to show it to be spoken for, but did not grace the man with her regretful smile. Instead, she looked to the terrace, expecting to see Elijah hurrying her way, but the only thing she saw was Jude standing just inside the double doors, awaiting her time to walk into the garden and join Simon, who stood chatting with Vicar William Jakeston, Mr. Jakeston's elder brother, who'd traveled from London to act as their officiate.

Lord Beauchamp was also missing. Sam hoped it remained that way, at least until she could escape back to London and the sanctuary of Craven House. Her father had had the common sense to not show his face in the breakfast room either, leaving Sam blissfully to her thoughts of Lord Ridgefeld without the need to ignore her father's presence. She'd promised Jude she would not outwardly speak ill of Beauchamp or draw attention to their family strife. Her assurance had been fulfilled far easier than Sam expected.

If only Eli would join her and fulfill his promise to distract her, then all would continue to be well. She was seated across from Lord Gunther at the feast, but Eli would be at her side. Another welcomed occurrence, and Sam suspected it was Jude's doing.

Her maid had reassured her that Beauchamp was seated close to the head of the table—as was proper for the father of the bride—with all of Jude and Cartwright's family scattered through the guests.

The strings of a single violin started signaling for everyone to be seated before silence fell once more.

A flurry of nervousness fluttered within Sam as she glanced around. Guests hurriedly took their seats. She scanned each row but did not spot Eli anywhere. It would be the height of embarrassment for him to slip in during the nuptials.

Once everyone was seated, the violinist commenced a lovely song unfamiliar to Sam. The notes carried on the slight breeze, reaching far and wide across Hollybrooke.

The vicar cleared his throat, motioning for everyone to stand.

As Sam did, she turned to watch her sister's approach, catching sight of servants standing watch in the many windows of the manor.

Sam glanced longingly at the empty seat meant for Elijah.

Perchance he had been held up by some unforeseeable business and would join them for the meal to be served immediately following the ceremony.

Contemplation of the previous evening and the two missing guests fled Sam's mind as Jude, on the arm of Garrett, came into view.

Her sister was stunningly elegant in her cream gown with gold threaded through her long, curling locks and a sprig of burgundy blossoms clutched in her hand. Tall and graceful, everything a woman of the *ton* aimed to be. A sash of entwined gold and burgundy was tied loosely around her waist and trailed down the back of her dress, creating a fanning train, floating behind her as she made her way down the terrace steps and into the garden.

Ooohs and *Ahhhs* could be heard, as well as mumbled praise for Marce's excellent planning for a garden wedding.

Sam glanced toward Lord Cartwright where he stood next to the vicar, a shining smile upon his face. A few feet away in the front row, the soon-to-be Dowager Countess Cartwright held a smile much like her son's as she took in the woman who would birth the next Cartwright earl—the good Lord willing.

Sam glanced skyward to keep the tears of joy from spilling down her cheeks and ruining her gown. Not a cloud hung in the sky, and the breeze was barely more than a whisper in the trees as Jude walked slowly between the rows of guests. Her twin paused briefly, giving Sam an encouraging smile before Garrett pulled her farther toward her betrothed.

A single tear escaped when Sam witnessed the light that filled Simon as Jude took her place at his side. They were fated to be together—always and forever.

Could that lay in Sam's future, too? Did a man exist who would love and cherish her enough to keep her by his side for all eternity? Or was she meant to live her life one soirée, one opera, and one garden party at a time? Drifting from one social gathering to the next in an endless cycle of societal necessity.

A part of her wondered if a mundane marriage was for her. Certainly, after a spell, the usual *ton* gatherings would lose appeal, and Sam would seek something else to keep her occupied—and distracted. Just a short couple of days before, she'd desired nothing more than to return to the fancy ballrooms, lavish dinner parties, and scandalous outdoor playhouses of London.

At the moment, she wanted nothing more than a warm, male body taking a seat in the chair beside her.

Sam hadn't expected her wayward fantasy to be realized, but no sooner had she thought it then a man did indeed take the seat beside her.

Unfortunately, it wasn't the lord she'd hoped for.

Or any lord at all. It was her brother, Garrett.

"This seat is spoken for. Move," she hissed.

He glanced around as the guests resumed their seats with Jude and Simon standing before the vicar, their backs to the crowd.

"By whom?" he whispered back, gaining an evil stare from Marce.

"If you must know, I am saving this seat for Lord Ridgefeld." There was little chance Garrett had been told of what transpired—or nearly transpired—the night before. If Jude said she would hold a confidence, she did not betray that, even to her own kin. "Now, kindly move. Please."

The *please* was clearly an afterthought and only said to gain what she wanted—or more accurately, demanded.

Garrett only settled further, stretching out his legs and turning his attention toward the vicar as he spoke. "He left."

"No," she stuttered. "*You* need to leave. Now."

"I meant, Ridgefeld departed this morning. Before breakfast." He didn't even bother glancing in her direction, further confirming her brother was unaware of Sam's relationship with Elijah.

But gone?

"That cannot be," Sam argued in a hushed tone. "We are seated next to one another at the feast, and he has business to conduct with Simon and Lord Cummings."

"Business was completed, obviously, as I witnessed Ridgefeld, his valet in tow, leaving Hollybrooke before many guests had risen from their beds." Garrett looked at her from the corner of his eye, one brow raised. "As to the seating arrangement, I cannot say, but maybe his plans were changed without word reaching Marce. She will likely be a little peeved to have an empty seat at the table. It should be comical to watch her scramble to have the place setting removed and seats shifted at the last minute."

Garrett's continued monologue blended in with the sound of the vicar speaking to the guests. Speaking of Jude and Cart's unlikely meeting, their commitment, mutual love for one another—and their plans for the future.

None of it penetrated the haze that had settled around Sam.

Elijah had left Hollybrooke without so much as a farewell to her.

"He must be returning before nightfall." Sam wasn't sure why she felt the need to rebuff Garrett or what he'd claimed to see. "Mayhap a day trip into town for business."

"Don't think so, dear sister."

Their bickering garnered them a loud *"Shhh"* from Lady Chastain—Ellington—who sat directly behind them.

"How can you be so certain?" she leaned close to whisper as Simon and Jude turned to face one another, clasping hands.

"They loaded his trunk, and the servants changed out his bedding. His room was across the hall from mine," he offered.

Cheers sounded around her as guests stood, clapping and chanting their good tidings to Lord Cartwright and the new Lady Cartwright. Her sister…a countess.

But all Sam could hear was the tearing of her heart as it was ripped piece by piece from her chest. She didn't want it to be true. She longed for Garrett to be mistaken.

Lord Ridgefeld, Elijah, would not depart Hollybrooke in such a manner, without a proper goodbye. Or at least a note of explanation for his hasty departure.

He'd made her a promise.

Sam pressed her lips together to stop any further denial. It would only serve to make her appear senseless and dimwitted. Of all people, Elijah was aware of the amount of scorn, disgust, and anger she held for her father, the first man to leave her without a backwards glance. To continue on with his life as if she and Jude were little more than a wrong turn taken, though his path was quickly righted and his course set as if he'd never embarked on the detour at all.

The inconvenience of two daughters, forgotten.

Had she been an inconvenience to Eli? Had he departed only to forget her before he reached the nearest town?

Guests milled about around Sam, congratulating the newlywed couple, offering advice on a successful marriage, and expressing appreciation for the feast to come.

People laughed with good cheer. Sam only longed to cry in despair.

People moved about. Sam could not bring herself to stand.

People spoke of good tidings to come. Sam's voice was lodged in her dry throat.

As the day progressed, the guests ate until they were full and moved inside as evening fell. A night of dancing and cards had been planned in honor of the newly joined Lord and Lady Cartwright.

It was all a blur around her. Sam suddenly found herself standing against the wall bordering the dance floor with no recollection of how she'd come to be dressed in her evening gown of midnight blue silk, though the hue perfectly matched her mood.

Her neck tight and her hands clutched mercilessly before her, she searched the room once more, as the final strings of denial fled her, leaving her shoulders sagging.

Lord Ridgefeld had truly departed Hollybrooke Manor, and he was not to return.

Her chin trembled, and she sniffed to keep her sob at bay and her tears where they belonged…unshed.

Certainly, she'd been mistaken about Elijah and his character.

He was not the white knight who'd rescued her from the storm.

He was not the kind gentleman who'd allowed her to cry on his shoulder.

He was not the empathetic man who'd told her of his own heartbreak at his parents' hands.

He was the marquis who'd inspired a deep passion within her, but without the rest, Sam knew her desire for him would wane with time.

Even now, she sensed her heart hardening to him—any thought of the man, in fact.

Elijah, the Marquis of Ridgefeld, was no better than Sam's scoundrel of a father.

# # #

"Mathers!" Eli pounded on the side of the coach. "Stop the conveyance. I am in need of air."

It was a bit of an understatement—in need of air. Elijah needed far more than air to turn is life right-side up once more. He desired Samantha Pengarden...at his side and in his home, forevermore. Had this been the affliction his father had faced when meeting his mother? He'd given so much thought to Alice Watson, and rarely thought of the man he'd only known through the musings of his grandfather.

The coach rumbled to a stop only three short hours after departing Hollybrooke. That time was all Eli could spend locked in the conveyance alone, with only this thoughts—filled with remorse and regret—as company.

He'd stood outside Sam's bed chamber door for as long as possible before guests began stirring and preparing for the late morning wedding in the gardens. He'd flipped through the thin volume he'd taken from Cummings' private study. He'd debated returning the book to her, allowing her to gain the knowledge he could never share with her, but that she so desperately longed to know.

He could not do this to himself. He'd made the correct decision. The only decision that would benefit everyone involved.

"My lord?" Mathers asked, opening the door wide.

Eli jumped from the confines of the conveyance, happy to do away with the restrictions imposed by the enclosed coach.

"Shall we turn about and start back to Hollybrooke?" Mathers' brow rose in question, and a spot of hopefulness shone in his tone. "We can arrive before the meal is served—"

"No." Eli slashed his hand through the space between them before pivoting to pace alongside the road. "Give me a few moments, and we will continue on our way."

"Very well." Mathers averted his glare before climbing back up onto his perch and taking the reins in hand to await Eli's next command. Blast it all, but Eli hadn't meant to be harsh with his servant. The man was loyal to a fault, and one of the few men Eli considered a friend despite the fact that he paid Mathers' salary. It was something Mathers rarely forgot and because of it, he made himself available to Eli but rarely spoke of himself.

Eli turned and strode to stand below Mathers' perch. "My apologies." When his valet—and occasional carriage driver—only nodded but refused to meet Eli's eyes, he climbed up next to the man, rubbing his open palms down his face. "I did not mean to speak harshly. My troubles are my own, and I know this."

"May I speak freely, my lord?" The man's hands tightened on the reins, his knuckles turning white with strain.

"Of course," Eli sighed.

"I do not believe you wanted to leave Hollybrooke," Mathers confided.

"No, I did not." Truly, he hadn't wanted to leave Sam and whatever the draw between them was. "Originally, I came to Derbyshire to escape the strain from Grandfather's passing and the regret of failing to bring my mother home. Unfortunately, my troubles followed me here."

In truth, he hadn't gained the courage to knock on Sam's door that morning and return the books because he knew it was a selfish act. Eli had wanted to see her one final time before he departed, though he knew full well he would never confess to her that he was leaving Hollybrooke. So, instead, Eli had discovered where Cummings had hidden his treasures, slipped the book back into its hidden spot, and fled.

It made him no more honorable than his mother, who'd snuck out of Liverpool during the dead of night. At least she'd left a note for Grandfather. Eli hadn't so much as grown the nerve to do that.

Mathers flicked the reins, and the coach started once more.

Elijah settled in, enjoying the feel of the fresh breeze against his face, though it did nothing to clear the muddle of concerns he carried with him.

He freely admitted his family had a tendency to flee—disguised as travel or exploration trips—to run away from the things that haunted them. His grandfather had initially sought out adventure after his wife died, not thinking the impact it would have on his son and grandson. His own father had taken on far more risky exploits after learning of his wife's pregnancy and expelling her back to England. And his mother had fled England altogether as soon as it was possible. Elijah's father's death was too much for her to handle. Having to care for an infant was entirely out of the question.

Fleeing Liverpool had been a way to escape anything and everything that reminded Eli of his failures and the things—people—he would never have back in his life. And now, he'd bolted from Hollybrooke for similar purposes. He could never possess Sam, had no right to set his sights on her; and everyone—including her family—had deduced as much. Even before Elijah had come to the realization.

The cycle continued. Eli was helpless to change his course.

"Miss Samantha is a rare thing of beauty," Mathers said, glancing at Eli from the corner of his eye.

But Elijah would not allow his true feelings for the woman to escape him. It was too late for that.

"Truly enchanting." Bloody hell, he hadn't meant to speak the words aloud.

"I agree, my lord." His servant wisely kept his gaze trained on the road before them, but he was unable to hide his smirk.

No matter how much Elijah wished to debunk his previous mindless uttering, it would be an outright lie to say he found the woman anything other than what he'd said: enchanting.

They barely knew one another, but there was something there. Something that pulled him to Sam. Gave him no other option than to be near her, listen to her every word, and pray that it continued.

It was the most convincing reason why he needed to leave Derbyshire. Cartwright had spoken the truth: Sam should be allowed the time and opportunity to know her father. But it had been the immense draw Elijah had felt to her that had influenced him to heed Cartwright's warning.

What if Samantha's feelings for him were only what they were because of the strain placed upon her by Beauchamp?

Elijah could not live knowing he'd come to care for—be connected to—a woman who did not share the same affection.

"When do you suppose we will arrive home, Mathers?" Elijah shouted over the din of the carriage wheels and galloping horses.

Chapter Eighteen

June 1819
London, England

Eli sat tall on his mount, surveying the crowded streets as he led the half-dozen wagons behind him, each heavily loaded and packed with extreme care, carrying his grandfather's most valued treasures. Decades of memories, travels, and foreign lands all carefully arranged in forty-eight large trunks and several crates. Twenty-seven hours spread over three days journeying from his estate outside Liverpool all the way to London. Four broken carriage wheels, and two thrown horseshoes.

Exhaustion infused every inch of his body.

The final day, Eli had escaped the confines of his traveling coach to ride astride. He was glad he had. The city was impressive, vast beyond his childhood recollection. The streets varied between unsavory to well-kept as he moved toward Lord Cartwright's townhouse.

Nothing could have prepared him for the sight of his country's greatest city. It rivaled his time in South America and the Mayan ruins, the great Pyramids of Egypt, and the slow-moving rivers through the Amazon jungle.

Why had his grandfather kept the majestic nature of their homeland from him?

No doubt remained that Eli had selected the correct museum to house his grandfather's amassed treasures.

A man walking down the street, keeping close to the storefronts, nodded in Elijah's direction. He tipped his head in return. He likely appeared as someone far grander than he was as six wagons and his traveling coach followed him through the London streets.

He understood why Sam was so desperate to return to London. Excitement filled him at the mere thought of her. They'd known one another for such a brief period of time, yet Eli was hard-pressed to think of a moment spent without her coy smile, fiery hair, and hellion demeanor coming to mind. He'd fled his home to escape all the memories of his grandfather, but returned with a new ghost shadowing his every moment.

He had viewed his home in a completely different fashion following his trip to Derbyshire. Suddenly, he no longer favored the masculine presence in every corner of the sprawling estate. And found himself thinking back to the places of female whimsy that had existed during his early years—the last remnants of his mother. However, they'd slowly disappeared as his grandfather continued to collect, and his mother's lilac drawing room was converted to house Grandfather's pottery assemblage. Alice Watson's sewing room gradually turned into a place where the marquis hung his prized sword collection. In the end, even his mother's bedchamber—a room that had been floor-to-ceiling pink—had been transformed into a reading room.

The day he and Grandfather had returned from a trip to France and saw his mother's personal space stripped of every memory of her life had been the day Eli had known she wasn't coming back—ever. He'd been twelve and nearly a man, but he'd given in that day and cried…allowing his anger, despair, and abandonment to surface. He'd slept for two days after. And promised himself he'd never allow a woman to bring him to tears again.

He'd come close to breaking that long ago promise when he'd sought out his mother in America.

"M'lord," one of his drivers called. "Mayfair is that way. We be continue'n on ta the museum."

"Just so, Carter." Eli smiled over his shoulder. It had been good to travel with such a large party. It reminded him of his grandfather and their many excursions. They'd even spent one night camped under the wagons in a particularly desolate part of Buckinghamshire. It had rained the entire night, and they'd all awoken sopping wet and cold. Nevertheless, Eli had enjoyed their trek immensely. "They will be expecting you. Lord Cartwright and I will be round tomorrow to sort through everything. Please return to Mayfair when you're done. A hot meal and dry bed await you."

"Verra kind o' Lord Cartwright to house us all," Carter shouted over the noise of carriage wheels and hooves as they journeyed down the cobbled lane. "But I be honest in say'n I canna wait ta return ta Liverpool on the morrow, m'lord."

Not long ago, Eli would have said the same.

Eli waved as he and his traveling coach turned into Mayfair and the wagons continued on to the British Museum. A weight lifted from him. He didn't relish parting with all his grandfather had worked so hard to collect, but he knew the items would be properly cared for and appreciated. Something that was impossible for one man to accomplish in the middle of Lancashire.

The narrow streets were less crowded, giving Eli a clear view of the roads as he passed—each with grand townhouses on both sides, manicured shrubs, and well-tended drives. He would certainly need to visit a tailor if he planned to stay longer than a fortnight in town. He would gain the title of the country bumpkin with only three proper coats. Though a man only needed so many fine garments when he rarely left the presence of his servants.

Sorting and storing for proper transport had taken more time than Eli had expected, delaying his trip by almost two full weeks. The added time had hopefully given Lord Cartwright and his new bride the opportunity to settle in to town life before Eli arrived and took up their space and time.

He'd sent word to Cartwright, indicating his expected arrival date. He should have sent word to Miss Samantha about his arrival, as well. Possibly been so forthright as to request an audience with her or a turn about Hyde Park. He'd read that women—and men, as well—spent many hours per week in or around London parks or attending the arts at Pall Mall. The activity appeared cumbersome and time-consuming to him.

It was also possible Sam had forgotten all about him and secured a beau in London. A gentleman more accustomed to moving within society. Truly, he wished he'd have remained at Hollybrooke long enough to tell her of his affection for her, but Cartwright had made a valid point…and Eli hadn't yet the notion of his tender for the woman. As many have written, absence makes the heart grow fonder.

And one thing Eli was aware of was his affection and longing for Sam. In fact, he'd never been so certain of anything in his life thus far.

He steered his mount into the Cartwright drive and dismounted as his coach came to a stop behind him. Mathers, his valet, exited quickly and hurried to the door to announce Elijah's arrival. It seemed an overly aristocratic gesture to him, but if he were going to make a sterling impression, society rules need be adhered to.

"Ridgefeld!" Lord Cartwright hurried outside, his butler and two footmen close behind as Eli brushed the traveling dust from this overcoat. "You've arrived. The museum has added additional staff to assist in unloading, sorting, and organizing your grandfather's expansive collection. Since you wrote of staying in London until the task was complete…I feared without help you would be here long past the Christmastide season." He waved wildly toward the door. "Do come in. Let us have a drink and discuss your travels."

He looked between his driver, valet, the footmen, and Cartwright. "Do you think—"

"Do not worry," he said, rubbing his hand through his sandy light brown hair and rocking back on his heels. "They will see to your things. Let us go inside."

Cartwright didn't wait for Eli to respond but pivoted and started back toward the door.

There was no other option but to follow the man or be left behind.

"We can handle this, my lord," Mathers confirmed.

"Thank you." Elijah hurried to catch Cartwright as he walked across the foyer, mumbling under his breath with each step he took.

"Pardon, my lord?" Eli finally fell into step beside him. "What were you saying?"

"Oh!" Cartwright's steps faltered as if he hadn't realized he'd spoken aloud. "It is forty-seven steps to my study from the front door. I have a thing for counting…and when I am overexcited, I tend to take smaller, quicker steps. Very ungentlemanly. If I count, it helps."

Eli only smiled and nodded at the earl's rambling.

"It is a pleasure to see you again, Ridgefeld," Cartwright gushed. "It was a pity you departed Hollybrooke when you did."

"Yes, well…" Eli wondered if Cartwright remembered that he'd all but demanded Eli leave the wedding celebration early. "I am happy to have arrived safely—as well as all the wagons—in London. It has been many years since I've seen the city. I do hope your bridal tour was enjoyable."

Cartwright rounded his desk and sat, motioning for Eli to do the same in the guest chair. "As far as bridal tours go, it was dreadful, I must say. I had the unfortunate task of evicting paying tenants from my country manor. When my uncle absconded with much of the Cartwright coffers, it was necessary for me to take on leaseholders at many of my properties to afford their upkeep and such." He shook his head with remorse. "Since my fortunes are beginning to improve—and my family is soon to grow—I thought it only right to revert my estate for family use."

He wondered if the earl was accustomed to oversharing with his business guests, or maybe Cartwright was in need of a friend. Besides Cummings, Stanford, and Gunther, Cartwright had had no other male guests not connected to Miss Judith in attendance at Hollybrooke. And the trio was more business associate than friend.

"Nuisance, the lot of it, though I am certain you are not concerned with all that. May I offer you a drink?" Cartwright asked.

"Oh, no, thank you," Eli said. It was far too early for spirits, and tea had never been a favorite of Eli's. "Thank you for offering me a place to stay while in London. It is quite embarrassing to admit that I do not have my own residence here."

"It is the least I could offer for your generosity to the museum. And I dare say my new bride would be appalled if I allowed you to find lodging in a boarding house or to stay at an inn while in town." A screech sounded from the somewhere deep within the house, and Cartwright cringed. "Although, you may still want to seek other accommodations. My dear mother is still adjusting to being called dowager, and without Theo in residence, she is completely unoccupied." He paused, massaging his temples as another yell echoed from the second floor. "If you do decide to find other housing, would you ask my dear wife if I might join you?"

Elijah chuckled at the man's unintended—and unexpected—wit. "I've heard escaping one's mother is difficult, and I fear evading a wife is all but impossible."

Light footsteps sounded behind Eli, and he turned, his breath hitching. For a brief moment, Eli thought it was Sam who'd entered the room, and his heartbeat sped.

His hopes were dashed when Miss Judith—err, Lady Cartwright's—lyrical voice greeted him. "Lord Ridgefeld. It is lovely to see you again. I do hope Simon is not keeping you from resting after your long journey." She raised a questioning brow at her husband.

"I have not—" Cartwright began but wisely clamped his mouth shut.

"I have had a room prepared for you," the countess continued. "At the opposite side of the house as the dowager, never fear. I am confident you must be exhausted. I can have a footman show you to your room."

"Yes, you are correct, my love," Cartwright agreed. "Rest...and a proper bath are just what is needed after travel."

The countess smiled, turning back to Eli. "If you are rested by this evening, you are welcome to join Simon and me. Lord and Lady Chastain are hosting a ball in our honor—to celebrate our union—and introduce us properly to society. You truly must come."

He stopped himself from asking if Miss Samantha would be in attendance. Of course, she would not miss an event celebrating her sister and Cartwright.

"I will have my valet ready my evening attire," Eli said with a smile, hoping his unease was not too visible. "It will be my first soirée, excluding the small country dances held outside Liverpool, of course." There was no need to mention the many tribal rituals he'd partaken in over the years, but he'd more accurately served as a witness and bystander at those.

"Lovely." Lady Cartwright clapped her hands with delight. "Do not fret overmuch. There will be at least a dozen familiar faces, I assure you."

Odd that any nervousness dissipated quickly at the idea of being in Sam's presence once again.

Chapter Nineteen

"Lord Proctor!" Sam's deep, throaty laugh echoed down the deserted corridor as the chords of a waltz drifted through the large house until the sound reached the spot of privacy that she suspected the baron had planned to lead her to all evening. "You are highly improper."

"My sweet, Sammy, you have no notion how improper a man can be!" His hand slid up her thigh as he spoke, sending a hum of warning through her. The nickname he'd dubbed her with was almost as offensive as his skills on the dance floor—hence why she'd allowed him to lead her *away* from the ballroom. "Just one tiny kiss, my sugar dumpling."

Sugar dumpling? The man certainly knew nothing of her to think she was sweet in any sense of the endearment. Sam wondered if he'd think her saccharine if she twisted his ear until he gave her a bit of room to breathe.

Proctor—Eric as he demanded she call him—was said to be dashing, wealthy, and connected. Every debutante's dream with his jet-black hair…a bit too dark for Sam's liking. His piercing blue eyes…a bit too intense for Sam's comfort. His aggressive arrogance…a bit too forthcoming and in conflict with Sam's own forceful demeanor. However, he was an eligible, unattached man with an estate in Devon, a house in Bath, and a grand townhouse befitting a prince. Certainly, he wasn't an earl like Jude's husband—nor a marquis.

Why did Elijah spring to mind at that exact moment when she was in the arms of another man?

Sam had done all in her power to forget the blasted scoundrel. She'd embraced town life as the sister of a newly minted countess. London's most fashionable homes were presently open to her, even before Jude and Simon had returned from their bridal tour. Marce had been up in arms regarding whose invitations to accept, and which to reject.

Closing her eyes and tilting her head back, Sam concentrated on the baron's hand, currently traveling up her side to cup her breast. As it settled, she noted the minuscule size of his pal. Surely a man's hand was meant to be twice the size of a woman's?

She pushed the wayward thought from her mind as his warm breath cascaded over her neck; the aromas of the evening's goose pudding filling her nose, assaulting her senses.

This was not working. *He* was not working. Neither had Sam been able to feel desire—or anything resembling it—during her time at the opera, ensconced in Lord Harborborn's private viewing box.

She pushed free from Proctor's hold as his lips settled just below her ear.

The old Sam would have purred, maybe even issued a subtle moan of delight.

Now, she couldn't think past the clammy nature of his hands and the man's weak bottom lip when their mouths met.

It obviously spoke volumes of the man: sweaty, tiny hands...beady, shifty eyes...and lips that likely allowed drink to dribble down his chin. Young misses spoke of his dashing good looks; however, he only appeared a gaping-mouthed fish to her.

"I think it is time we return to the ballroom, my lord." Sam took a step in that direction. "People will have certainly noticed our absence by now."

Proctor grasped her hand before she could slip farther away. "Would *that* be so dreadful?"

"What are you implying?" Sam had a hunch, but she wanted to hear him say it.

"I think my meaning is clear, Miss Samantha." He made the grave mistake of raking his gaze up and down her body before attempting to pull her close once more. "You've accompanied me to the park, Abernasher's garden party, and I've placed my name on your dance card a half-dozen times in the last fortnight. I believe it is obvious, not only to you but society as a whole."

There was little reason to inform Proctor she'd also enjoyed similar outings with four other suitors since her return to London.

Her eyes narrowed. How had she ever thought him dashing? Or the least bit thrilling?

"Come now, Sammy," he continued, disregarding the warning in her glare. "I cannot be the first man to propose such an arrangement to you."

"An...arrangement..." Sam stuttered. "You—"

"I am willing to procure a lovely townhouse for your use in Mayfair or St. James...or, just a few days ago, I discovered a quaint cottage bordering Hyde Park. The morning breeze through the trees lining the grassy area would please you, I am certain." Sparingly, he finally took note of her dumbfounded expression. "Oh, I will also include an allowance for gowns, jewelry, and travel. And a carriage for your daily use. I am not an ungenerous man."

Sam took a firm hold of her gown and lifted her skirt high enough for her foot to strike out and thump him soundly in the shin.

"Ouch." He leapt back and out of her reach. "I certainly should have suspected a cottage would not do for the daughter of Madame Sasha. I will contact my man of business to secure you a grand residence. Does that soothe your temper, my sugar plum?"

The man clearly held no self-preservation. And, quite possibly, lacked a fair amount of sense.

"I shall like to return to the ballroom *now*," she seethed, pivoting sharply and starting back toward the soirée.

"But, Sammy, we have yet to discuss the sizeable allowance I am willing to settle upon you while our arrangement continues," he called at her fleeing back. "Come now, this is what you desired!"

Sam had half a mind to slip her foot from her slipper and throw the shoe at him; however, her soft footwear would not be able to satisfy her desire to maim him.

To make her point known, she stomped down the hallway, her feet making almost no sound, only serving to infuriate her all the more. How dare he suggest she'd agree to be his mistress—a common ladybird, kept caged, wings clipped—however well fed and guarded.

Is this what her sister's advantageous marriage had gained her? The opportunity to be some lord's trollop.

She rounded the final corner and stepped into the ballroom through a side door, inching her way along the wall, settling close to a potted fern. She needed a moment to compose herself, to allow her temper to cool and her fury to drain.

Proctor would rue the day he'd met her if he even so much as glanced in her direction again.

Crossing her arms, Sam set her stare on the dancers swirling about the floor. Gowns of every color, hats of every size and style, sparking adornments, and lords and ladies of every age twirled, swayed, and laughed.

Sam attempted each day to find the enjoyment she'd felt before departing for Derbyshire: the thrill of a turn in the park, the allure of a night dancing beneath hundreds of sparkling candles, and delicious meals spent in the company of refined men. No more did an evening at the Theatre Royal partaking of a performance by Charles Mathews or John Liston make her giddy with excitement and anticipation.

It was difficult to find a companion that sought to discuss any topic more significant than the weather or the latest fashions. Sam did not care a whit if a hat were adorned with small apples or pears, or whether the bird perched in the décor was a canary or a bluebird. Whoever thought it sensible to stitch an imitation animal to a headpiece in the first place? It was made all the more morbid when some of the *ton*'s matrons boasted that their hat ornamentations had once actually been alive.

Revolting.

A round of giggles drew Sam's attention farther down the wall from her hiding spot slouched behind the potted fern. The insipid titters inspired images of a flock of geese, the group of pastel-clad debutantes did nothing to deter her impression of them as they moved in a swarm toward the refreshment table, speaking in pairs and trios about their upcoming dance partners and plans for the remaining season.

Maybe these were her only two choices: join the group of simpering maidens fresh from the schoolroom, or accept a lord's offer to be his courtesan. Neither spoke to a particularly attractive future. Her fiery auburn hair did not suit well with lavender, peach, or powder blue, but ran more to bold colors: midnight blue, Brunswick green, and carmine. Sam preferred her hair swept high atop her head, her throat and earlobes decorated with rubies or sapphires, not pearls.

She had nothing in common with the latest crop of debutantes.

However, she did not see herself finding kinship with the many mistresses littering the room, either.

Did ladybirds flock together as simpering innocents did? The name certainly implied they did.

Again she wondered how she could have mistaken Proctor's intentions so completely. He'd done all that a gentleman was supposed to: sent her flowers and gifts, paid social visits to Craven House, invited her for walks in Hyde Park, and placed his name first on her dance card.

Could courting a new mistress be the same as courting a future bride? It was unthinkable to consider the notion.

Appalling!

Sam scanned the ballroom once more, noting an elegantly clad woman hanging on the arm of a pretentious man, holding her fan high to hide her smile as she batted her lashes. A seductive game to be certain.

Another woman, a widow of indeterminable age, coyly pressed her body along the length of a portly, stout man old enough to be her father—and a dated periwig admirer. Sam need keep a close watch on the pairs and note if they departed the ballroom together or left in separate conveyances.

There was only one cause for it all: Lord Ridgefeld.

She'd been perfectly oblivious to the mundane nature of society before he'd stumbled across her in the wilds of Derbyshire. She'd been unaware of how a weak bottom lip could negatively affect a kiss. She'd been unconcerned with how others perceived her. She'd been happy, fulfilled, and content.

Presently, her life held none of those feelings.

Instead, Sam felt her boredom crushing her, her lackluster enthusiasm noted by her family, and the void within her growing by the day.

Even an innocent dalliance in a darkened hall had been unappealing, though that was likely due to the man she'd chosen as her companion. Her stomach soured when she was unable to spot a single gentleman who would not prove unappetizing—in either demeanor or appearance.

She'd put a curse on Elijah if she knew how.

He'd ruined her, and not in a scandalous way; although that would be preferable to her current situation.

Sam huffed, tapping the toe of her slipper on the polished floor.

The marquis had taken from Sam her most treasured traits: her frivolous tendencies, uninhibited leanings, and pessimistic inclinations.

If he were here, she'd demand he return her to her former self.

Take back his kisses, their moments of complete honesty, and his assurances that the future could be bright if only she would allow herself to forgive and let go of the past.

She looked towards the entry doors, swung wide for guests to come and go.

When Lord Gunther noticed her glare, he nodded and started in her direction. The evening could not get any worse—the man was overly obnoxious and boring—persistent to the extreme. He'd badgered her into one dance already this evening. There would not be a second.

She imagined taking aim at Gunther's shin, much as she had with Proctor; however, the man was so unmindful, she'd likely injure her foot long before he understood her point.

Joining the other debutantes at the refreshment table was not overly repellant the closer Lord Gunther came to Sam.

It was either that or slip back through the door and out of the ballroom, though that may very well send her into the clutches of Proctor once more. Her reappearance would convince him she'd altered her mindset on accepting his offer and agreed to their arrangement. Which she most certainly had not, nor would she ever.

Sparingly, Gunther paused to speak with an elderly nobleman, and Sam was able to slip through a grouping of debutantes and out onto the terrace. The evening air was cold against her face and the skin of her neck. Her nipples instantly hardened within her bodice. It would have been wiser to seek sanctuary somewhere other than within the elements on the terrace with no shawl for protection. But between falling victim to the freezing night air or being caught in another mind-numbing conversation with Lord Gunther…her decision was clear.

Sam inched her way into the shadows, hoping to remain. The elevated terrace was blissfully abandoned as the ball was only now becoming crowded. As the room heated, people would seek the outdoors to cool themselves—and her peaceful reprieve would be shattered.

Her time at Lord Chastain's home was limited, though she and Lady Chastain—Ellington—had nearly grown up as sisters. Ellie had married Alex not long ago, and the pair embarked on a journey to make this townhouse their own. If Sam remembered correctly, if she took the main stairs down to the lawn below and turned left, she'd quickly find the doors leading into the library, with the ladies' retiring room down the hall. She could then take a few moments in the retiring room and rejoin the ball when most of the men had migrated to the card tables.

She cast a quick glance back toward the ballroom. Lord Gunther scanned the crowd in search of her.

When his back turned, Sam fled down the terrace steps and moved around the side of the townhouse, the evening dew dampening her slippers and soaking clear through to her stockings. They would be a filthy mess and utterly ruined by night's end. The loss of her shoes was little penalty for escaping Gunther.

The man had intensified his pursuit of her since she'd arrived back in London. Sam had made it very clear at Jude's wedding that she hadn't any interest in him; however, that did not deter Gunther from sending gifts and requesting to pay social visits to Craven House.

The only light to guide her in the dark night came from two guest bedchambers above and hardly made it possible to see three feet in front of her. Her knee banged against something solid, and she squeaked in pain, doubling over to rub the offended area. Blast it, Jude was the twin more acclimated to slinking around at night through unfamiliar surroundings. Sam's shin continued to throb as she hobbled toward the library door, praying with each labored step it was unlocked and not as pitch-black as outside.

"The door should not be far," Sam mumbled as a branch snagged in her hair, pulling several pins free. Her decision to outmaneuver Lord Gunther may have been a rash choice, but she'd set her course, and she very much intended to follow through.

Blessedly, her feet touched stone. She'd reached the cobbled area outside the library door. Sam grasped the knob and turned, half expecting it to protest and not budge, but she heard the mechanism click, and she pushed the door open a few inches. The warmth of the room caressed her chilled arms as she slipped into the cavernous library, each wall set with shelves. The door stood slightly ajar, and a sliver of light could be seen from the hall beyond.

Sam owed her sister a sincere apology for insisting she be the one to enter unfamiliar homes for their purpose of thievery, but that time had ended with Lord Cartwright's courtship. Maybe one day, in the far distant future, they would discuss their past misdeeds. The present time was not ideal for either of them.

Only a moment of remorse flared at the thought of her mud-soaked feet marring Ellington's new rug. Though it too receded when she neared the door and the footsteps beyond.

Someone was coming.

Spectacular.

Sam glanced around, a shiver traveling down her spine as she searched for a place to hide if someone were to enter the room. It was too dark to see anything beyond the hulking shapes of furniture. The footsteps suddenly halted before starting again, their noise tapering off. She counted ten paces before the footsteps once again stopped and grew louder once more.

Whoever it was, they were pacing outside the study.

Could Lord Gunther—or worse yet, Proctor—have discovered her plan? There was little chance Gunther was even aware she was avoiding his advances, and she could not have made her feelings more well-known with the latter.

Sam held her breath as she inched toward the door, determined to get a look at the man whose pacing kept her trapped.

"…you see, I have known my affection for you was…" He cleared his throat. "It is with great love in my heart that I request... No, no, that is all wrong. Think, think," the man hissed. His lowered voice made it impossible for her to guess his identity. "The words must be perfect. My dearest Miss—"

He turned once more, and his voice grew lower as he strode away from Sam. "Mayhap I should start by requesting a dance. Oh, quite right. And then step all over her delicate slippers. That will not enter me into her good graces."

His tone tickled at her memories as if Sam should know the voice. Match a face to the familiar speech.

The words making their way to Sam made her believe he was wrestling with something—and if she had to guess, it was about making a favorable impression upon a woman he cared for. It would be to his benefit if Sam sprang from the room and told him of his folly, that in the end, even if his feelings were declared, they would only hurt one another. Leaving at least one unlucky person with emotions they were unprepared to handle. Betrayal, regret, and remorse to name a few. No, the man would be better suited keeping his tender affections to himself and continuing on with his life at present. It would save him much heartache, not to mention the disruption of his sleep due to his mind's wanderings in the late-night hours.

Her fury ignited once more, burning as hot and bright as it had the evening of Jude's nuptials when she'd finally accepted that Elijah had left Hollybrooke...and would not return. The man had drawn her in, used all his persuasive powers to make Sam feel like she never had before: that to him, she'd meant something more, *been* something more. He hadn't realized the impact his kindness had had on her, and truly, neither had she until he'd disappeared.

It might have been his intention all along, and if he'd stayed longer, Sam might have made the ultimate mistake and given him a part of her she could never gain back.

It was her duty—no, her obligation—to warn the poor fool in the hall not to entangle himself with matters of the heart. It was not worth the suffering that would come when the fairy tale ended—dissolved like the morning fog off the moors.

If his interest were merely dealing with matters of the flesh, then that would be a far more righteous and enjoyable path, for certain. As long as one chose their companion wisely. Sam had not, and to her continued dismay, she'd learned that a skilled kisser not every man made. Elijah's lips had contained the perfect amount of warmth, held the right degree of pressure, and even thinking about their private moments together sent her blood racing. She hadn't experienced the same rush of pleasure with any of the men she'd spent time with since returning to London.

She refused to ponder the reasoning for this.

However, that did not stop Sam from laying the blame squarely on *his* shoulders.

The man outside pivoted again, and his voice rose loud enough for her to comprehend his words. "…antha, I have missed every moment since departing Derbyshire. I do wish I could have remained, to stay by your side. There were matters out of my control…no!" He sighed dramatically. But Sam's ears perked at the mention of Derbyshire. "Miss Samantha, I will be as forthcoming as I know how. I find I care for you greatly, and if you, in turn, have a similar attraction—no, that is far too forward—if you happen to feel a similar tender for me. Yes, that is better."

Ridgefeld! He was here…in London…at Jude and Simon's first ball as a wedded couple.

Her stomach clenched, and she held her breath, waiting to hear what he mumbled next. Elation soared within her at the same time her rational mind told her not to think too much into his reappearance. Told her to be angry he'd show his face here after leaving Hollybrooke without a word.

Sam had known he'd be journeying to London, his grandfather's collection in tow, but no one had let it slip that he'd arrived. She'd spent most of the afternoon with Jude, and she hadn't said a single word.

Nor had he called on her. Not that she'd expected him to call on her at Craven House.

Elijah owed her nothing. If anything, it was she who was indebted to him for rescuing her from the storm's fury—and awakening a passion she hadn't known lay dormant within her.

She'd begun a dozen letters to him since her return to London, burning each one in her bedroom hearth, unwilling to allow her weakness for Elijah to be forever recorded in ink. It would only serve to injure her further, a detriment to her future—wherever it may be headed. From his words, he'd been thinking of her as much as she'd thought of him, which only served to increase her irritation with him.

Sam had spent nearly six weeks laboring over what she'd done wrong, what mistakes she'd made, and why he'd fled without so much as a goodbye.

And now, he thought to show his face—at her sister's ball—and declare his affection for her? Things were not so simple. Sam could not wipe from her memory the many nights she'd wept into her pillow until she fell into a fitful sleep, fearing all the while that one of her sisters would hear and come asking what had upset her so.

Embarrassing.

Crying over a man…had she learned nothing from her mother's mistakes?

Thankfully, Jude had been with Simon on their bridal tour. Her twin was the only person close enough to note her pain; their connection was so complete. With time, the tears had stopped, but what was left was worse than a thousand sleepless nights. A sense of loss in the pit of her stomach churned every day. A constant reminder of the spark of passion she'd been privy to and denied. It ached to know it was gone…and hurt even more that she had no idea why.

If Elijah thought he could return and all would be forgiven and forgotten, he was decidedly mistaken.

Had they not discussed her inability to forgive others for past misdeeds, or was it only she who remembered every word they'd spoken that day in her guest chambers at Hollybrooke?

No matter how much she longed to forgive him and act as if they'd never quarreled, Sam was uncertain she could.

Chapter Twenty

Eli turned sharply, pacing down the corridor once more. His mind swirled with the words he couldn't seem to place in the right order. And there was no room for error when he finally spoke with Sam. To declare his warmth for her immediately, or take a slower, more paced approach and start with a walk on the terrace or a social call on the morrow or even a ride through the park? His time in London was limited. How limited, he hadn't decided, but keeping residence with Lord Cartwright and his new bride for any period of time seemed an invasion of their privacy.

Which led Eli to his current predicament. He'd arrived at the ball after the meal had been completed and stood in the shadows of the room, watching Sam flirt with several gentlemen, dance with still more, and in the end, slip from the room with a man whose midnight hair and tanned complexion had coils of jealousy coursing through Eli. She'd given several lords the coy grin he'd thought only for him. And all the while, she'd ignored Eli's presence, acted as if she hadn't seen him lurking on the fringes of the room.

This all should have reinforced that their time together had only been a convenience and not mutual affection and attraction; however, it simply increased Eli's need to be with her, share his deep feelings for her, and pray she returned them. It had been pure and utter torture watching another man swirl her around the dance floor while another fetched her a flute of champagne.

He should be her dance partner. *He* should be fetching her refreshments. *He* should have slipped from the room with her held close. Not those men who certainly knew nothing of Sam past her outer beauty.

He'd never envisioned himself a possessive man, but maybe it had only been that he'd never possessed something worth fighting for, worth coveting, worth protecting at all cost. A large portion of him knew his extreme sentiments were unjustified and verging on obsessive, though that reality hadn't taken root until he'd spied her on the arm of another man; a man who was far more learned in the ways of the *ton* than he, a man who'd certainly played the coy game of cat and mouse as he acted unaffected by her coquettish grin and lowered lashes.

Bloody hell, Eli was affected, and he'd stood across the room from the pair—not directly before her. It was utterly maddening. The vexing woman had been on his mind since he'd happened upon her along that deserted road. One could say he'd been blessed; though lately, it settled on him more like a curse.

Sam had enjoyed herself…immensely, while he'd hidden in the shadows. She'd laughed. She'd playfully tapped her fan on a gentleman's arm. She'd flitted between guests. Always poised and graceful.

And then, in a final dagger to his heart, she'd slipped from the room with the dark-haired lord. She'd stood too close. The man had tilted his head in her direction. She'd whispered something in is ear.

Eli's blood had boiled, and his heart beat erratically.

Jealous. Eli was jealous.

His jaw ached from being clamped shut to keep in his shout of anger—at himself, at Sam, and at the man who dared take Eli's place at her side.

That should be him, not that…rakehell. Eli knew nothing of the man, but he did not approve of their association on principle. Even Eli, who'd been sheltered from society, understood the scandal that could result from a man escorting a lone female about a darkened home without a chaperone.

Certainly, even with a proper lady's companion trailing them, there would still be gossip.

Miss Samantha enjoyed herself…and Eli had no right to interfere, even if the pair were on the brink of ruination. Maybe she'd been properly courted and had gotten betrothed while he'd been in Liverpool these six weeks? It would not be honorable of him to impede the course she'd settled on.

Lord Cartwright had been correct. Sam's outward display of affection for Eli had been false, brought on by the shock of her father's reappearance and her sister's wedding. Their connection—something Eli had thought ran deeper than any he'd ever known—had been nothing but a woman's need to grasp on to something tangible as her life spiraled out of control.

Odd to ever imagine Sam not being fully in control of her life, and that of those around her.

She'd overcome all the obstacles set in her path. Her sister's marriage and resulting departure from Sam's daily life, her father's sudden and unexplained interest in his twin daughters, and lastly, him. She'd moved on from him. She was happy.

He should allow her to be happy.

Yet, Eli was miserable.

He squeezed his eyes shut and twisted around once more, noting how his footfalls matched the beat of his heart.

He had been miserable for a long time. Far longer than he'd realized. Before his grandfather's untimely passing, before his decision to find his mother, possibly as far back as his time at Eton. Only he hadn't known it wasn't something that was missing but *someone*.

He'd mistakenly assumed finding his mother would fill the void so clearly taking over every part of him. When that hadn't worked, Eli had wagered the only way to move past it all was to remove all the reminders of his grandfather from their home and donate them for all to enjoy.

The spark of life had clearly infused him during his short stay at Hollybrooke, and it had led him to believe his decision was the correct one. Belatedly, he'd discovered it had all been due to Miss Samantha Pengarden. It had been his destiny to happen upon her that fateful day. He hadn't fully comprehended it then, but now, he had no doubt.

Eli paused once more and pulled at his neckcloth.

After his return to Liverpool to sort, pack, and transport the late marquis' treasures, she'd haunted him.

Every day. Every night. While he worked. While he ate. While he met with his steward. While he bathed. When he'd tried to find peace in slumber, his dreams were filled with images of her. If they hadn't been disturbed in Cummings' library that night. If they hadn't been interrupted in her bedchambers that afternoon. If he'd been man enough to cast off Lord Cartwright's warning and remain in Derbyshire to escort her to the wedding and feast that followed…

He quivered when he thought where their private moments alone would have led.

But he hadn't stayed to discover what could have transpired between them, and he was miserable all the more.

The difference was, now he could not deny it. Now, he knew the source of his discontent. Now, he was given no alternative but to claim her for his own or walk away and allow her to live the life she'd chosen for herself.

Neither choice was easy. Neither decision would mean contentment for Elijah.

Sam could very well rebuff his advances. She may be in love with the raven-haired man, with Elijah a distant memory.

What would Eli do then?

He could not return to Liverpool as if none of it had happened, push his affection and longing for her to the side and continue on with life.

Possibly attend the country parties hosted by neighboring lords, meet a young miss, and marry, forgetting the blaze within him only a certain fiery-haired hellion could bring to life. Continue with a mundane life of caring for his estate, being an attentive husband, and praying a horde of little Ridgefeld children populated his home. How was that fair to anyone, especially him?

Eli shoved his hands deep into his pockets, frustrated that he'd allowed such a mess to develop.

His grandfather hadn't embarked on any journey that did not suit his needs and wants. The old man had wanted to see Africa, and so he did. Longed to travel along the clear beaches of Greece. Felt inspired by the ruins in Egypt. He'd traveled near and far because it gave him pleasure, happiness, and purpose.

The late marquis would want nothing less for his grandson.

That Eli's happiness lay with a woman should not make it less important.

Happiness was happiness, no matter the form it took.

However, the evening had shown Eli one very important thing: Sam appeared happy without him. While his future depended on her, Sam's may not be contingent on him.

"I should leave now, depart—return home," he mumbled. At some point, he'd stopped pacing and stood stock-still, his eyes unfocused as his mind swirled. Certainly, it would injure him far less to never voice his deep affection for her as opposed to speaking out and having his feelings thrown back in his face when she informed him that she'd chosen another. "It is ludicrous to think matters of the heart are worth all of this—"

A sharp inhale and the groan of an opening door had Elijah spinning around, an explanation on the tip of his tongue. Dreadfully embarrassing to be caught mumbling to oneself in a darkened, deserted hallway in an unfamiliar house.

"My apologies—" He could not bring himself to utter another word through his tightened throat. His eyes widened as a gowned figure stepped from the room down the hall.

His eyes focused on her feet as she walked toward him, her muddied, slippered toes peeking out from below her long, satin dress. As she came near, his gaze traveled to her narrow waist, a sash tied about it, and farther heavenward to her daringly low bodice. As much as he tried, Eli could not keep from taking in the beauty of her face, her auburn hair piled high atop her head with a ribbon pinned within her curls, and the teardrop earbobs that only brought attention to her long, graceful neck.

How much of his ramblings had she heard?

The only question overshadowing that thought was where the raven-haired lord had disappeared to. Did he await Sam's return in the dark recesses of the room she'd exited? The thought of another man having impure thoughts about Sam—touching her, kissing her, holding her—caused spots to invade his vision.

"Miss Samantha!" Though he'd kept watch on her from afar all evening, up close, she was exactly as he remembered. His mind's wandering over the long six weeks had never veered far from the truth: her delicate, unblemished skin was that of a proper English rose; her straight back and lifted chin showed her confidence and trust in her own worth.

She was elegance personified. She was demure, yet commanding. She was well-spoken and poised.

What her narrowed eyes, and silent perusal of him said was a mystery.

Her lips pulled back in a smile, a grin he'd never witnessed before though it was familiar, sparking memories of a long ago time…in a place far from London.

Her assessing glare, solid yet unassuming movements, and the hypnotic sway of her hips kept him focused solely on the progress she made toward him. He was helpless to look away. Unable to say a word.

Powerless to run, yet incapable of screaming for help.

She was the lioness of the African safari…ready to attack.

And Eli was her prey.

As she bore down on him, he noted the fury in her eyes, the anger in her steps, and the solid set of her shoulders.

Yet, he was too weak to break eye contact, too fragile to even know he should run.

He was caught in her snare, entranced—so much so he truly believed he would revel in her wrath.

Chapter Twenty-One

Her gaze flashed red as she stopped before him, and he instantly reached out for her, wrapping his arms tightly around her.

How dare Elijah show his face tonight—of all nights—at a ball thrown in her sister's honor? After everything he'd done—or not done, as was the case—to waltz into Lord Chastain's home and pretend he had any sort of tender for her. Ridgefeld could not be so foolish as to think she would believe anything he said.

Sam flinched at the contact before stiffening to resist his hold. Her arms hung loosely at her sides as she waited for him to release her. The urge to accept his warmth, to melt into his embrace and give in to her desires for him was strong. No matter what delusions spun through her mind, she always returned to the bottom line: he'd left her.

Without a backwards glance, without a note of parting, without a final word.

Elijah Watson, Lord Ridgefeld, had elicited emotions from her Sam never dreamed possible. He'd stood by and listened to her family's darkest secrets, comforted her during a difficult time, and pledged to be at her side until she departed for London.

Instead, he'd proven that every man was as she'd feared: the same as her father and Lord Proctor. Their intentions were to lie, cheat, and steal until they gained exactly what they desired. Elijah was no different. His actions had proven it to be fact.

He released her and stepped back. With that movement fled the smell of him: sandalwood and musk. As if he'd spent his day hard at work in a stable.

She needs must remind herself she was in the right and that Elijah had been in the wrong.

"Miss Samantha," he stammered. "I was preparing to look for you."

"Is that so, my lord?" Sam crossed her arms when he made to step toward her once more and leveled her stare on him. "Whatever for?"

"Yes, it—"

"Ironic, because I searched for you at Hollybrooke the morn of my sister's wedding. Imagine my surprise when I discovered you'd left…without so much as a parting word to me." She would not express how much it had injured her that day. His abandoning her had cut deeper than any wound her stranger of a father could inflict upon her. "Envision my feebleminded appearance as I argued with my brother over the misconception. You, Lord Ridgefeld, had made a promise to me. There was no way you would turn tail and run."

"That was not the way of things." Elijah held his arms out to her, begging her with his eyes to step into his embrace, but Sam only took a step back, increasing the distance between them. "I have much to explain."

"Unfortunately, I have no wish to listen." Hear his excuses, his rationalization, his need to explain away the injury he'd caused her. "And even less desire to be standing here with you."

"I do not understand…" His eyes widened. "Sam, I would do you no harm, ever. You must believe me. It was not my idea to depart Hollybrooke. I would have stayed if it were an option; however, it was not. The decision was not mine to make."

Sam focused on her anger on him, allowing his words to wash over her, unheard. She'd believed him once and had been made a fool. That would not happen again.

"Miss Samantha," he continued. "Let us return to the ballroom. I will fetch you a drink. We can stroll about the terrace and talk."

"No." One word, but it tore at her heart to utter it. She needed him to hear her and walk away…before her resolve crumbled.

"Then tomorrow. I will call on you. We can spend the afternoon at Hyde Park."

"That will not be happening."

His eyes went vacant, and he wavered where he stood. "I have journeyed all this way."

"To deliver your family treasures to the museum."

"But that is not the only reason," he rushed. "I could have arranged the transport without seeing to it myself."

"Your comings and goings are of little concern to me," she muttered. It would be wise to turn and return to the ballroom, pray he didn't follow her, hope he didn't continue to spout his words of defense. "I bid you good eve, my lord."

He grasped her arm but quickly loosened his hold and settled his hand lightly on her forearm. His touch didn't prevent her from departing; it was his eyes that kept her frozen in place. They held the softness she was used to seeing, but there was something more there. Something reaching farther than the storm clouds that waited just below the surface. It was exactly what she'd noted in him that first day: something within struggling to break free of the sorrow that shrouded him.

Sam shook her head to clear her thoughts and push down her body's treacherous betrayal.

"Please, Sam," he whispered. "Allow me to escort you back to the ballroom, and I will explain everything. But you must know that I care for you deeply."

She shuddered to think how he would have treated her if he didn't *care for her deeply*. Her heartbeat spiked as her thoughts turned even more treacherous; his arms around her, his lips pressed to her throat, and the hard length of his arousal unmistakably pressed against her, creating a longing, a desire she'd only dreamed of in recent weeks.

"I will remain in London…fulfill my promise to you," he said, running his hand through his hair, disheveling his locks. "I will stay as long as you think it will take for me to satisfy our previous bargain. Or any new arrangement that suits."

She wanted to believe he spoke the truth, longed for him to stay in London, but instead she asked, "What leads you to believe I am in need of your company now that I've returned home to London?"

She raised a brow as he remained silent, forcing him to speak.

"I, well—" he started before pausing to take a deep breath. "If you are spoken for or find yourself enamored with another gentleman, I will do the honorable thing and step aside."

"I did not say anything about another gentleman." Could Elijah know of Lord Proctor, have seen their intimate embrace? Certainly not. "It is only…"

"What?" he prodded. "Sam, I will do anything to prove that my devotion to you is pure."

Sam tapped her chin as she thought over his proposal. There was the fiasco with Proctor to consider. The man thought her in search of a benefactor. It was appalling and insulting. And she could not forget Gunther's continued interest in her. As one of Lord Cartwright's friends, it would be hard to dissuade Marce and Garrett if Gunther sought a true courtship. The man was titled, wealthy, and would provide for Sam in a manner befitting her needs.

"You swear you will not leave again?" Hurriedly she added, "—until I say your promise is fulfilled?"

"Of course, you have my word." The tension seeped from his shoulders, thinking he'd won their battle. There was much the man need learn. "Do you accept?"

Why did she sense that more than his stay in London hinged on her answer? "I have not decided as yet." She would not give in so readily…and maybe… "However, I fear our original agreement will no longer suit."

He frowned, and his brow furrowed. It was the first instance of unease she'd noted since she'd confronted him. If he suspected she was assessing how to use his offer to her greatest advantage, he didn't speak to that fact.

"Then I will bid you a pleasant evening," he said with a curt bow. "Do accept my apologies for interrupting you."

He made to walk past her without so much as offering his arm to escort her back to the ball. Yet, that was exactly what she'd wanted him to do only a moment before.

Now, she wasn't so sure.

Two could play at this game. She turned swiftly, setting her arm on his sleeve, falling into step beside him.

"May I propose a new agreement?" she asked, not daring to glance up at him. As much as Sam would have relished allowing him to walk away, making him to feel a small measure of the pain she'd felt, she admitted to herself that she needed him. No...she *wanted* him at her side. It was preposterous to contemplate. He'd abandoned her, but only after burrowing into her heart. He'd taken a piece of her with him. It was only proper she return the favor.

His steps faltered. "Certainly. I owe you at least the opportunity to set new terms."

Sam couldn't help but wonder why he cared if she pushed him away. He'd left her, not the other way around. What did this change in him signify? Why seek her out at all?

It made little sense to her.

However, if she could lead Proctor and Gunther to believe she was spoken for, then it would serve her purpose. "London is far different than our time in Derbyshire. Society standards dictate something far different than the blasé nature of country house parties. There are appearances to uphold. Places to be seen. People to charm. Is this something you are willing to navigate with me?"

They approached the ballroom, and with it their freedom to speak freely.

"You have my attention, Miss Samantha." He halted before they joined the other guests.

A sense of victory filled her. It would not be difficult to ensure that Elijah fell head over heels in love with her. She was stunning, charming, and a diamond of the first water. Only then would she do to him what he'd done to her.

Sam risked a glance at him from the corner of her eye.

She inhaled sharply. Certainly, his smirk did not mean he thought he held the cards.

Chapter Twenty-Two

Eli pulled Sam as close to his side as propriety allowed as they stepped through the open double doors and into the ballroom. Many people turned in their direction—some expressions filled with surprise, others with envy, and many with indifference. On the surface, he and Sam were only another pair of finely dressed people entering a room filled to bursting with other extravagantly adorned couples. Yet, he knew there was much more to his and Sam's connection.

How far he'd have to go to prove that point was still to be determined.

Surveying the room, Eli located Lord Gunther and then the raven-haired lord.

Never once did he allow his smile to falter, though envy clawed at his insides. On his arm was the most enchanting woman in the room. Her cunning only added to her allure. Eli dared any man to disagree.

From the raw, jealous stares sent his way, not a single man—spoken for or not—would argue with his assessment.

"I am yours to command," he reassured her. "You only need say the word."

"Firstly." She stepped down into the ballroom. "You shall attend me at all social functions."

"That is much as it was at Hollybrooke." He nodded his agreement.

"Secondly, you will escort me when I wish it," she paused, smiling to a couple as they passed. "Good eve, Lord and Lady Michaelson. I do hope you enjoyed the meal." She returned her focus to him. "Wherever I wish to go."

Eli nodded to the unfamiliar pair as they passed, noting the way the man kept a close watch on Sam, and the lady narrowed her eyes as her husband gawked.

"We did, thank you," Lord Michaelson said as the couple moved on.

Sam leaned toward him and whispered. "They are unsure if I am me or Judith."

"A pity." He steered her toward the far wall that led to the refreshment table, and away from Lord Gunther. The raven-haired lord had disappeared into the card room. "Do enlighten me on where exactly you would have me escort you."

She waved her hand, as if to say it wasn't important. "I have yet to decide, my lord."

"And the third condition to our agreement?"

"If I become entangled in a conversation I wish to be rescued from, I will give you a signal, and you will come to my aid, no matter who I am speaking with."

It sounded simple enough, and much in line with what Eli had hoped for them. She was asking him to court her...in not so many words, but her meaning could not be any clearer. He would oblige her until she was able to admit she too felt attraction for him.

"Am I allowed a question, or two?"

"Certainly, my lord." They reached the refreshment table and accepted flutes of champagne from a servant before turning. He maneuvered her toward the terrace. However, she seemed agreeable to his intended destination. "I might even allow three."

He took a sip of his drink to hide his smile before clearing his throat. "In our previous agreement, I was also reaping a benefit. With these new terms, what will I gain?"

"The same, of course," she retorted. "I will keep the marriage-hungry maidens at bay."

"And…"

"And what?"

"You are now asking for more in this arrangement. It is only fair that things continue to be mutually beneficial to us both." He knew he risked having her walk away, call off the arrangement altogether; however, he could not allow her to treat him like her own personal lap dog. He longed for nothing more than to continue their relationship, but at the expense of his manhood? That was not an option for him.

She remained quiet as they stepped out onto the terrace. The nightly breeze had subsided, and the cold had turned to a mild chill, though not many braved the elements in the outdoor area. It served Elijah and his need for privacy.

Sam gave a short laugh. "My lord, it is you who owes me, not the other way around."

"Be that as it may," Eli continued, "I haven't any notion what exactly you expect from me."

Sam touched her fingertip to her lip in thought. "A kiss."

"A single kiss?" A single kiss would never be enough to satisfy the ever-increasing need within him.

They paused at the terrace railing, and she removed her hand from his sleeve, placing both gloves on the cold rock wall. "A kiss is a most generous offering."

"I did not say it was not." He matched her stance and stared out into the dark night beyond. "However, no contract is legally binding nor in good faith if both parties do not receive mutual satisfaction."

"And what do you suggest to make this arrangement more…*mutually beneficial* for us both?"

"A kiss for each time I escort you. A kiss for each task I complete." In a way, he knew this new proposal played greatly in his favor. If anything were to spark a deep desire in her, it was another kiss. Many more kisses, if he were lucky. "Simple and uncomplicated."

She eyed him suspiciously. "Very well. A kiss in return for each favor I request."

Eli smiled into the night, happy with their agreement. In essence, he would court Miss Samantha Pengarden, and if all worked in his favor, she'd be deeply in love with him before she realized his ploy to make the woman his.

#

It only took fourteen hours for Eli to realize he'd made a grand mistake by striking a bargain with Sam. And thinking that, at any point, he'd had the upper hand, now proved how misguided he'd been. She'd soundly duped him. He threw the letter down on his dressing table and rubbed his face before reading it once more, but the words remained the same.

The Mistress Enchants Her Marquis

Dear Lord Ridgefeld,

Thank you for your gracious acceptance. It is my wish to see a gentleman's boxing club. Do arrive at eleven sharp, and we shall attend the morning rounds at Gentleman Jackson's. I hope I am not mistaken in assuming your status can gain us entry.

With kind regards,
Miss Samantha Pengarden

She could not actually mean to request he secure them entrance into a lord's gentlemen-only establishment such as Gentleman Jackson's. The comical—or possibly better called, *sad*—part of the entire debacle was that Eli hadn't been to a boxing club before. It would be a first for both of them. Certainly, he'd witnessed competitions of strength and honor during his travels, but never had he entered a proper establishment meant solely for physical exertion as opposed to righting a wrong or returning honor.

With her note in hand, Eli summoned his carriage and arrived to collect her from Craven House—a rather sprawling townhouse on the edge of Mayfair. The residence was on the fringe of propriety: two blocks in either direction would place the home in an elite area or a section bombarded by growing poverty and hard financial straits. Its immaculate landscaping and fresh paint told Elijah that Sam and her family took pride in their home. A sign hung proudly, displaying the manor's name: *Craven House*.

Mathers quickly opened the carriage door and set down the steps for Eli to depart. "May I knock to announce your arrival, my lord?"

Eli feared he'd never gain a familiarity with Mathers addressing him so formally. He and the servant were of a similar age and had grown up as friends. His valet—and sometimes carriage driver, footman, and confidant—had been the grandson of the late marquis' own valet. It was only natural Mathers serve the Ridgefeld family as his family had before.

"No, thank you," Eli said, hopping down from his carriage with more gusto than the moment called for. "I can collect Miss Samantha."

With heavy steps, he made his way up the drive, uncertain what Sam had told her siblings about their outing. Lying was not an option for Eli, as he knew deception never favored a man. And he wanted nothing more than to make a notable impression on Sam's family. Over the coming days—and possibly weeks—he would do all in his power to court her properly…maybe a proposal of marriage even awaited them. However, that would be impossible if he lied and her family ever learned of it.

A bolt of dark green moved behind the hedge at the side of the townhouse, catching Eli's attention and bringing him up short before he took the final steps to knock at the front entrance. The figure had moved far too quickly to be a servant at work on his chores. He scanned the place where he'd seen the movement but saw nothing but well-trimmed, square shrubbery.

"Lord Ridgefeld!" Eli spun back toward his waiting carriage where Mathers stood, slack-jawed, and staring at Sam. "I see you received my letter. I was uncertain you'd be at the museum to receive my note."

Two things were clear. Firstly, Sam did not trust him to keep his side of their bargain. And secondly, she had no intention of telling her family where they were headed, that she was with him, or that they did not have a proper chaperone.

"I gave my word and will uphold it." Eli retraced his steps toward the carriage. "I thought I would speak with your family."

Clutching a large bag tightly to her chest, she glanced over his shoulder and then back at him. "They are out for the afternoon, my lord. If you had arrived only ten minutes ago, you would have caught them before they departed for Hyde Park." He raised a brow as a serene smile spread across her face. "Shall we?"

Mathers stepped forward and offered his hand to assist her into the carriage.

Eli frowned. Since when did his servants take orders from others?

"Where to, my lord?"

"Gentleman Jackson's." Eli regained his side in the carriage, sitting across from Sam, who still clung to the duffle she held, certainly a bag too bulky for their afternoon plans. "It is good to see you again, Miss Samantha."

"And you, Elijah." The breathy way his name left her lips sent his pulse racing. "Thank you for accompanying me on this outing."

She said the words like he'd had a choice in the matter—besides breaking his promise to her.

"My pleasure, I assure you." He eyed the bag once more. She pulled it closer as if to hide it in her skirts. "May I ask what you brought?"

"Of course, you may."

He waited, but she said nothing further. "What is in the bag, Sam?"

"My boxing gloves—err, Garrett's boxing gloves."

"What do you plan to do with them?" Something told him he did not want to know the answer, especially if it had anything to do with Eli donning the gloves and entering the ring.

"Step into the ring, of course." As if to punctuate her words, his carriage jerked into motion.

"Absolutely not." Eli vehemently shook his head. He would put his own person at risk before allowing her to participate. "I made a promise; however, I cannot, in good conscience, keep that promise if it will put you at risk. I will not do it. A woman entering a gentleman's boxing club is outlandish and unheard of. But entering the ring? Preposterous."

"*Humpf.*" She turned and pulled the curtain aside to watch their progress. "If you insist, I shall leave my gloves in the carriage."

"That is very gracious of you," Eli said, rubbing his palms down the velvet seat at his sides to dispel the nervous sweat that had gathered. If she'd persisted with her foolish plan, would he have given in to her demands? He'd had a difficult time as it was securing a way into Jackson's without anyone noting Sam's attendance. Thankfully, it seemed the proprietor was not completely shocked by his written request, and had actually hinted at the fact that Eli's bid was quite commonplace. "May I ask why you are interested in Gentleman Jackson's?"

Her face brightened, and a mischievous grin settled on her lips.

Lips he would relish kissing when their afternoon was complete, and he had fulfilled her first wish.

"I suspected you would never agree to accompany me to White's. The next best thing is Jackson's." Her smile only intensified, as he finally understood the brilliance of her plan. "Though it is only a boxing club, I will gain a rare sight of what it would be like to live the life of a gentleman."

The late-morning traffic was light, and his carriage sped through town without much delay, swinging around to the back of the large building housing the boxing club. On any other day, Eli would have enjoyed attending the establishment, watching two men in a bout of fisticuffs, and the thrill of donning the gloves himself. But not this day.

"Where are we?" she asked, allowing the curtain to fall back into place as she turned to face him. She bit her lower lip, hard-pressed to keep her skepticism from showing. "This is not Gentleman Jackson's."

It was Elijah's turn to look smug, knowing he'd be able to keep his promise but also keep her reputation intact—for at least another day. "It certainly is."

"B-but..." she stuttered. "We are in an alley."

"Directly *behind* the boxing club." His bravado soared, even as she narrowed her eyes. Mathers opened the door and set the steps, just as the back door of the club swung open to reveal a broad-shouldered man with a neck as thick as an ox. He must be the owner—and an avid boxer. "Your private entrance to debauchery awaits."

Eli stepped from the carriage and reached his hand out to help Sam.

One glance at the man holding the door, and her eyes rounded as big as saucers.

"Lord Ridgefeld." Their host bowed to Eli and turned to Sam. "Miss Samantha Pengarden. I am Mr. John Jackson. It is a pleasure to have you both at my esteemed establishment. Your private ring awaits. Right this way."

Jackson stood back and allowed them entrance before bustling inside to lead the way down a well-lit corridor.

"I asked to witness a boxing match, not"—Sam paused, motioning to the vacant hall before them—"this."

"It was a surprise to receive your request, my lord," Jackson threw over his shoulder as they turned a corner and stopped before a closed door. "I had occasion to meet your grandfather several times, and even your father once or twice, though he was only a lad."

Eli clasped his hands behind his back and turned his eyes to the floor as his pace slowed. The last thing he wanted either Sam or Jackson to see were the tears threatening to escape at the mention of his sire and grandsire.

"I have readied my own private ring for your viewing." Jackson pushed the door wide and allowed Sam and Eli to enter. A large, square boxing ring stood in the center of the room. Several rough benches had been pushed against the walls to allow room for two overstuffed armchairs, precisely positioned to gain a full view of the ring. Several men huddled in the far corner. "I have two of my prized purse fighters preparing to spar for you."

The proprietor waved them to their seats.

Eli guided Sam to their place as she took in every detail of the room, from the cream-colored walls, to the hanging gloves, to the large hand-drawn posters of men dressed for sport, to the telltale signs of dried blood on the wood floor—stains either forgotten or incapable of being scrubbed clean.

"This sport is not one for delicate eyes, Sam," Eli leaned close and whispered. "We can leave whenever you say the word."

She bit her lower lip, pulling her arms and legs close as a smooth, expressionless look overtook her normally lively face. "I requested this outing and know the sights in store for me." She tucked her ankles below her chair and folded her hands primly in her lap.

Never once had Eli witnessed this reserved side of her.

Was she nervous of the display to come?

Jackson had assured Eli in his note that he'd instructed his fighters to spar lightly: no blood was to be drawn from either party.

"I need speak with Mr. Jackson. May I retrieve anything for you? A drink perhaps?"

"No, Elijah," Sam said. "Thank you."

"Very well." He stood and moved toward Jackson to offer his thanks for seeing to his outlandish request. "Mr. Jackson, thank you for organizing this, especially on such short notice."

The man chuckled softly, the sound a few notes too high for a man of his immense size. "You may not believe this, my lord, but female members of the aristocracy—from elderly matrons to young debutantes—routinely set up private fights. It is only right I allow them entrance, so long as they do not interfere with my male membership."

"Their husbands and guardians do not find issue with this?"

"I have learned that men and women of the *ton* do not always question how the others spend their time." Jackson glanced toward the men donning their gloves.

"However, business is business. If it keeps food on my table and my doors open, ladies may request private gatherings here." He looked to the ring. "The men are ready."

Eli would have never imagined that women's delicate sensibilities could endure the flying of fists and knuckles meeting flesh. Had Sam attended a private gathering at Jackson's before? From the stiff set of her shoulders and her gaping mouth as she watched the men enter the ring, he suspected not.

Sliding into his seat, he patted her clenched hands. "Are you ready?"

"I believe I am, my lord." She gave him a tight-lipped smile. "I have long wanted to see what my brother does when he says he is off to his boxing club."

"Jackson is certain to have a show for you." Eli relaxed in his chair. Only time would tell if he'd made a grand mistake by agreeing to bring Sam to such a violent affair.

Chapter Twenty-Three

Sam's entire body hummed with excitement. She felt invigorated—liberated—though a bit dismayed at the sheer violence of the match as she exited with a satisfied smile while Mr. Jackson held the door. That Elijah would make good on his promise and accompany her to Gentleman Jackson's had never actually seemed like a viable outcome. She'd expected him to send word that he could not attend her that day or arrive and outright forbid her to go to a men's sporting establishment.

Though it wasn't only the sight of the shirtless fighters, their hands gloved and raised for battle that caused a flutter of anticipation to course through her the second they'd entered the private room. Sam could think of only one thing after they had departed Craven House: the kiss she would owe Elijah at the end of their outing.

She'd dreamed of pressing her body close to his, setting her lips upon his, allowing her tongue to explore…since their night in the study at Hollybrooke.

In fact, his lips had no more left hers that long ago night than she was already longing for another kiss.

Remembering the scandalous image in *In Physica Educationem in Caritate: Volumen Unum* had not dulled her need. The sight had filled many lonely nights in the last six weeks. Several times, she'd wondered if Eli had returned the book to Cummings' study before he departed. She could not be so lucky to learn he'd absconded with the volume.

The sun shone brightly, assaulting her eyes after their time spent in the dimly lit interior of Jackson's private sparring room. It had all been exciting, yet far less grand than she'd expected. Garrett hurried off to his club every Tuesday afternoon at precisely one o'clock. Could it be that her brother was truly in need of exercise?

"Miss Samantha?"

She focused, pushing the thoughts from her mind to see Elijah's offered hand. His carriage waited in the alley where they'd left it. How long had they been within the club? The sun had crested and started its descent toward the western horizon.

Mid-afternoon.

Her sisters, with any luck, would still be attending Jude: settling her into her new home, offering suggestions for renovations, and keeping the dowager Lady Cartwright from sinking her claws into her new daughter-in-law while Simon handled his affairs at the museum.

It had been far too easy to slip from the house without notice. Before Jude's betrothal to Simon, Marce had been like a hawk, hovering over her siblings, waiting for one to step out of line. Now it seemed they could come and go as they pleased; though, certainly, her blessings would not continue. Their manservant, Mr. Curtis, was sure to see the carriage return to deposit her at her doorstep. Possibly worse was if the elderly servant spied Sam kissing Lord Ridgefeld.

The Ridgefeld carriage was comfortable and maintained—if dated—but still far more luxurious than the Craven House coach. The dark burgundy seats showed off her dark green gown to its finest. She much liked the way the two hues paired and silently committed to finding a sash of the exact shade to wear with her gown.

When the carriage started out of the alley, Sam met Elijah's stare, and she knew he too thought of the kiss to come. Maybe she should pull the curtains, shimmy across the carriage to sit beside him and give him his reward before they reached her home.

"You are flushed, are you overly warm?" he asked with a hint of concern.

She could not admit it was the anticipation of their parting that brought heat to her cheeks, though his concern did bring to mind another reason. "No, my lord. Quite the opposite, I must admit. The breeze from the open curtains is cold against my face."

Without another word, he turned to both sides and pulled the cords free of their holds, releasing the material to cover the windows, casting a shadow across his face. She didn't favor the way it hid his deep cocoa-brown eyes or the dark lashes framing them. Concealed the way his lips parted when he smiled and his dimple appeared. Sam had no need to see them now in reality, as her memories conjured them whenever she closed her eyes. She fought the urge to allow her lids to lower and the pleasurable sensations to take hold. She would not allow herself even the briefest moment of fancy while the real man sat mere inches from her.

So close…yet so incredibly far away.

If she were to reach out to him, would he come to her willingly?

Did the mere thought make her a wanton woman, unworthy of a man such as him?

Sam could not—would not—think in those terms. Similar to men, women had needs. So far, besides a few not so intelligent decisions, she'd managed to harness her desires since gaining a peek at the wickedness denied to unwed ladies. If she asked politely, would Elijah show her all she'd been unable to see in her limited time with *In Physica Educationem in Caritate*?

If she'd been thinking correctly the previous evening, Sam would have added it to her list of demands in recompense for his ungentlemanly departure from Derbyshire.

The likelihood that he'd continue to answer her demands—or that she had many others planned—had a sense of urgency filling her. They would arrive at her townhouse shortly.

Sam pushed from her place and came to rest next to Elijah on his bench.

His eyes barely registered the shock of her movement when his hands slipped around her back and beneath her knees, lifting her to settle across his lap. The muscles of his thighs could be felt through her many layers of underpinnings and his woolen trousers.

Her pulse quickened at the same time she allowed a groan to escape.

Sam didn't hesitant a moment before anchoring her arms around his neck and scooting closer into him. The heat from his body warmed her.

"Are you claiming your compensation, my lord?" The question left her on a sigh as desire pooled at her core. The slight sway and jostle of the coach added a sensual rhythm to their embrace.

A shudder ran through him, and his mouth landed against hers—crushing, demanding, controlling—utterly captivating her. His hands moved along her back slowly, at odds with their kiss. She tangled her fingers in his hair, holding him securely to her as she pressed him into the seat. The need to be closer to him—to feel more of Elijah against her—was more than she could bear, and Sam hastily released her hold on him. Grabbing her long skirt, she adjusted to straddle him, her knees on either side of his hips on the bench.

The position allowed her to feel his desire for her: the hardened length of his manhood straining against the flap of his trousers. Begging to be freed. As if of their own accord, her hips pressed into him, and she shivered with need.

She'd never straddled a man, but her body knew exactly what to do as she gently started to rock back and forth. She pressed her core to his rigid length as the heat between them grew.

So focused by the friction their bodies created, Sam almost lost pace with their kiss.

But when Elijah's hands dropped lower, cupping her bottom and lifting slightly, her most intimate place lost contact with him. The shift in position pressed her breasts to his chest, and his mouth moved from her lips, tracing kisses across her cheek to her ear.

She moaned as he took her lobe between his teeth and nibbled…so gently, Sam thought she'd imagined it.

But then his mouth moved to the spot behind her lobe and sparks of longing coursed through her. A hidden spot. Did all married women and experienced men know of this delicate place that could send a woman into a frenzy of need?

She didn't know, but the one thing she did understand was that she did not want Elijah's lips to leave that sensitive place.

"Elijah." Her head tilted back, and her eyes opened to see the roof of the enclosed carriage. She attempted to focus on a tiny tear in the material above her, anything to keep her from thinking about the storm building inside her with each second that their bodies remained pressed together. "Do not stop."

Elijah's only response was to drag his lips farther down her neck.

Her bosom heaved as she struggled to bring air into her lungs…and remember what to do after it was there.

It was all too much.

Yet, not nearly enough.

Every inch of her flooded with increased warmth, so hot she felt she would, at any moment, perish in the flames of her lust. She sensed the inferno's ever demanding pull.

Sam stiffened, preparing to fall into the pit of desire…willingly.

Oh, so readily she would go if only to feel this sensation forevermore.

The warmth turned to an extreme awareness of where her hands rested, the feel of her breasts pressed against his starched linen shirt, the way his neckcloth grazed her exposed bosom above her neckline.

Sam commanded her fingers into action, determined to give him an ounce of the pleasure he was giving her. Gently kneading, her hands caressed Elijah's neck and down across his shoulder blades—solid muscle. Gained from years exploring the farthest reaches of the known world.

In a way, Sam was now an explorer—an adventurer with a course set to discover everything that matters of the flesh had to offer.

And that started with Elijah Watson, Lord Ridgefeld, a most proper marquis.

Chapter Twenty-Four

The carriage slowed, causing their easy sway to halt—though it did not deter Eli's lips from continuing their path along the exposed mounds of her breasts. He nipped softly, and her resulting shudder of pleasure was all the confirmation he needed to reach between them and tug the neckline of her dress down to reveal more of her expansive porcelain skin. She was on the cusp of utter inhibition, her breaths coming in ragged bursts, matching the beat of her heart that pounded against his trailing lips.

Elijah knew the folly of his actions, the deplorable nature of his thoughts, and the ruination that could soon follow if they continued down their chosen path of pleasure. He should set things to rights; return her to the bench across from him, right her gown, and repair her hair, hoping that her swollen and red lips returned to normal before she entered her home.

However, he was long past rational thought. Even if he spoke to the subject, it was unlikely Sam would hear him—her need matched his.

He allowed his mouth to travel the final few inches to take her dusty rose-colored nipple between his lips. He sucked gently, and she rewarded him with a deep moan, her head still thrown back in ecstasy.

Eli pulled away, enchanted by the raw, pure beauty of Sam.

She was perfection.

A flawless goddess he desperately needed in his life.

The drive to hold her, keep her, protect her consumed him.

But what must he protect her from?

"My lord," Mathers' call waded through his desire-filled daze. "We have arrived."

Suddenly, protecting Sam from his lust-filled longings was paramount. She was a lady, and deserving of far more respect than he'd shown her thus far.

While he coveted her, and his need to possess her and make her his was almost overwhelming, she was *not* his. The liberties he'd taken went far beyond what was proper and acceptable, even for a couple in the throes of a courtship.

Eli stilled Sam's hips as they ground against his manhood. "Sam," he murmured, attempting to gain her attention, to stop her hands from their wildly enticing path down his sides to the waistband of his trousers. "The carriage has stopped…outside your home."

The grave nature of his words—and the repercussions that could follow—did not so much as slow her exploration of his body.

He clamped his eyes shut, concentrating on the feel of her hands through his shirt. He desperately wanted to shout for Mathers to continue around the block…through town…and on toward to the country. Anything to gain more time with her.

"Who in the blasted hell is blocking the drive?" Eli's eyes sprang open at the angry bellow at the same time Sam stiffened in his lap. "You, man, whose carriage is this?"

"Lord Ridgefeld, sir." Mathers called in response.

"If he is within the house, kindly take your vehicle round to the stables."

"My master is still within." The hesitant tone in his servant's voice had Eli quickly lifting Sam and setting her on her own seat.

She righted her gown with trembling hands, though she did not make any move to depart.

"Your hair," Eli said, feeling around on his seat and collecting her scattered pins that'd been freed from her curls. Several tendrils hung loosely about her shoulders. "Here."

Sam took the pins from him and expertly pushed them into her hair, repining her curls. They were not as precise as when she'd departed her home, but Eli hoped her brother would not notice.

There were many expressions he'd expected to see on her face: eyes wide in shock, lips pressed tightly together in fear, or even her posture slumping in disbelief.

But she kept her eyes locked on his as she worked hastily to right her appearance. Her tongue darted across her lower lip as her chin lifted a notch and her lids lowered. She was the picture of sensuality, all flushed cheeks and plump lips.

Eli hardened further. An almost painful arousal.

"Either instruct Ridgefeld to depart his carriage or move aside."

"It is my brother," Sam whispered after her hands had appraised her hair. "And he is livid. How does my hair look?"

"Almost as it did when I collected you." He'd wanted to make a good impression on her family. He'd planned to woo Sam sisters with his charm. The only thing he'd managed to do was infuriate her brother.

"Wonderful," she said, her coy smile returning. "I will distract Garrett while you depart. I look forward to our next outing."

Their next outing? Eli was uncertain he'd make it out of her drive without Garrett challenging him to defend his sister's honor.

Sam pressed a kiss to his lips and flung the door wide, giving him no opportunity to respond as Mathers stepped into view to place the steps before Sam hopped from the carriage unassisted. "Thank you for a wonderful afternoon, my lord. I do look forward to our phaeton ride in Hyde Park on the morrow. I will await your arrival at one sharp."

She spoke far too loudly, and there was no chance her brother did not hear every word.

"Of course, Miss Samantha." The carriage was empty and cavernous without her. "I look forward to our next outing."

She glanced over her shoulder and winked before addressing her waiting brother. "Good day, dear brother." Her husky tone was smooth as honey, and Eli could see from his vantage point within the carriage that Sam gave her brother her most charming, sweet, and unassuming smile. "I did not know you were visiting today."

"I visit every day," he said gruffly as the carriage door swung closed. "What is Ridgefeld doing here? And why are you in his carriage? Where is your lady's maid?"

"He is returning me home, silly." Her muffled reply drifted through the curtained window, and the carriage jostled as Mathers took his perch. Eli noted she'd avoided his other questions. "Now, tell me, Garrett. I saw you dancing with the beautiful—and highly desirable—Miss Mallory Stewart…can the family expect her and her parents for supper soon?"

Eli chuckled at her skill for distraction.

A splinter of light shone through the slim crack between the curtain and the window frame. Sam's brother looked between the carriage—his eyes bulging—and his sister. The man was certainly suspicious, though Eli wasn't sure if he questioned his sister's presence in a man's carriage without a proper chaperone, or if his worries lay closer to Eli's intentions where Sam was concerned.

She slipped her arm through Garrett's and tugged. With one last look at the carriage, her brother allowed Sam to pull him toward the townhouse.

"The chit hasn't a single thought of value in her head. I assure you, we shall not be entertaining her or her hoity-toity parents…ever." Garrett chuckled. "Though she is blessed with a bosom and hips that have many men falling all over themselves to touch."

"Garrett!" Sam's voice hitched on the word. "That is highly inappropriate for a gentleman to comment on. At least until the pair is wedded and bedded."

"And what do you know of being wedded and bedded, my dear Samantha Eugenia Constantine Pengarden?"

A part of Eli longed to be with the pair, laughing and bantering alongside them—sharing in a rare moment of camaraderie; however, he sensed it was a private occurrence that could only be enjoyed and embarked upon by siblings. Something forbidden to Eli. No matter how much he tried to deny it, he longed for the closeness of kin.

He wanted to stay to hear Sam's response to her brother's question, but the siblings had journeyed into the house, disappearing from sight.

"To the museum," Eli called when the front door slammed shut.

"Of course, my lord," Mathers shouted. With barely a jingle of the reins, the carriage started its slow trek toward the British Museum—and the days of work that still lay ahead for Eli. Cataloguing, organizing, and preparing his grandfather's treasures for display. Thankfully, the work was a mindless task and would give him ample time to think over all that had transpired between him and Miss Samantha Pengarden—and ponder what tomorrow would hold for them.

Chapter Twenty-Five

Sam inched toward Elijah on the high perch of the phaeton as he expertly maneuvered the conveyance through Hyde Park. The sky was clear, and there was barely a breeze, making the afternoon perfect for their ride. Orange sellers shouted to passing carriages as the fruit's crisp scent hung in the air.

The phaeton belonged to Jude's husband, meaning Elijah was staying at Lord Cartwright's residence. Odd that her sister hadn't informed her of this fact during her morning social call to Craven House, nor the morning prior—or even at the ball two nights before. More peculiar still, Sam hadn't wondered where he'd found lodging.

"I hope your evening was pleasant." Elijah kept his cautious stare straight ahead.

He hadn't said much since collecting her, preferring to focus his attentions on driving the phaeton. He'd said it had been many years since he'd driven one, and Cartwright's was rather ancient and not the best maintained.

"It was as many nights are at Craven House," she said. He hadn't asked after her and Garrett's conversation the day before. "Marce hosted a card game, and I was charged with keeping Payton upstairs and out of sight, something that was once Jude's responsibility."

"Card games?" He turned toward her with a raised brow. "Your mother was once the proprietor of a bordello and your sister now runs a gaming hell in your home?"

"That is better than a bordello, is it not?" Sam couldn't help but laugh at his shock. "But seriously, yes, she hosts card games. Only a few rules; men must remember their manners, refrain from overdrinking, and keep their hands to themselves…other than that, bring your coin. The house takes a cut, and the men are free to play late into the night so long as no arguments start. It allows us to retain our financial freedom."

He remained silent as an enclosed carriage pulled alongside them, and a young woman leaned out the window. "Good day, Miss Samantha!"

"And to you, Miss Mallory," Sam replied. "May I introduce Lord Ridgefeld, my companion for the afternoon?"

"A pleasure, my lord." The girl's eyes traveled the length of Elijah, and tiny coils of jealousy sparked within Sam. "Lovely weather for a day in the park, is it not?"

"Certainly, Miss Mallory." Elijah nodded in agreement. "It is delightful to make your acquaintance."

Sam narrowed her eyes on Miss Mallory when the girl tittered, covering her mouth with her fan. She thought the chit interested in Garrett, so what in blazes was she doing making cow eyes at Elijah?

"Have a wonderful turn," Sam called. She tugged at Elijah's sleeve, signaling him to move on and away from the flippant girl. "That is the debutante who's smitten with Garrett."

"She seems nice enough." He flicked the reins, and the horses began a four-beat walk.

"Miss Mallory is a vulture, and her mother is far worse. Thankfully, Garrett has no title, no house of his own, and limited funds." It made the girl's interest in him all the more puzzling. It could be nothing more than her need to rebel against her family's wishes by seeking the favor of an unsuitable man. "However, I will not allow the girl to get my spirits down. Not on a day as beautiful as this." She tilted her face toward the bright sun overhead, the edge of her bonnet falling back slightly to allow the warm rays to reach her face.

"Were you in any trouble after I departed yesterday?" he asked. "I certainly would have walked you to the door and spoken with your brother."

"Everything was perfect." And it actually had been. It had only taken one mention of Mallory, and Garrett had been distracted long enough to forget all about Elijah's carriage in their drive…with his little sister inside. Sam did not relish manipulating Garrett; however, if the need arose, it had to be done, especially if she and Elijah were to continue their arrangement without unnecessary questions from her siblings. "And your evening went well?"

Elijah remained quiet for so long, Sam glanced at him.

"Are you unwell, my lord?"

"My apologies." He rubbed his free hand across his face and massaged his neck. "I spent the rest of the day at the museum. Unpacking, organizing, and cataloguing all my grandfather's possessions. It was very strenuous, and the task is not any closer to completion."

Sam felt the tiniest bit of guilt. "And here I am, demanding you waste precious time on a carriage ride through the park."

"I cannot spend every waking hour at the museum," he said with a smirk. "This outing is a welcome respite. Especially with you for company."

Sam glanced away as a blush blossomed. "Good day to you," she called to a trio of matrons walking the path alongside the carriage trail, hoping they attributed her scarlet cheeks to the warm weather. "I enjoy your company, as well, my lord." Meeting his eyes while she made her confession was too much. He would see how true the declaration was, and Sam was not ready for that.

"Then I suppose it is a good thing I will be extending my stay for several days."

"That is awfully convenient, Lord Ridgefeld," she conceded.

"It is Elijah, remember?"

In her mind, she'd thought of him as Elijah since their night together in Lord Cummings' study, alone but for the book filled with wickedness. Sam hadn't dared slip into the room and collect another volume after Elijah had departed Hollybrooke.

Broken. She'd been broken and hurt after he left. No drive had remained to explore the intricacies of the marriage bed. But after their time in the carriage the day before—and the heat of his thigh pressed against hers now—Sam longed to be alone once more, not on the high perch of a phaeton for all the see, with no privacy for even the smallest kiss.

Would he demand his reward for their outing today? Would Sam be forward enough to oblige, even knowing any number of people could witness their intimacy?

Blooming bullocks. Sam would press her lips, as well as every inch of her body, to his right here. Right now. In the middle of Hyde Park, with any number of society members as witness to her ruination. But a most sweet, public ruination it would be.

It would certainly discourage Lord Gunther and Proctor.

"Eli." She allowed the shortened name to escape her. Two syllables that had heat pooling at her most delicate spot. "It is a manly, strong name."

"Thank you," he said with a chuckle and a sideways glance. "It was bestowed upon me at birth by my grandfather."

"Your grandfather named you?"

"Yes, there was no one else willing to give me a fitting name."

"What of your mother?" Sam inquired in a whisper as another carriage rolled past without slowing for a greeting. "Did she not have a name selected before your birth?" His faraway look returned. "I do not mean to pry."

"It is all right, Samantha," he said, but the heaviness did not leave him. "My mother barely noticed she was pregnant once she learned of my father's death. She did not leave her bed...she barely ate...and conversed with no one. So, if she had selected a name for me, she voiced it to no one before she fled shortly after my birth. She stayed long enough for a portrait to be painted depicting her and me, but then her attention quickly turned to other…things."

"That is horrible." And not so far from her own story, though it was her father who'd abandoned her mother. "I do not mean to bring up such delicate matters."

He led the horses to the side of the carriage path and pulled them to a stop, tying the reins to the wooden peg next to him before shifting to face her. Sam did not dare look around to see if they'd garnered the attention of anyone. Everything faded with his eyes trained on her.

"You are the first person I've told of the circumstances surrounding my birth," he confided. "My servants are aware. Possibly even Lord Cartwright has an inkling, but I have told no one. Not even my classmates at Eton."

"Why tell me?" They'd shared a few brief moments of intimacy but never had she expected that to lead to a confession of his most private secrets. "Do not misunderstand, I am grateful you think so much of me as to share this…but…"

He took her gloved hands in his, his stare never wavering. "I trust you, Samantha. Since my grandfather passed away, you are the closest thing to a friend I have found. I believe stumbling upon you on that deserted road was fate; it was meant to bring us together."

A heavy feeling settled in the pit of her stomach. Elijah had been her distraction, something to take her focus off her father's reappearance and to keep Lord Gunther at bay. It had hurt greatly when he'd departed Hollybrooke without a farewell, but fate?

Certainly, their association had naught to do with any lasting entanglement, least of all fate.

"I do not understand, my lord."

"Sam, I left Hollybrooke to allow you the opportunity to connect with your father; something I have longed to do with my mother but have been denied."

"What would lead you to believe I would ever want to connect with my father?" she hissed. "He abandoned Jude and me. He left my mother with not a single look back after discovering she had the misfortune of birthing a girl…and twin girls at that. He left us to live barely above poverty while he wed his proper bride and tried for an ideal family." Sam chuckled, not her usual deep, throaty laugh but a manic cackle. "Imagine his misfortune to discover his wife was not a broodmare able to give him an heir and a spare, let alone a daughter."

"My presence was a distraction, everyone knew that."

"Who is everyone?"

"Your family—"

"My family?" she asked. "Did my family request you leave without saying goodbye?"

He shook his head. "They did outline the reasons I should depart; however, it was entirely my decision to leave immediately."

He had only been a distraction for her…that is what they'd agreed upon.

Sam hadn't expected any attachment to develop beyond the physical attraction, which was undeniable. But there was little other explanation as to why she'd insisted on Eli accompanying her on outings. She was back in London. It was far simpler to avoid unwanted attention from men she found not to her liking. Sam wasn't in need of Elijah to protect her against…what had she expected him to protect her from?

She was a capable woman. She led a decent life. She had a family who greatly cared for her, and she returned that feeling with all of her heart.

But still, she was drawn to Elijah. Longed to have him close—and not only for what he could teach her about pleasure.

"Who bid you leave Hollybrooke?" Sam demanded. "I need to know who would do such a thing. It was Marce—no, Garrett—who stepped in unbidden to try and steer me down a path not of my choosing. Was it not?"

"It was not, Sam, I promise you that."

"Then whom?" Her voice cracked as she spiraled out of control.

Elijah glanced around before retaking the reins and bidding the horses continue down the path.

She needs must know who in her family would so outwardly betray her without so much as consulting Sam to see where her intentions lay.

"Tell me who, Elijah." She infused the demand with all the sternness she possessed, her tone strong to let him know he would not get away with keeping the truth from her.

"It was Cartwright; however, he admitted the advice had come from Miss Judith, err, Lady Cartwright." Elijah cleared his throat when Sam remained silent. "She thought it best I allow you the opportunity to decide if you wanted a relationship with your father. I was a distraction from the serious matter at hand. Which I believed to be true. We both know she was correct."

Her own twin had done this to her? It seemed impossible Jude would wish such hurt upon Sam. How dare she run off with her new husband and leave Sam alone, even taking Eli from her company.

"...and so you left?" Sam couldn't keep the sorrow from her voice or her vision focused as it blurred, her head spinning. She shouldn't have pressed him for an answer. It had taken weeks, but Sam had worked through the hurt of Eli disappearing. It would have been far better not to know the reason for his hasty departure. Maybe even continue to think he'd been called away on important business. It hurt to know the one person who should care for her above all others had sent him away.

But that was no longer true or even possible. Jude had Simon now. Her allegiance belonged solely to her husband, not her twin.

"I think it is time I return you to Craven House." His shoulders slumped.

"I think that is for the best, my lord."

Chapter Twenty-Six

"It was your best interests they were concerned with, Samantha." Eli kept his hands tight on the reins as he navigated the path leading out of Hyde Park. He had to wonder how his day had taken such an unexpected turn. She'd been all smiles and laughter until discovering his reason for departing Derbyshire. However, how could she be angry with her sister? It had been he who had left without saying goodbye. He had made a promise to her that he hadn't stayed long enough to fulfill. "If you seek to be angry with someone, it should be me."

Elijah longed to pull her close once more, her fingers tangling in his hair and the scent of her surrounding him. Anything but the sight of the woman next to him presently, her shoulders bent forward as she wrapped her arms around herself and stared off into the distance…focusing on nothing.

He turned onto the main street leading back toward Craven House. The time of day was not late, and most of society was shopping, promenading around one of the many parks in London, or making their rounds of social calls, thus leaving the streets less crowded than any other time of the day. They passed several carriages and men on horseback, but not so many as to slow their travel.

Eli had the horses at a solid trot as they moved through town.

He stared straight ahead but risked several glances in Sam's direction. She alternated between focusing on something in the distance and picking at the stitching of her overcoat.

The need to comfort her drew him; however, Eli was conflicted on how to soothe the pain he'd caused.

"Miss Samantha!" a male voice shouted behind them. "Samantha!"

Eli glanced over his shoulder to see the raven-haired man who had escorted Sam from the ballroom two nights prior. Though he was curious about him, Eli's jaw clenched with jealousy as the man shouted for Sam's attention once more.

"Do you wish me to stop?" Eli asked

She turned slightly and glanced behind them to the man creating the commotion.

"Lord Proctor," she hissed, flipping back around, her shoulders straightening. "I most certainly do not wish you to stop, my lord."

"We may not be able to avoid it," Eli said, throwing another look over his shoulder before flipping the reins. "His carriage is picking up speed, and he will be alongside us before long."

"Then for heaven's sake, let us increase our pace, as well."

"I am uncertain this phaeton can go any faster."

"It is a blasted phaeton, it is meant for speed, my lord," she shouted, grabbing for the reins. "Give the horses their heads and let us outpace Lord Proctor."

He wanted to question her reasoning, but when she took control of the horses and flipped the lead, they went from a trot to a full gallop. The horse directly in front of Eli bucked slightly, unhappy with the sudden change in pace.

"Miss Samantha," he called, grasping the bar beside him. "I do not think this safe—or prudent—on a busy London street."

"Where is your sense of adventure, my lord?" she shouted over the pounding of hooves.

At the bottom of the Atlantic Ocean, not far from the Chesapeake Bay. Eli bit his tongue to stop the words from escaping. There was only so much he was willing to share with Sam. The true depths of the guilt he felt over his grandfather's death wasn't something he was ready to share with anyone, least of all Sam. He'd generously admitted a speck of the fault that plagued him, however, it would only serve to lessen the purity of his remorse to speak of the weight with another. Maybe one day…but that was not at present.

Instead, Eli hooked his boots under the front edge of the conveyance and held on as they careened around a corner, narrowly missing a cart heaped with coal. He had no idea how Sam kept her seat as the carriage swayed and jostled.

"The bloody fool is still trailing us," Sam shouted.

The wind from their speed had sent her bonnet from her head, and it hung down her back. With each moment that passed, more of her hair came loose and flew behind her. Even her eyes shone like he'd never seen before.

They were alight with…life.

Adventure.

The thrill of danger.

"Turn there," Eli shouted, recognizing the wide road leading toward the countryside. Certainly, the man would not chase them from the city. "Why does he seek your attention so?"

She glanced quickly in Eli's direction, and her smile wobbled. "We shared a brief conversation at the ball the other evening. That is all. He likely seeks to continue our discussion."

"And you do not wish for that?" His brow rose.

The road before them cleared as they traveled from the well-maintained city roads to the wood-packed, rutted roads leading out of London proper. The phaeton hopped and bounced on the uneven surface.

They needs must slow down before anything disastrous occurred.

"Lord Cartwright will be cross with me if I damage his conveyance, Sam."

"Then let us pray Lord Proctor gives up his chase soon."

They bumped and jostled down the path, passing several men on horseback and a wagon hauling fruit to the market.

"He is falling behind," Eli shouted. "Do slow down."

"Not until he is out of sight."

They rounded another bend, and the phaeton let out a loud crack as the ride became ever rougher.

"Something is not right." Eli leaned over the side of the phaeton as they slowed to see a wooden plank protruding from the underside of the carriage. "Blast it, I think we broke the axel."

"The what?" Sam inquired, her eyes widening. "Is it easily fixed?"

"I haven't much experience with carriage repairs, but we certainly will be stuck here if I am unable to mend it." They came to a stop, and Eli jumped down from the phaeton and assisted Sam with doing the same before they both squatted to see the damage done to the underside of the vehicle. "It is a wonder the wheel did not fall off entirely. As much as my pride hurts to admit this, I think this is far beyond my level of skill with repairs."

Eli straightened, brushing the dust from his trousers. A glance in both directions showed him that they were alone—not another carriage in sight.

"At least we lost Lord Proctor," he mumbled. "Why would the man go to such great lengths to gain your attention?"

She shrugged, digging the toe of her slipper into the soft dirt at the side of the path.

"Very well," he said. "Keep your secrets."

Her eyes rounded, and she stomped her foot. "I am doing no such thing. The man is a nuisance, and I have no interest in associating with the scoundrel."

Scoundrel? Eli raised his brow at her venom.

"Shall we?" He held out his arm.

"Shall we what?"

"Well, it is either we sit here and await nightfall—there are still animals hunting, even so close to London—or we start walking and hope to gain a ride from a passing carriage." He jiggled his arm. "Either way, it is unsafe to wait here where a highwayman could happen upon us and rob us blind."

"Do not fear, my lord," Sam said with a laugh. "I will defend your honor."

"I would expect nothing less since it is your fault we are in this predicament to begin with."

She slipped her arm into his. "*My* fault?" They fell into step alongside one another as she pondered his words. "If you hadn't stopped to collect me along the road in Derbyshire, I don't believe we would be in our present situation." She stared up at him, eyes full of laughter as she attempted to keep a serious expression.

"Very true," he conceded, stepping around a gaping hole in the road. "I should have left you to the storm. You likely would have succumbed to the elements and either floated away with the rain or froze by the roadside. I can now see the merit in that course of action."

"You would not have dared!" she stammered.

"And if I had?" he countered.

"I certainly would not have blamed you. I am a handful. My family can attest to that."

"Will you do me a favor?" He squeezed her arm.

"Depends."

"Do not blame Lord and Lady Cartwright for what happened in Derbyshire." He glanced at her, but her loose auburn hair blocked her expression. "They only wished for you to have the chance to mend your relationship with Beauchamp. Besides, we were caught in a position that was not altogether innocent."

The rumbling of wagon wheels against the rocky road behind them drew Eli's attention.

They turned in unison to see an empty cart being pulled by a single horse, driven by a farmer, his dirt-streaked face and toothy grin comforting as he stopped alongside them.

"That be ye fancy rig back there?" he called.

"It is, sir," Elijah answered with his own smile. "I don't suppose you are headed into London proper and would be willing to allow us a ride in your cart."

The man, at least thirty years Eli's senior, looked to his ragged horse and back at his empty cart. "Ye and the missus be stranded?"

"We are." Elijah shook his head with regret. "I'd planned a lovely picnic in the country with my wife, and our phaeton broke an axel. Barmy mistake I made not checking the thing before leaving town." He didn't risk a glance at Sam after referring to her as his wife.

The driver scratched his head. "Well, me own wife only sent me and me son ta town ta collect lumber for the barn repairs. Oh, an' flour. I left him with ye horses. I suppose she won't be know'n if'n I give ye a ride as far as the market off Piccadilly."

"That is perfect." Sam didn't wait for the driver to change his mind before moving to take a place in the cart, leaving Eli to follow. "Come, my dear, sweet husband. Our day is not completely ruined, after all. Thank you, kind sir. I am Miss—Lady Ridgefeld, and this is my husband, Elijah. We will certainly reward you for the transport."

"I be Ralph, m'lady." The man removed his hat and nodded his head. "It be a pleasure ta meet the pair of ye, but no coin be needed. I be goin' that way regardless. When I be pass'n back toward home, I be give'n me son directions ta deliver ye horses safe 'n sound, I will."

"Well, you are very kind, Ralph—and your son, as well." Sam smiled her most charming grin, and Ralph blushed as crimson as the sun setting on the far horizon. "My husband and I are very grateful for your assistance."

Elijah climbed into the cart and settled next to Sam, his wife for the present. He'd be lying if he didn't admit the sound of his name on her lips—in conjunction with the term husband—did not have him thinking all sorts of wicked thoughts…mainly the idea of making Sam a proper wife, his bride.

Certainly, a courtship between them was developing. Why else would she demand he take her on outings? It would not be long before a conversation with her guardian—was that Marce or Garrett?—would be necessary. He would make his noble intentions known…and pray that Sam's family approved of him.

Chapter Twenty-Seven

Sam slipped into the house and sighed, quietly closing the door behind her. Her face was still heated from her exciting escapades with Eli. Though he hadn't claimed his payment kiss, she owed him a huge reward. Leaning against the door, Sam set her fingers against her lips, and her eyes drifted shut as she imagined the kiss to come. She would be bold and wrap her arms around him, maybe slip her hands under his shirt to feel the muscles she knew lay beneath, hidden from view.

Her heartbeat spiked at the thought, and her face likely reddened further.

"Did you just climb out of a cart?"

Sam's eyes sprang open, and her hand fell to her side.

Marvelous.

She should have insisted Ralph drop them off at the market, which had been their original plan, but the man had insisted on seeing her all the way home.

Her youngest sister, Payton, stood right outside the drawing room, its windows facing the driveway.

Fabulous.

She'd seen everything...

"And was that Lord Ridgefeld with you?" She set her tiny hands on her hips. She'd grown into a woman without Sam noticing—and an observant woman, at that. "I am certain Marce will enjoy the story of my sister most regal climbing out of the back of a market cart like a common farmer's daughter." Payton smirked triumphantly.

"You would not dare!" Sam retorted, stepping toward her sister and crossing her arms. "I will tell Marce of your nightly trips to the gaming halls."

"You can prove nothing." Payton didn't bother denying her late-night outings, merely pointing out that no evidence of it existed.

Thankfully, Sam had been holding onto a little tidbit of evidence, in case the need ever arose for her to make use of it. "A note arrived several days ago...something about you owing a certain shopkeeper five pounds by next week." Payton's eyes widened in surprise, her mouth gaping. Sam continued, "So, I think it advantageous for both of us to keep each other's confidences. Do you not agree?"

Payton only nodded, her chocolate-brown curls bouncing with her exaggerated effort.

"Very good." Sam smirked. "Now, I should hurry to my room and freshen up for supper. That farmer must have transported a hundred pigs in that cart. I smell worse than a horse's stall in the blazing summer heat." Though Sam would not forget Ralph's kindness.

Sam strode confidently past Payton, certain her sister would never risk Marce learning of her ever-increasing gambling debts. Just as Sam would not delight in their eldest sister questioning her outings with Lord Ridgefeld—or worse yet, her intentions toward the man.

With the man.

They all had secrets, it was only a matter of finding the means to keep them hidden.

For now, Sam needs must figure out what her next outing with Elijah would be. She'd thoroughly enjoyed their time at Gentlemen Jackson's and Hyde Park. It wasn't even a stretch to admit that she'd enjoyed their reckless phaeton ride into the country, though her feet were a bit sore from their short walk until Ralph had happened upon them and offered assistance.

Not to mention her aching arms from holding onto the reins as the horses ran with abandon. There was no chance she'd admit she'd been frightened during their short jaunt out of London.

"You know, dear sister," Payton called, halting Sam before she started up the stairs. She didn't turn to face her youngest sibling. "When a man courts me, he will need more than a filthy horse and cart to woo me. I suppose not all women are as particular as I."

Sam's back stiffened, but she refused to turn, in no mood to neither argue with her sister nor defend Elijah. "Then I think it is a grand thing that Lord Ridgefeld is not courting me." She paused, debating whether to say more. "And, thankfully, for all gentlemen concerned, you are far too young for a courtship as yet, which will afford you ample time to improve your whiney, simpering disposition."

At Payton's gasp, Sam smiled to herself and started up the stairs.

No matter how much she teased Payton, Sam was certain the girl needed time to mature before setting her sights and gaining a tender for any man. For once her youngest sibling grew a taste of the pleasures a man could give, she would fall fast for the first gentleman who could bring her to the edge of ecstasy, and she'd jump over without needing a push. Not that Sam was naive enough to allow Elijah to bring her to the ledge. Nor was she trusting enough to throw herself off the cliff with only him as her guide.

"Have a wonderful afternoon, Payton." Sam turned the corner at the top of the stairs and continued down the hall to her room…and blessed privacy.

She needed solitude to decide what outing she'd undertake next with Lord Ridgefeld. His presence was certainly a boon for her, bringing amusement and a sense of leisure to her normal routine since joining society. It was a constant wake up, dress, eat, social calls, afternoon entertainment, meals, and evening soirees. The pace left no time for satisfaction of the grand moments she'd experienced in the last several months.

Once safely in her room—all of Jude's possessions gone—Sam sighed in relief.

A lovely pink gown hung from her wardrobe in anticipation of her evening out. She hadn't any notion what entertainment was planned for her that night, but the dress was certainly demure, a soft blushing color that suddenly seemed far too innocent for Sam to wear convincingly. Would society look at her in the gown and suspect the pleasure she'd experienced with Elijah?

The mere thought of their intimate moment in his carriage sent heat flooding her entire body. She stripped her overcoat from her shoulders to ward off the warmth overtaking her as she hurried to her window, unlatching it and throwing it wide to allow in the breeze.

Sam scanned the driveway and street below, but Elijah—and the cart—was gone, disappeared from sight. A spark of remorse filled her. Certainly they had quarreled, but if she hadn't insisted they try and outrun Lord Proctor, Cartwright's carriage would not now be deserted outside the city and Sam might have been able to convince Elijah to extend their outing. He'd mentioned a picnic in the country. Something entirely uninteresting to her, but with Eli…she rather thought she'd enjoy the outing. Maybe that would be her next request. Or the opera. Her mind swirled with possibilities. Covent Garden outdoor playhouse with its darkened garden paths and private audience boxes.

However, Marce would never agree to allow her to journey to the opera or Covent Garden unchaperoned with Lord Ridgefeld. It would be highly unseemly and certain to gain undue attention—which only increased Sam's desire to do exactly that.

Besides, she owed Elijah a reward for their afternoon outing.

What better way to give it than to request his accompaniment to Covent Garden that very evening. Certainly, he would not turn down her request, it was innocent enough. Especially if she could convince Jude and Lord Cartwright to join them. Her twin owed her much more than a mere night at the playhouse for her hand in Elijah fleeing Hollybrooke.

Sam hurried to her writing desk and jotted off a quick note, requesting that Jude and her husband accompany her to Convent Gardens. As their houseguest, they would have no option but to invite

Lord Ridgefeld to join them. But, hastily, Sam added Elijah was welcome, as well, just in case Simon was too obtuse to realize it would be rude not to bring Ridgefeld along.

Sam replaced her quill and dusted the page with sand to make sure the ink did not smudge after she'd folded the note. She could not risk any of her message being illegible when Jude read it. Would her sister—her closest friend and confidant—suspect Sam's clandestine intentions behind her invitation?

Truthfully, Sam was unconcerned with how Jude interpreted the note. She was determined to see Elijah again—the sooner, the better. There was much more she sought to learn from him before he disappeared once more to the far reaches of Liverpool.

# # #

Eli entered the museum, unable to dispel his smile. He'd thought the brisk walk from Piccadilly to the museum would give him time to put Sam from his mind, at least until his afternoon of work was complete. Once he'd returned to Lord Cartwright's townhouse, and his room, he would be free to allow his thoughts…and desires, to return to her. For now, he had a task to complete, and if he did not wipe his satisfied grin away before meeting with Cartwright, the earl would certainly suspect Elijah had something altogether different on his mind that had naught to do with his family's treasured collection.

The exhibits were busy with meandering men, women, and a few well-behaved children as Eli made his way to the door leading to the offices and the workroom hidden in the far reaches of the large building. He'd relish the opportunity to bring Sam here to wander through the displays and disappear into the darkened maze of corridors, exploring not only the hidden treasures not on public display but also each other.

"Ridgefeld," Lord Cartwright stepped into his path. "I've been trying to gain your notice since you entered the museum."

"My apologies, my lord. It is rather loud in here."

Cartwright glanced around. The museum was as it always was, quiet as a mausoleum. He shook his head as if he'd missed something important but was unwilling to admit it. "I was not expecting you this afternoon. I am on my way to meet Garrett at White's for a meal. Join us?"

He'd hoped to spend several mindless hours sorting through artifacts and jotting notes for display cards, not sitting with the two men closest to the woman he could barely take his mind from.

Bloody hell, maybe a meal and drink would help him sort through his coming dilemma. The possibility of his intention to court Miss Samantha properly—with her brother and brother-in-law's approval—could be discussed over their meal.

"If you have other plans—" Cartwright's brow rose.

"No," Eli insisted. "No, I do not. I would very much enjoy joining you."

Cartwright clasped his shoulder and turned toward the front door. "Wonderful, my carriage is being brought round to take us."

At the mention of conveyances, Eli remembered Cartwright's damaged phaeton abandoned on the road leading out of London. If he planned to broach the subject of courtship, it would not be in his best interest to mention the broken carriage until *after* Cartwright and Garrett seemed amiable to his pursuit of Sam. Hell, maybe he should hold off telling the earl until all the betrothal papers were signed.

The carriage ride to White's passed quickly, Cartwright lost in his own thoughts and not bothering with chitchat.

It gave Eli time to brush the dirt from Ralph's cart from his trousers. He'd offered the man money in exchange for transporting them into London, but the farmer had refused, only promising to check on the phaeton on his way back home to make sure vandals hadn't set upon it.

His grin returned at the thought of Sam nestled in the filthy cart, with nary a complaint as they were jostled and jarred the entire journey. It was not hard to picture her, a heavy pack on her back and garbed in thigh-hugging trousers as she kept at his side while they explored the desert or used machetes to cut a path through the South American jungle.

She continued to surprise him with each hour they spent together. In Derbyshire, she'd appeared much like the spoiled, well-mannered debutante she was, but even then, Eli sensed a deepness to her. A part of her that she hid from others. Chances were if he hadn't happened upon her in Cummings' study, looking through that scandalous book, he would have never discovered the enchanting creature she was.

Sam did not trust easily, but she had good reason. A reason Eli understood better than most.

She was quick to divert a subject if she sensed it was not to her liking—another skill Eli was adept at.

Sam had no qualms about gaining what she wanted—by any means necessary—be that an education in intimacy or an outing all too unsuitable for an innocent maiden. Elijah envied this trait in her. He tended to push others away, deny himself what he truly longed for in an attempt to keep others at bay, in turn, guarding himself against hurt and loss.

However, he was determined to change that. His goal for prolonging his stay in London was to court Sam properly. Do anything and everything to make her happy; bring the light to her eyes he'd first noted at Hollybrooke. That Sam appeared to revel in their time together also gave Eli hope for his future—*their* future.

He would wait in anticipation for her next note requesting his company on an outing. Or was she prepared to invite him into her home, Craven House? Maybe it was his turn to take the lead and call on her, make a plan of his own?

Bloody hell, but he had no idea what activities a couple did when courting, especially in London. In Liverpool, he might invite her to the harbor and take her out on one of the many schooners to watch the sun set. Or invite her to the Sunday gathering at his local parish for a meal with his local community. Even an afternoon at Tidbell's Inn for a spot of tea.

Eli's connections and knowledge of town life—or lack thereof—was no more glaring than in that moment.

Focusing on Cartwright on the opposite bench, he watched the man scribble in a small journal he held close, his pencil feverishly moving across the paper as if he sensed if he slowed down, his thoughts would evaporate.

"What are you writing?" Eli asked.

Cartwright glanced up, puzzled, as if he'd forgotten he was not alone in the carriage. "Oh, I am making notes of topics to speak about with my dear sister, Theodora, when I travel to her school in Canterbury."

Eli pictured the precocious girl he'd met in Derbyshire, no more than thirteen, but destined to be a true beauty with an intellect to match. "I hope her journey to school went well. If I remember correctly, she was to set off for Canterbury when you and Lady Cartwright started your bridal tour."

The man's eyes widened. "Correct, Lord Ridgefeld. I hadn't expected you'd retain such inconsequential information."

"It is not every day a man meets a young woman destined for greatness, Cartwright." Elijah wondered if he spoke of Lady Theodora or Sam. "I look forward to one day speaking with your sister about the merits of girl's boarding schools as opposed to private tutors."

"I am certain Theo would enjoy a spirited debate on the subject." Cartwright nodded, a lock of his fair hair falling across his face.

The carriage slowed to a stop, and the door opened to reveal the famed gentlemen's club White's. Until now, Eli had only been privy to stories of the place's grandeur: the dark, masculine interior, the male camaraderie found within its exclusive walls, and the relaxation of sharing a private evening reading *The Post* and drinking port.

"Coming, Ridgefeld?" Cartwright called from the walk outside the carriage.

Eli hurried to join him and hide his anticipation of being inside. It would be unbecoming to show his exhilaration at embarking on an age-old tradition among society men. His grandfather had brought Eli's father here many years ago. And if the late marquis had been afforded a few more years, Eli was certain they would have come here together, as well.

Instead, Cartwright stood beside him, and Sam's brother waited inside. Could these two men fill the void his grandfather's demise had left within Eli? Would they become his friends? His family?

"Well, Ridgefeld." Cartwright slapped him on the back. "Let us enjoy a bit of peace and quiet before returning to my townhouse and discovering the evening entertainment my dear wife has planned for us."

Eli gulped. "Both of us?"

"You are our guest, and Jude informed me it is only proper to entertain one's visitor for the duration of their stay." Cartwright recited the words slowly, much as he had the morning of his wedding in Cummings' office when he bid Eli to depart. The earl was only a messenger, and therefore, held no responsibility for the repercussions Eli faced with Sam. "Shall we?"

The door opened as they neared to allow them entrance, and swung just as quickly closed to keep the prying eyes of the loitering individuals outside from invading and disturbing the sanctity of the club.

Would Elijah give up his quiet existence in Liverpool for a life surrounded by the extravagant nature of town society? The answer was simple…if it were Samantha's wish, he would grant it.

Cartwright waved to Lord Garrett Davenport and the man moved toward them.

"You did not say you were bringing him." Sam's brother nodded at Eli, leaving no room for misunderstanding. "But I guess he can stay. This way."

Eli's first thought was that the man jested. They were barely acquainted with one another; there was little opportunity for the man to make any decisions one way or the other about Eli in such a short time. That did not stop the pang of hurt he felt, though.

The trio moved to a table set for them before the roaring hearth as a manservant added a third place setting.

"I hope you don't mind I selected the grouse and wild salmon for our meal." Garrett dropped into his seat, a drink already in his hand, obviously unconcerned if either man took issue with the selected fare.

Elijah turned to admire the great bay windows at the front of the establishment, the dark mahogany wood walls that matched the furniture to perfection. Even the servants' garb was highlighted with a dark blue, the same hue used for the upholstery of the overstuffed chairs scattered about the room in some organizational arrangement that eluded Eli's understanding.

Behind him, Eli heard Garrett speaking in hushed tones with Cartwright. *Phaeton...London countryside...repairs...bloody inconvenient...no one hurt...just a carriage*, where the only words he could make out between the pair. Sam must have sent word of their phaeton ride misfortune to her sister.

"On the road leading out of London?" Garrett shouted loudly behind him, before hissing, "That is very far from Hyde Park, do you not think? What where they doing all the way out there? Did you think to question that?"

"Certainly, I did," Cartwright's squeak said he hadn't thought to question any of it—and Eli was content with that. It was a conversation to be had at a later time. "But Garrett, the probability of a carriage having trouble is quite high, especially with a phaeton of its age and usage. I do not think it warrants further discussion."

Eli continued surveying the room, anything to keep away from the discussion of the damaged phaeton. Not that he was avoiding the conversation, it was only that Cartwright was a much more agreeable and understanding man without Garrett near.

Chuckles and a shout of outrage had him spinning to watch a table across the room. A group of men sat relaxed as a game of faro was underway. He wandered closer, the need to be part of the revelry overtaking him. A man in a shockingly bright mustard-yellow coat shuffled a deck of cards with ease, keeping up a steady stream of conversation with the players gathered around the table. If Cartwright and Garrett were not waiting on him to dine, Eli would be tempted to take a seat at the table and test his luck at a hand. He'd never thought of himself as a particularly providential man—especially after his grandfather's death and his mother's disinterest in reuniting with her only son—but since meeting Samantha, things had improved.

Not things.

He had improved.

Elijah's views on life and his future had altered in an uncanny and unexpected way.

For a brief moment, he actually desired to belong here among the wealthiest members of society—Sam's world, not his.

"Let us have it, Calhoun!" The round, balding man who shuffled the cards called. "Record the bloody wager and allow me to deal another round. Some of us have other entertainments this evening."

"Then be off with you," a man mumbled—obviously Calhoun—hunched over a large tome with a quill fresh with ink. "I need make certain the wording is correct, or Applegate will likely try to wiggle his way out of making good on his debts…again."

A lanky, freckled faced man sat up straight with indignation. "I have always paid my debts. I have an enraged father to show for it."

The table erupted in another round of laughter.

Elijah wondered if he'd been raised closer to London if he'd know why Calhoun was fretting over the verbiage of a written wager or why Applegate's enraged father gained such a jovial response from the men around the table.

With a flourish of his hand, Calhoun sat back and smiled. "Very good. I look forward to seeing you attempt to extricate yourself from this one, Applegate."

Before the man dealt the cards, a servant bustled forward to remove the large book from the table—obviously, the famed White's betting book.

The servant made to whisk the leather-bound book away, but noticed Eli's interest and halted. "Would you care to place a wager, my lord?"

"Have him bring the blasted book over here," Garrett shouted, waving Eli back to their table, their heated discussion about the phaeton blessedly at an end. "You can peruse the thing at your leisure once you have a drink."

Garrett was obviously not in favor of Eli joining them. A fact that would normally concern him, but at the moment, the man's brash attitude mattered little. He followed the servant back to their table and took one of the two open seats, his back directly to the flames from the fire. It gave Eli ample opportunity to survey the room—the crowd growing with each moment as men flooded into the club in groups, pairs, and a few singles.

As he searched the sea of unfamiliar faces, the black-and-blue-garbed manservant set the betting book on the table before him. Elijah ran his hand slowly over the worn leather cover to caress the cracked binding as the smell of aged paper and history settled about him. How many men had filled this club, entered their name and wager in this very book? This would have been a very unique treasure to collect.

Elijah closed his eyes and breathed in deeply as Cartwright and Garrett spoke. He lost track of their words when he opened the tome to a wager recorded in January of 1797. A chuckle escaped him when he read the stakes of the bet—a rather mundane wager—but the victor was entitled to submit a full-page advertisement in *The Post* regarding the minuscule size of the loser's manhood.

Had Lord Argyll followed through after he'd won their wager?

Oh, to locate a copy of the newspaper from late January 1797.

"Something comical?" Cartwright asked.

Elijah turned to more recently recorded wagers. "A Mr. Marcus Bosworth wagered his father could not be tricked into purchasing a lame horse. Unfortunately, the elder Bosworth was duped into buying the horse, and therefore, Lord Argyll was announced the victor."

"How much did Argyll win?" Garrett took a long pull on his drink. "A few shillings, a pound?"

"No." Elijah chuckled again, shaking his head. "He won the right to place an advertisement in *The Post*, denouncing the…ummm…grandness of Bosworth's manhood."

"Who would speak ill of an old man's part?" Cartwright's brow scrunched in confusion.

"Not the elder Bosworth's part," Elijah retorted. "But that of Mr. Marcus Bosworth. Wonder if the fool ever found himself a bride lucky enough to not read *The Post*."

"I have never understood the logic in placing a wager on an undetermined and unpredictable outcome." Cartwright sat back in his seat, his interest in the betting book gone. "Makes absolutely no sense."

"There is much you do that makes no sense to me, Cart," Garrett laughed. "I do enjoy a good shaming now and again."

Elijah read page after page of wagers on horse races, winter hunting expeditions, and even the occasional bet over who would claim the hand of a certain lady, or more shockingly, which gentlemen would be caught in a lady's marriage noose.

The work at the museum, and his pursuit of Miss Samantha, would extend his stay in London into the foreseeable future. Elijah flipped to the most recently recorded wagers. Maybe he would wager a spot of coin on an open bet. Something with moderate stakes and a high likelihood of a payout.

He was almost nearing the final recorded wager when a familiar name stood out to him, written in the bold, sharp handwriting of a man.

Who shall take Miss Samantha P—as mistress?

The page was divided into five columns; Lord Gunther, Lord Proctor, Mr. Tobias Shillings, Lord Meyton and...

Lord Ridgefeld?!

"What in the bloody hell?" Under each name, men had been placing wagers—large wagers—on who would take the woman to bed as their mistress first. Even more startling, his name only had one man betting he would take the prize: Mr. Harold Jakeston? "That...well..."

Before Eli could slam the betting book shut, run from the room, and burn all evidence of the scandalous wager before either of his companions saw, Garrett pulled the book from his grasp.

Samantha's brother's face went from a leisurely smile to a tight line of disbelief to utter outrage as his nostrils flared and he pushed his chair back to stand. Garrett's hard stare lifted to meet Elijah's.

"I would never," Elijah protested. "Have never so much as thought—"

Garrett planted his palms on the table and leaned toward Elijah. "You'd bloody damn well better not be caught with my sister in a compromising position of any sort," Garrett seethed. "I am not so forgiving as to accept your proposal of marriage after you ruin her. Oh, no, you will see the blade of my sword or the end of my pistol before I agree to any such thing."

Garrett immediately pivoted and walked out the front door.

"And the man says I am the odd one," Cartwright mumbled, withdrawing his journal from his pocket. "Lord Garrett has a tendency for dramatics, do not let him convince you otherwise. He is much like his sisters in that regard." Cartwright nodded as if agreeing with his own words. "No matter, there will be more food for us."

Elijah ripped the page from the betting book and slipped it into his pocket without Cartwright glancing up from his scribbling.

"My lord, you cannot—" The servant who'd delivered the book to their table hurried back over. "That book is a piece of history. It is not to be tampered with in any way. I must demand you return what you took."

Cartwright glanced up at the stammering man, confusion etched on his face. "I brought this journal, my good man. Now, off with you before our meal grows cold."

Eli risked a glance at the servant, his face red and flustered, and he did what any marquis would, he nodded in dismissal to the man. Reluctantly, the servant bowed, took hold of the book, and moved across the room, keeping a close watch on Elijah as he did.

No one would ever place a wager regarding Miss Samantha again—or they would answer to him.

Chapter Twenty-Eight

Sam waited in the foyer for her carriage to be brought round to take her to meet Jude and Lord Cartwright. Her afternoon had crept by as she waited for a reply from her sister. It had arrived during supper, and their housekeeper had delivered it immediately to Sam—to Marce's disapproving glare.

It had taken a bit of convincing before her eldest sister acquiesced to Sam's pleas. It was only an evening at the outdoor playhouse, and she'd be properly chaperoned by a respectable, married woman—yes, she'd stooped so low as to dare Marce to refute Jude's newly acquired respectable status as a countess—and now Sam was almost free of the confines of Craven House. The most shocking aspect of the entire situation was that Marce had not bid Sam take Payton with her.

With any luck, the new Lord and Lady Cartwright would be too enamored with one another to notice if she and Elijah slipped away.

To appease her sister further, Sam had donned the demure, high-necked, pink evening gown with cuffed shoulders and white gloves. Her beaded ivory reticule and matching fan went splendidly with her dress and didn't take attention away from her pearl earbobs. She'd gathered her hair low on the back of her head and allowed her locks to hang free over one shoulder.

There was no need to glance in the looking glass again. Elijah—and any man with proper eyesight—would see how stunning she looked. Graceful, poised, and every inch a lady.

Now, if only her carriage would hurry.

She was ready to be anything but a lady.

Jude expected her shortly, and they'd not want to be late and face the crushing crowd of people hurrying to their seats before the curtain rose.

The front door opened, slamming against the doorframe when Garrett stumbled in.

His face flamed red, his shirt untucked, and his hair mussed.

"Heavens," Sam yelped, her hand lying against her chest to settle her erratic heartbeat. "Whatever is the matter with you?"

"With me?" His cynical laughter filled the room as he set his hand against his own chest, mimicking her stance. "Never mind. Where are you going?" He took in her fancy garb and neat hair, as he looked her over from her crown to her toes peeking from beneath her skirts.

Sam took a deep breath, refusing to look away from his intense glare. "Jude invited me to accompany her and Lord Cartwright to the playhouse." A moderately adjusted form of the truth. "Marce gave me permission to attend. She is in her office if you'd like to check for yourself."

Garrett narrowed his eyes, huffed, and started off down the hall toward their sister's office, the stench of liquor following in his wake.

Her nose wrinkled at the horrid smell. Very unlike her brother to imbibe overly…and then dare show his face at Craven House. Marce was no fool. The only thing she despised more than scandal was a man who drank in excess.

Odder still, her brother had never taken much interest in his siblings' comings and goings. There was little reason now for him to take more than a passing notice of Sam's evening entertainments. While he was the only male member of their family, it was common for Garrett to leave the rearing of his younger siblings to Marce.

The hair on the back of her neck prickled despite the warmth of the foyer. Anything out of character for Garrett unsettled Sam.

The jingle of horse riggings sounded outside.

Her maid had insisted she take her shawl and muff, as well as her jacket. The outdoor playhouse was known to be a bit on the frigid side into the late evening, and Sam thought it wise to listen. Especially since she planned to slip away from the lighted areas for a few moments alone with Elijah.

Sam hurried outside, and Mr. Curtis handed her into the carriage before they were off. It was only a short ride to Lord Cartwright's townhouse. With no one to invade her musings, Sam allowed her thoughts free rein. They immediately focused on Lord Ridgefeld. The cut of his broad shoulders. The way his eyes matched the shade of his hair almost perfectly: dark with hints of gold. The way a single dimple appeared high on his cheek when he smiled. His strong hands.

Those same hands holding the naughty book at Hollybrooke, his eyes aglow with surprise but quickly fading to a deep, lust-filled stare. In her altered memory, no servant had disrupted them. They'd stayed wrapped in each other's arms as their lips and hands explored to their hearts' content. When they'd explored as much as possible being fully clothed, Eli had swept her into his arms and carried her to the chaise lounge, laying her down gently as her hair fanned around her like a halo, all her hairpins suddenly gone and forgotten.

Elijah's body did not follow her to the lounge. No, he had other plans for her.

Her body shuddered at the thought.

Instead of joining her, he kneeled and used his hands to push her skirts up to reveal her slippers. Those same hands gently removed them, his fingers trailing along the bottom of her stocking-clad feet before traveling up to her ankle and farther still.

Sam's head fell back, and she moaned, just as she did in her own imaginings of that night.

His fingers caressed up her calf to the bow just above her knee. With a swift tug, the knot came undone, and Eli rolled her stocking down. He smiled at her in wonder before pressing his lips to her leg and following the path his hands had taken to remove her other stocking.

Why did she long for his hands to move higher on her leg, between her legs, not downward?

She swallowed, altering her own memory. Now, his hand did follow the path she imagined. Higher and higher until his hand brushed her most sensitive spot.

Warmth flooded her, centering at her core as she shifted to allow Elijah easier access to push her drawers to the side and…

"Samantha?" Jude cleared her throat. "Are you sleeping?"

Sam's eyes popped open, and she attempted to focus, but all she saw was the ceiling of the enclosed carriage, her head still thrown back and yet another moan struggling to escape.

How had she journeyed all the way to the Cartwright townhouse in the blink of an eye? Certainly, it was not possible. Maybe she was asleep, and Jude was invading her dream. Sam glanced to the open carriage door, her sister poking out, her head tilted to the side and her lips pursed.

No such luck; she had indeed arrived.

No matter how much she wished to return to her musings of moments before, it was impossible.

"Are you ill?" Jude demanded. "We can have you taken back home if you wish."

Sam sat up straight and felt along the seat for her muff and handbag, her shawl was still draped across her shoulders. "Heavens no." Sam moved to depart, and Jude stepped back to allow her room. "I am quite well, I assure you. And looking forward to a night at Covent Garden."

"Very well." Jude assessed her sister from head to toe. She often wondered if when her twin looked at her, she felt as if she was staring into a mirror. "My carriage awaits."

Sam followed Jude to the Cartwright transport, glancing over her shoulder to see Simon standing by the conveyance. But Elijah was not in sight. Was it possible he'd turned down the invitation? Or more likely, Simon hadn't extended the invitation at all.

An entire evening trapped with Jude and her doting new husband would be more than she could handle. Claiming ill did not seem the worst idea.

It was obvious Elijah had had his fill of her—and her antics.

Did Simon know it was Sam's fault his phaeton lay abandoned on the road leading out of London?

His welcoming grin when she and Jude joined him said he did not. This was a relief, but had Elijah taken the blame? Had Simon and Elijah argued over the damaged carriage? Had Eli been asked to leave the Cartwright townhouse? Knowing she need take responsibility for her part in the incident, a rock settled in the pit of her stomach.

However, Simon would not look so…happy, if he and Elijah had indeed had a row over the phaeton.

"Shall we depart?" Simon asked, holding his hand out to his wife. "I find I am looking forward to the play."

Jude swatted at his arm with a laugh. "You are in no way excited or so much as the least bit anxious to attend Covent Garden. You and Ridgefeld would have enjoyed spending the entire evening entrenched in a card game at White's—or sorting ancient, dusty artifacts at the museum—much more." She wiggled her finger in his face. "The first rule of marriage is not to lie to your wife."

Jude dropped a quick kiss to Simon's cheek and took his arm.

Sam had to remind herself she was happy her sister had found a love match, a man who suited her perfectly in every way…even if their outward displays of affection had Sam dwelling on her own lack of connection to others.

A spot of movement caught Sam's attention as they rounded the carriage.

Taking her eyes off her sister, she noted through the open door a figure already seated in the conveyance.

And any thought she had of claiming ill evaporated.

Elijah.

He smiled tentatively, something different about the set of his shoulders.

"Good evening, Lord Ridgefeld." Sam's smile was in no way timid. "I was unaware you'd be joining us."

His furrowed brow told her he didn't believe her words for a second.

"Yes, well," Simon cut in. "My dear wife says it is only proper—and expected—our guest be invited to join us. She also says it would be rude on Ridgefeld's part to turn down the invitation." He paused, looking to Jude for approval. Her scowl conveyed her words were not meant to be shared. "Anyways, here we all are. Two of us wishing to be anywhere else…"

Sam raised an eyebrow at Elijah, her question clear: did he wish to be anywhere else?

When he only shrugged, Sam accepted the footman's assistance into the carriage and took the seat next to Elijah.

"I am most certain my dear sister and I can find a pair of gentlemen who would be more than willing to escort two beautiful ladies to the playhouse," Jude teased with a pout.

"No chance of my wife joining another man for an evening out."

The couple entered the carriage and had no more sat before the door closed.

Sam adjusted on the bench, sliding her thigh to rest against Eli's. The dim interior—and the volume of her skirts—hid her subtle move from sight, but Elijah's sideways glance told her he was aware of her every move, though he did not draw away.

Interesting.

"It is my understanding that tonight's performance is to be a tragedy."

"Taming of the Shrew?" Simon inquired.

"That is a comedy, my dear husband."

"Any beautiful woman transformed into a shrew is certainly a tragedy," Simon retorted. "Then it is the one where the king loses his head?"

"No, guess again."

Simon tapped his chin in thought, and Sam could practically see him thinking through all the works of Shakespeare.

"It is Romeo and Juliet," Sam offered before Simon became any more flustered. "A grand love story with an ill-fated ending."

Simon huffed with irritation. "I have read the work, studied the aged writings of Shakespeare. Of all his plays, I think it his most implausible story."

"How so?" Eli asked, breaking his silence.

"No man or woman so deeply in love would go to such lengths to prove their affection. It is ludicrous." Simon nodded, as if his decree were fact and there was little point in refuting its validity.

Just the thought made Sam shake her head. Her time spent around Simon had increased so much she'd started thinking much like him: validity. She hardly knew the meaning of the word, yet was able to use it in a proper sentence, even if only in her thoughts.

"The notion is not ludicrous," Jude countered, turning to face Simon. "I know a certain woman who was willing—and prepared—to turn herself over to the magistrate to prove her love. Primed to spend an indeterminable amount of time locked in The Tower. And she would have done it without a second thought if only to show her love for another."

Jude clearly spoke of herself and her past with Simon, though Elijah likely did not know the story. She'd need share it with him at a later time, but this evening was about them…and Sam finding out what would happen next in her dream of his hand inching ever higher up her leg. Her body seemed to understand what came next, but Sam craved the physical knowledge over her own imagination.

"You are correct, Judith, as seems to be your habit."

"May I have you commit that uttering to paper and have Sam and Lord Ridgefeld sign as witnesses?"

"Not a chance," Simon muttered with a chuckle. "And do stop scaring Lord Ridgefeld. He must think the pair of you overbearing and demanding. The man will never set his sights on a leg shackle if you two are an example of the ladies to be found among society."

Elijah stiffened beside her. "I certainly have no aversion to marriage, my lord."

Sam risked a glance in Jude's direction and noted her sister's knowing grin. While Sam had no aversion to marriage, neither did she plan to step into the role of wife quickly.

"Call me Simon—or Cart—and every sane man should have a healthy aversion to marriage, or they will never survive the ordeal."

Jude straightened in her seat and crossed her arms. "You best be jesting, my lord, or you shall not survive the night!"

"As I said, Ridgefeld, marriage is utter insanity," Simon continued. "Thankfully, I am also a firm believer that a man must be a bit insane to hold any sense in his head."

"Oh, you!" Jude uncrossed her arms and slipped her hand into Simon's. "I knew you loved me."

"Against my better judgment—and the advice of the Dowager Countess Cartwright—I do adore you." He squeezed her hand. Many would think he kidded, but Simon rarely joked. In fact, Sam was certain that unless there was a written numeric formulae for creating a jest, her brother-in-law was incapable of it. "Now, let us not monopolize the conversation. Ridgefeld and I have made startling progress with his grandfather's collection over the last two days."

By not monopolizing the conversation, Cart clearly meant he sought to refocus the discussion on another topic that interested him: anything to do with antiquities or collecting objects of advanced age.

"I expect it will take us another two days, at most, to sort through everything and confirm all the details on each piece." Elijah lit up much like Simon at the shift in conversation.

Would he be happy to be done with his time at the museum? What were his plans after that?

Sam would not expect him to stay in London over returning home…even for her.

Though she held no hold on him as he held no hold on her.

He was a distraction, and once he left London, Sam would need find another means of keeping the likes of Lord Gunther and Proctor at bay. The men sought a most scandalous association—much to Sam's dismay. She would be no man's mistress, no matter the promises such men made.

"I worked with my servants for over a month's time preparing everything, but I fear the collections multiplied on my journey to London." Both men laughed at Elijah's witty comment; Simon's an open, heartfelt chuckle, while the laugh of Sam's bench mate would be better described as reserved. "There are many memories hidden within mere objects. An adventure to Greece, a near-death experience off the coast of a tropical island when our ship took on water, or the time my grandfather was determined to climb a sheer vertical cliff in the Congo."

"You must have lived an exciting childhood, my lord," Jude sighed. "My sister and I were confined mostly to London and ventured farther than an hour's ride only a handful of times until last year."

"I must admit, you both appear intelligent and worldly. I never would have suspected the pair of you had never left England."

"But you would be surprised where we've traveled *inside* of England." It was Sam's and Jude's turn to laugh, while the men looked uncertain about what Sam spoke of. Jude had confessed she'd spoken with Simon about their combined past: their time spent stealing into and out of London's finest homes without anyone the wiser until Lord Cartwright discovered their nightly escapades and demanded Jude give up her scandalous activities…and return the items she and Sam had worked so hard to steal. "We are worldly in our own way."

"Even if you had been kept in a cell for your entire life, I still would have thought you captivating," Simon gushed.

"You go too far, my lord." Sam turned a pointed stare on her brother-in-law. "If she'd seen that fate, her skin would be pasty, her hair limp and dull, and she'd be as feral as a wild cat."

Sounds of revelry invaded the interior of the carriage, and Simon gazed out the windowpane. "We have arrived. Lord Haversham was kind enough to give us use of his private box so we will have no need to mingle with the general masses."

Sam only smiled, knowing she planned to do her best to keep herself—and Elijah—out of the private box and deep in the shadows off the lighted paths.

#

The trio interacted as if they'd known one another for longer than the current London Season. Elijah was undoubtedly the outsider in the group, yet he enjoyed the back and forth between Sam and her sister, as well as Lord Cartwright's input. The earl never intended to incite laughter with his comments; however, the man possessed an unknown talent for making a jest. And as they traversed the crowd within the outdoor theater, their easy conversation continued.

Despite the paper crammed in his trouser pocket, Eli found he enjoyed their company immensely, and his pride swelled at having Miss Samantha on his arm as they collected drinks and hurried to their box before the play began.

He'd debated calling on the other men listed on the betting sheet, but he'd been stumped as to what to say to them. Brandishing threats or instigating a duel would be no more proper in this situation than demanding Sam stay far away from the group of lecherous men hell-bent on ruining her before all of society.

He felt his blood boil at the very thought of the group's nefarious designs. Betting on Sam's innocence like one would on a horse race…unthinkable, despicable, and uncivilized.

"Lord Ridgefeld," Sam asked, tugging on his arm. "Is all as it should be?"

"Very." He managed a weak smile, but felt the strain to keep his anger within. "However, I think I would relish a spot of fresh air before continuing to our box. I am unused to such crowds, and I am feeling a bit overwhelmed."

She eyed him suspiciously, knowing there was something more than a sense of claustrophobia that clung to him. "I will come with you."

"This is not necessary—"

"Of course, it is," Cart said. "Samantha knows the location of Haversham's box; otherwise, you might very well be wandering the theater in search of us long after the performance begins. If I am to sit through the entire blasted thing, so are you."

"It is the only noble option, my lord," Eli answered. "Miss Samantha and I will return before the play is underway."

"See that you do." It was Sam's twin who offered the warning, her glare squarely on her sister.

If Eli didn't know women were strictly forbidden from entering White's, he'd believe Lady Cartwright was privy to the wager he'd ripped from the betting book. Maybe he should speak with the countess and discover the best course for keeping Sam out of harm's way. Eli's offer of marriage would certainly be the most direct way of keeping Sam's reputation from being tarnished by the men's petty wager.

But would Lady Cartwright offer him assistance, or would she rebuff his honorable intentions with Sam?

"This way, Lord Ridgefeld." Sam steered him from the crowd to several lit paths bordered by shrubs and hedges on each side. "The trails are notably untraveled at this time of the evening."

The buzz of conversation and laughter from the playhouse crowd faded the farther they walked toward the paths that seemed to travel outward and wind around the outdoor theater. Eli guided her down a narrow path just wide enough for them to walk side-by-side, her top occasionally snagging on a wayward branch.

They continued past a private nook with a bench.

"Your gown is stunning this evening. And your hair, I have not seen it styled in such a fashion before." The words tumbled from his mouth, one after the other. Eli was little better than a smitten schoolboy with his first infatuation. Shockingly, he realized, Sam was, indeed, the first woman he'd felt anything more than friendship for. Fondness and affection were growing rapidly. Almost more rapidly than was comfortable. "I think sedated hues suit you."

Now he sounded a true English dandy; the kind who flitted around like a butterfly with garb colored to match.

She kept her gaze trained on the ground before her as they ambled. "I've always favored bright, bold fabrics over muted tones, but I think you are correct, Elijah."

Would there ever be a spoken word as sweet as his name on her lips?

A dandy and a poet. Very fitting they were to watch a Shakespearean play.

"My lord." She halted, causing Eli to either pause beside her or leave her behind—and he had no intention of leaving her. Why did the thought ring true for more than just this moment? "I owe you a reward," she breathed softly.

His reward? Her company was reward enough to keep him satisfied for many days to come.

Eli kept silent as she stepped closer to him, pressing her body to his. He feared moving—or even breathing—as it would surely sever the connection between them and douse the fire that resided in her intense gaze and rocketed through his entire body.

"You owe me nothing." How to explain it was he who owed her? Besides the late marquis, Eli had never felt close to another person, never trusted another not to hurt him by leaving. But Sam…everything about her was different. She threw her entire self into every outing they shared, damn the consequences. She was light, yet inside, he sensed a darker, deeper soul who had experienced her own hurt, but never did she allow that to cast a shadow over her present. "I have a confession, Sam."

Her form, a moment before melting against him—curving to fit the contours of his large body—now stiffened. Eli wrapped his arms around her to keep her close. He would never find the courage to say what must be said if she was not in his arms.

"Elijah?" The question had barely left her lips when she rose to her tiptoes and pressed her lips to his.

The kiss was instantly demanding, drawing from Eli, and he gave himself over to her as her hands encircled his neck and ran through his hair.

Needy. It was the only way he could describe it.

She needed him.

He needed her.

The only question was: Were they searching for the same thing within the other?

It didn't matter. Eli would give her whatever she demanded.

Attention. Complete adoration. Love. Possessions. Fancy gowns. Costly jewels. His home.

Anything she desired, he was willing to give her if it was in his power to do so.

The only thing beyond his power was walk away. Leave her. That he could not—would not—do.

A trumpet blared, signaling the performance was to start momentarily.

Reluctantly, Eli pulled back when every instinct told him to hold tight and never let go.

She looked up at him, her eyes hooded with lust—and dare he hope something far deeper?

Her usual coy smile returned. "I believe we are now even once more, my lord."

They were nowhere near even. However, his confession need wait for another time as she set her hand on his arm and they started back toward Lord and Lady Cartwright, waiting in the Haversham's private box.

Chapter Twenty-Nine

Eli stared up at the darkened townhouse before him, pulling his riding jacket tighter to ward off the chill. No light shone from any window, and no activity outside led him to believe anyone was home. The night was growing late. His borrowed horse stomped its hoof on the cobbled drive and tossed its head, showing displeasure at being out in the cold when he could be warm in the Cartwright stables.

It had been an entire day since Eli had seen or heard from Sam. Over twenty-four hours spent eating, sleeping, or laboring away at the museum, but his every thought had revolved around her. Her perfect rosebud lips, her scorching red locks, her unsettling stare that always seemed to find the tiny things Eli wished to keep hidden, but then she would just as seamlessly transform into the coy hoyden.

Eli had finally given up on his day's work when he'd mislabeled a saber from the Orient as a scythe sickle from the wheat fields of England used after the Great Fire of London. It was a mistake no true collector would have made, and thankfully, Lord Cartwright had not discovered the error before Elijah had. He'd decided then it was time to return to the Cartwright townhouse; a meal, warm bath, and sleep were exactly what his body—and mind—craved.

Besides Sam in his arms.

He pulled the note from his pocket, a single line jotted on pristine, cream paper.

The Cartwright butler had handed him the note, addressed to him, when he'd returned from the museum.

14 Saint George Street, Hanover Square – 10 o'clock, sharp

Maybe the sender meant ten o'clock in the morning, not that night; however, Sam's elegant script was unmistakable, and Eli would not risk missing another outing with her even if it took place in an unfamiliar part of London, at an unfamiliar home—with no explanation as to why. Eli spied a post where the drive disappeared behind the house. Tying the reins securely, he searched each window for any sign that someone was within.

The sound of carriage wheels and hooves sounded in the near distance, drawing Eli back toward the street, flanked on each side by neatly kept homes. He took shelter next to a tall shrub, keeping himself hidden from view as the carriage approached from the same direction he'd journeyed from. To his surprise, the coach slowed to a crawl before turning into the drive at 14 Saint George Street and stopping a mere several paces from where he stood in the shadows.

He was intrigued, there was no question about it. What exactly had Sam planned for their evening?

Sam exited the conveyance as if reading his thoughts. Her shimmering gold gown became visible only for a moment before she pulled her long cloak tightly around her. Eli noted that her hair was pinned under a cap, masking its vibrant color, but he still knew it was her: from the graceful curve of her neck, the confident set of her shoulders, and the tilt of her chin. That he also recognized the coach and driver from the previous evening only confirmed it was her.

The carriage pulled away, leaving her standing outside the residence, clutching her handbag in one hand as something else hung from her other.

"Miss Samantha," he called, stepping from the shadows.

"Shhhh, my lord," she hissed, meeting him halfway. "Take this. Tie it tightly."

Sam held a black domino mask out to him, her own disguise matching but in gold and outlined in silver.

Eli took the mask and turned it over in his hands. "What is this?"

"Do hurry and don your mask, my lord, before anyone happens upon us." She did not hesitate to tie her golden disguise securely to her face, a simple bow at the back of her head as her handbag dangled from her wrist.

The loud bells of St. George's rang through the crisp night, sounding the ten o'clock hour.

"Come, it is to begin, and we cannot be tardy." Her eyes fairly glowed in the dark with her excitement, and any lingering doubt on his part melted away as he quickly secured his own disguise.

His grandfather had been wrong. One did not need travel the seven seas to find adventure. It lay about

London proper in great abundance if one had the right guide.

She grasped his hand the moment he was finished and pulled him toward the darkened house.

"There appears to be no one in residence."

"Oh, my lord—I will refer to you only as such this evening—what lay beyond the front door of this townhouse is certain to shock you," she said breathlessly as they reached the front stoop.

"What shall I call you?"

"Whatever you'd like, my lord." Her teasing tone mellowed to something else as if his chosen endearment meant much to her. "But you must decide quickly before the door opens."

Sam knocked loudly on the door, and footsteps sounded within.

"Do not delay…" She raised her eyebrow, challenging him to answer.

"My fair maiden," he replied without further thought. When she scrunched her nose, he tried again. "My perfect English rose?" He thought the play of a red rose and her burnt color hair was perfect, yet her expression said the name did not suit her at all. "My enchanting marchioness?"

Her eyes narrowed behind her mask before she chuckled deeply. "Splendid. No one will suspect who I truly am."

Unease settled heavily upon his shoulders as the door opened to reveal a manservant, smartly dressed in green and black with his own mask in place. "Welcome," he said in greeting. "My master is pleased you are here. Do remove your overgarments and come this way, the game is preparing to start."

Sam did as instructed and started after the man, but Eli held her back and whispered, "Where have you brought me? And what *game* does he speak of?"

"Heavens, my lord, can you not tell a lark at play? I do not know who lives here. Nor will any of the other guests. I overheard Payton—" her voice dropped with a hiss when she uttered her sister's name—"speak of the thrill of a night such as this, and I simply had to know more, see more, experience more. And so, here we are!"

The manservant pulled open a set of double doors and stood aside for Sam and Elijah to enter the room. "Enjoy your evening. Do let any servant know if you are in need of anything. You will not know my master from any other player."

"Are you ready, my lord?" she asked with a wink, and he knew her mask hid her smile.

Elijah was in no way ready as his gaze set upon the room before them. At least five tables were spread around the large space, each filled with masked men and several women dressed as if they were attending a grand ball—a masquerade ball. Two servants were posted at every table; one handing out drinks perched on a silver platter held aloft, and another seated among the guests.

"A card game?" he asked.

"Not just any card game, a high-stakes card game where more is at stake than coin." Sam moved from his side, and the sway of her hips as she entered the room held his attention. "Come, my lord," she beckoned over her shoulder like the siren she was.

It was then he noticed her gown plunged in the back, almost to her rounded derriere. Where had she gotten such a risqué dress? Certainly, her family could not know of its existence, or Sam's nighttime outing wearing the alluring golden creation. He strode to her side, wondering if her neckline was as daring.

Elijah had no need to see for himself. Every eye in the room had turned to watch them enter, and he was not foolish enough to think anyone noticed him at her side.

He'd hailed her as enchanting.

He could not have imagined how accurate that was. His only regret was that he had, as yet, failed to request her hand as his marchioness.

From the lecherous stares hidden not at all behind the masks of many men…and the envious glares of the dozen women in attendance, he should not wait long to ask.

Chapter Thirty

Sam stilled her nerves, pressing them down as she moved through the room, hips swaying with each step. Not that she sought attention; however, she did hope her sensual appeal had players letting their guards down and loosening their purse strings enough to afford Sam a few large hands. Her coin purse dangled at her side, full of her monthly pin money—and the bit extra she'd taken from Marce's emergency box in her office.

Elijah's presence at her side, one step behind her, was felt by all in the room.

Her protector.

Why did that fill her with a sense of rightness?

Never had she needed another to look after her, care for her, or in any way feel responsible for her well-being.

"My enchanting marchioness." His voice caressed her neck. "I fear the game will not begin at all this night with your presence distracting so many."

It was true. Even the servants had stopped setting drinks before guests or shuffling cards and distributing chips.

Sam found a table with two open seats and started toward them. If her confidence were going to last, she'd need Elijah close for the entirety of their evening. The players at the table were total strangers as each followed the house rules, their faces covered with disguises of every shape and color. Dominoes, fairies, butterflies, Grecian gods and goddesses, feathered and furred animals sat at each table.

It was like stepping into a dreamland…the princess of all with her prince at her elbow.

"Do sit," a man called, motioning Sam to take the open seat next to him, the other vacant chair stood two players down.

Something in the man's tone had Sam moving past the chair he'd motioned to and sitting between a portly man and a rail-thin woman in modest garb, leaving Elijah to take the seat next to the offending man. She lowered herself into the plush, high-back chair as a servant set a flute of champagne at her elbow.

"Thank you," she mumbled, unconsciously lightening her normally deep tone.

She caught Eli's eye across the table after he too had accepted a drink—and quickly drained it before nodding for another.

Yes, the man was interesting. An entertaining distraction and an agreeable companion.

She stopped short of adding his talents for pleasure as her face heated at the thought. Thankfully, her golden mask did its job and hid her discomfiture well.

How had Payton known of such a gathering? Sam shuddered to think of her young sister attending without some sort of protection against the lascivious stares. She would think only of the game at hand, not about her safety.

"I am Viggo, my lady," the offensive man leaned slightly forward, blocking Elijah from her line of sight. "May I request what I am to call a woman as beautiful as you?"

Viggo? Certainly not his true name.

"How, may I inquire, do you know that beauty lies behind my guise?" She hadn't meant the question to be flirtatious, but the sparkle she noted in the man's eyes told her he'd taken it as permission to set his attentions on her. "I could be pockmarked from disease or lacking teeth."

Sam thought she heard Elijah chuckle at her outlandish words, though he was still blocked from view.

"It is your soul which is beautiful, my lady." His words flowed sweet and easy as honey.

"And if I am not a lady?"

"You can still be beautiful, even with lacking pedigree."

"She is *my* enchanting marchioness." Elijah announced to the table at large.

But Viggo didn't move his stare from Sam. "Your coquettish wordplay wounds me, *my lady*."

It was hard to determine if the man's words sounded more like a snake's slither or a cat's hiss. Either way, both were repulsive. And it stung to think a man thought her so easily claimed. Sam had come for a spot of fun, not to find herself on the receiving end of yet another scandalous proposition.

"Do tell me your evening is not spoken for."

"Her evening is most certainly spoken for. And the one after that, and so on, Viggo."

Sam gasped at Elijah's thunderously booming voice. He was angry, yet Viggo was harmless enough and was certainly no cause for drawing undue attention to them or reason to insult their host by disrupting his party. Her stern look did nothing to keep Elijah in his seat as he stood, tapping Viggo on his shoulder to gain his full attention.

"My lord," Sam purred. "Do sit. It is obvious to all who witnessed us enter I *belong* to you." She put added emphasis on belong, suspecting Viggo did not seek a lady but more along the lines of a courtesan. "Let us enjoy a rousing game of cards."

Elijah regained his seat, and Viggo turned his attention to the servant announcing the card game to be played. Vingt-et-un was simple mathematics, and Sam was admirable at figuring numbers in her head. The table next to them was set up for Hazard, favoring dice instead of cards.

She set her coin pouch on the table and withdrew a note to exchange for playing chips, several other players doing the same. The first hand was dealt, and both Sam and Elijah were forced to give up their ante for the round. The next several hands went in much the same way with Viggo winning far more than he lost. Blast it, Sam should have listened more when Payton instructed her in card play: what hands to discard, and which to stake a sizeable pot on. Before long, only a half-dozen chips were stacked before her, and she was worried her evening would end far earlier than desired.

A miserable failure.

Not that Sam expected to win, but her first time gambling outside Craven House should last longer than a walk in Hyde Park, certainly.

Elijah's chips were at least triple hers.

One more hand and she'd request Elijah escort her to another game table, one more to her liking.

The servant dealt two cards to each player, and Sam quickly picked hers up, holding them close to keep the other guests from seeing her hand. Two tens.

A total of twenty points…the optimal hand was twenty-one.

Marvelous.

Though no one could see behind her mask, she knew the importance of not giving away her hand, a tell as Payton would say. The upturned corner of the mouth, the nervous twitch of an eye, or even the fidgeting of cards were enough to signal your confidence in your cards. She would win her first hand.

The guests either threw in their cards, added a wager, or passed to the next player. Elijah passed, not raising the chip count, and then it was Viggo's turn. He threw added chips in just as often as he discarded his hand—however, this time, Sam was lucky. He pushed his entire stack into the center of the table.

It was easily four times as much money as she'd brought with her—and ten times more than what was stacked in front of her.

"It is your turn, my lady," the portly gentleman on her right said.

Sam bit her lip. She still had a few coins in her handbag, but even with that, it was not enough to match Viggo's wager. Her hand went to the opal bob dangling from her ear. She'd brought nothing else of value with her.

Twenty was a better hand than most that'd won the past dozen hands.

"I am happy to lend you enough coin to match my wager," Viggo said gallantly. "If you win, you can return my funds. If you lose…" He let his words trail off, but Sam was in no way disillusioned to the fact that the man would demand she pay her debt in less reputable ways.

She took one last look at her hand before setting her cards face down and removing her opal earbobs and pushing them to the middle with the other chips. The woman next to her gasped, her hand pressing to her covered bosom as if to keep her erratic heart in her chest.

Elijah cleared his throat in an attempt to gain her attention. Though it would anger him, she avoided his stare and smiled behind her mask.

"I think my opals make the wager even," she said. "Do you agree, Viggo?"

The other players threw their cards down in defeat, Elijah with them.

"Show your hands," the servant called.

Sam gulped when Viggo triumphantly showed his cards—an ace and a ten.

Twenty-one.

Sam slid her cards across the table, face-down.

Viggo chuckled, knowing he'd bested her. "It is a shame you will lose such a precious keepsake," he tsked as if remorseful for being the one to take her opal earbobs.

"Do not fret. I was well aware of the risk involved when I placed them upon the table.

"I wish all men played with as much grace in losing as you, my lady."

She stood and noticed Viggo's eyes narrow behind his mask when Elijah also pushed back his chair to depart.

"Do not go," Viggo said. "Mayhap you can fulfill your debt and retrieve your jewels."

Sam didn't like the insinuation in the man's tone, and feared Elijah knew exactly where the man's thoughts lay when he growled.

"Come now, pretty lady," Viggo coaxed. "I am certain you do not wish to return home without your treasure. I only ask for a private moment with you."

# # #

Elijah had had bloody well enough of the vile, despicable man and his inappropriate comments. "Viggo, you have overstepped the bounds of propriety. You will apologize at once for your audacious behavior and crude manners. No noble gentleman speaks to a proper lady in such a disrespectful tone."

His knuckles turned white from his clenched fists when Viggo only let out a loud cackle. Three men at the table stood, deciding another game would not be had at this table anytime soon, and moved off to find vacant seats at other games.

"Proper lady?" Viggo continued to chuckle around his words. "Your *enchanting marchioness* has already admitted she is no proper lady. And if I am honest, it would not be hard to ensure she becomes *my* enchanting marchioness—at least for one evening. I will call her any title she desires as long as she fulfills *my* desires."

"I think it wise we depart, my lord." It took Eli a moment to recognize the tug on his sleeve was Samantha. He shook off her hold and stood from his chair suddenly, it fell over backwards, knocking into a man at the next table. "El—my lord!"

"We will not depart until this scoundrel apologizes to you," Elijah bit the words out, each syllable harsher than the last. "Now, Viggo…do you have something to say?"

The offending man had also stood. A single raven-black lock of hair falling forward to cover part of his mask, his body relaxed and unprepared for the fight that would ensue if he did not issue a request for forgiveness.

Eli had sensed he knew the man when he'd first offered Sam a seat beside him, but the man's voice had been unfamiliar. Now, the raven hair and beady eyes…

Lord Proctor.

The man's name written in bold, self-assured script on the betting book page. Had he recognized Sam behind her mask and hair covering? Worse yet, had Sam known it was Proctor and openly toyed with him?

Suddenly, remaining a moment longer in the vile man's presence was more than Eli's restraint could handle. His fists threatened to lash out at Proctor, no matter how much his good sense was saying to walk away before things got out of hand and Sam's identity was exposed.

"My lords," a jovial man chuckled, stepping between the men. "Do resume play or depart. This is meant to be a friendly spot of fun at the gaming tables, not a competition of force."

Sam had retreated a few steps, leaving her lost earbobs on the table all but forgotten.

Certainly, it would be wise to leave.

Eli looked Proctor in the eye with his next words. "My apologies for disrupting your evening. I am man enough to admit and remedy a situation when I am at fault. Thank you for your kindness." It was meant for their host, but his threat was evident. "Do enjoy your evening."

His hand flung out and snatched Sam's forgotten opal jewels—unconcerned with Proctor demanding their return as their rightful owner—and slipped them into his pocket for safekeeping until he could return them to her.

With a nod to their host, Eli pivoted and joined Sam as they made their way from the gaming room. It did not escape his notice that she kept a few feet separating them as they departed.

Was she angry or embarrassed at the man's lewd insinuations?

If she wasn't, Elijah was furious enough for both of them.

The manservant quickly helped Sam into her cloak before assisting Eli with his.

And as speedily as they'd entered the townhouse, they were once again standing outside—alone. His horse still remained tied to the post, and the Craven House carriage was nowhere in sight. The temperatures had plummeted further since their arrival, and a bone-chilling gust caught the edge of Sam's cloak and whipped it around her legs.

She ripped her mask from her face, not bothering to untie it, and swung around to face him.

He expected to see tears, anguish etching her delicate face; instead, there was only fierce rage.

She threw her mask to the ground and stepped toward him. "How dare you claim me like a piece of chattel. I am not something to be possessed, *my lord.*"

She was furious with him? "I only meant to stop the man from casting doubt upon your character."

"This was to be an enjoyable evening, garbed in disguise, my identity protected. The man was harmless, his words held no insult to me. He did not know me…it was only meaningless fun. The night was to be a time for everyone present to act out of character…"

"He propositioned you before the entire table," Elijah thundered, removing his own mask with a quick tug. He needed her to see his face, know he only meant to protect her. "Any gentleman would not stand by and allow such dishonor to be leveled upon a woman."

She crossed her arms. "His insinuation, his *proposition* as you call it, did not fall too far from our own agreement."

The accusation had him stumbling back, her words cutting deeper than any dagger.

"Companionship and reward," she continued, closing the distance between them and pressing her body to his. She lifted up on her tiptoes to kiss him but paused a mere inch from their lips connecting. "And speaking of rewards, I do believe I owe you for accompanying me this evening, though the night did not progress how I expected."

He turned his face away, her lips landing at his jawline. "No. My part in our agreement was not to—"

"Your part of our bargain has been satisfied, Elijah," she whispered. "Your company as a distraction from my mundane life is no longer needed. You may return to Liverpool—or wherever you call home—with a clean conscience, your side of our arrangement repaid in full."

"This has never been merely an arrangement to me—sordid or otherwise," he confessed.

"Unfortunately, I only sought a few days of dalliance."

She could not mean that; however when he searched her face, he saw only determination. "And I sought a courtship, Samantha."

She shook her head.

"I care for you. Very deeply." It was her turn to turn away from him. "Look at me, Sam." He reached forward and set his fingers against her chin, pushing her to look at him, to truly see what his eyes held and believe every word he uttered. "I did not come to London merely to deliver my grandfather's collection to the museum. If that were the goal, I would have sent the lot of it with trusted emissaries and remained at my home."

When she remained silent, he continued, "I agree, I may have reacted excessively to the situation tonight, but I only meant to protect you from harm."

"There is a thin line between the need to protect or possess. And I have no intention of being possessed. Neither do I need protection." She made to push past him as the sound of carriage wheels against cobblestones sounded. Their host must have been kind enough to send for her driver. "Now, I will bid you goodnight and Godspeed on your journey back to Liverpool."

"I have no intention of leaving, Sam." He would not abandon her again, no matter how many times she turned him away. Even if Cartwright—with Judith in tow—were to bid him keep his distance from Sam, Elijah would be unable to. The blasted woman had infiltrated his every thought…his every desire…his every hope for the future.

"Well, I have no intention of continuing our acquaintance, the distraction it once offered is no longer appealing to me." She bent and retrieved her discarded guise before lifting her chin and pushing past him. Her driver held the carriage door open and assisted her in before he climbed aboard. "Home, Mr. Curtis," she shouted.

Elijah stood frozen, watching the carriage depart without Sam so much as glancing at the window as she rolled away.

A distraction. A dalliance. Of no consequence.

Her angry claims assaulted him one by one, bringing back memories from his journey to America and another woman who had no room for him in her life.

He'd tucked his tail and run then…straight back to his ship to sail for home.

Elijah had less than a day's worth of tasks remaining at the museum.

Was he destined to repeat his actions?

Put distance between him and Sam and pray that his heart mended with time?

Though he suspected when a man's heart was shattered as many times as his, there was no way to locate all the splinters to piece it back together.

But every inch of him shouted there was nothing he wanted more than to try.

Chapter Thirty-One

Sam allowed the tears to fall as her carriage hurried toward home, her weeping masked from Mr. Curtis by the sound of the wheels. Every part of her threatened to fragment into tiny pieces and scatter in the wind, but she'd made it to safety, and in the privacy of her darkened coach, did not have to worry about hiding her suffering. Her weeping turned to gut-wrenching sobs as she pulled her legs up against her chest on the bench and did her best to disappear into the oblivion of her wrap. The heavy black garment was certain to be the only thing remaining when the carriage arrived at Craven House.

She snuffled into her cloak.

The mask, handmade that afternoon to perfectly match her gown, lay forgotten on the seat next to her. How had she ever thought attaching herself to Elijah would be wise?

Sam grasped the loose fabric of the seat and wrenched until her fingers ached from the pressure.

Their outings—the boxing club, the phaeton race outside of Hyde Park, and tonight, gambling—were all things no proper lady would do. They were exactly the activities a man did with his mistress. So why did it hurt her so when another accused her of being nothing better than a courtesan?

Had that not been the game she'd planned all along? There was no one to blame but herself—and her inability to keep her affection for Elijah a secret. Truly, she'd never meant to care for him, only punish him.

Why had she treated Elijah so horribly for protecting her honor—her reputation—from being sullied? He was kind, he was loyal, and he had a tender for her.

Sam had never expected to see the man again. Worse yet, to learn he traveled to London for her and her alone. He'd left Hollybrooke without a single thought about her feelings or the injury his dismissal of their new association might cause.

Sam wiped a tear from her cheek as it blazed a path down her face. A tousled curl hung across her forehead, and Sam hastily reset her hairpin to return it to its place.

In truth, Elijah had been far more to her than a mere distraction from the moment he happened upon her in the gathering storm. She didn't want him to be anymore. She wanted his attention…but any mention of affection would only serve to hurt her more when he removed himself from her life.

Elijah had admitted he cared for her and that he intended courtship.

Had he only said those things because of Viggo's insistent flirtation at the card table?

Viggo…something about the man's voice, his looks, and his persistence reminded her of someone. His indecent comments had indeed alarmed her, making her all the more grateful for Elijah's presence.

She'd been the one to act excessively. Why push Elijah away when she longed for him: his tender touch, his caressing words, and his passionate kiss. Worse still, she'd said the most horrid things, utterances sure to guarantee he never wanted to see her again. The lump in her throat blocked her sob of remorse.

Salted tears streamed down her face, falling to the delicate silk of her gown. The material was ruined, but Sam continued to let her anguish out, unconcerned with the state of her expensive frock.

All too soon, her carriage slowed, and Mr. Curtis climbed down to open the door.

She brushed the tears from her cheeks, though there was no helping her disheveled appearance. Her face was certainly splotchy with upset, and her eyes surely must be a red to match her hair hidden under her cap. But the hour was late, and with any luck—not that her luck had been stellar of late—she could slip into the house and up to her room without anyone the wiser. The darkness would hide her appearance from Mr. Curtis well enough, the elderly manservant's sight having been compromised by age years ago.

"Will you be need'n anything else, miss?" he asked when she accepted his offered hand.

"No, thank you."

"Ye have a good slumber, Miss Samantha." He kept his gaze on the ground as she fled toward the door.

Mr. Curtis had been with Craven House long before Sam and Jude were born, having fled with their mother—Madame Sasha—when she, Marce, and Garrett were thrown from their home after Marce and Garrett's father, Lord Buckston, had passed away. Curtis was a kind and compassionate man, never overstepping his role among the houseful of women, but keeping a close eye on her and her siblings.

"And you, as well," she called over her shoulder when she paused before opening the front door. "Thank you."

She didn't wait to see the man's questioning look regarding what she was offering him thanks for, but pushed the door open and stepped into the warmth and security of her home. A place Marce did all in her power to keep for their family. A place Garrett hadn't resided in years. A place Jude had sought to escape. A place where Payton was free to hone her skills at cards. And a place where Sam would likely remain all her days.

Her father had abandoned her, as had her mother to death, and Jude to marriage.

Those who should love her above all else.

She did not deserve Elijah's kindness after the horrible things she'd said to him, especially knowing he'd lived a similar life to her own. His mother abandoning him, and his father and grandfather succumbing to death.

His isolation was far more startling than hers.

Her lip quivered, and she sensed another sob rising from her chest.

She pushed herself toward the stairs, knowing she could not keep her cries at bay for long.

"Where have you been?" Marce asked, her candle held high to illuminate her face as she traveled down the staircase, Garrett only a few steps behind her. "We have been worried half to death."

"You should not be concerned with me," Sam retorted, her tone harsher than she'd intended. Her siblings fretted over her—two of the few still around to care anyway. "I am home…and unscathed."

Partly unscathed, she longed to add. Though they could not see her wound, for it resided inside, certain to fester with no possibility of healing.

Garrett pushed past Marce to stand on the landing above Sam. "Bloody hell!" He threw his hands wide. "You think you are unscathed?"

"What is your interest in my whereabouts, Garrett? You have never bothered with much more than a simple greeting or hurtful tease." It was another thing she resented, though she hadn't fully understood that until now. Her only brother was close to Jude, and, of course, Marce, but he rarely paid any mind to Sam or Payton. "I do not answer to you. You are neither my father nor my guardian."

His eyes narrowed with the insult, and a jolt of remorse at her cruel words coursed through her.

"Let us take this to my office before we wake the household." Marce's petite frame floated past both her siblings to the foyer and then toward the room she used as their household office. Sam and Garrett followed obediently in her wake. "Now, where were you all evening?" Marce asked once more when Garrett closed the door behind the trio.

Marce walked to her desk before setting down her light and turning to face Sam. Her expression was serene, as usual, but her lips were compressed, the only sign she was upset—possibly even furious. Opposite of her eldest sibling's settled nature, Garrett strode purposefully across the room to the far bank of windows and back again, his agitation obvious.

Sam's unease grew at their reversed roles. Garrett was normally the blasé brother who took no interest in her, while Marce's disciplinary standards matched that of a taskmaster.

"I attended a private card game."

"A gambling party?"

"I wore a disguise, so it is doubtful anyone recognized me." She held up her gold and silver mask. "I was not careless."

"If you are worried about someone recognizing you, then it was obviously a place a proper lady should not be." Marce raised a brow in question. "Who hosted this party?"

Sam thought about lying but knew Marce would see through her deceit. "I am unsure. No names were given, but the house is on Saint George Street in Hanover Square."

"Saint George, you say?" Garrett stopped pacing and spun to face her. "Oh, bloody hell, it was Damon, Lord Ashford's card party. How did you hear of the gathering? Whom did you attend with?" He didn't slow his questions long enough for Sam to answer, not that she wanted to answer his questions at all. "A woman can only gain entrance if they are *escorted* by a man of good standing."

She could not admit she'd heard of the party from Payton. Could she?

They had never been close, Payton being younger than she and Jude and therefore an outsider. Did she owe the girl any loyalty?

Certainly, their blood tie required Sam not speak her name. "Lord Ridgefeld was kind enough to escort me." There it was. Her sibling would have no objection to Elijah; he was known to Cart, a patron of the museum, and a nobleman.

Garrett threw his arms in the air and swung his head toward Marce. "Did I not inform you of the man's intentions?" he snarled.

Did they know Elijah sought to court her with marriage in mind? Was it possible he'd already spoken with Cart and Garrett about his intentions? "What do you know of Elijah's intentions?" Sam demanded, settling her hands on her hips.

"Oh, so you do not deny it?" her brother countered. "…and it is Elijah now?"

"I do not know what I should be denying!"

"Hush!" Marce's fingertips massaged her forehead, and Sam noted for the first time that her sister was gowned in an ethereal, billowy, white nightshift, her equally white robe thrown over, the sash untied as if she'd been awakened suddenly. Even her normally expertly styled hair hung haphazardly in one long plait over her shoulder. "The pair of you are giving me a headache."

Garrett threw himself face down on the low chaise lounge with an exaggerated sigh.

Sam took her usual seat on the long, high-backed couch she normally shared with Jude and Payton. But she did not drop her gaze to her lap in preparation for a scolding. No, she kept her chin high, her shoulders straight, and her eyes level.

"Tell her!" Garrett said before burrowing his face deeper into the lounge. "I cannot."

Marce's eyes squinted shut and she held the bridge of her nose, forgoing massaging her forehead.

"What is going on?" Sam looked from Marce to Garrett and back again.

"Did you agree to be that *scoundrel's* mistress?" he asked, his voice muffled because his face was still pressed to the plush cushions of the lounge.

"Of course, not," she denied. "He propositioned me in a dark hall at Simon and Jude's introduction ball, but I soundly kicked him in the shin. The rascal took my meaning and hasn't approached me since."

"You just admitted he escorted you Lord Ashford's gambling party!"

"No." Sam shot to her feet. "I said, Lord Ridgefeld escorted me to the party, not Lord Proctor."

"Who is Lord Proctor?" Marce sighed.

"Another man from the betting book," Garrett seethed.

"I am utterly confused!"

"That makes two of us," Sam agreed. "What betting book?"

Garrett pushed to a seated position, his feet planted on the floor, his Hessian boots gleaming in the candlelight. "The blasted betting book at White's. Men record bets of all sorts, and wager everything from money to landholdings to farm animals."

"And my name is mentioned in this book?" she stammered. "Why would it be there?"

"It seems…" Marce's mouth pulled into a severe frown. "That men are wagering large amounts of coin on who will take you as their mistress first."

"*Were*," Garrett corrected.

"That is preposterous!" Sam laughed, garnering a stern look from both Marce and Garrett. "I have no intention of being any man's mistress, I assure you both."

"So Lord Ridgefeld has not made any inappropriate advances?" he prodded.

It would not do to speak of their arrangement, their evening in Lord Cummings' study, their outing to Gentleman Jackson's, or their phaeton race; however, their time in Hyde Park or their evening at Covent Garden was innocent enough so long as she did not speak of their moonlit stroll along the darkened paths.

Based on Garrett's reddened face, twitching eye, and flaring nostrils, it would be wise to admit nothing. "He most certainly has not. And what do you mean *were?*"

"Ridgefeld tore the page straight out of the betting book and stuffed it in his pocket."

"Then all record of the silly wager is gone?" she asked.

"I certainly hope so," Marce commented. "For your sake, of course. But why would Lord Ridgefeld take the wager page?"

"It was obvious he wasn't the one to start the bet. It was his first time at White's."

"Who else besides Lord Proctor and Ridgefeld were listed?"

"There were more?" Sam squeaked. "I cannot imagine—"

"Lord Gunther, Mr. Tobias Shillings, and Lord Meyton, though I have never made the acquaintance of the last two." Garrett stood and continued his pacing.

"You swear on your place in this household that you have not become some man's mistress?"

Sam should be offended by the question. Outraged her brother would even think she'd stoop to such a level. But, truly, their mother had been little more than a high-priced courtesan, and many thought Marce had also taken up the *family* business after their mother's death. How else could a young, impoverished female take care of four siblings and a large house? She and Jude had even begun to think their sister was bargaining her body as a means to keep food in their pantry and a roof over their heads. Never had Garrett so much as lifted a finger to help support their family financially.

"Of course, Samantha would never jeopardize her future by accepting such an unsavory offer," Marce said, coming to Sam's defense, but not surprisingly, her words lacked a bit of conviction as she eyed her sibling, searching for any indication she had, indeed, become what Marce had worked so hard to avoid for her family. When she didn't see what she feared in Sam's expression, Marce continued, "Now, I think it best we all find our beds. The night is growing late. I will have the housekeeper prepare your old room, Garrett."

Her brother moved toward the door. "Do not bother, I will return to my lodgings."

"It is late, and you are in no condition to travel." Marce spoke softly, attempting not to mention the stench of liquor on their brother. "At least allow Mr. Curtis to see you home in the carriage."

Garrett paused, his hand on the doorknob. "That is kind of you, dear sister, but I can see myself home."

"Very well." Marce collected her candle. "I will see you to the door. Sam, I shall see you in the morning. Do not sleep through breakfast."

Though the words were said softly, it was a demand. Sam nodded.

"Sleep well, Samantha." Garrett pulled the door open and thundered down the hall, Marce quick on his heels, shushing him the entire way.

There was nothing left to do but for Sam to find her own room. Slipping from the office, she used the servants' stairwell to avoid seeing Marce as her sister saw Garrett to the door and then climbed the main staircase.

Neither had noticed her distress or reddened face from her tears. Normally, she'd seek to hide her turmoil. This night, she'd longed for guidance, someone to notice her unusually despondent demeanor. Instruct her on what to do, how to fix the mess she'd made. She'd spent so many years keeping things to herself—rarely so much as allowing Jude into her inner workings—that she was unsure how to ask for what she needed.

Maybe a good night's rest and a bright morning would bring her answers, or at least the means for finding some semblance of closure with Elijah.

Chapter Thirty-Two

Elijah hunched over a crate, removing two identically wrapped square objects. The crate must have been packed for shipping by one of his servants because he had little idea what lay within the tightly bundled paper. Not that he was overly concerned with any of it. He had two crates and one trunk remaining then he would return to Liverpool.

And forget about his time in London.

Though, putting Samantha from his mind was an entirely different and likely impossible task.

A loud thump, followed by a yelp, sounded deep within the cavernous storerooms behind the museum proper. Eli made to stand, but several sets of feet rushed down the corridor outside the room he worked in.

Maybe travel would assist him. He'd had no urge for worldly adventure since his grandfather had passed away and his mother had crushed his spirit. Eli's journey to Hollybrooke had helped, but how much of that was due to Sam's unexpected presence? Honestly, London had been more enjoyable than he'd anticipated, as well—again, mostly because of Sam.

A leather-bound journal was wedged into the crate between another wrapped treasure and the wooden side. As he grasped it and opened to the first page, the scent of his grandfather surrounded him as he noted the man's neat script on the first page. Elijah set the journal aside. It was not the time for him to travel down the path of memories. Possibly he'd allow himself the luxury on the long journey back to Liverpool.

His time at White's with Lord Cartwright and Sam's brother was a unique time he'd hoped to repeat, that was until he'd spied Samantha's name—with his own linked to it—in that blasted betting book. He had no qualms about him and Sam being connected. His intentions were of the purest nature; however, the other men listed and the nature of the bet were highly inappropriate.

She'd insisted she would never seek to become any man's mistress; though her coquettish banter with the raven-haired lord—disguised as Viggo—spoke to the contrary. Had she enlisted Eli's accompaniment only to meet the man at the party? He could not handle such deception on her part. With any luck, he'd be gone and would never learn the extent of Sam's duplicity. He would depart before nightfall that very night, despite Lord and Lady Cartwright's insistence he stay as long as he desired.

Elijah preferred to depart immediately, yet obligation dictated he remain long enough to finish his work at the museum and see the late marquis' collection properly arranged and catalogued.

After that, his debt would be paid, his responsibilities fulfilled to both his grandfather's legacy and his promise to Lord Cartwright and Lord Cummings.

"My lord!" a male voice sounded from the door. Eli turned to see Ames, the young apprentice assigned as his helper during his time at the museum. "I did not expect you until later today. I came in early to organize things for your arrival."

"Sorry to startle you." Eli stood from where he'd hunched over the crate. "I could not sleep and decided to arrive early. The night watchman let me in. I do hope I did not overstep."

"Oh, certainly not, my lord." Ames hurried across the room. "Lord Cummings and Lord Cartwright gave specific instructions you were to have full access to the museum until further notice."

Eli couldn't help but smile at the man. Ames had been overly accommodating since being assigned to him. "That will be today, Ames. I plan to finish and depart London before sundown. I have been away from my estate too long as it is. I cannot have the place falling apart while I'm away."

Ames nodded in agreement but held his tongue before setting to work.

It was a lie. The Ridgefeld estate needed little oversight to run properly and efficiently. His steward had grown used to the late marquis' long absences, and truly, Eli being underfoot all the time was likely a hindrance. However, since Eli had taken his place as marquis, he'd been much like a ship without sails, tossed around by the wind and sea, trying to gain some sort of course that always eluded him in the end.

Eli set back to his task, unwrapping the two identical square objects.

He'd mistakenly thought he'd found his intended course, discovered where his future lie and how to fill the void created by his grandfather's death and his mother's indifference.

With Sam by his side.

There was no lack of irony in the notion that one woman's negligence had led him into the arms of another.

That he'd been so foolish as to allow Sam to burrow under his skin and nestle in a place he'd never intended to let another soul was inconceivable.

He shook his head in disgust of his deep-seated need to have someone close, to share his secrets, losses, and fears with. And she'd thrown them all back in his face.

"May I assist you, my lord?" Ames asked. "I am nearly finished with this trunk, and I can catalogue everything you've unpacked."

"Thank you for all your help." The man was eager to please. Cartwright had shared the man, fresh from Eton, was hopeful for a paid position with the museum. "I think you will make a wonderful addition to the staff here."

Ames beamed with pride. "It is an honor to assist you with such an impressive collection, my lord."

"It was my grandfather's life's work, all these antiquities." Both men paused to scan the huge storeroom, almost every inch covered by assorted objects, ready for museum goers to enjoy. "I was with him when he collected half of these."

"I, myself, have never been farther than the Scottish border."

"Then I think it imperative that if your life allows, you journey and explore the world at large." The vacant place within him from his grandfather's passing opened again as memories flooded him: fond memories, exciting memories, harrowing memories, and…sad memories.

How many nights had he spent alone? How many days had he been left in camp while his grandfather explored areas too dangerous for a boy? How many times had he met great people in far-off lands, felt a part of their life and them a part of his, only to journey to a new place and leave them behind? After many years, Eli had learned never to get too close. Always knew tomorrow would mean a new place and new people.

How had he forgotten this self-taught lesson?

Bloody hell, he'd even pictured himself spending afternoons at White's with Cartwright and Garrett, evenings dining with Sam and her large family, and holidays in the country.

He could almost hear his mother's cackle at his delusional thoughts of rescuing her from the clutches of some evil man—or place—in America and bringing her home to England.

He was an inept simpleton who'd been turned by a pretty face and enchanting manner.

"What would you call this?" Ames inquired, holding aloft a scepter encrusted with green gemstones. "A spear?"

"It is a scepter from the Aztec ruins." One of his grandfather's most prized discoveries and, without a doubt, the most valuable piece of the collection. "It is said to have belonged to the second king of

Tenochtitlán, Huitzilihuitl in 1400. My grandfather thought it comical to carry it around our estate and use it to point out things."

"I would have much enjoyed meeting the late marquis." Sadness seemed to fill Ames as if he understood the immense loss and emptiness Eli had faced in recent months. "Lord Cartwright speaks very highly of him."

"He was a kind, caring, and compassionate man. Not to mention, a man of great patience and understanding."

Eli had barely thought of his grandfather during his time in London, beyond thinking the old man would have enjoyed gallivanting about the city. Phaeton races, the play, and a scandalous card game.

It would be hard to enjoy the memories now. Sam's image would taint them all. He could not think of one without thinking of her: in his arms, bodies pressed together, heated lips exploring. His heart fluttered for a brief moment before crashing once more.

He would return to Liverpool to be haunted by not one ghost, but two.

The life he'd had stolen away from him when his grandfather had passed.

And the life he'd almost had which was never fully realized.

Lord Cartwright—and Jude—had been correct when they'd cautioned him against thinking that Sam's feelings were true when all she'd sought was a means of escape during her time at Hollybrooke, made all the more complicated when her father appeared. She'd been honest with him. He'd known the terms of their agreement. It was his foolishness that had led him to believe he meant more to her than a mere companion while in town—a distraction from her mundane life and a way to keep away the many men who sought her physical charms with no other promise for the future.

He'd held a true affection for her, and thought she'd felt the same.

It was a mistake to think she'd accept a proper courtship from him. His only saving grace was that he hadn't mentioned his plans to Cartwright and Garrett the other evening. How embarrassing to have to look the men in the eyes and for all to know Sam had refused his courtship.

Distance, and time. That was exactly what Eli needed.

Two things he would not obtain if he remained in London with Lord and Lady Cartwright…for no other reason than Lady Cartwright was identical in appearance to the woman he meant to forget.

In no other way were they similar. Sam's appealing, honey-toned, husky voice was at complete odds with her sister's high-pitched, singsong speech.

Their auburn hair was a similar length with Sam's being ever so slightly longer, but their preference for style could not be any more dissimilar—Sam favoring upswept curls or long locks falling over one shoulder, exposing her long neck and graceful, confident poise.

Her choice of bold, rich fabrics only added to her allure—teardrop earbobs of cream with flecks of every shade or iridescent hues accompanying every gown.

Eli reached into his pocket and withdrew the jewelry she'd lost at the card table the night before. He hadn't gotten the opportunity to return them to Sam. Making a mental note to leave them with Lady

Cartwright before he departed, Eli made to stuff them back into his pocket for safekeeping, but Ames noticed them first.

"Those are beautiful opals," he commented, seating himself next to Eli. "My mother never left the house without her opal necklace with matching bracelet. Are they for the collection?" He held a notebook, ready to scribble notes about the earbobs.

Eli shook his head. "No, they belong to a friend. I must return them."

His only regret was that he would be unable to return them himself.

Sam had made it perfectly clear she had no wish to see him again; his presence as a distraction was no longer required.

# # #

Sam pushed further into the warmth of her bed, having only given herself over to sleep as the sun crested on the London skyline. Her eyes could not have been closed more than two hours, at most; her head pounded from hours of sobbing and lack of rest.

Quiet. An entire day spent abed. It was all Sam longed for. Not *all* she longed for, but the one thing available to her. She'd instructed her lady's maid not to disturb her until Sam rang for her assistance. Marce would likely sleep late as well after their midnight discussion in her office.

Something had drawn her from the slumber that had finally claimed her.

But what?

She was warm. Her bed plush and comforting. Her room dark as night.

The pounding continued, though it wasn't in her head.

"Samantha Pengarden!" Jude said sternly on the far side. "Open this door this instant before I call Mr. Curtis to knock the thing down."

Sam flipped her bedding back, revealing her neat room with the drapes pulled tight. Jude's bed still resided not far from hers, untouched since she'd married Lord Cartwright and moved out of Craven House. Sam's eyes ached as they focused in the dark, a sliver of light peeking under her door.

It hadn't been her brightest idea to throw the bolt on the door before allowing her tears to fall unrestrained after dismissing her maid the previous night.

She slipped her stocking-covered feet over the side of the bed and stood, the cold floor seeping through to her toes as she padded across the room to allow her sister entrance.

Jude entered with a stern frown, her hair loose about her shoulders as if she'd left home in a hurry, not sparing enough time to properly prepare for her day.

"Why are you still in bed?" Jude demanded, grabbing Sam's arm when she attempted to climb back beneath the covers. "It is almost noon!"

"Noon, that is all?" Sam pulled away and threw herself on the bed. "If only I could sleep another two, possibly three days. I am exhausted."

"What is the matter with you?" Jude sat on the bed next to her, glancing at her old bed. "Ever since Hollybrooke, you have acted strangely. I wrote every day while away after the wedding, and not one response came from you. And then, I arrived back in London, and you have yet to visit me at my new home. I barely saw you at the ball the other evening, and then I received a note from you requesting Lord Cartwright and I accompany you to Covent Garden. Only you disappeared with Lord Ridgefeld, and barely spoke when you both returned." Jude paused, taking a deep breath after her long ramble. "And now you are staying in bed all day—"

"Stop, Jude," Sam pleaded, bringing her hands to cover her ears—not that it would block out her sister's rant completely. "Everything is fine. I am feeling unwell today. That is all."

"Did you think me ignorant enough to truly think you wanted to attend the play with Simon and me?" She scooted farther onto the bed. "You knew proper decorum dictated we bring Lord Ridgefeld along."

"So?" Sam was not having this conversation right now. Her headache had returned with a vengeance.

"So…I spoke with Marce," Jude admitted.

"You conversing with our sister should strike me as odd now that you are a countess, married to a fine lord?"

"Do not think to use that tactic with me, Samantha," Jude warned. "You know exactly what our sister told me."

"That I favor a future similar to our mother's?"

"Sam…"

"What?" She pushed to a sitting position and tucked her legs beneath her long nightshift. "She told you of the wager in White's betting book. A wager, I might add, I knew nothing about. I am not, nor do I ever plan to be, a harlot. I will never sell my body for finery or exchange my independence for a fancy townhouse."

"That is good to know; however, I never expected you'd do such a thing." Her sister eyed her in the dim light coming from the open door. "I am here about Lord Ridgefeld."

"What about him?" Had he told Simon of their quarrel?

"You care for him, do you not?"

Sam had rarely been accomplished enough to lie to her twin. They shared a connection far greater than that of mere blood sisters. They'd shared everything from birth—their clothes, their tutors, their bedchambers, and more than all that, they shared their identical looks. Had shared a womb.

At the moment, Sam saw her inner sorrow and pain reflected in her sister's identical eyes.

"I do not need to hear your answer." Jude shook her head. "I know you have feelings for him. I've known since Hollybrooke. I suspected that when he arrived in London, you'd continue your companionship."

"Then why did you bid him leave Hollybrooke?" Sam had wondered, but as her sister had said, she hadn't spent enough time in Jude's company to ask.

"Because," Jude took hold of her sister's hands and turned to face her directly, "I feared your feelings for him were only inspired by father's unexpected arrival. That your affections for Lord Ridgefeld were only to distract yourself from the turmoil you felt over my wedding and Beauchamp's appearance."

Sam could not deny it. "True, my draw to Lord Ridgefeld—Elijah—started as a means to keep my boredom at bay and the thought of losing you a dull pain to be acknowledged at a later time. Also, he helped to keep Lord Gunther from fawning all over me."

Jude laughed, and Sam gave a weak smile.

"And then, well, I enjoyed his company greatly. We spoke easily." Sam remembered their time in Cummings' study…her naughty thoughts and his flirtatious nature. "But then when Beauchamp appeared, Elijah was there to talk to. A shoulder to cry on. I could not burden you with everything. It was your special time. You had Simon, and I had no one save Elijah."

"You could have come to me." A tear appeared in the corner of Jude's eye and trickled down her cheek. "I was in pain, too. I was confused. I was hurting. We could have mourned together. At least tell me Lord Ridgefeld was kind and compassionate."

"He listened to me, allowed me to cry, and told me of his own past—not so different from my own."

"That is good to hear. If I wasn't able to be there for you, he was."

"But then he left Hollybrooke without a word of farewell."

"I am truly sorry for my part in that," Jude confessed, pulling Sam close. "It was not my intention to harm you, only give you the opportunity to listen to what Beauchamp had to say…he is our father. Family."

"You are my family. Marce is my family. Garrett and Payton are my family. Simon is now my family. Beauchamp is not my family." Sam tried to suppress the anger rising in her. Jude was not the person she was angry at. Even Lord Beauchamp was not the target of her fury. "For our brief time together, I saw Elijah as family."

"But not any longer?" Jude whispered.

"No."

"I am sorry to hear that, Sam. Lord Ridgefeld is a good man."

Pain swelled in Sam's chest, threatening to double her over from the sharpness of it. "I am sorry, as well."

"Then I suppose it is best he is departing London." Jude averted her eyes and busily straightened her skirts on the bed, arranging them about her legs to cover her exposed ankles. "The townhouse was crowded with him in residence," Jude mused. "Entertaining houseguests is a lot of work. His carriage is being loaded now, and he will be off before late afternoon."

Elijah was leaving London? It shouldn't surprise her. He did not belong in London. He was an adventurer, an explorer, and a man used to travel.

It would not be long before he found a woman better suited to him and his life, one far more suitable than Sam could ever be.

"If you wish to say your goodbyes," Jude continued, "he can be found at the museum, finishing his tasks and verifying that everything is prepared for his grandfather's exhibit."

"You know I do not favor the museum as you and Simon do." Sam attempted to keep her voice level, to not betray the remorse and misery threatening to take over. No, those emotions were better felt alone…with no witnesses. Every part of her ached to go to Eli. To tell him that she cared for him, possibly more than he cared for her. That was what scared her most. What if she gave her heart to him, confessed her love for him, only to have him leave her? Not today, not tomorrow, but one day, he would leave her.

As her mother and his father had done in death.

As her father and his mother had done by running away.

As Jude had done by falling in love and marrying Simon.

Eventually, Marce and Payton would do the same.

She and Garrett had never been close, but even he would become more distant.

Where would Sam live if Marce married and moved to her husband's home? Would Craven House be sold? Sam hadn't the means to care for the property. A future as a spinster, shuffled between the unwelcoming homes of different family members seemed likely for her.

It was that or trust in another person to care for her.

The closest she'd been to allowing another into her life was Elijah, and in the end, she'd pushed him away, too. She'd clung to him for as long as she could before a decision had to be made.

A permanent attachment with confessed feelings of mutual love and devotion…

Or end their association before she had the chance of getting hurt.

But she was already hurting. Saying what she had to push him away the previous night had driven a spike into her own heart. The agony of losing Elijah would not disappear anytime soon.

"I think it is best I go." Jude stood and shook out her skirts. "I can see you are not feeling well. Do call on me when you are in better health."

Jude leaned forward and placed a quick kiss on Sam's cheek.

"Farewell," Jude called over her shoulder as she left, closing Sam's door behind her.

Chapter Thirty-Three

Elijah loaded the final empty crate into the waiting wagon, preparing his convoy to return to Liverpool. His task was complete, every object accounted for, the catalogue triple-checked for accuracy. There was nothing left for him to do but return to the Cartwright townhouse, collect Mathers and his personal carriage, and be on his way. With the wagons not loaded down with all the antiquities, they would be able to travel at a faster pace back to Liverpool.

Home.

A familiar, comforting place—as much as any place felt like home to Elijah.

Why was he stalling?

The sun had crested in the sky hours before. If they wanted to travel outside of London proper before nightfall, they needs must be on their way.

Instead of mounting his horse, Elijah walked back into the museum in search of Ames. The man had been a great help, a pleasure to work alongside with a work ethic that would have pleased the late marquis greatly.

"My lord," Ames called, weaving through the many piles of collectibles. "I thought you had left. Is there something more I can help you with?"

The young man's welcoming smile had been a constant the past few days, and for some unknown reason, Eli needed him to know how much that meant to him. "Ames." Eli held out his hand for the man to shake. "It has been a pleasure working alongside you."

"For me, as well." He eyed the offered hand for only a moment before grasping it and giving it a firm shake.

"I want you to know that if the museum does not appoint you to a paid position—a long-term position—then they are fools."

The man's cheeks blossomed with embarrassment. "It is my intention to work diligently until the day comes, my lord."

"Very good, but if the day does not come—or does not come soon enough—please write to me. I may be coordinating a few expeditions in the near future." Elijah had thought about travel but had made no sure plans. He was uncertain why he'd mention the possibility to the man. "I would enjoy having you on my team when the day comes."

Ames's eyes rounded, and his arms hung limply at his sides in disbelief. "My lord," he stammered. "I do not know what to say. I would be honored to accompany you on your journeys."

"And mayhap, when we return, we can promise the museum a new exhibit—as long as your employment is part of the deal." It was a brilliant idea, one that would keep Eli occupied and his mind off a certain woman. But it could also secure a future for Ames. "I will send word after I arrive home and sort out my other business matters."

The man's eyes drifted over Eli's shoulder to the door beyond and then immediately hit the floor. "Lady Cartwright, it is a great—" The man dropped into a deep bow. "I had not expected you." Ames was stumbling over his every word.

Elijah turned slowly, dreading the wisdom Sam's sister was here to impart. She'd left the task to Cartwright the last time, but Eli certainly did not have luck on his side. Had the woman heard of the betting book wager or his and Sam's outing to the gambling party? He deserved any scolding or outright rebuff she was here to convey.

But the woman standing just inside the large storeroom was not Lady Cartwright.

His heart stopped at the sight of her and then began again, an erratic beat that nearly brought him to his knees.

If Ames were to work with Eli, his eyesight needed to be checked.

There was not a speck of him that thought the woman was Lady Cartwright.

Even across the large room, Eli knew Samantha—her air of confidence and grace. The tilt of her chin. The bold color selection of her deep blue gown. The way her hair swept over her shoulder. Suddenly, he remembered the opal earbobs in his pocket.

"Ames," Eli said, pulling his stare away from Sam long enough to bid the man to leave them. "Can you give Miss Samantha and me a moment of privacy?"

His gaze snapped back over Eli's shoulder. "My apologies, Miss Samantha…I did not…I mean to say—"

"Do not fret," Sam replied, moving farther into the room. "Even my siblings have a difficult time telling me and Jude apart…we are identical, after all."

"Almost identical, but vastly different in many ways." Eli's words were spoken softly. They were not likely heard by Sam.

Ames quietly departed the room as Elijah watched Sam make her way toward him, stopping to examine objects along the way, her fingers trailing across an ancient tapestry from China. But she did not stop to admire the beauty of the woven fabric. She kept walking toward him, her eyes never leaving his.

What was she doing here? It didn't matter if she'd come to tell him all the ways she'd used him as a distraction, a means for escape from her townhouse, or that she never planned to see him again.

Eli only wanted one last moment with her—to brand *this* imagine into his memory.

The sway of her hips, the uplift of her coy smile, the delicacy of her touch.

As she drew close, he noted her smile fade to unease. Her hand trembled where it touched a terracotta pot. Her footsteps faltered and then halted several feet from him as she searched his face, her eyes intense.

Without further thought, he took the final steps to meet her, opening his arms.

Elijah wasn't sure how he knew she'd accept his embrace and all but collapse into his arms, but he did. And if he were being honest, he needed to hold her far more than she could possibly need his arms wrapped around her.

Her warmth against him, her cheek resting against his chest as he tucked her head below his chin, told Elijah their time together had been born of true affection for one another.

"Elijah, I—"

"Shhhh," he mumbled. He didn't want any words, declarations, or apologies to taint this moment.

However, Sam pulled back. "I have much I need to say. Things I should have said last night, instead of the awful lies." Eli's heart skidded to a stop and his breath hitched, waiting for her next words. "Nothing I said was the truth, Elijah, you must believe that."

But what she'd said was exactly as he'd expected—deep down, at least.

"I was scared."

"Scared of what?" he asked.

"Of letting you in, of letting *anyone* in." She drew a deep breath before continuing. "Our connection was instant—our brief encounter on that deserted road—and so powerful I feared my affection for you must be stronger than yours for me. And then when you left Hollybrooke, I knew it to be true. I spent those six weeks trying to forget you, to forget our time together, and believe another would kiss me the way you had. That I would find someone who would allow me to cry on their shoulder; who would know my past and not pass judgment on my future. But the attention of others was not what I needed, and never what I desired."

She looked up at him, her eyes open, and Elijah saw to her very soul. He understood her hurt. The pain she'd silently endured her entire life. The added injury he'd caused her.

He needed to repair the damage he'd done—and do his best to wipe away the hurt others had inflicted upon her.

"Then you appeared at the ball, and I thought I would make you pay for abandoning me in Derbyshire," she whispered. "I thought I would use you until your company no longer interested me and then it would be my turn to abandon you. Send you back to Liverpool as hurt and rejected as I felt in Derbyshire."

"Then why are you here?" he asked. He wanted to hear her answer as much as he dreaded hearing her say the words aloud. She was here to reinforce, for a final time, that his affection for her would never be returned. Could he stand to hear the words? Would he survive…find a way to mend his heart…or at least collect some of the shards?

If only he could piece back together Sam's shattered soul, then his would mend along with hers.

"I am here…" Her words trailed off as if she were losing her confidence. "I am here because I love you. I've loved you since the moment in Lord Cummings' study when you found me with that most inappropriate book. When you did not laugh at me or think me childish or unworthy of knowing matters of the flesh."

"I think I have loved you since my carriage stopped alongside you during the storm." It wasn't a competition…who'd known they loved the other first. However, Elijah needed to say the words, make his own declaration before it was too late.

"I thought I could ask any ridiculous thing of you and you would agree, which you have." She took another step back, and Elijah's arms fell to his sides. "It was unfair of me, selfish and petty. Especially with people gaining the notion you'd taken me as your mistress. It was not what I intended, though neither did I expect you to think of our arrangement as a courtship. For that I am truly sorry."

And now she was to tell him…for the final time, rip his still-beating heart from his chest and crush it under the heel of her boot.

"With each outing, I found I looked forward to the next. Each time you accompanied me out, I fell more and more in love with you. I am unsure when I realized how much you loved me in return, but you proved it over and over. And it scared me. Not your love, but the thought that I continued to love you even after promising myself I wouldn't allow anyone to hurt me again."

Elijah sensed there was more she wanted to say, that Sam still searched for the final words to tell him that though he loved her—and she loved him in return—it would not work. She could not remain at his side. That she did not have the amount of trust within her to believe Elijah would never walk away and leave her behind, brokenhearted.

When she remained silent, he took hold of her hands and spoke from his heart…or what was left of it. "Sam, we are much alike. I have felt the same hurt, pain, and abandonment. I know the repercussions and anguish when you love another but that love is not returned. I know the loneliness and despair of not knowing what the future holds, or even *if* it holds anything of worth beyond the mundane day-to-day. I have not witnessed a prosaic moment since meeting you." He paused to draw her closer, longing for an ounce of the confidence she normally wore like a shawl upon her shoulders. "Even when I returned to Liverpool, each moment was spent dreaming about returning to you. Each night spent dreaming of the way you'd feel in my arms once more. How I would show you that we were meant to be together—though, I had no right to expect that."

"However, it is what I led you to believe. What I unknowingly wanted myself." She rose to her tiptoes, bringing her eyes in line with his and their mouths a mere inch apart. "I want you, Elijah. No matter my own insecurities, I trust you will never leave me. My love for you will have no end. You are the man I never dreamed I would make mine, never thought I deserved. You understand me far better than even my twin. It was only you who noticed my pain at Hollybrooke for what it truly was—a sense of great loss—and you soothed me, allowed me to cry, and truly heard every word I said."

"As I would every day until the end of time," he mumbled. *As I will*, he corrected in his own thoughts.

"Then I beg you, make me yours." She leaned forward and set her lips to his, insistent and demanding yet unsure. Too soon, their lips parted. "Your enchanting marchioness."

"Say no more." Elijah pulled her against him and swung her into his arms as he strode across the room toward the door. They needed a special license to wed—and privacy, though he was uncertain which they'd find first. But Eli spotted the tapestry she'd lovingly ran her fingers along as she'd walked to him earlier. He snagged the woven heirloom with one hand and spread it in an open area between the stacks of his grandfather's most prized possessions.

Gently, he laid Sam down, her auburn tresses cascading across the fabric.

But he paused.

She reached out toward him, her eyes hooded in lust—or was it love?—as she moaned.

Elijah reached into his pocket and retrieved her opal earbobs.

"My enchanting marchioness wears opals," he commanded, handing them to her, and she quickly returned them to their rightful place at each ear.

In that moment, surrounded by all his grandfather's worldly treasures, Elijah knew the only treasure he'd ever need in his life was lying before him, her arms again reaching out to hold him.

"I love you," Sam whispered. "My sister may have stolen an earl, but I have enchanted my very own marquis."

Elijah had known since their first meeting that he loved Miss Samantha Pengarden. All that was left was to show her exactly how much. And he would start with her lips, continue down her neck, and lavish sweet love upon every inch of her body until there was no doubt remaining in her that Elijah loved her wholly, madly, and deeply. And would for the rest of eternity.

Epilogue

Sam tightened her hold on the railing, allowing the breeze sweeping the harbor to push her hair from her face and out behind her. The fresh air and scent of salt would be commonplace to her soon enough—as soon as her dear husband gave the word to pull anchor and set sail. The gentle sway of the water below her would take longer to acclimate to; however, she did not fear the change from solid ground to unpredictable, dark, rolling waves beneath her—not as long as Elijah Watson, the Marquis of Ridgefeld stood at her side.

Husband.

Her husband.

Samantha Watson, the Marchioness of Ridgefeld.

She should feel adrift shedding the final vestige of her youthful life.

After a few years, would anyone remember her link to Craven House, or was it possible her past would fade as quickly as it had for Jude?

Shouts from behind her had Sam releasing her told and turning to face a group of men charged with loading her trunks, packed for extended travel—with love—by Marce and Payton.

"What can m'lady pack that be so bloody heavy?" A burly man strained under the weight of Sam's newly acquired wardrobe: gowns of the finest silks and satins befitting a marchioness, gloves, kid boots, slippers, hats, underpinnings, and stockings. More clothes than she ever imagined would belong to her…and her alone. She would not be made to share these with her twin, though that did give her a twinge of loss. "I have half a mind ta let the trunk fall to the harbor, I do!"

"It will be your head if Lady Ridgefeld's trunk ends up submerged," Ames shouted, trudging across the desk. The young man, eager for adventure, had gladly accepted the opportunity to travel with Sam and Elijah. Though he was not seasoned in travel—as Elijah said—he was fervent to please, which was worth a decade of experience, her new husband assured her. "Now, take it below deck to my lady's quarters, and if so much as a nick is found on her lovely trunks, I will report it to Lord Ridgefeld."

Both men sighed and shook their heads at Ames's exaggerated ramblings.

Ames met her smiling stare and nodded in her direction.

No, she would not lack for entertainment or fine company in the months to come. Dare she admit that it might be far superior than any London ballroom? She'd even packed a deck of cards from Payton, in case Elijah was willing to participate in another game.

"Are you certain you wish to see America?" Jude asked.

Sam had almost forgotten her sister's quiet presence next to her. "I am."

"It is a long, harrowing journey."

"That I know, dear sister," she reassured her twin as she reached out to grasp Jude's hands. "But Elijah received a letter from his mother and he has always told me that if she were to reach out, he would never turn his back on her."

"But you only just wed," Jude sighed, blinking to hold in her tears. "Can you not settle in London or Liverpool first before departing England?"

Ironic, all this time Sam had been worried about her sister abandoning her, forgetting their bond, because she married. And yet, Jude was as upset and forlorn as Sam had felt only a month prior. "Judith, I love you. Likely far more than I love myself. Elijah and I will return as quickly as the winds allow, hopefully with his mother in tow. I cannot deny him this. I love him too much. I want him to be happy for as long as it is in my power to do so."

"Just the sight of you, my enchanting marchioness"—Eli stepped forward, gaining a giggle from both women and made to take Jude's hands, but quickly chuckled and turned to Sam—"would be enough to solidify my eternal happiness."

Sam averted her eyes as heat flooded her cheeks at his softly spoken endearment. "And I am content to follow you to the ends of the known world, Elijah."

"Thankfully, I will never ask that of you." He released her hands and turned to Sam's sister. "I make a solemn vow to return Samantha to you whole and unscathed by the heathens in Baltimore."

His eyes danced with merriment as Jude laughed once more.

It was something Sam would never tire of: Elijah's smile, his presence at her side, his vow to protect her at all costs. He was everything she'd ever sought in her life.

"My lord!" Ames waved his arms frantically to gain their attention. "Last of the trunks have been loaded and only a few crates of supplies remain. A carriage arrived just now. A fancy gent is making his way aboard. Shall I greet him and ask his business here?"

"No," Elijah called. "I can handle that. Thank you for your assistance thus far, Ames."

Jude hurried to the railing and peered over, leaving Sam and Elijah alone. Her husband did not waste a moment, as he immediately leaned down and placed a soft kiss upon her lips.

They were wed and the need to hide their affection was no longer a concern. Sam wrapped her arm around him, pulling Elijah along the length of her body. She felt his desire stir as she opened her mouth and deepened their kiss.

In the fortnight since the small, intimate ceremony that'd made them man and wife, Elijah had delighted in showing her all she'd longed to know about what happens between a man and a woman after marriage, though they did not always wait to be behind their closed bedchamber door.

"Sam." Jude tugged her from Eli's arms, pulling her to the side of the schooner. "It is the viscount. Whatever is he doing here?" Her twin's eyes narrowed and her shoulders stiffened, anticipating the argument to come when Sam confronted their father once more.

"Calm yourself, Lady Cartwright," Elijah said with a chuckle. "Sam invited him to see us off."

"You…what?" Jude sputtered. "That cannot be…Sam…you invited him?" The woman threw her arms wide, to take in the entire harbor. "—you invited him here?!"

"Why do you make it sound so unlike something I would do?" Sam asked before turning to Elijah. "Will you go meet him? Jude and I will join you in a moment."

"Of course." He placed a quick kiss to her cheek before sauntering across the deck, his steps sure as if he'd spent a majority of his life on a rocking boat, his entire body used to the fickle movements aboard a ship.

"Have you a change of heart, dear sister?" Jude raised a brow, crossing her arms and blocking Sam's path.

"Not a change of heart exactly, but if Elijah has taught me one thing, it is to willingly accept people who put forth an effort, even after many years of neglect." Sam smirked at the thought, and the immense change her husband had brought around in her. She'd always thought herself incapable of change, especially of bestowing forgiveness on those who'd wounded her. Yet, Elijah had shown her that unless one is willing to give a person a chance, they cannot ever *earn* forgiveness. "Has Father written you since your arrival in London with Simon?"

Jude averted her stare and her shoulders tensed once more. "Yes," she confessed. "And I have written back. I visited his London townhouse soon after returning from Simon's country estate. I never told you because—"

"That is not important, Jude. You were under no obligation to tell me, but I thank you for allowing me to come to my own understanding of the situation and how to proceed. As much as we look alike, we are far different people. Our own selves. It is time that *we* realize that, as well as others." If Jude had told Sam she wished to know their father, start an actual relationship with him, Sam would have laughed in her face; then lectured her on the many mistakes she was making. But recently, she'd learned family—especially those who sought a relationship—should be embraced and not pushed away. "He wrote me, as well. It is only that it took a bit more time—and Elijah—to show me the importance of forgiveness. And even I am capable of such a thing."

"He is not a horrible man." Jude met her stare, pleading for Sam to believe her words.

"I will give him a chance, I promise." With a reassuring hug, likely the last she'd share with her sister for several months, the pair turned toward Elijah and their father. The viscount nervously looked between the women, and Elijah leaned close to whisper something to him.

"Samantha." He nodded, and she was struck—not for the first time—at the resemblance between her and Beauchamp. "Wedded bliss adds a glow I would recognize anywhere."

"Father." Sam tested out the word, still foreign and awkward. "Thank you for coming to see us off."

"There is not another place I would rather be than here…with the pair of you." He cleared his throat. "And you as well, Lord Ridgefeld."

"It is lovely to see you again, Father." Jude stepped forward and embraced the man. It appeared so natural, as if they'd been close all their lives and not newly acquainted.

"And you, Jude," Beauchamp said, glancing around the deck. "Is Lord Cartwright with you?"

"No. He had business to tend to and wanted me to spend some time with Sam before she departed." Jude returned to Sam's side. "He will return for me shortly."

"That is good. I was going to offer to see you home."

"Thank you for accepting my invitation." Sam needed to say her piece before the captain informed Elijah it was time to depart while the wind and sea were cooperating. "Elijah and I would like you to join us in Liverpool upon our return—Jude and Simon will also come—to celebrate our wedding."

Beauchamp's eyes rounded and he stood a bit straighter. "Of course. I would be delighted to attend."

Sam stepped forward and embraced her father, surprised to discover the hug did not feel out of place or unnatural in the slightest.

"That is wonderful, my lord." Elijah settled his arm around Sam's waist when she stepped back. The reassuring squeeze let her know he was proud of her.

Sam wanted to please her new husband—in every way possible.

And if she also found peace with her past, that was truly a positive.

"M'lord," Misgaviage, their captain, called. "It be time."

"Very well." Elijah nodded. "It is time we say goodbye. Not forever, but for now. I will give you a few moments, Sam." With a quick peck on the cheek, Elijah went to converse with the captain, leaving Sam alone with Jude and Beauchamp.

"I will miss you—" Sam started, adding, "—both of you."

A tear streaked down Jude's cheek and her twin brushed it away. "And I will miss you, but I plan to write. In fact, I have already written my first letter. It will be sent tomorrow and will greet you when you arrive."

"We will stay at the McDowell Inn and Tavern in Baltimore."

"Elijah informed Simon last night at supper."

"And I will also write, my daughter." Beauchamp smiled, and the man looked ten years younger than when they'd met in Derbyshire. "It has come to mind that there is much you and Judith do not know about me, my family, and my time with your mother."

"I look forward to reading all about it," Sam confessed. Shockingly, she did. The man knew a part of their mother that Sam and Jude had never been privy to. A time in Sasha Davenport's life that she'd been happy, thought she'd found her forever love.

It was the same with her and Elijah. Yet, their relationship, their love and devotion, was far more than Beauchamp and her mother had ever achieved.

"Goodbye, sister." Sam embraced Jude.

"Not goodbye," Jude countered. "Safe travels. May the wind be always in your favor."

"Thank you." Sam looked over her sister's shoulder to where Elijah watched, keeping a close eye on his bride. "I think it is time we set sail."

"Certainly." Beauchamp offered his arm to Jude. "I will escort Judith to the dock and we shall wave you out of port."

"I would enjoy that." The trio joined Elijah by the plank leading from the deck to the dock. Hugs were shared all around before Beauchamp led Jude from the schooner.

Sam was immediately in Elijah's secure hold once more as so many emotions flooded her. She loved her family. She would miss each one—even her father. But, she'd found her forever love.

And come hell or turbulent waters, Sam would never let Elijah go.

"A penny for your thoughts, Lady Ridgefeld?" he whispered close to her ear before setting his lips to the tender spot below her earlobe.

A shiver traveled through Sam's entire body. "I was thinking that you have given me a truly rare gift—one I may never be deserving of."

"Oh, do share, my lady." He trailed his lips down her neck to her collarbone and nipped gently. "I am ravenous to hear."

"Beyond love, you have given me hope…"

"And you are undeserving of hope?" He pulled her back against him as he massaged her waist. "I find that difficult to believe."

"Before meeting you, I would have said yes, I was very undeserving of hope."

"What changed?"

Sam looked up to see her sister and father waving from shore with Lord Cartwright at their side.

"Not what, but whom," she mumbled, waving back at her family. "You showed me the importance of forgiveness. Not of others but for myself."

"Remorse, regret, and ill tidings toward another will weight a person down."

"And without them, I am filled with a great amount of hope."

"That is certainly good because we may face insurmountable odds when we arrive in Baltimore to convince my mother to journey back to England with us." Elijah stood straight and waved to the gathering on the dock.

"It is with luck you have married a most persuasive woman, my lord." Sam's throaty laugh echoed on the breeze. "I love you, Elijah Watson."

"I am convinced I love you far more, Samantha Watson."

"Impossible, my lord," she retorted, giving a final wave to her family and turning in Elijah's arms. Sam pressed her body into Elijah's and felt the familiar hardening in his trousers. "Now, dear husband, show me to our quarters. We have a long journey with many endless days and nights to fill."

"Then it was advantageous of me to bring along our wedding gift from Lord Cummings."

"A wedding gift?" Sam's mind swam. "Whatever do you mean?"

"We will have to adjourn to our chambers below deck to find out, my enchanting marchioness," he teased, settling his lips against hers.

However, Sam had a hunch she knew exactly what awaited her below deck. In their short time as a wedded couple they'd explored all realms of the naked flesh, but there was always more to learn.

"Then, by all means, lead the way, dear husband.

Books By Christina McKnight:

Lady Archer's Creed Series

Theodora (Book One)

Georgina (Book Two) – Coming 2017

Adeline (Book Three) – Coming 2017

Josephine (Book Four) – Coming 2017

Craven House Series

The Thief Steals Her Earl (Book One)

The Mistress Enchants Her Marquis (Book Two)

The Madame Catches Her Duke – Coming 2017

The Gambler Wagers Her Baron – Coming 2018

A Lady Forsaken Series

Shunned No More, A Lady Forsaken (Book One)

Forgotten No More, A Lady Forsaken (Book Two)

Scorned Ever More, A Lady Forsaken (Book Three)

Christmas Ever More, A Lady Forsaken (Book Four)

Hidden No More, A Lady Forsaken (Book Five)

Standalone Title

The Siege of Lady Aloria, A de Wolfe Pack Novella

A Kiss At Christmastide: Regency Romance Novella

For The Love Of A Widow: Regency Romance Novella

About the Author:

Christina McKnight writes emotional, intricate regency romance with strong heroines and maverick heroes.

Christina enjoys a quiet life in Northern California with her family, her wine, and lots of coffee. Oh, and her books . . . don't forget her books! Most days, she can be found writing, reading, or traveling the great state of California.

Email: Christina@ChristinaMcKnight.com
Follow her on Twitter: @CMcKnightWriter
Keep up to date on her releases:
www.christinamcknight.com
Like Christina's FB Author page:
ChristinaMcKnightWriter

Author's Notes

Thank you for reading *The Mistress Enchants Her Marquis (Craven House Series, Book Two).*

If you enjoyed *The Mistress Enchants Her Marquis*, be sure to write a brief review at any retailer.

I'd love to hear from you!

You can contact me at:
Christina@christinamcknight.com

Or write me at:
P O Box 1017
Patterson, CA 95363

www.ChristinaMcKnight.com
Check out my website for giveaways, book reviews, and information on my upcoming projects,
or connect with me through social media at:

Twitter: @CMcKnightWriter
Facebook: www.facebook.com/christinamcknightwriter
Goodreads: www.goodreads.com/ChristinaMcKnight

Sign up for my newsletter here: http://eepurl.com/VP1rP

There are several people I'd like to thank for staying with me through the emotional journey of writing this book.

To Marc, my amazing boyfriend—thank you for always being *you*!

To Lauren Stewart, my critique partner and best friend, you pushed me to explore new avenues of thought that I never dreamed possible. If we were in a true relationship, it would be one based on co-dependency, but in a good way. My writing would not be what it is without your comments, criticism, suggestions, and guidance.

I'd also like to thank the wonderful women who've supported me in both my writing career and life, including (but not limited to): Amanda Mariel, Debbie Haston, Angie Stanton, Theresa Baer, Erica Monroe, Ava Stone, Roxanne Stellmacher, Laura Cummings, Dawn Borbon, Suzi Parker, Jennifer Vella, Brandi Johnson, and Latisha Kahn. I know I'm forgetting people…You have all been very patient and wonderfully supportive of my eccentric ways.

A very special thank you to my editor, Chelle Olson with Literally Addicted to Detail, your skill and professionalism surpass all that I expected. Chelle Olson can be contracted by email at literallyaddictedtodetail@yahoo.com.

Also, a special thank you to historical and developmental editor, Scott Moreland.

And to my proofreader, Anja with Hourglass Editing, thank you for embarking on yet another journey with me.

Cover and wraparound cover design and website design credit to Sweet 'N Spicy Designs.

Finally, thank you for supporting indie authors.

Made in the USA
Columbia, SC
05 May 2017